PRAISE FOR

The Good Mayor

WINNER OF SCOTLAND'S
SALTIRE SOCIETY FIRST BOOK AWARD

"An exuberant, whirlwind read." —*The Guardian* (London)

"Every now and then, a first novel reads like the culmination of a lengthy literary career. . . . *The Good Mayor* is a case in point."
—*Financial Times*

"A smoldering siren and likeable hero delight in a romance with charm. . . . Nicoll convincingly builds and maintains the sexual tension between his leads in a way that will keep readers hooked."
—*The Sydney Morning Herald*

"A literary novel and gorgeously written, old-fashioned romance."
—*The Australian Women's Weekly*

"Audacious in conception, inspired in execution, this fable-like novel of love, loss and friendship set literary tongues wagging. . . . A dexterity and lightness of tone that plies its way between tongue-in-cheek whimsy and world-weary omniscience."
—*The Canberra Times* (Australia)

"A wonderfully warm and comforting experience . . . *The Good Mayor* is a marvellously satisfying tale, evocative, moving and gently funny in a manner that recalls Jane Austen."
—*Herald Sun* (Australia)

"A story of love, dreaming and loss, magical realism . . . You will not be disappointed." —*The Observer* (London)

The Good Mayor

A NOVEL

ANDREW NICOLL

BANTAM BOOKS

A Bantam Books Trade Paperback Original

Published in the United States by Bantam Books, an imprint of The Random House Publishing Group, a division of Random House, Inc., New York.

Originally published in hardcover in the United Kingdom by Black & White Publishing Ltd., Edinburgh, in 2008.

Library of Congress Cataloging-in-Publication Data
Nicoll, Andrew.
The good mayor: a novel / Andrew Nicoll.—Bantam trade paperback ed.
p. cm.
ISBN: 978-0-385-34312-1
I. Title.
PR6114.I255G66 2009
823'.92—dc22 2009014065

Printed in the United States of America

www.bantamdell.com

2 4 6 8 9 7 5 3 1

Text design by Steve Kennedy

AN

L

AW

The Good Mayor

IN THE YEAR BLANK, WHEN A-K WAS GOVERNOR of the province of R, Good Tibo Krovic had been mayor of the town of Dot for almost twenty years.

These days, not many people visit Dot. Not many people have a reason to sail so far north into the Baltic, particularly not into the shallow seas at the mouth of the River Ampersand. There are so many little islands offshore, some of them appearing only at low tide, some of them, from time to time, coalescing with their neighbours with the capriciousness of an Italian government, that the cartographers of four nations long ago abandoned any attempt to map the place. Catherine the Great sent a team of surveyors who commandeered the house of the harbour master of Dot and lived there seven years, mapping and remapping and mapping again before they finally left in disgust.

"C'est n'est pas une mer, c'est un potage," the Chief Surveyor memorably remarked, although nobody in Dot understood him. Unlike the Russian nobility, the people of Dot did not express themselves in French. Neither did they speak Russian. For, despite the claims of the Empress Catherine, the people of Dot did not count themselves as Russian. Not at that time. At that time, the men of Dot—if anyone had cared to ask them—might have spoken of themselves as Finns or Swedes. Perhaps, at some other time, they might have nodded to far-off Denmark or even Prussia. Some few might have called themselves Poles or Letts but, for the most part, they would have stood proudly as men of Dot.

Count Gromyko shook the mud of the place from his feet and

sailed home for St. Petersburg, where he confidently expected a new position as Her Imperial Majesty's chief horse wincher. But, that very night, his ship struck an uncharted island which had impolitely emerged from the seas around Dot and he sank like a stone, taking with him seven years' worth of maps.

The admirals of the Empress Catherine were left with a blank space on their charts which they were far too civilised to mark "Here be Dragyns" so, instead, they wrote, "Shallow waters and foul grounds, dangerous to navigation" and left it at that. And, in later years, as the borders of many different countries shifted around Dot, like the unreliable banks of the River Ampersand, it suited their governments to say no more about it.

But the men of Dot needed no maps to navigate the islands which protect their little harbour. They found their way through the archipelago by smell. They guided themselves by the colour of the sea or the patterns of the waves or the rhythm of the current or the position of this eddy or that piece of slack water or the shape of the breakers where two tides crossed. The men of Dot sailed confidently out of their harbour seven centuries ago, taking skins and dried fish to the ports of the Hanseatic League, and they sailed home yesterday with cigarettes and vodka that nobody else need know anything about.

And, like them, when Good Tibo Krovic went to work in the mayor's office each morning, he navigated confidently. He picked up his paper from the front door, walked down the blue-tiled path, through his neat little garden to the collapsing ghost of a gate where a brass bell hung from the branches of a birch tree with a chain ending in a broken wooden handle, green with algae.

On the street, Tibo turned left. He bought a bag of mints from the kiosk on the corner, crossed the road and waited by the tram stop. On sunny days, Mayor Krovic read the paper while he waited for the tram. On rainy days, he stood under his umbrella and sheltered his paper inside his coat. On rainy days, he never got to read his paper and, even on sunny days, likely as not, somebody would come up to him at the tram stop and say, "Ah, Mayor Krovic, I was wondering if I could ask you about . . ." and Good Tibo Krovic would fold his paper and listen and advise. Good Mayor Krovic.

City Square is exactly nine stops from Mayor Krovic's house. He would get off after seven and walk the rest of the way. Halfway there, he would stop at The Golden Angel and order a strong Viennese coffee with plenty of figs, drink it, suck one mint and leave the rest of the bag on the table. Then there was only a short walk down Castle Street, across White Bridge, through the square and into the Town Hall.

Tibo Krovic enjoyed being mayor. He liked it when the young people came to him to be married. He liked visiting the schools of Dot and asking the children to help design the civic Christmas cards. He liked the people. He liked to sort out their little problems and their silly disputes. He enjoyed greeting distinguished visitors to the town.

He enjoyed walking into the council chamber behind the major-domo carrying the great silver mace with its image of St. Walpurnia—St. Walpurnia, the bearded virgin martyr, whose heart-wrung pleas to Heaven for the gift of ugliness as a bolster to her chastity were answered with a miraculous generosity. St. Walpurnia who was twice blessed by God—first with a beard of monstrous luxuriance and then with a cataclysm of warts which covered her whole body and which she exposed to the men of Dot almost daily in a tireless effort to turn them away from sin. St. Walpurnia who, when the rampaging Huns threatened Dot, offered herself to them on condition they spared the womenfolk of the city. St. Walpurnia who, as the monks recorded, ran towards the Hun camp, calling out to them, "Take me! Take me!" and those beastly Huns, who thought nothing of slaking themselves in the hairy flesh of their camp animals, treated poor, saintly Walpurnia as a mere plaything. When she died, hours later, crying out, "Oh God, oh God, oh Jesus!," the legend said there wasn't a mark on her entire warty body. God granted her a heart attack as another mark of his extreme favour and, when her corpse was recovered, a smile of bliss shone out from beneath her velvety moustache as a sign that she had already entered into the delights of Paradise. Or so my legend says.

In the year Blank, when A-K was governor of the province of R and Good Tibo Krovic had been mayor of the town of Dot for almost twenty years, I had been here twelve hundred years longer, watching.

I am still here, on the very top of the topmost pinnacle of the cathedral named in my honour but also, in some way that I cannot explain, I am standing on a ledge set into that carved pillar which supports the pulpit far, far below. And I am standing on the shield above the door of the Town Hall and painted on the side of every tram and hanging on the wall of the mayor's office and printed on the front of every notebook that lands on every desk in every classroom in every school in Dot. I am spread-eagled on the bow of that filthy little ferry which arrives, intermittently, from Dash, salt crusted in my ridiculous beard, a woven hemp bumper slung around me like a horse collar.

I am carried on coloured cards in the purses of the women of Dot, blinking at the light as they pass from shop to shop, snoozing in the copper-chinking dark, nestled in kiss curls and baby teeth and souvenir ticket stubs. I hang over beds—beds raucous with wild love, beds chill with indifference, beds where children sleep plump and innocent, beds where the dying lie racked and as thin as string. And I lie here, at the very heart of the cathedral, bare bones wrapped in dry gristle and ancient crumbled silks inside a golden pavilion, studded with jewels, gleaming with enamels, gaudy with ornament, where kings and princes have knelt to weep repentance, where their barren queens have sobbed out pleadings, where the people of Dot stop to pass the time of day with me. I cannot explain this. I cannot explain because I do not understand how I can be in all of these places all the time.

It seems to me that, if it is what I wish, I can be wholly and completely in any one of these places. Everything that is Walpurnia can be here, on top of my cathedral, looking down at the city and far out to sea, or here in the golden box or there on the front of that particular school notebook. And yet it seems to me that, if it is what I wish, I can be in all of those places at one time, undiluted, not spread one atom thinner, everywhere, watching. I watch. I watch the shopkeepers of Dot and the policemen and the tramps, the happy people and the sad people, the cats and the birds and the yellow dogs and Good Mayor Krovic.

I watched him as he walked up the green marble staircase to his office. He liked those stairs. He liked his office. He liked the dark wooden panelling inside and the big shuttered windows that looked across the fountains in the square, back up Castle Street to the white mass of my cathedral under its copper-coloured onion dome where, every year, he led the council for its annual blessing. He liked his comfortable leather chair. He liked the coat of arms on the wall with its image of a smiling, bearded nun. Most of all, he liked his secretary, Mrs. Stopak.

Agathe Stopak was everything that St. Walpurnia was not. Yes, she was blessed with long, dark, lustrous hair—but not on her chin. And her skin! White, shining, creamy, utterly wartless. Mrs. Stopak, although she showed me the dutiful devotion proper for any woman of Dot, was not one to take that sort of thing to extremes. In summer, she sat perched on her chair by the window like a buxom crane, dressed in filmy floral prints that sagged on every curve of her body in the heat and moved with every gasp of air that came in at the window.

All winter long, Mrs. Stopak came to work in galoshes and, seated at her desk, she slipped them off and took from her bag a pair of high-heeled peep-toe sandals. Inside his office, poor, good, love-struck Mayor Krovic would listen for the clump of her galoshes when Mrs. Stopak came in to work and rush to fling himself on the carpet, squinting through the crack beneath the door for a glimpse of her plump little toes as they wormed into her shoes.

And then poor, good, love-struck Tibo would sigh and stand up and brush the carpet fluff from his suit and go and sit down at his desk with his head in his hands and listen to Agathe Stopak, clip-clip-clipping across the tiled floor of the office next door, putting something in a filing cabinet or brewing coffee or simply being soft and scented and beautiful and on the other side of the door.

From time to time during the working day, like anyone else, Mrs. Stopak would leave her desk to attend to ordinary human needs and invariably she returned with her make-up restored to a mask of perfection, trailing clouds of limes and lemons and bougainvillea and vanilla and exotic scents that Good Tibo could not even name. He imagined the places they had come from—Pacific islands wafted with spices and tinkling with temple bells where tiny waves sighed on pink coral sands. He imagined the places they were now—little puffs of scent squirted on to the soft plump mounds behind Mrs. Stopak's knees, on her blue wrists and dewing her milky cleavage. "Oh, God," Mayor Krovic muttered to himself, "when you snatched my atoms from stardust, why did you make me a man when you could have made me into little drops of perfume and let me die there?"

GOOD MAYOR KROVIC WAS UNHAPPY BUT SO was Mrs. Agathe Stopak. On cold winter nights, she lay, shivering, in bed, listening to the rain drumming on the window, watching the curtains billow in the draught and wondering if they moved because of the wind outside or because of Stopak snoring beside her. He lay there, flat on his back, dead straight down one side of the bed as if a sword lay between them, with the sheets belled over his huge hard belly like a circus tent. The wind whistled down the chasm between them but, even without it, the bed was icy.

Stopak smelled of putty and whitewash. There were spots of paint on the grey vest he wore in bed, it clung under his fingernails and he snored like the steamroller she had seen spreading tar along Ampersand Avenue on the way home from work.

Stopak had always snored but, years ago when they were first married, she hadn't minded. Back then, the bed was warm and Stopak would go to sleep every night, collapsed on her plump pink body, his head nestled between her big ivory breasts, his body covering hers like a blanket, one arm stretched down her belly and between her legs, the other doubled under the pillow. And he would snore, exhausted, and Agathe would lie there, glowing, and twine her fingers in his hair and whisper love to him as he grunted the night away.

She fed him well. She would race back from her job in the mayor's office with good things in her bag and have them cooking by the time Stopak came through the door and sat down at the kitchen table with its yellow daisy cover. But, in those days, Stopak never sat down before he had rushed up like a charging bear and grabbed her from behind and goosed her and kissed her and polkaed her round the kitchen until she beat him back with laughter and a potato masher and forced him into a straight wooden chair.

"Stop it!" she'd bark. "You'll need your strength for later." And then she'd kiss him with a promise and feed him tournedos Rossini and home-made game pie and roasted potatoes and clotted egg custards under crunchy sugar lids and apple crumbles and good cheese and, as he ate, she would tell him everything about the day—who had been to see the mayor, the school party that had toured the Town Hall or how the Police Chief's hat had fallen off the desk and landed in Peter Stavo's bucket of bleach and come out as white as a nun's knickers—and they'd laugh.

And then, when Stopak had eaten, Agathe would leave her place at the table and hike her skirt up and straddle him in his chair and hold him in her arms and pull his hair and kiss him again and again until they fell into bed and, eventually, slept and the dishes could wait until morning. She loved him in those days. She still loved him, but not in the same way. Not that way. Now she loved him the way you would love an old blind dog. A pitying sort of love. The sort of love that's not quite strong enough to reach for the gun over the fireplace and do the kind thing.

She loved him because he was the first man she had ever loved, the first whose bed she had shared, and, for a woman like Agathe, that would always mean something. She loved him because they made a beautiful daughter together and because, years ago, Stopak had stood beside that little cot like a broken scarecrow, screaming, weeping over their dead child. She loved him because his business was a failure, because he was broken and pathetic. She loved him as one might love an old teddy from childhood—not for what it is but because we remember what it used to be and what it used to mean. And that's not how a man should be loved.

Stopak, for his part, did not love Agathe as a woman like Agathe should be loved. From the day they buried the baby, he never touched her again. He came home from the cemetery, still bowed down by the enormous weight of that tiny white coffin, dark earth spotting his trouser cuffs, and, when the door closed on the last, damp-eyed guest, Stopak slumped into a chair, crying.

Agathe had crossed the room to kiss him quietly on the top of his head. She took his hand. It was limp as a fish. "Shhh," she soothed and cradled his head against her spinnaker bosom. "Shhh, we still have time. We'll be happy again. We can have more babies. Not like her." The tears were rolling off Agathe's chin. "Never like her. Not to take her place. Other babies for us to love and we'll tell them about their big sister in Heaven. Not now. Soon."

But Stopak only sat there with the look of a felled ox and, between sobs, he gasped out refusal. "No. No more. Babies. Not. Again. No. More." He meant it. Life in the little flat changed. Stopak started to come home late from work. The food Agathe made for him dried in the oven or disappeared, like cinders, into the rubbish bin by the sink. But she loved him. She knew she could save him so she waited every night in the kitchen until he came home—whenever he came home—and mouthed her way through spoiled, parched meals with him. He ate everything without a word as if he was shovelling coke into a furnace. Once she even tried to trick him with soup, then cherry pie, then lamb chops but he ate it all in silence, just as he would have done if she had piled everything into one big basin and dumped it on the table in front of him.

The next evening, to make up for it, Agathe hurried home with a brace of pheasant. In the kitchen, she trimmed off their breasts and wrapped the meat in thick slices of dry, oak-smoked bacon. While it was roasting she sliced carrots and boiled potatoes and laid the table. It was ready when Stopak arrived and he ate it as if it was porridge.

Agathe looked at him in disgust and disbelief, pushing her fingers through her thick black hair, almost tearing it out with frustration. "For Christ's sake, Stopak!" she screamed. "Say 'That was nice' or something."

"That was nice," said Stopak and he took the evening paper from the pocket of the jacket hung over his chair, flapped it open and began to read.

Agathe was heartbroken but she wasn't ready to give up. She was a woman and she understood a man's appetites. Above all, she understood Stopak's.

The next day, as soon as the first peal of bells from the cathedral announced her lunch hour, Agathe left her desk and went into the mayor's empty office. She wrapped a scarf round her head, turned to face the coat of arms hanging on the wall and murmured a hurried prayer. "Good Walpurnia, you gave yourself to be ravished by the Huns for the sake of the women of Dot. Well, I'm a woman of Dot and I want a Hun for my husband tonight. A Hun! It won't save all the women of Dot but it might save one man. Help me. Please." Then she dipped a polite curtsey that showed off her pretty legs and hurried out the door.

Agathe clipped down the Town Hall's marble stairs in her high heels and trotted over White Bridge to Braun's department store where she squandered a purseful of notes on several, almost invisible, items of underwear. "It's all so expensive," she gasped, "and it's hardly even there."

The elderly shop assistant smiled. "That's because it's made by fairies—woven from the cotton they find in the tops of aspirin bottles on the night of the full moon. Hans Christian Andersen wrote a story about it and some genius developed an entire mathematical formula to explain why the price of knickers rises as the size of knickers falls. Do you want them?"

"Yes, I'll have them."

"You'll freeze to death. Listen, for the price, I'll throw in a nice thick undershirt. Wear it." She wrapped everything carefully in layers of pink tissue and sprinkled broken lavender heads between the sheets and tied it all in ribbons. Then she put the whole thing in a shiny red cardboard box, with "Braun's" written on it in gold, and tied up with a yellow raffia cord.

It dangled hopefully from Agathe's little finger as she hurried back to work and it sat in her in-tray all afternoon. When the sun came through the office window and warmed it, wafts of lavender began to drift round the room. The scent of it thrilled her.

Agathe spent the rest of the day glancing from her work to the little red box and from the box to the clock above the door to Mayor Krovic's office. She was tingling. Her stomach was fluttering. She went to mark up another entry in the mayor's diary but her hand trembled so much that the pen left an ugly blot on the page. Coffee. Time for coffee. She must have some coffee.

As she stood by the machine watching the coffee splutch, splutch, splutch into the glass lid, Agathe danced from foot to foot, singing a song about "The Boy I Love" that her granny had taught her when she was a little girl. She had sung it to Stopak when they were first walking out together. It was only then, when she was older, that she had understood how naughty the words were. It made her happy. It made her happy to remember Granny and the old days with Stopak and the thrill of it—and the naughtiness—and it made her happy to think of that little red box and the naughtiness to come. She was happy anyway. It wasn't the song. It was the box and hope that made her happy. A little box full of hope, like Pandora's box but without the bad stuff. Just the hope and a little bit of naughtiness and she would be glad to let that escape out into the world.

The coffee machine gave a final snort, like Stopak just before he rolled over in the night, and Agathe poured out two cups—one for her and one for Good Mayor Krovic. Then, with a couple of ginger biscuits balanced in the saucer, she wiggled through the office, past her desk and towards the mayor's room. Before she even opened the door, she heard him whistling "The Boy I Love."

"I haven't heard that song in a long time," he said, taking the saucer. "My grandmother used to sing it."

"Mine too," said Agathe.

"She was a wicked old woman, my grandmother."

Agathe laughed. "Mine too. She was the child of pirates, you know."

"She was not!"

"No, truly. The child of pirates or a lost Russian princess.

Nobody knew. They found her when she was very small, wandering along the beach one morning, sucking her thumb and cuddling a velvet blanket with red and gold stripes. A kind farmer took her in and made her his own. But I think she must have been more pirate than princess. Imagine teaching a young girl a song like that!"

"All things are pure to the pure," said Tibo. He pointed with his pen and asked, "Is that for me?"

Agathe was puzzled.

"The Braun's box? A present for me?"

She was surprised and a little embarrassed to see the scarlet package swinging from her left hand. "This? Oh, this! This. No. Not for you. Sorry, I bought it at lunchtime. I must have picked it up by mistake. No. Not for you. Sorry. Just for me. Well, that is. No." Agathe began to back out the door but Tibo called her back.

"Everything all right, Mrs. Stopak? I mean things at home. I know you and Stopak . . . well, a sad time. We were all very sorry. If you could do with a day or two off work, we can manage. I can get one of the girls from the Town Clerk's Office to come in. It's not a problem."

Agathe put on a solemn face. "You're very kind, Mayor Krovic, but, honestly, things are fine now. Things have been bad but they're better now. Honestly. Much better."

"I'm glad," said the mayor. "Look, I won't need you any more today. Why not take the rest of the afternoon off?"

That made Agathe very happy—after all, she had some new clothes she wanted to try on. She thanked him and left the office. From behind the door, she heard him shout, "And thanks for the coffee." Good Mayor Krovic.

The sun was still sparkling in the fountains of City Square as Agathe left the Town Hall. With her coat thrown over one arm, she crunched over the gravel along the boulevard on the banks of the Ampersand. She strolled along the avenue, switching from pools of sunshine to dark blobs of elm-shade and back into sunshine, swinging her handbag as she walked in time to "The Boy I Love" playing inside her head. At Aleksander Street, she stopped at the delicatessen to buy some bread and cheese and cooked ham but she came out with all that and more—a green papier mâché carton of strawberries, the first of the season, a bottle of wine, a bar of chocolate and, at the bottom of her bag, alongside the little scarlet package from Braun's, two bottles of beer. "If St. Walpurnia does her job, he'll need to build his strength up," she said to herself.

There was a black kitten curling itself round the bins at the bottom of the stair that led to the Stopaks' little flat. Agathe stopped to pick the cat up and pet it. "Black cats are lucky," she told it, "but I've got all the luck I need in this little box so you'll just have to stay here for tonight." And she put the cat back on the pavement and began to climb the stairs.

Her bag was becoming heavy and the string handles were cutting into her fingers but she hardly noticed. The little red box made everything seem light.

Agathe bumped the door of the flat shut with her bottom and emptied her groceries on the kitchen table. She took a sharp knife and cut the bread, spread the cheese and ham neatly on a plate, arranged everything just as it should be with the beer bottles wrapped in a wet cloth on the window ledge.

She was satisfied. "Nothing to burn, nothing to dry out. Ready to eat." But she decided to leave the wine for Stopak to open. That could be his job—a man's job. Then she took the little box, locked herself in the bathroom and turned on the taps.

Steam rose and filled the room as she undressed. Agathe unbuttoned her dress. In the mirror above the sink, another Agathe did the same. The Agathe in the bathroom, our Agathe, looked at her appraisingly. The Agathe on the other side of the glass looked back and smiled. Both Agathes let their yellow dresses fall from their shoulders and whisper to the floor. Our Agathe picked up her dress and hung it from a hook on the back of the door. She would need it later. The Agathe in the mirror probably did the same but it was impossible to be sure, since she had drawn a modest curtain of steam across her window. On this side, in the Dot where traffic drives on the right and where Agathe's beauty spot was just a little above her left lip, this Agathe took off her underwear and rolled it into a ball. She would not be needing that.

Naked and plump and luminously beautiful, she undid the package from Braun's. The sensible thick undershirt, the make-weight gift from the old lady in the shop. That was a kind thing. Agathe smiled and put it aside on top of the green wooden bathroom stool. And then there was a layer of pink tissue paper. A scattering of lavender flowers fell to the floor as she opened it and Agathe giggled and stooped to pick them up again, pinching them from the tiles between finger and thumb. She did not notice how the movement stirred her own scent through the steamy room. Tibo would have noticed.

In a moment or two, Agathe had retrieved her new lingerie. She held it up to the ground-glass window and admired it, admired its opalescent transparency, its softness, its barely-thereness. She leaned over the steaming bath and hung it from the string where she usually hung her stockings to dry overnight. Pinned there she could admire it while she lay in the bath.

Agathe carefully gathered all the tissue paper from the package and folded it into a neat book. "I'll save that for Christmas," she said. At the bottom of the Braun's box there was still a purple layer of lavender blossom. It smelt wonderful—clean and bright and sharp and summery. With her nose in the box Agathe breathed it in deeply, held the smell of it in her lungs, savoured it. Then she emptied the box into the bath and stirred the blossoms round.

She put the little red box on the floor, well away from damaging steam or water splashes—it was a keepsake to treasure—and stepped into the bath.

She was a goddess. Titian could not have done her justice. She was Diana bathing in a forest pool out of sight of mortal eyes. The water rushed back in ripples, eager to touch her. It lapped the rim of the bath as she moved, sinking down deeper, sighing with relaxed enjoyment. Agathe piled her hair up to keep it out of the water and dark tendrils coiled on her neck in the rising steam. She looked up at her extravagant new underwear and smiled. She imagined Stopak's reaction, what it would urge him to, what she'd submit to—eagerly—for his sake.

She looked down at her body, pinked by the heat of the water, little toes wriggling under the faraway taps, melony, rose-tipped breasts awash in lavender-scented water and, between, dark fronds that moved like black anemones in the beat of the bath-tide.

Agathe, so long without a touch, caressed herself. And stopped. She reached for the soap. Soaping was permissible for a respectable married woman but only soaping. Through clenched teeth she gave a little growl of fury and frustration. "Oooh, Walpurnia, you'd just better!" Then she held her breath and sank under the water.

WHEN STOPAK CAME HOME FROM work that evening, Agathe was sitting in her chair by the window, wearing the yellow dress again. She got up at the sound of his key in the lock and hurried to the door to meet him.

Stopak stood like a gatepost as she kissed him and, though Agathe pretended to herself that she didn't notice, even that was another acknowledgement of another tiny rejection, another chill draught in the house. She took him by the hand and led him to the kitchen.

"I got some wine," she said, "for a treat, since it's such a nice day. But I can't open it. You do it, Stopak, you big strong man." And she "oohed" and "aahed" over his muscles.

Stopak sat at the table and pulled the cork. It was the only sound in the flat and it went off like a pistol shot. There were two glasses on the table. Stopak put the bottle down between them. The wine stayed unpoured, a red exclamation mark upside down on the table.

"Pour me some wine, then, you silly man," Agathe said and managed a laugh.

He filled two glasses and handed one to her. She took a sip.

He emptied his and filled another. She forced another laugh. "My word, lover, you must be in the mood."

"These days," he said, "I'm always in the mood."

"Good. Oh, good," said Agathe. "I like a man with an appetite."

And, under her breath, in a panicky whisper, she said the name "Walpurnia."

She made a hasty step towards the table. "Here, let me help you." She sat down and began to pile bread and cheeses and ham on to a plate for him. She made a huge open sandwich, glistening with yellow butter on bread with a crust that gleamed as if it was varnished, and heaped with salt ham. She picked it up and held it out to him. She wanted to feed it to him, as mothers feed their children or lovers feed each other.

"I can feed myself," he said coldly. "I'm not a . . ." but he didn't say the word. Even now, months later, he couldn't say the word.

Instead he started to reach out across the table, grabbing things for himself, slapping them down on the plate in front of him, wolfing them down angrily.

Agathe pretended not to notice. She stuck to the plan. She was going to enjoy a picnic with her man. Not quite warm enough to take a basket to the park but they'd have it here and then there would be love again.

She had a conversation planned, things to talk about, and she kept talking about them even when it was obvious that she was the only one talking. "I thought we might go on a trip over the holiday weekend. There was a brochure, well, a big pile of brochures, on the front desk at the Town Hall. They're bringing the pleasure steamer back—you remember, the old thing they used to have, almost an antique now. I wonder where it's been, but it's coming back. We could go over to the islands. We could see your uncle in Dash. We haven't seen him for a long time, apart from, well, that time, but not for a long time. You like him. I like him and he's always been nice to us. I wouldn't ask him to put us up but, if we stayed in that little boarding house down by the smokery, we could manage. It's a bit fishy but it wouldn't be expensive. We could afford it and we could do with a couple of days away. You must be due the time off and the whole town shuts down for the holiday weekend anyway. There's no point staying open just to watch nobody coming in."

And on and on like that she heard herself, rattling on and on like a sewing machine spooling out an endless seam of words, mouth noise because it was the only thing that would hold off the quiet and, if it was quiet, she would have to look at him, saying nothing, and he might glare at her with that mixture of boredom and disgust which must mean that he found her boring and disgusting when she was not boring and disgusting. She was not. She knew she was not. He was wrong about that. It was Stopak who had gone wrong. But she could cure him and table talk wasn't part of the cure. The plan said the cure would come later, just a couple of hours later.

"And curtains for the bedroom. I thought red would be a nice change. Cheer the place up. They usually have a sale at Braun's about this time of the year and there's bound to be some old offcut lying round in their basement. I'll bet I could find something that would just be perfect for curtains and I might even cover your old chair." And on and on until, "Had enough? But don't you want some strawberries? I got them specially. Save them up for later. I bet I can tempt you later. Go and have a seat and read your paper. I'll clean up. You've had a hard day." And the scraping of the chair and the flap of the newspaper and the sigh of the sofa springs.

Agathe stood by the sink, mopping the dishes and singing "The Boy I Love" softly to herself, but there was a catch in her voice and her eyes stung. When she was finished, she emptied the sink and carefully mopped all round it. She dried everything and stacked it and put it away. She hung the damp towel from the rail in front of the oven to let it air and she took an old knife from the drawer in the kitchen table and began to hunt for grease. Agathe ran the blunt blade along every edge in the room—round the enamel rim of the stove, under the hood where the flue passed out through the wall, on the tops of cupboards, along skirting boards. Tiny, almost imperceptible shavings of grease spooled off the blade and clung there. She washed them away in the sink and filled a bucket of hot soapy water and rinsed everything down.

She had calculated it would take almost exactly two hours—just as long as it would take Stopak to wring every last drop of ink out of the evening paper. She knew. That was how long it took every night. Nobody could get value out of the paper like Stopak. And then, when it was done, the kitchen would be clean, the kitchen where they would meet across tomorrow's breakfast table as lovers again, the kitchen where he would hold her and look into her eyes and acknowledge that she had saved him. It would be so wonderful. Like the morning after their wedding. Like a new wedding. She was drying the last of the cupboard doors when she heard the springs creak in the sofa again and Stopak got up to go to bed. He left without a word. No goodnight. No warning that he was leaving. Silence. She heard him sit on the bed. A shoe dropped. Sighs. A shoe dropped. Agathe took her bucket and emptied it into the sink. She looked down at her hands. Pink. Rough. She turned the cold tap on hard and held them under the flow of water until the pipes began to screech and knock in the walls. Better. Calmer.

Anyway there was a jar of cream on the dressing table. She thought about taking handfuls of it and smearing it on Stopak. No. No. No. Not the plan. She tidied up and walked through the flat to the bedroom where Stopak lay like a corpse in the bed.

"Hello," she whispered teasingly and lit the lamp on her dressing table.

Stopak made some grudging acknowledgement. "I was trying to sleep," he said.

"I know. I'm sorry. I won't be long." Agathe let the yellow dress fall to the floor at her feet. She kicked it away with the toe of her shoe and stood there, more naked than naked, wrapped in whispers of pink gauze. She bent over unnecessarily to pick up the dress and stepped to the wardrobe where she hung it over the door. Stopak's eyes were boring into her.

"What do you think?" she asked, preening herself, running her fingers over the slivers of cloth that decorated her.

He lay in bed and said nothing.

Agathe crossed the room again and sat down on the little stool by her dressing table. Her stockings whispered against each other as she crossed her legs elegantly and there was a metallic sound as she unscrewed the lid from a jar of lavender-scented cream. She scooped a little out and began to rub it slowly into her hands. Slowly. Watching him in the mirror as she did it, blowing him kisses and making baby faces at him.

"You mustn't hate me. It was so expensive. And it barely covers me here . . ."—and she pointed—"or here . . ." and she pointed again. "And it's so thin. I bet you can see right through it, you bad boy. You mustn't peek."

She saw in the mirror that Stopak couldn't take his eyes off her and she pretended to scold him. "See! I told you not to peek and you're peeking. You're looking right at me. Naughty, naughty Stopak. Very naughty." She made a little pout at him in the glass as she stood up again.

"But I don't blame you. It's such pretty stuff and quite good value when you think about it. The lady in the shop told me that fairies make it from bits of cotton they steal from aspirin bottles on the night of the full moon, so that must make it very precious but . . ." She began to crawl from the foot of the bed towards him, writhing like a tigress. "If a big, strong man like you got a hold of it, you could probably just tear it to ribbons. You could probably just bite it off me with your teeth like a wolf, couldn't you, you bad, bad man?"

Stopak threw back the covers. "I have to go to the bathroom," he said.

"Now? You have to go to the bathroom now?"

"Yes. Now. Go to the bathroom."

"All right, then. I'll wait. I'll just wait. Don't be too long, you naughty boy. I've got so little on I'll freeze to death without big, strong Stopak."

Stopak did not come back. After a time, Agathe took off her shoes and climbed under the covers. When she woke up again, Stopak's side of the bed was still empty and she could hear noises coming through the flat. She got up and wrapped herself in a dressing gown and stumbled down the hall. Under her feet, she could feel the knotholes in the floorboards where they were wearing through the linoleum. There were tearing sounds coming from the bathroom. Agathe was alarmed. She tried the door but it was locked. "Stopak! Stopak, are you all right? What are you doing in there?"

"I'm fine. I'm working."

"What do you mean, 'working'? Stopak, it must be three in the morning. What are the neighbours going to think?"

He came to the door. Agathe could hear him just on the other side of the thin board panel. "I'm just working. That's all. I thought the place could do with a bit of a tidy up. It's been a while since we decorated in here."

Agathe was almost screaming. "For God's sake, Stopak, it's been a while since we did a lot of things. Come to bed. Do some of those things. To hell with you and your decorating, Stopak. Come to bed. There's some men in Dot would be glad of an offer like that."

"Name one!" he screamed. "Just name one!" But the door stayed shut.

Agathe stood outside in silence for a moment or two until she heard the sound of paper peeling off the walls again, then she went back up the hall, threw her underwear on to the floor and climbed into bed, naked this time, and wept.

IN THE MORNING, WHEN IT CAME, THE HOUSE was silent again. Agathe got up and shambled to the bathroom. The walls were bare and it smelled damp. Stopak had repainted all the woodwork and filled in a lot of little holes in the plaster but he'd left the place tidy apart from a couple of tiny curls of paper Agathe could see hiding under the bath. She shuffled to the sink and groaned at her reflection in the mirror. What a mess. A gorgon. No wonder he wouldn't. She ran the taps and scrubbed her face clean. Her eyes were still red but there was nothing to be done about that. Agathe was exhausted. She felt as if she had spent the night sleeping on a pile of rocks. Her throat burned from sobbing, her chest was thick, her nose was blocked and swollen to the size of a beetroot and she creaked in every joint. "This is what it's like to be old," she said.

But mirror Agathe said, "You're not old. Don't let him make you old."

Agathe reached to the bathroom stool where the makeweight undershirt still lay neatly folded. She picked it up and slipped it over her head. She failed to notice the tiny impacts of the last few lavender blossoms as they fell to the floor. "See! An old lady in an old lady's undershirt!" It wasn't true.

The sad red-eyed figure in the mirror was more alluring and erotic than the seductive strumpet she had tried to be the night before.

The thick undershirt clung to her curves like syrup and barely skimmed the outer edge of decency. Agathe could not look anything less than sumptuous—it was beyond her. She walked flat-footed to the kitchen. She had intended the place to be filled with the smell of bacon and coffee and cinnamon bagels. Instead it smelled of bleach and turpentine from the brushes Stopak had washed in the sink. She groaned, took them out, put them in an old cup and scoured the remains of the paint away. "Oh, what's the point?" she muttered. "What's the bloedig point?"

Agathe stopped cleaning. She threw the scouring pad in the sink and put the coffee pot on the stove as she stamped angrily out of the room. She stamped angrily back again and took the coffee pot off the stove.

She left again and sat down on the stool in front of her dressing table.

"What's the bloedig point?" This was going to take some time. "What's the *bloedig* point?" She combed her hair furiously. It fell around her face in deep dark coils. "What *is* the bloedig point?" She stood up and went to a chest of drawers, took out a clean pair of knickers, visible knickers, enormous knickers, boiled grey, cheese-holed, comfortable knickers, and put them on.

"Undershirt and knickers. Old lady undershirt and old bloedig lady bloedig knickers! Bloedig! Bloedig! Bloedig!"

Agathe sat in front of her mirror and did her make-up, never halting her mantra of curses except when that tiny little brush, loaded with dark red paint, was hovering over her mouth. Then she cursed inwardly. It meant she had to hold the fury inside until she had blotted the paint away with a tissue-kiss and then, through perfect lips, she spat vile things at the mirror.

Then she felt better. "Better. Yes, a lot better. Get a bit of slap on, girl, and face the world." In the mirror, the rumpled bed lay like a relief map of the Andes. "To hell with the bloedig bed—let Stopak make it." She reached into the wardrobe and pulled out her blue dress, the one with the white piping, slipped on her shoes and walked out of the flat.

It was dark on the stair. She walked carefully with one hand on the old wooden banister, one hand on the central stone post. Agathe was glad to reach the street. She stepped off the last unsteady tread of the stair and she was about to hurry off to work when . . . "Good morning, Agathe!"

Agathe's hand shot to her chest. Hektor. She hated Hektor. She hated him because he was gorgeous—all dark and tall and dangerous. Always that same black coat sweeping the pavement winter and summer, his hair all lank and floppy, his face so pale, his eyes so hot like a saint or a devil. Women looked at him and wondered things out loud—women Agathe knew, decent married women who should know better, women who should know the value of a good man with a steady job instead of talking that way about a waster like Hektor. So Agathe chose to hate him, family or not.

She hated everything about him from his unpolished shoes to his ludicrous moustache. It made him look ratty. And he was dirty, stinking of drink and cheap cigarettes. That boy could do with a wash. She looked away quickly from his ice-blue eyes and hated him some more.

"Good morning, Hektor. I'm sorry. I can't ask you in. I'm going to work."

"Oh, that doesn't matter." He flicked a lock of black hair back behind his ear. "I've come to see Stopak anyway."

"Stopak's not in either. What do you want with Stopak anyway?"

"Agathe, I'm surprised at you. What kind of way is that to talk? You don't have a cigarette, do you? No, you don't do that sort of thing. Not you. Not Agathe. And why do I have to have an excuse to come and visit my own cousin? My favourite cousin in the whole wide world. My own darling cousin."

"Well, he's not here. I don't know where he is but I do know this—he hasn't got any money so you can just leave your darlingest cuzziny-wuzziny alone!"

She moved to go but Hektor refused to stand aside and stayed, smiling down at her as she squeezed past him and hurried on to the end of the road. At the corner of Aleksander Street, she could have caught the tram to work along the Ampersand but it was still early so she decided to go for a coffee at The Golden Angel instead.

Agathe crossed the road and stood by the corner of Green Bridge, waiting for the Castle Street tram. She was watching the end of Aleksander Street nervously. Sure enough, Hektor came down the street. He saw her. He looked right at her and curled his lip. She saw his moustache hike up a little at one side. Stupid smirk. What was that supposed to mean? Looking at a decent woman like that as if he knew something. He couldn't know anything. What could there be to know?

The tram was coming and she put out her arm to flag it down. The driver clanged his iron bell to warn that he was stopping and Agathe stepped neatly on to the platform at the rear. As the tram pulled away she looked back and saw Hektor outside The Three Crowns—a rough sort of place with men who would take bets and fight. On Saturday nights, they would spill out on the pavement and spit and quarrel. Agathe saw Hektor walk up to a man in a torn sweater. They spoke. The man gave Hektor a cigarette. He was still looking right at her as the tram crossed the bridge and turned away.

The tram juddered. Agathe turned her eyes to the front. All over Dot people were going to work in the sunshine. Agathe watched them as her tram rolled through the city. A couple who kissed goodbye for the day at the very next tram stop, the woman turning to wave as she skipped on to the back platform. A little boy in shorts kicked a red ball along the pavement as he brought the morning paper home, a yellow dog bouncing on a string beside him. She heard its yaps fade away as the tram hurried along the long avenue that leads to my cathedral. Agathe looked up coldly when the shadow of the vast dome fell across the passing tram. There should have been dramatic organ chords or the sweep of angel choirs. Nothing. She felt nothing. No awe, no protective glow, nothing. Maybe a little anger and disappointment but, apart from that, nothing.

May sunshine filtered through the thin young leaves on the limes of the avenue and Agathe saw, in silhouette, tiny birds flying between the branches. They flapped furiously—faster than the eye could register—and it seemed to exhaust them for they would suddenly fold their wings and fall through the air like tiny, resting torpedoes, fall, fall, fall, for a heartbeat then unfold their wings and flap again. They were everywhere among the trees, flapping, flying, falling.

Agathe craned her neck to watch them as the tram rattled along. "Look at them," she thought to herself. "Why are they doing that? What can it mean?" And then she felt suddenly foolish and concentrated very hard on the handbag propped on her prim knees. It didn't mean anything. It was just what they did. Some birds stretched out their wings and glided endlessly over oceans, some had to flap like clockwork toys to go from branch to branch. What can it mean? Nothing! What does it mean for a grown woman to look for a meaning in that? Some birds fly this way, some birds fly that way, the leaves come on the trees, the leaves fall off the trees, a man wants you, a man stops wanting you, a baby's born, a baby dies. That's all there is to it. There is no meaning in it. It doesn't mean anything.

Agathe felt her eyes fill and she hurriedly reached into her handbag for a tiny handkerchief and dabbed away the tears with a folded edge before they ruined her make-up.

The tram conductor clanged his bell. "Castle Street next stop!"

She stood up, swayed to the back of the tram and stepped off. The Golden Angel was just across the junction. Agathe stopped at the edge of the pavement, waited for the traffic to clear and crossed the road. As the heavy glazed doors of the cafe closed behind her, all the noise of the street disappeared, politely excluded as if by some solicitous major-domo. Inside, the place breathed calm and steam and coffee smells and cinnamon and almonds and peace and welcome. It was a coffee cathedral and, in the heart of it, like a vast organ gleaming under burnished copper domes and wrapped in polished brass pipes, the huge, steaming coffee machine spurted toccatas of flavour.

Agathe gave a heavy sigh and took off her gloves. All the tables were full but the high stools along the counter were still not taken. Agathe hated sitting there. It wasn't ladylike. She felt that, perched there, people would look at her. She was right, people would. Men because they couldn't help it, women because they knew they couldn't.

Agathe sat down on the stool at the very end of the counter. It was awkward. She had to hitch her skirt a little higher than she would have liked. It stretched over her hips a little tighter than she would have liked. People looked. Men noticed the way her stockings wrinkled a little at the heel. Women noticed them noticing.

At the other end of the bar, the owner, Cesare, was standing like a carved figure. Everything about him was black except for his sparkling white shirt. His hair was brilliantined black. His moustache, pencil thin, was carbon black, his eyes, his suit, his tie, his gleaming shoes that turned up at the toe, all black, and the spotless white cloth that hung over his arm only made everything else all the blacker.

He moved to take Agathe's order but a voice came sharply from somewhere in the depths of the coffee machine. "I'll do this, Cesare."

"Yes, Mamma," he said and he went back to standing very still. Cesare was good at standing very still. He could do it for a long, long time.

And then, from out of the coffee organ, Mamma Cesare appeared. She was tiny, barely able to see over the counter, but she was formidable—a pocket battleship of a woman. Everything that was black about Cesare was iron grey with her. Hair pulled back in a tight bun the colour and texture of iron, iron-grey wool stockings on bow legs, shoes that should have been black but were scuffed down a few shades from constant wear as she waddled for miles every day between the tables and a dress that had been black when she put it on in the first days of her widowhood. But that was decades and countless yester-washes ago.

Mamma Cesare rocked her way from hip to hip down the passage behind the counter and stopped in front of Agathe. From down there, on the floorboards she had polished with nearly fifty years of feet, Mamma Cesare looked up at Agathe balanced on her high stool and smiled like a shark. "Voddayavont?"

"Coffee, please. And a Danish pastry."

"Have the coffee. The Danish you don't need."

Agathe bristled. "I'd still like one. Coffee and a Danish pastry, please."

"Just the coffee."

"Look, who's the customer here? The customer is always right."

"Not when she's wrong," said Mamma.

"Do you talk to all your customers like this?"

At the other end of the counter, Cesare was starting to move. He may even have cleared his throat but Mamma held up a hand and he stopped.

"The customers I talk to like this are the customers that need talked to like this. You don't need the Danish. Danish will make you old. Don't let him make you old. You're not old."

Agathe slumped on her stool. "Just coffee," she said.

Getting the coffee took some time. Mamma Cesare had to shuffle back to the coffee organ and pour milk into a tin jug and grind her special mix of blue-black beans and coax steamy whistles from the pipes and flip levers and push buttons and build a crescendo of cream into a swelling finale that frothed in the cup.

She carried it back to Agathe and, reaching up, placed it carefully on the counter.

"Coffee," she said. "No Danish." Then Mamma Cesare gently turned the saucer. There, at one side, there was a mouth-sized block of chocolate—two layers, white on the bottom and bitter-dark on top, stamped with the image of a tiny coffee cup. "No Danish."

"How did you know?" Agathe asked.

"Sometimes I know. Sometimes I see things. Sometimes people tell me things."

Agathe was embarrassed. "What people? Who knows? Who else knows my business?"

Mamma Cesare gave her hand a reassuring pat. "Not these people. Just people I know. They come here, they talk to me sometimes. Drink your coffee. Let's talk."

Agathe took a sip of coffee and looked deep into her cup. "I don't know what to talk about," she said.

"How about him?" Mamma Cesare nodded towards the door where a tall man stood at a high table built round an ornate iron pillar. "That's Mayor Tibo Krovic."

"I know," said Agathe. "I work for him. Didn't the voices tell you that?"

Mamma Cesare harrumphed a little but pretended not to notice. "Every morning, Good Mayor Krovic, he comes in here and stands at that same table. Every morning, he orders a strong Viennese coffee with plenty of figs, drinks it, sucks one mint out of the fresh bag he brings every day and leaves the rest of the bag on the table. Every morning. Always the same, regular as the Town Hall clock. And he does this why? He does this because he is absent-minded and forgetful? No! Not Good Mayor Tibo Krovic. A man can run a town like Dot who is absent-minded and forgetful? No. He does this because he knows I like mints and, if he came in here every day and gave me a bagful, I would have to turn them away. Politely, of course, but it would still very likely cause offence and I would lose a good customer and he would lose a place to drink good coffee. Clever Good Mayor Krovic."

"He's a very nice man," said Agathe. "I like working for him."

"A nice man—pah! Eat some chocolate."

Agathe lifted the block between two dainty fingers. She felt it melt a bit under the heat of her skin and she wanted to eat it all in one lump but, instead, she bit it carefully in two and put the other half back in the saucer. A few tiny crumbs stuck to her lipstick. She flicked them away with the tip of a kitten tongue. Men looked. It took ages.

"All I'm telling you," said Mamma Cesare, "is that you need a man. I know, I know—you look at me and you think I don't know. I know. This one," she gestured back along the counter at Cesare standing like a black statue, "where do you think he came from? And all I'm telling you is, when you need a man, make sure it's a good one. Anybody can get the bad ones. The bad ones there are a lot of. The good ones are harder."

Agathe almost laughed. "Mayor Krovic is my boss. He's not interested in me—and I'm not interested in him. I'm a respectable married woman."

"Who sleeps alone. Tell me I'm wrong."

Agathe looked into her cup again. "No, you're not wrong."

"Coffee, chocolate. Drink, eat."

Agathe obeyed like a schoolgirl.

"I'm not telling you to jump into bed with Tibo Krovic. But the time is coming, my girl, and you could do a lot worse, a lot worse. Finish your coffee."

Agathe gulped it down. It left her with a frothy white moustache.

"Now turn the cup over, spin it three times and give it back to me. Use the saucer. Don't touch the cup any more."

Now it was Agathe's turn to look disapproving. "You're making fun of me," she said. "You can't read my fortune in a coffee cup. Nobody reads coffee cups. It's tea leaves. People read tea leaves."

"Just give me the cup!" said Mamma Cesare. "Tea leaves, coffee cups, it doesn't matter. In the old country, I am strega from long line of strega. If I tell you I can read the future in your bath water, you should listen." Mamma Cesare turned the cup over and looked closely at the milky patches inside. "Huh, like I thought. Nothing. I knew it."

"Don't say that. I must have some future. Don't say 'nothing.' Tell me what you see! Tell me."

Mamma Cesare made an impatient noise in her throat. "I see you are making a journey over water to meet the love of your life, I see you are coming back here to talk to me at ten o'clock tonight and I see you are going to be late for work."

Agathe sat up straight on her stool and looked anxiously at her watch. The high table by the pillar was empty except for an almost-full bag of mints, and the big double doors were closing quietly. "I have to go," she said. "I'll be late for work." She got down awkwardly from the stool and her dress rode up improperly over her thigh.

"Ten o'clock," said Mamma Cesare. "There's something I want to show you. Now run."

"For goodness' sake, I can't come back at ten. It's late."

"Ten o'clock. Pay for the coffee then. I won't wait."

Agathe banged the door on the way out and hurried into Castle Street.

Outside, the sun was still shining brightly. Agathe stopped in front of the big curved window of The Golden Angel, put on her gloves and checked her reflection in the glass.

Mamma Cesare waved at her from behind the counter, a tuberous hand appearing above the mahogany, like the last glimpse of a drowning sailor about to vanish beneath the waves. Everything was neat, everything was straight, Agathe was ready for work but she would have to hurry.

Above the noise of the traffic she imagined she could hear machinery starting to whirl up in the towers of the cathedral, weights shifting, chains uncoiling, great metal gears whirring. Agathe hurried down Castle Street without even bothering much to watch herself in the shop windows. By the time she reached Verthun Smitt's, the big double-fronted ironmonger's, she could see Mayor Krovic up ahead, just stepping on to White Bridge. Somewhere up on the hill, doors were opening above the cathedral's great west front, a painted copper apostle with a shiny brass halo was getting ready to roll out on his trolley and a black enamel devil was getting ready to run away for another hour.

Mayor Krovic had crossed the bridge and he was stepping smartly into City Square but Agathe was close behind him, a little out of breath. She hurried on.

An old woman raised her red umbrella—honestly, an umbrella on a day like this—and waved it. "Mayor Krovic, Mayor Krovic, a word please. It's my grandson's school."

And Good Mayor Krovic, because he always stopped to listen to the people of Dot, stopped to listen to the old woman with the red umbrella as the first, deep, bronze-throated stroke of nine o'clock filled City Square and Agathe trotted past towards the Town Hall steps. "Good morning, Mayor Krovic," she panted and he nodded at her politely. Agathe never even noticed the queue of ducklings quacking in the waters of the Ampersand she had just crossed.

INSIDE THE TOWN HALL, PETER STAVO WAS clanking away from the bottom of the green marble stairs with his bucket. "I've washed that!" he yelled as Agathe ran for her office.

"Sorry, I'll be careful." She slipped off her shoes and trotted upstairs. When he came in from the square a moment later, Good Tibo Krovic saw the image of Agathe's toes was still evaporating from the stone and he sighed.

Halfway along the corridor to his office, Tibo stopped in the middle of the thick blue carpet and looked admiringly at the big picture hanging outside the council chamber—*The Siege of Dot.* And there were Mayor Skolvig and half a dozen friends, holding out in the tower of the old Customs House, still firing at the invaders as they pillaged the town. The graceful stonework of the windows was half shot away, everybody but Skolvig was battered and bandaged and he stood there, in a manly suit of black and a stiff lace ruff, his arm raised in heroic encouragement, urging them on to one more fusillade. Tibo found himself standing in front of the picture as if it was a mirror, raising his arm to mimic Skolvig and, as he posed there, he wondered, "Would I? Could I?"

Tibo's name was already written in gold on the wooden panels that recorded all the mayors of Dot—"Tibo Krovic" gleaming in last place at the end of a long line that ran through Anker Skolvig and back to times before there were surnames to "Vilnus, Utter, Skeg," men lost at the bottom of a well of history who existed only as bits of broken seal on scraps of parchment locked in the charter box.

Inside the council chamber, all around the walls and on either side of the stained-glass windows hung portraits of the mayors of Dot—men with magnificent whiskers in respectable, broadcloth suits, fading into the shadowy darkness of treacle-tarry varnish. In the quiet of the empty chamber, Tibo sat for a while in his grand chair and picked out a spot on the opposite wall. "There," he thought, "I'll go there, I think." And, for a moment, he imagined all the councillors' desks cleared away, the chandeliers lit and the chamber filled with guests drinking to his health before he walked out of the Town Hall for the last time. And what then? There would be time to fix that garden gate but, after that, what?

Tibo pictured himself doddering back into the Town Hall on a cane, just at the hour for morning coffee, and slipping into the councillors' lounge. He saw himself giving wise advice to a new mayor and a new generation of councillors who met, every week, under his portrait and grew up fed on stories of what Tibo Krovic had done for Dot. He saw their embarrassed smiles. He saw them looking at their watches and recalling urgent meetings as they tried, politely, to get away. "But do call in again at any time," they would say. "Always a welcome for Tibo Krovic. No. No. Stay and finish your coffee. Help yourself to biscuits." And the door would bump politely shut and he would be alone.

"That's years away," said Tibo sadly and he went back out into the corridor and past *The Siege of Dot* again. In spite of the blood and the gun smoke, Anker Skolvig looked suddenly smug. "You had it easy," said Tibo and he opened the door to his office.

Agathe was already at work on the morning post when he arrived and he smiled at her as he walked past her desk and on into the inner office. He couldn't help it. He'd tried but everything about her just thrilled him—the way she was holding that envelope, her sharp, efficient wielding of the paperknife, the dainty way she dropped the "special" stamps into that old jam jar on her desk, the tip of her tongue held in the corner of her mouth, her eyelids opening and closing, the smell of her, her smile. "Good morning again, Mayor Krovic," said Agathe.

"Hello, Mrs. Stopak. Sorry I'm late." And the lush municipal carpet felt as queasy as molasses under Tibo's feet as he covered the last few paces to his desk. She was watching him. She knew. She could see how he felt. He knew it. But, when Tibo looked back from his doorway, Agathe hadn't even moved in her chair. She sliced through the last envelope, removed the folded letter inside and added it to her pile. Without so much as turning round, she called, "I'll bring the post in shortly. Would you like another coffee?"

Tibo put his jacket on a wooden hanger and hooked it over the hat stand in the corner of his room. "I've just had one, thank you," he answered. And then, "*Another* coffee? How did you know?"

He reached into the inside pocket of his jacket, took out his pen and sat at the desk. From the other side of the room I looked down at him like a motherly Santa Claus suspended on the town coat of arms.

"Much help you are," he told me angrily.

Agathe overheard him from the door. "Did you say something?"

"No, I was just talking to myself," said Tibo. "It's old age catching up with me."

"Sometimes it's the only way to get any sensible conversation." She handed him his letters. "The mayor of Umlaut has written. Something about celebrations for the anniversary of their town charter. He's inviting a delegation from Dot. It's on top of the pile."

Tibo snorted. "That's as much as my job's worth. You know how much the Dottians hate the Umlauters. But I'll have to look at it, I suppose. Thanks for pointing it out. And what did you mean, 'another coffee'?"

Agathe realised that Tibo had no idea she was at The Golden Angel earlier and, for some reason, she decided that she didn't want him to know. "Sorry. Slip of the tongue. Nothing at all. Would you like a coffee? That was all I meant. Any coffee at all? No?"

"No, thanks," said Tibo.

"Right. As you like. You're on duty at the Magistrates' Court at ten thirty. Just to remind you. The clerk says it's the usual routine stuff. Mostly drunks and wife-beaters." Agathe closed the door on her way out.

Tibo got up, walked the long way round his desk and opened it again. For the hour or so until he left for court, there would be glimpses of her.

By nine twenty-five, he had gone through the post. Most of it was rubbish and could wait until the afternoon. At nine twenty-seven, he asked Agathe back to his office so that he could dictate some urgent letters. As she sat down and crossed her legs, Tibo looked very hard out the window, studying the dome of the cathedral.

"To His Honour Mayor Zapf, Town Hall, Umlaut," he said efficiently. "I need two copies of this. Begins. Dear Mayor Zapf, The mayor and council of Dot have received your invitation to attend celebrations marking the anniversary of the Umlaut town charter. After due consideration, the mayor and council of Dot have decided to reject this thinly disguised insult. You cannot believe that Umlaut's history of treachery, deceit and double-dealing can be wiped out by the offer of beer and mouldy sandwiches, knocked up in that unhygienic brothel which passes for a Town Hall. Speaking for myself, I would rather be the plaything of a Turkish cavalry regiment than soil my shoes by visiting your sordid little village. However, I understand the Turks are fully occupied with the wives of the councillors of Umlaut. Yours etc. Can you read that back please, Mrs. Stopak?"

She did.

"I don't like 'brothel,'" said Tibo. "Harsh word. Make it 'bordello.' Much nicer."

Agathe made a few tiny marks with the point of her pencil. "Bordello," she said. "Two Ls and two copies."

Tibo looked back at her from the window. "Ready for the next one?"

She nodded.

"To Mayor Zapf of Umlaut. Begins. Dear Zapf, Thanks for the invitation. Hope to return the favour soon. I'm planning a fishing trip the weekend after next. Usual place. Bring beer. Best, Tibo. Just one of those, Mrs. Stopak, and send it in a plain envelope, not the city stationery, and nothing on file, thanks. Oh and you'd better mark it as personal. Thanks, that's all for now."

Agathe stood up to leave and Tibo watched her go, waiting for the very last sight of her before he sat down again at his desk. Agathe's typewriter began to click and whirr in the room next door and Tibo listened, imagining.

At ten o'clock, the bells of the cathedral rang out over the square again. Tibo checked his watch and got ready to leave for court.

The three letters were already waiting in a folder on Agathe's desk. She held it up to him as he passed. "For signing, Mayor Krovic."

Tibo tapped his pockets, found his pen and signed two of the letters. He wrote something quickly over the last envelope, folded it roughly and placed it inside his wallet. "That's a very nice dress," he said. "You're looking very nice today. Well, as usual, that is. Very nice."

"Thank you," said Agathe, modestly.

"Very. Nice." Tibo was beginning to stumble. "The colour. Nice. And that . . ." He gestured vaguely at the piping Agathe had taken so long to stitch into place. "It's very . . ." Tibo hated himself then. He could stand in front of the entire council and talk about anything, argue about anything, persuade anybody about anything, order anything but, in front of this woman, he was left mumbling "nice." Still, with Agathe, even "nice" seemed to please her. It did please her. Good Tibo Krovic was the only man in Dot who ever said "nice" to her. "Nice," he said again. "Right. Court."

Tibo put his pen back in his pocket and walked out of the office, past Anker Skolvig and his heroic hand gestures and back into the square.

The court of Dot is not its most inspiring civic building and Tibo's dread of the place grew deeper the closer that he got to it. The city fathers who built it skimped on the job. They chose a cheap, dung-coloured sandstone and the rain had soaked into it and bubbled it and winter frosts had sliced whole sheets of rotten stone off it.

Now my image carved over the door was indistinct and runny—almost bloated—as if I had been dragged from the Ampersand like a week-old suicide.

Outside, at the entrance, the court's "customers" gathered every day in dirty clumps, smoking, swearing, squabbling. The pavement there was dotted with foul blobs of spit and gum and cigarette stubs. Tibo despised these people. He hated them for making him their mayor. He wanted to be mayor of honest, hard-working people who swept their doorsteps and washed their children before tucking them into clean white sheets. But he had to be mayor of these people too. He was also the mayor of scum. Whether they bothered to vote or not, they were his. He had to protect them—from themselves and from each other—and he would give his life for them. He knew it—just like Anker Skolvig—but he didn't expect them to be glad of it or grateful or paint his picture in heroic poses or even say thanks. Tibo set his mouth into a stern flat line and walked firmly past them. Nobody spoke to him. One or two glared at him. Somebody spat but it landed on the filthy pavement and not on him.

Inside the courthouse it was just as bad—everything painted in shades of municipal sludge, bile yellow over baby-turd brown or dead-cat green, the smell of the bleach bucket mingled with the grease and old cigarettes of the crowd and, always, inevitably, one lamp, someplace, broken or missing.

Tibo looked into the courtroom. The place was deserted except for Barni Knorrsen from the *Evening Dottian,* sitting in the press box, reading a paper. The court would be quiet until the business started. Nobody liked to have to abandon their smoking and spitting until they really had to.

"Hello, Barni," said Tibo.

"Good morning, Mayor Krovic. Any excitement for us today?"

"I'm afraid not—just the usual drunks and wife-beaters, I'm told."

"It's been ages since we had a good murder!"

"And luckily that would be out of my league," said Tibo. "But listen, Barni, I was hoping I'd run into you here. There's a bit of something out of nothing that I wanted to show you—might make a tale for the paper. Here, tell me what you think." Tibo reached into his jacket and took out his wallet. There was Agathe's second copy of the letter to the Umlauters, bent to fit with "Private. In confidence" scrawled over one side in pen.

"No, that's not it," said Tibo and he put the slip of paper on the broad wooden lip of the press box. Barni was slow to notice so poor Tibo had to keep up a pantomime of burrowing into his wallet for quite a time. "No. No, that's not it either." Good God, there were only four pockets to go through. Small wonder Barni had never graduated to a big-league paper. "Maybe I should just take everything out and start from the beginning." Finally, Barni casually picked up his folded newspaper and flicked the letter on to the floor of the press box and covered it with his foot. "Does that man never polish his shoes?" Tibo wondered. He put everything back into his wallet. "Sorry to have wasted your time," he said. "It'll turn up."

"Don't worry about it, Mr. Mayor."

At the far side of the room, a door opened and the black-robed clerk nodded at Tibo. "We need you on the bench now, sir. Business is about to commence."

Tibo signalled his agreement. "Sorry, Barni, got to go. Busy, you know. Sorry. I'll be in touch about that other thing."

When Tibo took his seat on the court dais at precisely ten thirty, he looked across at the empty press box and smiled.

By eleven o'clock, Tibo had dealt with the first two cases of the day—an old drunk who had spent the night in the cells and a docker who'd come home from a night's drinking and hit his wife with the kitchen table when she asked where his wages were. The drunk was easy enough. There was no helping him. He had no money for a fine—every penny that he could scrounge from playing a wheezing accordion on windy street corners went to the cheapest rotgut vodka he could find. You could see him every day, sitting on a bench under the big holly tree in the old graveyard, guzzling it straight from the bottle. Nobody bothered him and that was how he liked it. Next winter would find him frozen to the ground on a shroud of stiff brown holly leaves and nobody would mourn—least of all him. But, last night, some zealous new constable had found him asleep, nursing a bottle wrapped in lilac tissue paper, and decided to do his duty.

"So you spent a night in the cells?" said Tibo in the sort of voice people reserve for deaf old aunts.

"Yezzor! Yezzor!" The old drunk spoke through vocal cords scorched by vomit.

"Better than sleeping in the graveyard, I suppose."

"Yezzor! Yezzor! Nuffadat to come. Yezzor!"

"Did they give you a good breakfast?"

"Yezzor! Yezzor, but I din eat it. I'm not muchava one fer fewd."

"No," said Tibo, "I imagine not. Right. Listen. This is what I'm going to do. I'm going to let you go with time served. But I don't want to see you again or the consequences will be severe."

"Yezzor."

"Is that understood?"

"Yezzor."

"Right, out you go."

The old man shuffled out of the dock. All around him, as he passed, others held back from him and the stench of his thick tweed coat, a vile blanket greased with years of his own filth. From his high chair at the front of the court Tibo could read on their faces exactly what he had felt for them. As low as they had gone, they were not so poor as to have nobody to despise. Tibo wondered who was looking down despising him.

"Next case!" yelled the clerk. "Pitr Stoki."

A little man with a swaggering stride sat down in the dock. Tibo watched him. There was a leery insolence about him. Cocky—a man who walked with his shoulders. Stoki sat down in the dock, looking from side to side with a challenge in his glance, sniffing repeatedly and brushing the tip of his nose with a curled finger.

Tibo leaned down from the bench. "Mr. Stoki, you are accused of assaulting your wife. Are you guilty or not guilty?"

Yemko Guillaume, the fattest lawyer in Dot, stood up to speak. Across the court, Tibo could hear his knees creak. Guillaume's belly was so vast that it hung in front of him in two lobes, he had breasts like jelly moulds and Tibo was left trying to outstare a hair-fringed navel that winked from his gaping shirt front. It brought to mind the county fair when fat farmers came in from the outlying places and tried to cheat the carnival folk by squinting at the sideshows through the gaps in their tents.

"I represent Mr. Stoki," said Guillaume. His voice came in strange wheezes, like the high pipes of an organ choked with lard. "Mr. Stoki pleads not guilty."

Then the clerk called the constable, a solid middle-aged man with respectable whiskers, who told of being called to Stoki's house when neighbours complained of screams and breaking furniture, and Mrs. Stoki's black eye and the story she told, which he noted at the time, word for word, in this very notebook, of what had happened.

"And was Mr. Stoki sober at the time?"

"No, Your Honour, Mr. Stoki was not sober at the time."

"So was Mr. Stoki drunk at the time?"

"Oh, Mr. Stoki was undoubtedly drunk at the time."

In the dock, Stoki sniffed some more and glared at the constable, jabbing his shoulders round like a bantamweight. The constable remained unimpressed and sniffed back.

On the dais, Tibo waved the end of his pen to signal that Guillaume was now free to speak.

"Constable, did you see my client strike his wife?" he asked.

The constable rocked on his big thick boots. "Good heavens, no, sir! In my experience, them as has the uncontrollable tempers and can't help themselves, always can when a constable's around."

Tibo snapped a reprimand, "Try to stick to the question, please, Constable."

"That is of no consequence, Your Honour, I have no more." Guillaume rolled back to his seat, descending gradually like a collapsing balloon and then suddenly crumpling into the complaining, squealing, straining chair.

"There's only one more witness," said the clerk, "the complainer."

Tibo recognised her. He had seen her in court every week. When the clerk said "the usual drunks and wife-beaters," this was the usually beaten wife. She was familiar—a pallid, stifled shriek of a woman with cowering eyes and a knuckled grip on herself. The same woman every week. The same blows. The same tears. The same screams. The same woman again and again.

Good Mayor Krovic stifled his fury and spoke to her in a flat and level voice. "I have to tell you, Mrs. Stoki, that you are not obliged to give evidence against your husband."

From the dock, Stoki nodded at her with a sharp jerk of the head and wiped his nose violently. She read the signal.

"No," she said. "I want to." She raised her hand to make the oath and, little by little, the story came out. Her eyes flickered between Tibo and the man in the dock as she told it.

No, her husband was not drunk. No, he had not stayed out that night. Yes, they had argued but that was her fault. It was nothing. She had nagged him. No, he definitely did not hit her.

Tibo saw the arm go back.

Yes, the chair broke but that was because she fell on it awkwardly. She was always clumsy that way—always falling and breaking things.

Tibo heard the slap. Tibo saw her fall.

It was all a mistake. The neighbours got excited about nothing. Stoki was a good man, a good husband.

Tibo saw a little boy, standing with his fists raised, tears streaming down his face and a father's giant fist beating him aside. It was all such a long time ago. That was what he must try to remember. All such a long time ago. He was not a little boy any more.

"Mr. Guillaume, have you any questions?"

"No questions, Your Honour. I would only invite you to rule in this case and excuse my client from the court."

Tibo laid his pen down on the notebook in front of him and pinched the bridge of his nose between tired fingers for a moment before he spoke. "Stand up, please, Mr. Stoki."

The little man stood up in the dock and shot his cuffs confidently.

"Mr. Stoki, it is my duty to consider all the evidence laid before this court, decide who is telling the truth and how much of the truth they are telling and come to a decision. Nobody tells all of the truth, no matter what they promise when they come here. I have to separate the wheat from the chaff. Having listened carefully to the testimony of your wife, I have come to the decision that she is as black a liar as I have ever heard and that you are as guilty as any man can be. The sentence of this court is one of thirty days' imprisonment."

Before Tibo's gavel fell, Yemko Guillaume was already gripping the edge of the desk and struggling to his feet. "Your Honour," he whistled, "this is the most astonishing miscarriage I have experienced in all my years of practice in the courts. Need I remind Your Honour that you are obliged to try the case on the evidence heard and only on the evidence heard—not what you think the opposite of that might be?"

Tibo looked bored. "That's true. But I am the master in this court and, if you want to appeal my decision, you can always ask the superior judge." He turned to the clerk. "Who's on the circuit at the moment?"

"It's Judge Gustav," said the clerk.

"Judge Gustav," Tibo told Guillaume. "And isn't he in Umlaut just now?"

"Yes, sir," said the clerk.

"Yes, sir," said Tibo. "On that big murder case?"

"Yes, sir," said the clerk.

"Yes, sir," said Tibo. "But he should be free in about a week?"

"Yes, sir," said the clerk.

"Yes, sir," said Tibo. "So there you have it, Mr. Guillaume. Judge Gustav should be here in about a week and I'm sure he'll take a very dim view of my decision and free your client. Until then, he goes to jail. Constable, take him down!"

Guillaume's giant belly was heaving. His face was turning blue with fury. "You'll be removed from the bench for this—for good!"

"Mr. Guillaume, I'm almost sure you are right and, if you are, I'll find myself with a lot more free afternoons, won't I? But that won't be for another week and, until then, that little man," he stabbed furiously towards the dock with his pen, "will be safely locked up." Tibo heard the blood singing in his ears. He had to fight against the urge to shout.

He kept his eyes fixed on Guillaume's fat face and said, "Mrs. Stoki, you have heard what has been said. Your husband is going to jail for seven days. If you are still in the house by the time he comes home again, then, God help you, you deserve all you get. This court is adjourned."

The first chime of the cathedral's eleven o'clock bell was lost in the blow of Tibo's gavel but, down in the town, on the banks of the Ampersand, along the canal, down at the docks, in the municipal offices that stood to attention round City Square, the bell called Dot to coffee.

Ladies shopping in Castle Street suddenly looked up and wondered, "The Golden Angel—could we risk a pastry?" In Braun's department store, the corsetry counter emptied, perfumery was abandoned, millinery was a desert and the coffee room on the top floor, where you can look across the street, eye to eye with a stone Walpurnia over the huge panelled door of the Ampersand Banking Company, became a forest of silver-plated cake stands, endlessly repeated in mirrored walls that would have done justice to Versailles.

In the mayor's office, Agathe put the coffee pot on the stove, waited a little, poured out two dark cups and went carefully down the back stairs to Peter Stavo's glass-fronted office. He saw she was sad. He said nothing. She said nothing. He ate two ginger biscuits and offered her the packet. She refused them so he ate the two she could have had. They finished their coffees and Agathe left. "Poor girl," said Peter, as he picked up his crossword.

Up at the courthouse, Tibo was in the magistrate's robing room splashing water on his face and saying quietly, "It was a long time ago. All a long time ago." The coffee that his clerk had brought him cooled on the desk.

An hour later, when the bells chimed again, Agathe began work on the second post of the day. As she worked, she looked at the spot on her in-tray where the scarlet box from Braun's had sat only a day before. She stopped thinking about it. She worked harder.

And then it was one. A single, basso profundo bong sang out across the town and sent a circling swirl of pigeons floating over the Bishop's Palace. Lunch. Tibo rose from the bench. The doors of the court were slammed shut and were locked, briskly, from the inside.

"Are you engaged for lunch, Mr. Mayor?" asked Yemko Guillaume.

Tibo meant to say something about sandwiches in his room but he was so astonished that no words came out.

"In that case, please join me. My treat. My cab is waiting. My cab is always waiting." Guillaume heaved himself out of the court's side door and into the waiting cab with Good Mayor Krovic shuffling behind like a tug nosing a great battleship out of harbour. Guillaume waved a huge hand vaguely. "Please sit in front, Mr. Mayor. I like to spread myself about a bit," he wheezed. "The driver knows where to go. I always eat at The Green Monkey. I trust that will suit." And, seemingly exhausted by the effort of it all, he slumped into his two seats like a collapsing soufflé and said nothing more.

As Tibo left the court with Yemko Guillaume, Agathe was crossing City Square for the baker's shop on the corner. Already a line of clerks and shop girls was queuing for sandwiches and cakes and freshly baked pies, chatting about the day, boasting about the night before, laughing. Agathe made a tight little mouth and refused to listen.

Eventually, after a long wait that ate into her lunch hour, Agathe reached the front of the queue and bought a cheese roll and an apple. "This is daylight robbery," she thought as she examined her change.

At The Green Monkey, Yemko Guillaume settled himself on a gigantic chaise longue in the corner of the room as two waiters in white uniforms with Prussian collars and gilded buttons wheeled a table into place against his intimidating paunch. The maître d' looked on approvingly. The celebrated lawyer Yemko Guillaume *and* His Honour Mayor Tibo Krovic lunching together here, in his establishment . . . Too, too perfect.

"No starter," said Yemko faintly. "Today, I would like to eat . . . I would like to eat . . . let me see . . ." His eyes rolled heavenwards and lingered on the pink-thighed nymphs gambolling explicitly on the painted ceiling. "I would like to eat something that tastes as good as that. A young gazelle, garrotted under a new moon by Nubian virgins and seethed in its mother's milk, served with the last bowl of rice from a starving Asian village, sweetened with the cries of an abandoned baby dying of thirst under a pitiless sun. No?" He looked quizzically at the maître d'. "You don't have that? Then omelette, please. And asparagus. And a glass of water. Mr. Mayor?"

Tibo managed to squeak, "That sounds fine."

The waiters withdrew, as obsequious as eunuchs.

"I don't eat much," said Yemko. "This . . ." he spread his arms to indicate his vastness, "it's a glandular disorder."

"I see," said Tibo. "I'm very sorry."

"To hear that I'm ill or because you thought me a gluttonous gourmand?" Everything Yemko said seemed to come with a raised eyebrow attached to the end of it.

Beside the fountain in City Square, Agathe chewed through the last of her stale roll. "I could make a better lunch than this for half the price," she thought.

Before she went back to work, she hurried up Castle Street to Verthun Smitt's double-fronted ironmonger's shop and bought a blue enamelled tin box. "From now on, I bring my own sandwiches," she said and turned back towards the square.

Just about then, a lopsided cab drew up outside the court and rocked on its springs as Yemko Guillaume extracted himself. "We must part again here," he said and enveloped Mayor Krovic's hand in his.

"Why did you ask me for lunch?" asked Tibo.

"Because you were right," said Guillaume. "That little turd smacks his wife. You must never assume that, simply because I am a lawyer, I have no love for justice. Never confuse justice and the law. Never confuse what is good with what is right. Never assume that what is right must be what is good. You did the right thing. No! See how easy it is? You've got me doing it now! You did the good thing. That is why they call you 'Good' Tibo Krovic—did you know that? 'Good Tibo Krovic'—like 'Alexander the Great' or 'Ivan the Terrible.' It must be almost worth living to have made a name like that. It was a good thing but it was not the right thing. The law is not to be mocked. It's the only shield the rest of us have to protect us from 'good' people. So I will report you to Judge Gustav. I have to do the 'right' thing. I have no choice. You're a dangerous man to have on the bench."

"I understand," said Tibo. "Thank you for the omelette."

The bells of my cathedral struck two. There was only one more case that day. The clerk called, "Hektor Stopak!" and handed the papers to Tibo.

"Stopak," Tibo wondered, "could this be Stopak, Agathe's Stopak? Surely there must be other Stopaks?"

Hektor stood in the dock. Quite a tall man, quite a dashing moustache, dark, good looking in a dirty, unkempt kind of way. Young. Too young to be Agathe's Stopak.

"Mr. Stopak, I see from the charge sheet," Tibo tapped the papers in front of him with his pen, "that you are accused of quite a serious breach of the peace in The Three Crowns tavern—a lot of shouting and swearing, quite a bit of damaged furniture and one of your fellow customers taken to hospital with a broken nose and a number of other, less serious injuries. I have the medical report here. Are you guilty or not guilty?"

Yemko Guillaume cranked himself to his feet again like a barrage balloon rising on the end of a cable. "I am for Mr. Stopak, Your Honour."

"And how will your client be pleading?"

"Guilty, Your Honour."

"Extenuating circumstances?"

"Is Your Honour disposed to hear them?"

"Not overly."

"Then let me only say that Mr. Stopak is an artist of some considerable promise—a painter. As such, he keeps somewhat," Yemko paused to attach another raised eyebrow to his sentence, "bohemian company. He is himself of an artistic temperament and his fellow artists share that fiery disposition."

"I hadn't realised that The Three Crowns was such a hotbed of artistic endeavour," said Tibo. "Is it an established school?"

"More of a 'haunt,' Your Honour," said Yemko. "The circumstances of the incident are very much as related on the charge sheet. A discussion amongst brother artists which became heated, drink having been taken . . ."

"Et cetera, et cetera, et cetera," Tibo interrupted.

"I had not realised that Your Honour was a Latin scholar. Yes, indeed, sir, a familiar story often rehearsed in Your Honour's court. However, I am happy to inform the court that, this very morning, my client has found employment with his cousin." Yemko turned with a wheeze and indicated a puffy-faced man with sad eyes, squeezed into white dungarees at the back of the court. "The senior Mr. Stopak is a businessman, a painter and decorator of impeccable character, unknown to the court . . ."

"Ah, not entirely unknown to the court," thought Tibo.

". . . who is prepared to offer my client full-time employment and a regular income."

"So he can pay a fine?" said Tibo.

"My client would now be in a position to make some form of redress to the court, yes, Your Honour."

"Very good. Mr. Stopak, please stand up. In light of the circumstances and your not inconsiderable record, the court will fine you one hundred. The landlord of The Three Crowns says you caused damage worth a hundred and twenty so that's probably more like sixty and another sixty for the man whose nose you broke."

"It was already broken," said Yemko.

"Can we agree on fifty, then? I make that two hundred and ten."

"At ten a week, Your Honour."

"No, Mr. Guillaume, I rather think thirty a week, now that your client has a decent job." And he leaned forward from the bench to warn, "Miss a week, Mr. Stopak, and you'll be painting the inside of a cell."

That was the business of the day.

It was nearly three o'clock by the time Tibo had finished the paperwork and strolled back through town to his office in City Square. Sandor the errand boy had already delivered the *Evening Dottian* and Agathe handed it to him wordlessly as he passed her desk.

Tibo unfolded the paper and sat down at his desk to read. The headline raved:

MAYOR KROVIC IN SNUB TO UMLAUT

And, under that, in smaller letters, next to a stock portrait of Tibo looking grim, there was a second deck:

REBUFFS INSULT BY UMLAUT'S ZAPF

and then, in tiny letters:

Exclusive, by Barni Knorrsen

with Tibo's letter knitted into something like a story underneath.

Agathe put a cup of coffee on the desk beside the paper, two ginger biscuits in the saucer. He thanked her. "Stopak—he's a paperhanger, isn't he?"

"That's right," she said. "He has his own shop. Why do you ask?"

"No reason. Was he busy today?"

"I don't know. I suppose so. He left the house very early—before I got up. Why, do you need some work done?"

"No, I don't think so. But I have got some work to do. Better get on."

Agathe tapped the folded newspaper with a scarlet fingernail as she turned to leave. "They misspelled bordello," she said. "Of all the words to get wrong! After you went to such trouble too." And the door shut behind her with a sigh of perfume.

As soon as she was gone, Tibo got up from his desk and opened the door again. He sat for a moment, sipping his coffee and admiring the view across the fountains, towards the cathedral before he started work. Agathe had prepared a neat heap of letters for him to sign. There was another stack in a red leather folder, which he knew he would have to read, and the contract for building the new police station in the northern section and that business about the school he had promised he would look into for the grandmother with the red umbrella. But, for now, Tibo sipped his coffee and watched the pigeons circling the cathedral, settling back to their roosts after their hourly alarums and excursions.

A breeze came in at the window. Tibo watched it approaching, stirring the elms on the avenue by the Ampersand, misting the fountains in the square, moving the fine curtains of his office, ruffling the papers on his desk and then on, invisibly, into Agathe's room. He knew it must have touched her, brushed her lips, filled her mouth—she must have breathed it and she must have taken it for granted.

"Mrs. Stopak," he called, "what's that perfume you're wearing?"

"Why on earth would you want to know that, Mayor Krovic?"

"It's nothing. Sorry. Forget I asked." Tibo opened the red leather folder and began to read.

"It's 'Tahiti,'" she said.

And Tibo said the word over and over to himself as he worked. "Tahiti, Tahiti, Tahiti." It mingled with the clatter of Agathe's typewriter and the sound of the fountains and the rumble of the trams as Tibo worked until it was too dark to see.

If he had asked it, Agathe would have sat all night to help but he did not ask and she cleared her desk and locked it a little after five. She could feel cold despair settling in her chest like a river pebble and rattling off each rib to land in the pit of her stomach where it lay. There was no point in going home but no point in staying away. As Agathe turned the key in the desk, she found herself saying, "Home is where they have to let you in." Granny had said that as a comfort—the reassuring promise that she would never be turned away. Now it seemed like the threat of a prison sentence and she said again, "What's the bloedig point?"

It was a long walk home. Not like last night, not a happy stroll to a happy place but a long and dusty tramp through hot streets at the end of a tiring day. She did not hurry. Her feet hurt, a stinging burning pain with every step that felt as if the skin on her soles was ready to part from the bones.

When she reached the delicatessen at the corner of Aleksander Street, Mrs. Oktar was out on the pavement, sweeping between the open crates of fruit that stood on display and brushing street dust off the piles of apples. She stopped to wave. Agathe waved back.

The black kitten that had wheedled round Agathe's ankles the night before was peering out from under a crate of oranges. "Is he yours?" she asked.

"No," said Mrs. Oktar. "There are always cats hanging round here. They breed. They spend all day lying out in the sunshine in the back yards and all night making kittens. It's not a bad life—and I wouldn't mind trying it myself—but I've got bills to pay and no smoked salmon to waste on the likes of him."

Agathe reached under the orange box and lifted the kitten up to her face, brushing his fur with a whisper of breath. "I like him," she said. "I'll take him home with me. He just needs some love."

"Like the rest of us," said Mrs. Oktar, "but also some milk and some flea powder and some smoked salmon." Mrs. Oktar was a wonderful saleswoman, a remarkable saleswoman but, like the rest of us, a victim of circumstance. And, although she ran a very fine delicatessen, it was, nonetheless, a delicatessen and, like every other delicatessen in Dot, it did not stock flea powder. "The milk I can do and we've got the smoked salmon but we haven't any flea powder. If I was you, I'd leave the cat until tomorrow. He's not going anywhere."

"I like him," said Agathe. "He's coming home with me. Just sell me the other stuff. I'll get the flea powder in town tomorrow."

"You're a silly girl but on your own head be it—and not just your *head* either. A word to the wise, Mrs. Stopak, take it from one who knows—every place you've got where you wouldn't let a man go unless he was Mr. Stopak, that's where you'll have those fleas. Tomorrow, when you're in town getting flea powder for Mr. Cat here, maybe you should think about getting some for yourself."

With an expert wrist, Mrs. Oktar flicked a brown paper bag full of air and put a carton of milk and a paper parcel of smoked salmon inside. The kitten squirmed deliciously in Agathe's grip, wrestling against her breast as she shushed it.

"Oh, be still, you bad kitten. Just wait a minute or two."

"That's 4.50," said Mrs. Oktar and she held out her hand. "For that, I'm prepared to throw in another bag for the cat. It wouldn't kill you to be a little bit hygienic, would it?"

Agathe dropped the kitten into the bag and he looked at her reproachfully from the bottom. His four moppish paws spread out in the corners but he seemed happy enough until she lifted the bag by its handles and swung him into space. Then he rocked unsteadily and stamped about on the uncertain floor of his cage, mewling pitifully. Agathe put her hand flat against the bottom of the paper sack to give him the reassurance of something solid beneath his feet and blew gently into the kitten's fur to attract his attention. "Shush, shush, shush, don't be scared, little cat. We'll soon have you home." She could feel the heat of his paws even through the thick paper bag and the delicious moving weight of him, hidden and dark and enclosed and unseen against her own flesh, brought back an old memory for her. "Soon have you home. You're like the rest of us—you just need some love. So come home with me and I'll look after you."

For the second night in a row, Agathe climbed the stairs to her flat with a parcel of hope swinging from a string at her finger but, when she reached the landing, she felt it leaking away out of the bottom of the bag to lie in a puddle at her feet.

The door of the flat was standing ajar. As Agathe went to push it open, she heard voices from inside—men's voices. She paused with her hand on the doorknob, listening. Stopak—she recognised his snorting laughter—and then that other voice. Agathe bounced the door open and walked in. "Hektor, what a surprise! And I was hoping we'd been burgled."

Stopak and Hektor were sitting together at the kitchen table, a platoon of empty beer bottles standing to attention between them.

"Aww, don't be like that," said Stopak. "It's just a little celebration. Me and my new partner." Stopak nodded the neck of the bottle in his fist across the table at Hektor.

"Your new partner? Your new partner!" Agathe was astonished. "All of a sudden the paperhanging business is so vast you need to spread the profits round a bit, is that it? You can't keep up with demand, is that it? And him! Why him? The things he knows about paperhanging you can count on the fingers of one foot!"

Agathe stamped out of the room and flung herself down on her bed—the only private place in the house, someplace where at least Hektor would never venture.

But he did. She was lying, face down on the pillow, her hair undone and piled in wanton mountains around her, her blouse loose and unbuttoned, still fuming over Stopak's news, when Hektor came in and spoke. "It's not like Stopak made out," he said.

"Hektor, go away."

"Look, I don't want to bother you or anything. It's just so you know—I'm not Stopak's partner."

"Hektor, just go away." Agathe's voice was half-muffled by the pillow.

"I'll go, I'll go. Just don't be angry with Stopak. He did a good thing. I had a bit of bother and he helped me out. He gave me a job but I'm not his partner and I'm not looking for a share of the profits. Nothing like that. It's just a job. Stopak's the boss. I'm just an employee."

Agathe lifted her face from the pillow. She was red-eyed and tearful again. These days, Agathe acknowledged to herself that she seemed to be always upset or on the verge of being upset. She pushed her hair back into its clasp, a gesture that made her blouse gape, exposing her sensible undershirt, and she flustered over the buttons and smoothed down her skirt. "Hektor, I don't care if he's hired you. I don't care if he hires Ivan the Terrible. I'm guessing he hired you because Ivan the Terrible got a better offer. Probably Ivan the Terrible would know at least as much about paperhanging as you do but I don't care! Hektor, just go away."

"All right," he said, "I'll go. But there's somebody else who wants to see you."

Agathe looked up from her last button expecting Stopak, shamefaced and shuffling. Instead, there was Hektor, holding out two paper bags. "I think he's hungry."

She took the bags and said nothing. Hektor waited hopefully for a word and, when it didn't come, he said, "By the way, we finished the bathroom." And he backed away and closed the door. After a moment, there was the sound of another bottle opening, the chink of thick brown glass and laughter.

"Bloedig stupid men," said Agathe. She poured the kitten out on the bed. "You are the only man I like," she said. "I don't like Hektor because he's bad. He might be pretty but he's bad so we don't like him, do we, little cat? And I don't like Stopak because he doesn't like me. So there! No, we don't like Hektor at all." Agathe looked at the bedroom door, safely closed, and let her fingers rest on the buttons of her blouse again, remembering that they had been open, wondering what Hektor might have seen. "Here," she said suddenly, "it's dinner time." She opened the milk carton and dipped her fingers, offering them to the little cat who lapped away enthusiastically with a rough pink tongue that tugged against her skin. "Try some of this!" She tore off a strip of smoked salmon and the cat lunged at it like a tiger. Agathe laughed. "I'll have to go to the circus for a whip and a chair, you bad cat. But don't go building your hopes up. We don't dine on smoked salmon every night in Schloss Stopak. This is just to welcome you. Tomorrow it's cat scraps from the fishmonger for you."

She fed the cat for a little longer and then, because smoked salmon is salty and it made him thirsty, she gave him more milk drizzled from the tips of her fingers.

A door banged in the kitchen and Hektor said something about "No more bloedig beer!" and then something about "The Three Crowns" and a chair scraped and the front door banged and the flat was quiet.

Agathe picked the kitten up and lay back on the bed with it nestled on her breast. It purred with the clunky purr of a coffee grinder as she scratched round its ears. It purred, she scratched. She scratched, it purred. Slowly and quietly they fell asleep together and Agathe would have lain there until morning if she had not been roused by the sound of the kitten relieving himself daintily against her curtains and doing back-heeled kicks across the carpet.

Agathe leapt up from the bed in a shower of greaseproof paper and salmon scraps. "No! Bad cat!" she yelled, and the kitten dived for cover under the bed. Agathe had no idea what to do about cat pee on the curtains. Granny would have known. She would have had some handy remedy—vinegar or turnip peelings and baking soda, something like that. But Agathe knew enough not to leave the stuff to dry in. She rushed to the kitchen and came back with a kettle of cold water which she poured on to the stain. "Let it soak," she thought. "It can't do any harm." And then, glancing out the window, she saw that evening had come on. She looked at her watch. Almost half past nine. Mamma Cesare! She put on her shoes and ran.

The street was empty and silent. The Oktars had shut up shop. There was nobody about and the sound of Agathe's heels came clipping back at her from the locked doors and closed windows on the opposite side of the road. As she hurried to the corner of Aleksander Street, she heard the distant banshee screech of the approaching tram, the clang of its iron bell. She imagined meteor trails of sparks spurting from the wheels on the big bend that leads to the bridge and she hurried on but, by the time she reached the junction, the tram was already waddling away from the stop and over Green Bridge.

Agathe walked slowly into the cast-iron shelter and sat down.

The next tram was due in ten minutes. She sat on the bench and did her coat up properly, straightened her stockings, buttoned her gloves. She flipped open her compact and looked in the mirror, sighed angrily, unbuttoned one glove again and pulled it off with her teeth, moistened a finger with spit and rubbed a disobedient eyebrow into place. She checked the mirror again. That would do—a bit more respectable. She held the glove in one hand and counted out coins from her coat pocket with the other. Enough to get to Castle Street. Sometimes ten minutes is a long time.

Agathe leaned back on the bench and looked down the road, a little fearfully, towards The Three Crowns. No sign of anybody coming and, when they were eventually thrown out, the last tram would have gone. Nobody coming out. She stood up and walked to the door of the shelter, holding on to a cast-iron pillar as she looked the other way up the street, across the bridge and towards my cathedral on its hill. The late evening sun was blazing from its domes and pinnacles and the cathedral was swirling a cloud of pigeons around its head like a matador's cloak. Agathe felt suddenly envious of those pigeons. Maybe they had no freshly painted bathroom but pigeons weren't too fussy about that sort of thing in her experience, and they had a place to sleep where they were welcome, where they would be warmly greeted, a place of tremulous, dancing, burbling physical contact, a place to raise their young, a place where, if they failed to arrive one evening after an accident with a hawk or a dustcart in the street, they might be missed if only for that night. She sighed. "What have I got? A kitten who pees up the curtains!" She felt lonely and ridiculous. She should be sneaking out of the house to meet a wealthy lover who would take her dancing and feed her steak and murmur hot-gasped nonsense in her ear before . . . before . . . Before what?

"I don't know before what," said Agathe, "but I'll know it when I see it and it's not 'before' waiting at the tram stop to go and see some mad old lady I never spoke to 'before' this morning."

She did a little dance, tapping from heel to heel in the tram shelter. "Ten minutes! Ten Minutes. I'll give them ten minutes. If it's not here by the time I count to a hundred, I'm going home."

And she began to count as she danced. "One elephant, two elephant, three elephant . . ." By the time she reached "a hundred and sixty-three," the tram was waiting at the junction, its single headlamp glowing in the dusk.

It clanked up to the stance, slowed, stopped, let Agathe hitch her skirt and climb aboard and clanked off again over the bridge.

Agathe had the tram to herself. She sat primly, knees together, holding her handbag on top of her thighs. The conductor said, "All right, dearie?" and Agathe hated that. She knew he was going to say something stupid like that.

Why couldn't he just have said, "Good evening, where to?" or "Yes, Miss?" or something polite and straightforward? But, no, it had to be "All right, dearie?" as if this chirpy display of bravado on an empty tram would suddenly ignite her libido and make all her clothes fall off. She gave him a cold glare, one of her "shrivellers" and said, "Castle Street," with a heavy strain on "please."

"That'll be . . ."

But Agathe cut him short, tipping a column of coins into her palm with a magician's ease. "I think that's right," she said definitely.

The conductor punched out a short green ticket from the machine that hung at his waist and went to stand on the back platform. He looked at her from there, dangling by one arm from the pole on the step, swinging out over the rushing pavement.

Agathe's disgust was bottomless. She refused to reward him with even a glance but the trees where she'd watched the birds that morning were passing by only as dark shadows now. She concentrated instead on reading the advertisements that ran along the edge of the ceiling, a small milky light bulb burning between each.

Tired, liverish, lost your fizz?
Try
Pepto Pills!

And there was a picture of an old man, leaping out of a bath chair to do cartwheels. His walking stick was flying through the air behind him. "Stupid," thought Agathe. "Silly. Why would a man in a bath chair need a stick? I mean, if you're wheeled about all the time, what's the point of a stick? I wonder how the cat is. What if he's peed in the bed—or worse? That would be a nice surprise for Stopak."

And then she thought, "First damp patch in that bed for a long while," but pretended that she hadn't because that would be a coarse and disgusting thing to say.

Palazz Kinema. New programme every Thursday.
Double Feature and Weekly Newsreel.
Telephone: Dot 2727

"Well, that's businesslike enough at any rate. Tells you all you need to know. I haven't been to the pictures for ages. Maybe . . ."

use

"ETHIOPIAN"

POLISH

AND YOUR SHOES WILL GLEAM LIKE AN ETHIOPIAN!

"I don't think that's very nice. I wouldn't want some nice African woman, sitting on a tram in Ethiopia, wondering if 'Dot bleach' could get her toilet as white as me. I wouldn't like that one bit. Do they have trams in Ethiopia? Do they have toilets? Oh, dear."

The conductor was swinging on his pole like an acrobat, dashing the length of the back platform and leaping and catching the pole and swinging round it back on to the platform. Agathe ignored him as violently and aggressively as it was possible to ignore anybody. "Of course," she thought, "the chirpy chatter failed so now behaving like a monkey is supposed to inflame me."

BORA-BORA COLA

THE TASTE SENSATION

THAT'S AS FRESH AS THE OCEAN

"Too sweet. I remember I tried it once on the ferry. I felt sick. Might have been the ferry but I don't think I could do it again. In fact, just looking at that sign is making me feel ill." She glanced away quickly.

The last sign in the row was printed in white letters on a red background. Very straightforward. No slogans. No gimmicks. It said:

ST. WALPURNIA'S HOME FOR CHILDREN.
HAVE YOU CONSIDERED ADOPTION?

"No!" thought Agathe. "Yes. No. No!"

The conductor rang his bell. "This is Castle Street. Castle Street next stop."

Agathe jumped off the tram and ran down the street, just as she had that morning, clipping over the pavement while the cathedral clock tower whirred and spun above her. The first bell of ten o'clock was already chiming when she reached The Golden Angel and the place was almost in darkness. Heavy vellum blinds had been drawn over the windows and the last of them was rolling down over the front door, tugged into place by a dark artichoke of a fist. Agathe rapped on the glass with a gloved knuckle. The blind halted. The artichoke fist uncurled a single finger that jabbed insistently to the left, back up Castle Street. Then the blind continued rolling down and the lights behind it clicked off.

Agathe was at a loss. She knocked again on the glazed door. Nothing happened. She waited. Nothing happened.

"Oh, come on," she said, "I wasn't late! Well, hardly late. Not late at all. I wasn't. I was right on time." She rapped on the glass again. Nothing happened. "Oh, for goodness' sake!" Agathe pouted deliciously. She gave up. She turned and began to walk away home but, just two shop fronts up the street, there was Mamma Cesare, standing in an open doorway.

She said, "You took your time. We said ten o'clock."

Agathe could only gape at her like a flounder and say, "But . . . but . . . I've been waiting down the street for the past ten minutes."

"Well, that was very foolish, wasn't it? Didn't you see me pointing?"

"But I had no idea what you were pointing at."

"You do now," said Mamma Cesare. "Come in quick."

She bent to pull Agathe up the step and urge her through the open half of a split front door and into a square vestibule, floored with tiny black and white chequerboard tiles.

The door closed with a forbidding click. Mamma Cesare spun an iron bar into place to secure it. "Now we are all nice and private," she said. With the two women in it, Mamma Cesare, tiny, brown and hunched, and Agathe, tall, buxom and ample, the little room was full to bursting. "On, out, come on," Mamma Cesare said, fanning her tiny hands as if Agathe was a stampede to be hurried up two more terrazzo steps and on through the peeling, half-glazed swing doors. "This way. This way. Follow me," she said but the passageway was dark and Agathe walked slowly, placing each dainty toe on the gritty crunching floor.

"Where are we going?" she asked.

"Oh, girl, stop fussing. Look." Mamma Cesare gave an ill-natured shove at a door on her right, invisible in the dark but known to her, and it swung open on The Golden Angel, lit by the lamps of Castle Street, tables all in place, chairs piled up with their legs in the air, awaiting the furious mop.

"See? It's the shop. We are coming by the side way is all. Happy? You need to be more trusting. No. What am I saying? You are a woman. Trust nobody. Especially do not trust yourself."

The door swung shut again, leaving them in the darkened corridor, rendered still darker by the light that had just been shut out. "Here are four steps," said Mamma Cesare.

Agathe heard her flat-footed shuffle and followed, one hand against the wall at her side, kicking each step with the point of her toe to be sure of where it was. And then there was a soft click, the sound of a handle turning and another door opening in the dark. Mamma Cesare's hand closed round her wrist and pulled her into the room. The door closed, the room filled with light and Mamma

Cesare leapt to embrace her, as eager as a puppy. "Welcome, welcome. Thanksyou for coming. Thanksyou. I am so very pleased to see you."

It was a strange room, eight sided but far from octagonal, just a space left over when the rest of the building went up around it. The walls were hung in old-fashioned French paper, printed with garlands of roses linked together by pink ribbons on a cream-coloured ground that had faded to buff. "Stopak wouldn't like that," Agathe said to herself. "Hard to match up all those ribbons. A lot of waste, especially in a room like this. Too many corners."

The place was old but clean and neat. There were two windows but Agathe couldn't imagine where they looked out on. Not on Castle Street, surely. Perhaps on some hidden courtyard.

There were pictures on the walls: the one of me combing my beard that every respectable Dot woman keeps in view of her bed; one of a gaudy fishing boat plunging through the sort of storm that would have sent the toughest battleship hurrying to port; one of ballerinas practising—but the viewer was supposed to understand that these ballerinas were of the poor but honest variety, the type who did not accept gentleman callers, who strove constantly for their art but couldn't afford to pay the gas bill and consequently danced on in the dark. And there was also, on the same wall as the image of me but somewhat lower down and a little to the left, a picture of St. Anthony, looking unhappy as a lot of devils tugged at his clothes and hair but sure of happiness just round the corner once he'd shaken them off—which he was about to do any minute, one felt sure.

There was a huge, dark, mirror-fronted wardrobe, so large it skimmed the ceiling, dripping with carved fruit that cut across a corner of the room and filled two walls, a brass-framed double bed covered by a home-made quilt which trailed the floor on both sides and a dressing table with a tilted mirror blocking a cupboard door. Agathe saw herself reflected endlessly between the wardrobe and the dressing table as Mamma Cesare waltzed her round the room in welcome.

"I am so pleased you are come. All day, I was wondering. Here. Sit." Mamma Cesare gave her a gentle push and Agathe plumped down on to the squeaking bed. "No chairs!" Mamma Cesare said.

She drew herself up to her full height, hands on hips, leaning back, looking at Agathe the way farmers look at fatstock in the show ring. It made Agathe nervous. She couldn't think of anything to say.

"Take your coat off," said Mamma Cesare. "I will make us some tea."

"Not coffee? You make wonderful coffee."

"That's for my job. For you, for a visitor, I make tea."

Mamma Cesare opened the wardrobe. There was a deep drawer at the bottom and it slid out with an easy sigh. She reached inside and brought out a black Japanese tray with a brown china pot, a tiny copper kettle on a stand, a spirit lamp, a box of matches, two fine china cups nestling together on a rattling layer of saucers, another saucer with a lemon and a knife and a tin box with a hinged lid covered in painted flags and golden images of swords and spears and, at the centre, the portrait of a magnificently bearded man in a red shirt.

Mamma Cesare picked up the empty kettle, excused herself—"Moment, please."—and bustled out of the room.

And that left Agathe to do what anyone would do in her place. She bounced on the bed once or twice, enjoying its extravagant squeaks, briefly battled her urge to snoop and then, because life is short and time is precious, gave in to it. Agathe was not the sort of woman to open drawers or look in cupboards but it is an accepted rule in polite company that what's on show on a dressing table is, most definitely, on show.

The mirror swung loose in its wooden stand, tilting slightly downwards and looking at the battery of pots and potions on the dressing table. There was nothing remarkable—the usual sort of lily-of-the-valley-scented Christmas presents you would expect for a lady of a certain age, a china dish with hairpins and some clumsy jewellery in it and a tiny photograph in a silver frame. When Agathe picked it up, she felt the velvet backing rub softly against her hand.

Red. Worn thin as if the picture had been handled often. Agathe imagined it—the little brown woman sitting before the mirror every morning, every evening, picking up the picture and kissing it. Was that what happened? Agathe looked again at the hidden velvet and fitted fingers against the worn pile. It could only mean that. A sacred thing. A relic. She looked at the picture in the frame. There was a tall young man, stick-thin, stallion-black hair slicked back over his skull, a moustache so thin and sculpted it must have been the result of fifteen minutes of breathless work with a razor or fifteen seconds with an eyebrow pencil. His cheeks were cadaverous. His eyes were coals. They spoke of ancestry reaching back through shadowed olive groves to Phoenician temples. He wore a heavy three-piece suit. The cloth looked bulletproof and there was a watch chain looping from the pocket of his waistcoat. He had one hand hooked through it by the thumb—a casual gesture when the rest of his body was poker-stiff and plumb-line straight. His free hand lay on the shoulder of the tiny woman in the chair in front of him—not so much a gesture of reassurance and connection as a policeman's grip, holding her there, forcing her down, keeping her in that chair whether she wanted it or not.

"That's my husband," Mamma Cesare said, closing the door with a heel. "That's Pappa. My Cesare. On our wedding day. We went straight from the mayor's office and we had our picture taken. Made everybody wait. So grand we were."

She put the kettle on its stand and a little water slopped on to the tray before she lit the wick of the spirit lamp. A ghost of blue flame danced in a lazy circle, sighed, burned steadily.

The little woman hopped on to the bed. Her feet waved well clear of the floor. She held out her hand to take the picture and gestured to Agathe to sit beside her while the kettle boiled.

"My Cesare," she kissed the picture, "such a man he was. Aiyy!" Mamma Cesare bounced on the complaining bed. "Hear that? Squeak! Squeak! Squeak! Twenty-eight years we were married and we wore this bed out." She bounced around a little more. "Not that I'm complaining. Such a life we had. Such a life you should have. This was a man. This was a real man!"

Mamma Cesare looked at the picture for a long moment and kissed it again and then she turned to Agathe at her side. "I know what you think. You are looking at me and you are seeing this tiny little old lady. Such an old lady. What does this old lady know of squeaking beds? This old lady," she clutched the picture close to her chest, "is knowing plenty about squeaking beds and, better than that, she is knowing plenty about love. There is love and there is beds. Love is good and beds is, is, is . . . beds is fantastico! But, when you are getting love and beds together in the one place," she slapped a hand down on Agathe's thigh, "this is the best. This is the good God spitting on his fingers and rubbing on the dirty windows where the angels forgets to clean and he's saying, 'Look in here. See what's waiting. See what it is I am doing for you!'"

"I haven't had that for a long time," said Agathe.

"Me too," said Mamma Cesare, "but I remember."

"And I forget."

"I know. This is why I am worrying so much for you. Look through the window with the wrong man and what you see is not so nice."

The little copper kettle began to splutch on its tray and Mamma Cesare jumped down from the bed to deal with it. She took tea from the painted tin, added water, stirred it and waited, stooping over the pot.

"Why did you speak to me this morning?" asked Agathe. "How do you know so much about me?"

"I am strega from a long line of strega. It's not so hard. You see a man who is starving to death and you know he wants bread. He doesn't have to ask. You see just by looking. Anybody looks at you, they can see you are dying of hunger."

"But my husband can't see it."

Mamma Cesare poured the tea. "I think maybe he sees fine. I think maybe he is a very hungry man, a man too frightened to share what he has with you, a man frightened to starve to death so he lets you starve alone. This is a very bad thing. Here," Mamma Cesare passed her a trembling cup and saucer, "drink this, every drop and say nothing. Not one word. Instead, listen."

Agathe untwined her knotted fingers and took the tea. Mamma Cesare settled herself on the squeaking bed beside her. It was like sitting next to Granny when the wind rattled down the chimney and the stories began, "Once upon a time..." Agathe sipped her tea. It was hot. A slice of lemon brushed her lip.

Mamma Cesare said, "A long, long time ago, in the old country, there was a war."

Agathe was about to ask "What war?" but Mamma Cesare quietened her with an eyebrow. "I told you to say nothing. And it doesn't matter what war. For people like us, it never matters what war. Generals and kings and presidents, they have different wars but, for us little people, there is only one war. All the same, I hope you never learn this. So, a long, long time ago in the old country, there was a war. But we were little people living high up in the mountains and far away. We did not care for their war. It is not touching us. Maybe, one day, we hear the guns like thunder from the hills, maybe, one night, we see their fires but everything is far away. Then, one day, there is shooting on our road and, at night, when it is over, there is a red soldier lying under a bush with no head where his head should be."

The room was quiet except for the sound of teacups on saucers. After a moment, Mamma Cesare said, "Then our village was itself again until, one night, there was fighting in our fields. Men were shouting. They hammered on our shutters and on our doors. The dogs bark. We do not open the door. In the morning, when it is quiet, there is a blue soldier sitting under a tree in my father's orchard with no heart where his heart should be. So we chase away the pigs and take him to the graveyard and bury him. That day, all the men meet on the steps of the church to decide what to do. This one says that we should keep out of the war, that it's none of our business. That one says the war is on our road and in our orchards and banging on our shutters at night—it's too late to keep out. This one says that our village has always been blue and the young men should go and fight for blue but that one says that blue is finished and red is going to win so we should join red. It went on all day. It got hot. I went home to make soup."

Mamma Cesare leaned across to check on Agathe's tea. "You finish? Say nothing."

Agathe tilted the cup to let her see. There was still a little left.

"Take the lemon out. Put it in your saucer. Drink every drop. So I make soup. And, the next day, when I go to the well, they tell me Cesare has gone to fight."

Agathe drained her cup in a gulp and placed it decisively in her saucer. "Which side did he join? Was he blue or red?"

"You finished?" Mamma Cesare investigated the cup. She was satisfied. "Nobody knows what side he joined. Nobody can decide who is best—blue or red. Nobody can decide who is worst. We hate them all but they made us fight. If we are red, then the blues will come and burn the village. If we are blue, then the reds will come. So the old men say we send our boys to both sides and tell both sides it is them we like. And they leave the village, the boys, and they toss a coin and they pick a side but they never tell anybody else because one side is going to win and one side is going to lose and both sides are going to die but somebody is going to come back and nobody is going to get the blame for killing nobody else. Not never!"

"You must have been terrified," said Agathe.

"I thought my heart was breaking," said Mamma Cesare, "and the worst thing is I can't say nothing because Cesare is not mine. Cesare is going to marry my best friend."

"Your best friend!" Agathe gasped with the thrill of it. This was as good as anything you could see at the Palazz Kinema on George Street—no, it was better! This was a true story of love and war. She imagined herself in the stalls with a bag of sweets on her knee, stirring trumpet chords playing, a drum roll, looking up, seeing that flickering rectangle of blue light beaming out from the projectionist's box, the cigarette smoke rising and curling through it, titles rolling up the screen: "The Red and the Blue. Starring . . ." Who should it be? Yes, "Horace Dukas as Cesare and introducing [a whisper of violins] Agathe Stopak as Mamma." That would need work. We have to find a better name. And a best friend—we need a best friend. And Cesare needs a best friend too and they have to leave the village together in the dead of night and then, on some moonlit road, they draw lots and—the horror—they end up on opposite sides and they try to make a deal with some other village boys so they can be on the same side but it's no good.

And here's Horace Dukas standing under a full moon, streaming with clouds, and he says, "Boys, this will never work. We can't pick sides here like it was a game of football in the village square. We can't leave the wheezy fat boy standing on his own waiting to see if he lives or dies. So you don't want to be fighting your brothers or your cousins. So what? Who would you choose to kill? Nobody wants to kill, nobody wants to die, so let's just take the dice as they fall and ride our luck. You are all my brothers and I wouldn't harm one of you to save the village but each of us would gladly die for our homes, our farms and our mothers. If we have to die, isn't it better that a friend should do it? At least then we don't die alone!"

The camera sweeps round the little group. With grim smiles, they shake hands, embrace, clap each other on the back. They go their separate ways. Cut to lingering shot of the full moon and fade to black.

"Your best friend—what was her name?"

"Cara."

"Pretty name."

"Pretty girl."

"Was she tall and blonde?"

"She was short and dark like me. Like all the girls in our village. Nobody got enough to eat. Very dark. She had a bit of a moustache."

"That's not so good," thought Agathe. "We can ignore that—artistic licence. Sometimes the cinema is more real than real. I'm seeing: 'With Aimee Verkig as Cara, her best friend.'"

Mamma Cesare said, "Turn your teacup over, spin it three times and hand it to me in your left hand."

The cup made a grinding sound as Agathe turned it on the saucer. "So what happened next?" she asked.

"Nothing. Not for a long time." Mamma Cesare turned the

cup over and began studying the tea leaves inside, looking for pictures, searching for stories. "Nothing here we didn't know. See, there's a ladder but everybody knows Stopak is a paperhanger and that drop of tea at the bottom, that's a journey over water."

"Oh, never mind about that. There's always a drop left at the bottom and you told me this morning I'd cross water to meet the love of my life."

Mamma Cesare gave her an encouraging look. "So you met him?"

"I haven't been anywhere. Just to work. Tell me about Cesare and the village and the red and the blue."

Mamma Cesare was quiet for a moment. She held the teacup tilted loosely in her hand as if it might slip from her fingers. Small bright eyes that had been probing Agathe's future a moment before were gazing now at a faraway past. After a while she said, "Nothing happened. We didn't hear anything. Of course we worried but the war stayed away so it looked like the plan was working. We stayed in the village all that summer. We had to work twice as hard in the fields with all the young men gone and then, in the winter with all the young men gone, it was twice as cold in our beds at night. The snows came. They protected us. Nothing could get through the passes. We went from house to house and sat together, telling stories and singing songs. It saved on wood when we all sat round one fire. But, always, our hearts were in the snow with our young men and Cara would sniff and sob on my shoulder about Cesare, how she loves Cesare and, please God, Cesare will come home and marry her. And I am sitting there, in front of a fire of cinders, my fingers blue, saying nothing, listening, listening to the wolves howling on the mountain, and hating her quietly."

Agathe pictured the scene—a tiny cottage, black against the blizzard, a single light shines from a small square window, the camera closes in. We see two young women in a humble kitchen. They are wrapped in shawls against the winter storm. Aimee Verkig, as Cara, speaks softly, movingly, of her love for the heroic Cesare, tears fill her eyes, she rests her head on the breast of the beautiful Agathe Stopak, who gazes out into the storm, impassive as marble, as cold as the blizzard, resting a motherly hand on Cara's hair aaand CUT!

"And then it was summer again," said Mamma Cesare, "and things started to go badly for the blues. Some of them came through the village in a hurry. They were in a bad way but they knew all about us and how loyal our village was and they told us we'd better get out because the reds were coming. We said we'd stay and they said they were very sorry but they were going to have to blow up the bridge on the far side of the village and that's what they did. They crossed over and they blew it up. Not that it was much of a bridge and they didn't blow it up very well, but they left a hole in the middle so we couldn't use it. Then, the next day, the reds came."

"I bet you fooled them. I bet you all ran into the street cheering to welcome them," said Agathe.

The shot opens with a close-up on trees in bloom, birdsong, open out to women, children, old men, running into the street throwing flowers at marching troops.

"You must be joking! We yelled at them. We called them every name we could think of. The old men stood in the street and demanded to know where they had been. The whole world knew this was the reddest village in the whole country—none redder—but, when those blue cowards ran through here, where were the courageous red forces? How could we defend ourselves when all our young men were away with the armies of red? Every woman of the village would gladly entertain a dozen brave red soldiers but, after the horrors inflicted by the diseased blue scum, that would be a dangerous and unpatriotic act. And all us girls howled and hid our faces in our shawls.

"The Captain was very impressed. He says how sorry he is and he extends a thousand sympathies for our suffering which is as great as anything endured by his men and all of it will count as part of the great national liberation effort and did we have anything to drink? And then, when they have drunk all the wine on show and all the wine we hid for them to find, the Captain says he is very sorry but there must be one more small sacrifice. He says they must repair the bridge and, a thousand apologies, that means they must blow up somebody's house and throw it in the gorge.

"The whole town is holding its breath but we know what he's going to say and, sure enough, the Captain says that the best house for blowing up, a thousand, thousand apologies, if you don't mind, is the house of Cara's father."

Agathe gave a little gasp of delight which she quickly transformed to horror behind a hand at her face. "No! She must have been distraught. Did she scream? Did she faint?"

"Oh, you never knew Cara. She is like ice. She walks up to the Captain and sits on his knee with her arms round his neck and she says, 'Oh, Captain, I know a much better house, much bigger, made with real good stones, much closer to the river and it belongs to the only lousy blue in this whole village. We chased him out of town. Now you can make sure he's never coming back. We don't need that sort round here.' That's what she said. I remember like yesterday. I see her face like I see yours."

Mamma Cesare was still for a moment and then she said, "You know whose house it was, don't you?"

Agathe's heart was pounding inside her chest. Yes, she knew. "It was Cesare's house."

"Cesare's house." Mamma Cesare nodded gravely. "Sure enough, that afternoon, we heard the explosions."

Agathe saw it all now. The beautiful but faithless Aimee Verkig laughing as she kisses the drunken red Captain (dramatically portrayed by Jacob Maurer) full on his cruel mouth. Outraged villagers look on in disbelief. They refuse to speak to her on the street. They turn their backs as she approaches. Labouring in the fields under a pitiless sun, no one will share a drink of water with her. Walking home in the dark, she hears her own curse whispered from the shadows. Terrified, she goes to the only house where she can be sure of safety. There, framed in the doorway, is the beautiful Agathe Stopak. Inside her humble cottage, the fire blazes warmly, a table is laid with fresh bread and summer fruits.

Aimee Verkig, portraying the faithless Cara, runs to her. "You must help me," she sobs. "I was wrong. I made a mistake. Hide me.

Take me in." The beautiful Agathe Stopak looks at her with contempt. She steps back, blocking the door. Her face is a cruel mask as she says, "We don't need that sort round here." She slams the door. Aimee Verkig collapses against it, weeping. Fade to black aaaaaaand CUT!

"How you must have hated her," said Agathe. "I bet the whole village wanted her dead."

"Not really. I hated her of course, but then I was her best friend and I was entitled to loathe her but nobody else had the right. I suppose they understood. Anybody would have done the same. My house, Cesare's house, let's blow up Cesare's house—who knows if Cesare's even coming home. But he did come home."

It is dawn. A little band of travellers is picking its way up the rocky valley. From the opposite hillside there is a loud shepherd's whistle. Another group approaches. A wave of recognition. The two groups of village boys meet at the same crossroads where they had parted under that full moon so long ago. They are tired and careworn, thin, tough, battle-hardened. Above all, they are fewer. Where is Francesco? Where is Luigi? Francesco won't be coming and Luigi stayed behind at Sand Ridge. But I was at Sand Ridge. We were all at Sand Ridge but we will never speak of this again. Grimly, the little band of survivors continues its climb into the mountains.

Cut to a door opening in the awakening village, the first of the morning. The beautiful Agathe Stopak begins her day's work, broom in hand, tidying her humble but spotlessly clean cottage. She begins the day—as she begins every day—with a prayer. "Heavenly Father, let this be the day that our boys come home to us but, if we must wait still a little longer, keep them safe in your care, until we meet again." We see Agathe in close-up, a lingering shot of her face, eyes closed, lips moving gently in devotion as soft organ chords play distantly. Her eyes open. She looks down the valley. Does she see something? Can it be? After all these months of waiting? Is it them? And is Cesare with them? He must be there. He must be safe. Agathe drops her broom and rushes out of the village.

Cut back to the returning soldiers, led by the quiet and courageous Cesare, tellingly portrayed by Horace Dukas. Already they see Agathe running towards them. They wave, they cheer. They meet. She embraces them in turn. She takes their hands in turn. "Darling Chico! Dear Zeppo! It's so good to see you, Beppo!" [we can work on the names later] and then she turns, the music swells, she is looking into the face of the man she loves with a secret passion. Cesare! "Welcome home," she says softly. She lays a sisterly hand on his arm. "Cara will be overjoyed." But there is a look in Cesare's eye, a look that says, "All these lonely months of fighting and killing and pain and suffering, I have carried the image of only one woman in my heart. Damn Cara to hell, it's you that I want. You and you alone forever!" And Cesare, sensitively portrayed by Horace Dukas, takes her in his strong hands and kisses her. Hold that shot, close in, resolve to pinhole aaaand CUT!

"It was the middle of the night when he got to the village," said Mamma Cesare. "The dogs are barking. Everybody knows what it means. Nobody is any more frightened. The war is over. I hear the noise. I look from my window. I see him. I say nothing. I keep my door shut. I say nothing."

"So what happened? Where did he go?"

Mamma Cesare nearly fell off the bed. "You crazy? This is a young man! For months he's been away at the war and all that time he's thinking about just one thing and when is he going to get it. You crazy? He went to Cara."

Agathe was aghast. "He went to Cara! After what she'd done? And you let him?"

"Sure I let him. It's not me who is crazy."

This was difficult. This was tricky. Agathe felt this might have to involve some really quite far-reaching script revisions—even for the sort of sophisticated audience who might be drawn to an Agathe Stopak–Horace Dukas vehicle.

"All right," she said, "you let him. Then what happened?"

Mamma Cesare said, "I wasn't there. How do I know what happened? All I know is he walks back out of the village before dawn and, this time, when he passes my house, I wait awhile and I follow him with my little bit of money and my little bag of clothes. And then, at the crossroads, he is waiting for me, looking back along the road as I come. And I say, 'Take me with you,' and he says, 'You'll do.' So that was it."

"That was it? That was it? That can't possibly be it. How could you possibly know he would leave the village again? Why should he? What's to make him? He's come home after a war to the girl he loves—why is he going to leave all that again? It's not natural."

Mamma Cesare shook her head. "I knew he'd never stay. Not when he saw that sign I painted where his house should be—'Cara did this' in big white letters. It must have glowed in the moonlight."

Agathe's jaw dropped. She didn't know whether to react with horror or admiration for a woman who was so determined to get the man she adored. She whispered, "So you left Cara to marry one of the other boys?"

"What other boys?" said Mamma Cesare. "Nobody else came home. That village died and I wasn't going to stay for the funeral. Cesare and me, we left for America."

"And ended up in Dot."

"It's a long story and I'm all of a sudden tired. This thing I wanted to show you, it will have to wait. Will you come again another night?"

Agathe said of course she would and Mamma Cesare must rest and she thanked her very much for the tea as they walked uncertainly together down the corridor to the street and especially for Cesare's story and, of course, for the fortune-telling.

"Oh, I forgot about that," said Mamma Cesare. "Tell me, who is Achilles?"

"I don't know an Achilles," said Agathe. "I know a Hektor and I don't like him very much."

"Your cup says you met Achilles. Maybe even today. I am never wrong. I am strega from long line of strega. You know Achilles. He is your friend."

Agathe said, "I'll remember. Goodnight." She pulled the door shut behind her and stepped on to Castle Street. High on the hill above, the cathedral bells struck midnight. And a few moments later, allowing for the time that the sound takes to travel over the city even on a clear Dot summer night, the driver and conductor of the last tram to run that evening got up from their seats on its back step, flicked their cigarettes away in bright curving shooting-star arcs, screwed the lids back on their coffee flasks and took the tram out of the depot. By the time it had rolled through town, past the darkened Opera House where the current production of *Rigoletto* had failed to impress the critics or the customers, through Museum Square, along George Street to find the manager of the Palazz Kinema waiting for his usual ride home and back in a lazy coat-hook loop to where Cathedral Avenue meets Castle Street, Agathe was already standing at the stop, spotlighted in a street lamp's yellow puddle. She sat at the back of the tram. She did not recognise the manager of the Palazz Kinema when he got off at the stop before hers. She kept her eyes fixed modestly on the floor until he passed and stood up almost as soon as the tram moved off again, holding on to the pole at the back as it crossed the Ampersand.

At the other side of Green Bridge, when the tram left her, she stood for a moment, enjoying the quiet, the rush of water under the arches, the whirring flight of two ducks as they flashed between the street lamps, the reassuring darkness of The Three Crowns, the distant, diminishing mechanical roll of the retiring tram, out of sight, invisible but still telegraphing its existence backwards through the complaining wires and reverberating rails. Agathe climbed the stairs to her flat, tiptoed into the bedroom, sloughed off her clothes like a dryad bathing in a moonlit pool and lay down, sadly, beside the snoring Stopak.

Before sleep took her, the little cat clawed its way up the bedclothes and burrowed, purring, under her hand. "Goodnight, Achilles," said Agathe and slept.

IN THE MORNING, TIBO'S SPAT WITH THE MAYOR of Umlaut was still front-page news in the *Daily Dottian*. When he stopped at the kiosk on the street corner to buy his morning paper, there was a big yellow bill on the board outside:

KROVIC & ZAPF–WAR

A wet stain marked where a passing dog had peed on one corner. In the queue for the tram, three men were reading the story—one of them holding the paper, two friends craning over his shoulders. It differed from the previous evening's version only by the addition of some quotes from Mayor Krovic who steadfastly refused to confirm anything. Halfway down the last column, under the word "DIGNIFIED," which appeared without warning in the middle of a sentence, Mayor Krovic had been prevailed upon to say:

> I have no idea how private correspondence between myself and Mayor Zapf of Umlaut could possibly have entered the public domain unless as part of some deliberate attempt to sow discord between our two cities. Consequently, I decline to rise to the goading of the Umlauters by commenting on this issue.

Fellow passengers saluted Tibo with approving nods. "You tell 'em, Mayor Krovic," said a fat lady in a felt hat and she stabbed a pudgy finger at the paper and laughed.

"Uppity Umlaut at it again," said the conductor. He clanged the bell.

Good Tibo Krovic found himself battling the temptation to feel guilty. Should he feel guilty? What was there to feel guilty about? Was he deceiving the people of Dot? Hardly. How could he be said to have deceived them? He had written an angry letter to Zapf. That letter existed. He had refused to say anything about it to the papers. So how could that be a deceit? Anyway, it was good for the Dottians to hate the Umlauters. It made the town football team play better, it made the schoolchildren study harder for the provincial spelling tests, it made the gardeners of the city parks department weed the flowerbeds a little more thoroughly and the Fire Brigade Band shine their brass helmets a little brighter. "Call that polished?" the bandmaster would say. "You're not in Umlaut now, laddie!" And, before he marched on to the bandstand in Copernicus Park with his mates on a Sunday afternoon, the man with the glockenspiel would polish his helmet thin. It was good for them. Tibo swallowed his conscience.

When he got to work, his desk was empty. No folders of council documents to wade through, no letters from angry ratepayers to deal with, no plans for new waterworks or demands for replacement trams from the transport department. Nothing.

"What's in the diary for today?" he asked Agathe.

"You've got a wedding to do at five o'clock. That redheaded girl from the ferry office. Rush job apparently. No fuss. Get it done and down the back stair quick but, apart from that, nothing." She snapped the book shut and looked at him with a smile.

"Nothing?"

"Not a thing."

"No letters?"

"There was one from a schoolgirl asking for information so she could do a class project on life in the Town Hall, and could she please come and visit?"

"Well, we must write back and tell her that she can," said Tibo.

"Done that. You always say that. All the time I've been here you've never turned anybody away."

Tibo sighed. "So that's it. Nothing."

"Not a thing. I'll bring you some coffee."

Tibo took out his pen and drummed it on the edge of the desk. Then he stopped—the number of pens he'd broken that way. He leaned back in his chair and puffed his cheeks out, pushed his fingers through his hair and made it stand up, smoothed it down again. Already he was bored. He began to draw in the corner of his desk blotter, random round shapes that joined up to become a plump and smiling woman who, coincidentally, looked very much like Agathe and, coincidentally, had no clothes on. She came back with his coffee to find him scribbling over it intently.

"Bored?" she asked.

"Very. I'm supposed to be the mayor. I'm supposed to be essential."

She laughed at him. "It's nearly the holidays. People are winding down. It's not your fault. You can't make business for the council to do."

"Still. I can't sit here all day. It's like taking money under false pretences."

"Go for a walk, then," she suggested. "Keep an eye on things. Somebody's bound to come up and bother you about something—some bit of broken pavement or some leaky drain or something."

Tibo was not enthusiastic. "What are you going to do?"

"I've enough to fill my days," she said firmly.

"Can I help?"

"No, you can't. Go for a walk." And she wiggled out of the room.

Tibo looked down at his blotter. It was just about possible to make out the shapes he had drawn there earlier. He traced round them again with the tip of his pen, brought them back to life then tutted angrily at himself and scored them out violently.

Good Mayor Krovic left his coffee cooling on his desk and strode out of the office. "I'm going for a tour of inspection," he said.

And Agathe called after him. "If anybody asks, I'll say you're out for a stroll."

Tibo walked down the cool green marble stairs and out into

the glare of City Square. He thought about a visit to the bookshop on the corner but ruled it out. Silly—he already had a house full of books. If he wanted more, Mrs. Handke, the City Librarian, would order anything he asked for. Not the bookshop, then. He left the square and turned left along the Ampersand, nodding at two old men who sat smoking their pipes on a cool, shadowed bench. "Fine day," he said.

"Fine day, Mayor Krovic," they said. That was all.

There was a lady with a big pram, loaded with shopping, and a sulking toddler hitching a free ride on the bumper and a blind man with midnight-blue glasses walking his panting dog. The man stopped, tucked his cane under his arm and took a bottle of water from inside his coat, holding it up high and pouring it out in spurts, randomly, where he guessed the dog's mouth might be. Some of it went in.

As he turned into George Street, Tibo made a note to talk to the City Engineer about having the animal troughs on the drinking fountains repaired. It would be a nice thing to do. George Street. Turn right to the Palazz Kinema. No, that wouldn't be right—not for a tour of inspection. Turn left to Museum Square. Yes—the new exhibition. Ideal. That was exactly the sort of thing that a mayor at a loose end should be investigating.

Long canvas banners hung between the pillars at the front of the museum, stamped with images of a winged lion and announcing:

THE GLORY OF VENICE

They flapped like the sails of a resting galleon as Tibo passed beneath and walked up to the half-glass doors where smart attendants in brass-buttoned jackets waited to welcome visitors.

"Good morning, Mayor Krovic," they said as they swung the doors open for him.

"Good morning," he said. "Just thought I'd pop in."

They nodded, smiling fawningly and somehow overcoming the urge to rub their palms together.

"Can this really be somebody's job," Tibo wondered. "Two

grown men standing here all day opening doors for people and bobbing at them. That can't be right. Good grief, there must be shifts of them, cover for holidays and days off and sick days, armies of men in fancy jackets, opening doors on the rates. That would need looking into."

The doors closed quieter than a coffin lid and Tibo breathed in the calm of the place. It washed him. He loved the museum. He had loved it from boyhood when his mother brought him, riding on the top of the tram. Tibo remembered the astonishment of it, the thrill of the Amazonian shrunken head in its case, dark and leathery, lips stitched shut with leather cords, eyelids peacefully closed, the whole thing the size of a fist and only the hair hanging down with the lustre of crows' wings to prove that it had once been a man, an unsuccessful warrior, a gambler with a losing hand but a gambler at least, a warrior at any rate. And the stuffed lion—well, half a lion, just the front half—charging from a stand of dry and shrivelled grasses, its mouth a gaping cavern of teeth and red death. Tibo remembered the first time he had seen it—how he'd turned the corner and found it and how the clutch of panic had seized his heart. He could picture himself there, a tiny naked hairless ape, frozen in terror on a savannah of brown linoleum, watching death arrive from a glass case and his lime lollipop, like a shiny green planet impaled on a stick, falling from his grasp to shatter on the floor.

He walked among the museum's granite pillars now and just ahead, in the shadows, he could see a little boy in a blue coat and a mother with packets of sandwiches in her basket to eat in the park later. "Whose pictures are these, Mother?"

"We share them, dear. They belong to everybody. You can come and see them whenever you like. They belong to you."

The joy of that. It had never left him. "Mine. They belong to me."

Tibo glanced behind the last pillar in the row. The boy and his mother were gone.

Good Mayor Krovic followed the shallow stair that curves upwards to the gallery, watched over by forgotten Dottians looking down from muddy stained-glass windows. Tibo thought the carpet very nice. "Not at all municipal," he thought. "Important. Metropolitan. Maybe we need door-openers after all."

The upper corridor of Dot Museum is hung with boring landscapes, silly treacle-coloured oils with cattle standing up to their knees in ponds and glaring out of enormous frames or sheep wandering drunkenly through impenetrable fogs and a few early devotional works, altar pieces dedicated in my honour and that kind of thing. Tibo ignored them and walked briskly on to the main gallery.

The Waldheim coffee pot collection tinkled in its case as he passed. He didn't notice. Tibo could see nothing but the vast canvas filling the back wall of the gallery. He hurried towards it. He wanted to rush up and hold it like a man who has been years in the deepest, darkest prison, suddenly released into the arms of his beloved. It was so lovely he forgot to breathe, indescribably lovely—or, at any rate, so Tibo thought but that's not the sort of thing that is permissible in stories.

In stories, description is compulsory so imagine a huge picture, all but life size. Imagine walking into a forest glade in summer, just as the handsome young hunter in the bottom left corner has done. Imagine hounds bounding beside you. Imagine a quiver of arrows on your back. Imagine bright sunshine pouring through the trees in great custardy dollops of light. Imagine the heat of it. Imagine the thirst of the young hunter and his dogs. Imagine how they have longed for that bright crystal pool. Imagine his astonishment when he pushes back the branches and finds a goddess bathing there, fleshy and white, great milky flanks, ivory shoulders, rose-pink breasts. Imagine serving maids, naiads or dryads or nymphs or some such, all colours, all sizes, in various states of undress or sopping-wet transparency. Imagine rich, figured velvets strewn over the rocks and leopard skins so soft and downy they ripple in the passing breezes. Imagine the frozen glare of the furious goddess, discovered at her toilet, humiliated, violated. Imagine the horror. That was what Tibo saw. That and the image of a beautiful city by the sea, rich with the plunder of her vast ocean empire where wonderful things like this went to be born.

He might have spent all day there, squandered the whole of his tour of inspection on inspecting just this one treasure but, when he remembered to breathe again, he noticed, filling the bench in front of the picture, the broad back of Yemko Guillaume. Tibo decided to leave quietly. He could come back later and he was just about to turn away when Yemko spoke. "Good morning, Mayor Krovic," he said.

"Oh. Ah. That is . . . good morning, Mr. Guillaume." Despite their lunch together the day before, there was something about Yemko Guillaume that left Mayor Tibo Krovic a little ill at ease and there was still that business about having him removed from the bench. "I didn't. That is. How on earth did you know I was here?"

Yemko signalled at the walls with his walking stick. "I caught your reflection in the glass of that unimpressive little Canaletto. I ask you—glass! Glass is anathema to oil. And Canaletto! Mere holiday snaps from the Grand Tour! The way these pictures have been hung, the curator should be hanged."

Mayor Krovic felt sure that Yemko had been waiting for some time for a chance to make that pretty verbal distinction. He passed no comment but, if Yemko was disappointed, he failed to show it.

"Won't you sit beside me, Mayor Krovic?" he invited. "Let us spend a few moments together, communing in silent adoration of the Masters."

Tibo managed to fit himself at one end of the huge leather bench which Yemko had annexed. It made a slight farting sound as he edged into position. He said nothing. He tried to banish from his mind all thoughts of how he must look. He chased the image of a penny-farthing bicycle from his head. He tried to relax. He tried to forget himself, forget where he was, who he was with, who he was. Instead, he imagined himself naked, wading into that cool green pool that lapped at Diana's feet. He imagined sinking in it. He imagined looking up and seeing . . .

"Don't you think Diana bears an uncanny resemblance to that secretary of yours—what's her name? Mrs. Stopak?"

"Definitely not!" said Tibo. People turned to look. He had been a little too definite. He modulated to a cathedral whisper, "And, anyway, how do you know my secretary?"

"Mayor Krovic, you are a personality in Dot. Everyone knows you. Everyone knows all about you and Mrs. Stopak shares your mythic status. I apologise if I have caused you any offence."

Tibo harrumphed genteelly.

They lapsed back into silence until, after a decent interval, Yemko said, "I have often wondered what people make of these lovely things," waving his cane at the walls with a wheeze. "Now that their Bibles serve only to gather dust on the shelf, now that we teach them nothing of Homer, nothing of the great myths upon which our civilisation is founded, what can these lovely, lovely pictures mean to them? A beautiful woman with flaming hair and a severed head on a plate, a pale nude in a woodland pool surrounded by serving girls, glaring at a man and his dog. What can that possibly convey?"

"Perhaps they understand them as beautiful things," Tibo offered. "It is possible, I think, to appreciate beauty without understanding it."

"You think perhaps they understand them as beautiful things?" There was a forest of raised eyebrows attached to the remark. "As beautiful things? You mean they look at that young woman with a dead head on a platter and say to themselves, 'What a lovely girl!'? Or they look at the pale luminous flesh of Diana, not knowing she is about to turn that baleful glare to a flash of divine spite and change poor Acteon into a stag for his own hounds to shred, and they say to themselves, 'My word, what a corker! Wouldn't mind taking her to the Palazz on Saturday night. And, by the way, what a nice dog.' Something like that?"

"Yes," said Tibo simply. "Something like that. After all, it is a very nice dog."

Yemko sighed. "Good Mayor Krovic, the most amazing thing about you—and I say this with genuine warmth and admiration—

is that you honestly believe it. You honestly believe in sharing these beautiful things with people who can never understand them and could never be made to understand them. You believe in it."

"You think me very silly, don't you?"

"Not at all. Not at all." Yemko gave a reassuring wave of his fat hand. "I admire your lack of cynicism. I wish I shared it. Truly I do. Truly."

"It's not a matter of silliness or cynicism. It's a simple fact of life. People can admire, people can love, even, and never come close to understanding. They love God but never claim to understand. I doubt if there's a man in Dot who understands his wife but they love them."

"Some of them," the lawyer observed.

"Oh, most of them! Anyway, I have to believe that it's right to share these things. I'm a democrat."

Yemko nearly laughed at that. "Yes," he said, "that quaint idea based on the polite fiction that all opinions are of equal weight. Somehow it only ever seems to extend to the field of politics, never to matters such as plumbing or oceanic navigation or translation from the Sanskrit." His vast body shuddered in a sigh. "Good Mayor Krovic. Poor Good Mayor Krovic, you must promise me you'll never disappoint these people you care so much for. They'd tear you limb from limb. You'd be their Acteon. And promise me that, if you should ever stumble on Diana in the woods, you'll allow me to help."

"It won't come to that," said Tibo, "but thank you and, if it ever does, I'll be at your door."

There was a pause. Tibo suggested lunch.

"No. Thank you, no. I don't think I could face it," said Yemko.

"Another time, then," said Tibo.

"Another time." And, with a great effort, Yemko held out his hand. "Goodbye for now, Mayor Krovic. If you don't mind, I think I'll remain here with Diana for a little while."

"Of course. She belongs to you, after all." And Tibo withdrew with a smile.

He had almost reached the corridor again when Yemko called

after him, "My clerk will be writing to Judge Gustav this afternoon. You do understand?"

Without turning round, Mayor Krovic said, "The offer of lunch is still open."

Tibo walked back down the corridor of gloomy landscapes and, just as the management of the museum demanded, followed the strange and circuitous route out of the building, past the diorama of the siege of Dot, past Admiral Gromyko's unpublished manuscript chart of the Ampersand and on, with a grim inevitability, to the gift shop.

Description is supposed to be compulsory in stories but there is no need to describe a place like that. One museum gift shop is much like another with its souvenir pencils and souvenir erasers and souvenir sharpeners, the sort of things which any self-respecting child would curl his lip at in normal circumstances but which, on a museum visit, become dearer than life itself, more to be coveted than rubies, prized above the riches of the Indies. Museum gift shops are built on a firm foundation of stationery and, piled on that, come layers of posters and replicas and sensible books of the kind aunts like to give at Christmas, explaining the workings of steam engines or the private lives of penguins.

Tibo ignored all that. He was an only child and nobody's uncle. Instead, he walked straight up to a wire rack of coloured postcards hanging on the back wall and took down one of Diana and Acteon. He looked at it closely. There was no doubt, in a certain light, seen at a certain angle, the casual observer might, if he didn't know any better, see, perhaps, a passing resemblance to Agathe Stopak—purely superficially, of course. Tibo reached to put the card back on the rack, thought better of it, dug into his waistcoat pocket for a few coins, joined the queue behind a bouncing child and its sighing mother and it was only then that he noticed, on another rack, another postcard. This one was different—not a souvenir card of the paintings on show in the museum but hung on one of those columns of rotating racks where the sign at the top advertised:

The World's Greatest Pictures

Tibo saw it flashing past, once a second, as the bouncing child whacked venomously at the creaking, spinning rack.

"Excuse me," he said to the sighing mother, "do you mind?" He reached over her and stilled the tower of cards.

The woman ignored him, tugged the child away and hissed something about being good.

Tibo reached out and took the card. It was another goddess but a goddess in a different guise, dark-haired, like Agathe, not the insipid blonde from the forest, nude too but not accidentally exposed, deliberately and provocatively naked and not glaring furiously from behind a raised arm either. This one was lying on a satin-draped couch, gazing languorously from a mirror, exposing her cello-curved back and those rounded buttocks (exactly the mouth-watering colour of Turkish delight dusted with fine icing sugar), piling her hair up off her shoulders in tendrils around soft white fingers and looking out from the mirror with eyes that said, "Yes, it's you at last. I've been waiting here for ages. Come in and shut the door." This one, this was Agathe. Good Mayor Krovic looked at the back of the card. There was the usual printed division with "This side for message," "This side for address" and a grey square with "Affix postage here" and in two lines at the bottom, it said, "*The Rokeby Venus,* The National Gallery, Trafalgar Square, London."

The queue moved on. Tibo handed both cards to the assistant. They trembled in his fingers. The noise of them knocking together filled the room. Mayor Krovic did not wait for his change.

The attendants, in their brass-buttoned blazers, standing by the door, startled him as he tucked the little packet hurriedly inside his jacket and ducked outside. "Good day, Mayor Krovic."

"Yes. Bye!" he squeaked and rushed down the steps.

It wasn't long before Tibo began to feel very foolish indeed. He had purchased two postcards—that was all. Postcards of the sort that were sold in the respectable surroundings of Dot Museum, not the sort of thing that sailors brought home from the markets of Tangier. They were images of a kind that could be shown to schoolchildren. They *were* shown to schoolchildren almost every day, for goodness' sake. Indeed, the mayor and council of Dot would be failing in their duty to the young people of the city if images of that nature were not widely available in every classroom. Those postcards were pure and healthy celebrations of the human form. They represented crowning pinnacles of European art and culture. And yet Tibo was unaccountably warm and, for the second time that day, he found himself battling the temptation to feel terribly, terribly guilty. He looked at his watch. It was almost twelve.

In Braun's department store, waitresses in crisp black uniforms would be collecting stacks of saucers and tidying away the coffee pots and brushing crumbs of choux pastry off the tablecloths with white horsehair brushes. Dot was thinking about lunch and Tibo had had enough of a holiday. He turned back along the Ampersand, heading for City Square again and, as he walked between the elm trees, he found himself, from time to time, patting his jacket pocket, just to be sure that the small rectangular stiffness was still there and, from time to time, between pats, he looked backwards at the pavement behind, as if he feared some helpful citizen might suddenly touch him on the shoulder and say, "Mayor Krovic, did you drop these?"

Nobody did. When Tibo arrived at the Town Hall, the cards were still in his pocket. They were still in his pocket when he bounded up the green marble staircase to his office, still there when he went in and still there when, for the first time since he sacked Nowak, the City Treasurer, for goosing three girls in the typing pool, he closed the door to Mrs. Stopak's room. Good Mayor Krovic took the cards out of his pocket. Without opening the bag he put them in his desk drawer and locked them away.

The cup of coffee which Agathe had brought him that morning was still on its saucer quivering under a skin of milk. Tibo moved it to one side and slid the paper out of his leather-framed blotter. He turned it over. The underside was clean and bare. He pushed it into place. He smoothed it down. He made sure his inkwell and his pen set and his desk calendar were all nicely squared up and standing to attention. He leaned back in his chair. Everything was right. Neat. Nothing odd or out of place. Good.

Tibo Krovic stood up and opened the door to Agathe's room again. She looked up from her typewriter and smiled. She had that same look, with her hair piled high and the soft tendrils that curled over her neck, that same look in her eyes that said, "You at last. I've been waiting here for ages. Come in and shut the door."

"Everything all right?" she asked.

"Yes, thanks. Fine."

"Sure?"

"Yes. Just the coffee you gave me. I forgot to drink it. I'll have to go and pour it out."

Tibo retreated back into his office and emerged a moment later with the coffee cup.

"I can do that," said Agathe.

"No, it's fine. Don't bother." And he made his way carefully down the corridor towards the marble security of the Gents, where he rinsed out his cup, squeaked away the tidemark ring of milk with his thumb under a running tap and took calming gulps of bracing, bleach-soaked air. Old Peter Stavo was nothing if not thorough.

Tibo's hands were wet. He pushed them through his hair and tugged his waistcoat down flat. In the mirror, he saw the Mayor of Dot again. The Mayor of Dot is not the sort of person to purchase questionable postcards. It was the Mayor of Dot who walked back along the corridor past the picture of Mayor Skolvig's last stand and the boards with the golden names of all his predecessors but it was Tibo Krovic who walked past Mrs. Stopak's desk and saw her and smelled her perfume and thought about those postcards and wondered. He hurried into his room and sat down.

"Do you want anything else? More coffee?" Agathe called. "Only I'm planning on going for lunch soon."

Tibo was about to tell her not to bother when he looked up and found her there, standing on the other side of his desk. "No. I'm fine, thanks. Honestly. Thanks."

"So how was your tour of inspection?"

"It was fine. Fine too."

"Spot anything that needs done? Something to get to work on?"

"Couple of things. Small things. Nothing too much to worry about. Maybe a little job for the City Engineer and I might have a word with the Director of Arts and Culture about staffing. We can talk about it later."

"All right," said Agathe. "After lunch."

"Yes." Tibo hesitated. "Do you have plans? I suppose you'll be meeting Stopak."

"No. I went mad and treated myself to a new lunch box and I made some nice sandwiches and I'm going to enjoy them in the square, by the fountain. Lots of the girls do it."

"Yes, I've seen them," said Tibo.

They had run out of things to say. So, instead of saying, "For God's sake, Agathe, let's just get out of here, run down to the ferry and sail away to Dash and get a room in a hotel and spend all night there drinking champagne and making love until we're sick and not come home until morning!," Tibo said nothing at all.

"Right, then," said Agathe. "I'll let you get on."

"Yes. Right. Enjoy your lunch." And Tibo burrowed amongst his empty in-tray until she had gone. He waited, listening. He went to the door that linked their rooms. She had definitely gone. He looked round the corner of the door towards her desk. She was not there.

Tibo walked out of the office, off the thick blue municipal carpet and into the cold, hard terrazzo corridor that led to the back stairs. If he went down and past Peter Stavo's little glass box, he could reach the square. He went up, past the Planning Department, past the City Engineer and the Town Clerk, past Licensing and Entertainments, up three floors until the stairs grew small and narrow and ran out against a blank door.

Tibo took a bunch of keys from his pocket and flicked through it. He opened the door and stepped into a small white room. Dust from the rotting plaster covered the floor. There were ladders and buckets stacked against the walls, nameless shapes draped in grey sheets and four wooden steps that led up to another tiny door. Tibo climbed again and walked out into the sky. He was surrounded by blue, like my statue standing alone on the topmost crag of the cathedral, wrapped in blue from the sky above his head to the dark smudge on the horizon that might be the ferry coming home. Blue.

He gazed down into the square, down amongst the pigeons and the shoppers and the Town Hall clerks heading to the pie shop, looking for Agathe, the shape of her, the walk of her. And there she was, sitting down on the edge of the fountain, leaning back, letting the sunshine fall on her face as she turned it up to the sky, her handbag and her lunch box safely tucked away under her feet.

Good Mayor Krovic looked at her, at her blue dress, her blue enamel lunch box, the blue of the wide-open sky over Dot reflected in the sparkling water of the fountain and all of them outshone by the cornflower blue of her eyes which he pretended he could see shining from the other side of the square and, suddenly, he found himself saying "cerulean." Tibo was like that. It happened sometimes. For no reason that he could tell, beautiful words would form themselves in his mind. "Sirocco"—that was one—and "caryatid"—that was another. Cerulean, sirocco, caryatid. And then, on other days, he would find himself struggling to remember things. "What's the word for a pillar carved in female form?" and "caryatid" would stay out of reach, just beyond his recall until he began to wonder, "Am I getting old? Am I losing my marbles?"

Lately, he had started finding thick, bristly tree trunks sprouting amongst his eyebrows. Tibo was not a noticeably vain man but he admitted to himself that he was having trouble keeping them under control and, the other night, he thought he might bleed to death after a less than successful attempt to shave away unwelcome hairs that had sprouted, wolf-like, from his ears. "Old. I am getting old," he sighed.

But at moments like this, moments when he looked at Agathe Stopak for as long as he wanted, when he was able to drink her in, Tibo didn't think of growing old.

A wind came in from Dash and curled the town flag around him. Tibo caught one corner in his fist and kissed it. He was still looking at Agathe when he let it go.

BEFORE LONG, THE CATHEDRAL BELLS BEgan to chime again. The clerks and the shop girls and Agathe started drifting back from lunch. When she reached the office, Good Mayor Krovic was already sitting at his desk, just where she had left him. The newspaper folded open at the half-done crossword, the empty coffee cup and the piles of biscuit crumbs—they all told a story.

"Mayor Krovic, you should eat better," Agathe said and she swept the crumbs into a cupped hand.

"I'll have something proper tonight."

"Just so long as you do. You want to do those letters now?"

She went to her desk for her notebook, came back, sat in the green chair opposite Tibo's desk and copied down his letter to the City Engineer and another to the Director of Arts and Culture.

"Do you think we need men to open the doors of the museum for visitors?" Tibo asked her.

"Is that all they do?"

"I think it might be."

"Then I'm not sure," said Agathe. "What are we paying them?"

"I don't know that either. That's why I want to talk to the Director."

"Well," Agathe was hesitant, "I wouldn't want to see anybody lose their job but, on the other hand, as a ratepayer . . ."

"Yes, that's what I thought."

"One more question," said Agathe, "then I'll decide. These door-openers—do they have them at the museum in Umlaut?"

"A vital question that goes to the heart of the matter as usual," said Tibo. "I'll be sure to ask the Director."

The afternoon passed slowly in clock ticks and typewriter taps and coffee cups. The *Evening Dottian* arrived and Tibo was pleased to see he had been pushed off the front page by a fire in Arnolfini's liquorice factory. Nobody hurt, production back to normal by tomorrow. The morning paper still lay folded on his desk, one clue of the crossword blaring its empty triumph to the room.

"My granny always told me you shouldn't look out the window in the morning," Agathe said.

"Because you might need something to do in the afternoon. Yes, thank you, Mrs. Stopak, I've always enjoyed that joke."

"Well, now you've got something to do. It's nearly five o'clock. The wedding, remember?"

"Yes, I remember. The ferry girl. What's her name again?"

"Kate."

As Tibo busied himself, putting on his jacket, straightening his tie, Agathe picked up his paper from the desk and looked at it for a moment. She said, "Twenty-four down. It's 'impi'—a Zulu regiment is an 'impi.' African troop says I am circular ratio. I'm pi. See? Impi."

"What?"

"Impi."

Tibo could only shake his head. "I sweated for hours over that. How do you do it?"

"I'm brilliant," she said.

"Yes, Mrs. Stopak, you are brilliant. A tribute to the schools of Dot. Kate?"

"Kate."

"And?"

"Simon. She's the redhead in the dress that's a little too tight for her. He's the spotty boy wondering how he got into this mess. All written down on the forms as usual."

"Kate and Simon. Kate and Simon. Kate and Simon. Right, show them in."

"On my way," she said and she left the room with that easy, hip-swinging stroll that amazed Tibo every bit as much as her crossword abilities.

A moment later, Agathe returned, herding the wedding party. Tibo had taken the wooden lectern from its cupboard in the corner and now he stood behind it under the arms of Dot, under my smiling image, smiling himself to welcome them. But they were glum.

Tibo looked at poor, fat red-haired Kate and the only word that came to mind was "unfortunate." An unfortunate dress, an unfortunate chin, unfortunate billiard-table legs and an unfortunate shade of ginger. Unfortunate. She walked behind the boy, Simon, pushing him along, driving him, unwilling, to make his declaration before the mayor. His face was a blaze of acne, a Biblical plague of pus-y boils—the sort of thing we saintly types would have condemned as a showy display of excessive zeal—and he wore a green suit which had certainly not been made for him.

Good Mayor Krovic came out from behind the lectern to shake their hands—his famous double-handed hand shake, the one where he gripped with his regulation, firm, dry grip and then wrapped his left hand over the top, just to emphasise the sincere depths of his genuine welcome. "Simon," he said warmly. "Kate."

They mouthed something at him.

"Are you alone?" Tibo asked.

They looked at each other. They looked back at him.

"Is there nobody else here?" Tibo tried again.

The boy said, "There was a lady who showed us in."

"Yes, Mrs. Stopak—my secretary. But didn't you bring a friend? How about your parents?"

Simon looked at his shoes or as much of them as peeked out from his gigantic trouser cuffs. "My dad wouldn't come," he said. "Says I'm crackers. Won't have anything to do with it."

"And my mum's working," said Kate.

Tibo looked at them. Kids. They were just kids. Children. He had no business marrying children. Certainly no business marrying children whose parents didn't care if they were married or not—didn't care enough to see it done.

"I can't marry you," he said.

"Yes, you can," the boy said. "We need to."

"You need to. Do you want to?"

They looked at each other, the spotty boy and the unfortunate ginger girl.

"We need to," they said together.

And Tibo realised with a wrench that he couldn't prevent it. He had no right to prevent it. They were just another couple of Dottians he could not protect, not even from themselves. But then, he thought, maybe he liked them better for that. Maybe they were better people—more like the sort of people he wanted for his town because of that. Ordinary, ugly people in bad suits who "had" to get married. Maybe that was what a town like Dot needed—a sense of shame as well as a sense of pride. One without the other would be meaningless. One without the other would be dangerous.

"I can't marry you without witnesses," he said and he called Agathe into the room. "Mrs. Stopak, these two young people would like you and Peter Stavo to witness their marriage. Do you think you could find Peter and ask him to come in?"

"Of course," she said. "I'll take Kate to help me look." Agathe held out her hand and gave a flick of her head. There was a smile in the gesture and, perhaps, something like a wink. Kate went to her. Simon and Good Tibo Krovic were left alone standing face to face across the lectern. Tibo cleared his throat. Simon smiled wanly.

Tibo decided to return to his chair and relax. "Maybe we should sit down," he said. "They could be a while."

"I'll just stand, thanks," said Simon.

So Tibo sat at his desk, looking at the boy's back. He had chosen to sit and it would be silly and awkward now to go back and stand. Simon had chosen to stand. He couldn't change his mind and sit. They were stuck there, facing the same direction, feigning fascination with me, spread-eagled like a bearded butterfly pinned to a shield. It did not aid conversation but Mayor Krovic had a perfect view of the back of Simon's neck, pink and angry where the barber's razor had passed that morning. The stumps of three pimples formed a row of bloodied volcanoes along his collar.

There was nothing to say. Tibo fussed over the evening paper for a bit. "Are you sure you wouldn't like to sit?" he offered.

"No, I'll just stand." The boy half-turned his head to speak. The movement sparked an eruption on his neck. A spot of blood rubbed along his collar.

"Fair enough," said Tibo.

And, eventually, after an age, Agathe returned. She had Peter Stavo with her, ordered out of his brown overalls, looking respectable and smart and she had worked a small miracle with Kate. The boy turned to look at her and his ravaged face split into a smile. Somehow, in the time they were away, Agathe had taken Kate and turned her into a bride. She had changed her hair, tied a silk scarf at her throat, done something with the little store of make-up she always carried in her handbag and Kate was holding in her hands a bouquet of blue flowers. Tibo recognised them. They came from the silver vase which stood in constant tribute in front of the picture of Mayor Skolvig's last stand. "Why not?" thought Tibo. This is at least as courageous as anything Skolvig did.

Peter Stavo came forward and stood at Simon's shoulder. They shook hands. "All the best," said Peter and Agathe took her place alongside Kate, smiling.

They were all smiling, Tibo realised. Agathe had taken this small, shabby, shamed thing and made it happy. He stood at the lectern and read the words and, when it came to the time for Kate and Simon to hold hands, Agathe took the little bunch of flowers away and stood at one side, holding them, looking down on them.

Tibo had read the words so many times before and now it seemed as if he had never heard them until that moment. Everything a wedding service in a church could provide, they lacked. There was no poetry and no grandeur and no emotion. It was a simple bit of bureaucracy, an official stamp like a dog licence or a hawker's permit but suddenly, today, Tibo found it strangely thrilling. He read the bland formula aloud for Simon to say, haltingly, after him and, as he read the words, he imagined that he was saying them for Agathe, to Agathe, in his own right.

There she was, in her blue dress, looking modestly into the heart of a borrowed blue posy as he promised himself to her and her only forever and he felt his own foolishness, he felt the foolishness of it all—that the same stupid sense of shame and convention and conformity which had forced those two kids together kept him apart from a woman like Agathe.

When he said, "You may kiss the bride," there were tears on Tibo's cheeks. Agathe looked up and saw them there and she gave a little sob too.

"You softie!" she mouthed and turned away to dab her eyes. They had fooled each other.

And that was how it ended then, not sneaking down the back stairs but there, on the front steps of the Town Hall, in smiles and laughter and a shower of confetti that Peter salvaged from the trays under a dozen paper punches on the desks of a dozen clerks and pulled from his pocket as Tibo yelled, "Cheese!" encouragingly.

There was time for a drink—"Just one. No, honestly, no more. Oh, all right, then, you're twisting my arm. But just one more and that's all!"—in The Phoenix and then they parted with hugs—"The scarf? Keep it. Don't be silly, it's a wedding present!"—and hurried home, Tibo walking quickly up Castle Street, Agathe waiting at the tram stop at the corner of City Square, Peter climbing the stair to his flat above Dot's second-best butcher's and the kids, Kate and Simon, running away together, laughing down the hill to the future—whatever that might be.

Agathe looked after them and tried to decide what it was that she was feeling. Envy? Pity? Nostalgia? Anger? She turned away with a sigh.

A cold wind blew up Castle Street and, before his tram arrived, it lingered near Tibo, bringing him the sound of Kate's laughter and the clatter of her feet as Simon hurried her over the cobbles. An unfortunate child—that was what he had called her. He chided himself for it now. They were plain, dull, ugly children both of them, lumbering blindly into plain, dull, ugly, blighted lives but at least they were not going alone. "Unfortunate?" thought Tibo. "Damn you, Krovic, when did you get so high and mighty?"

The tram came. He had missed the rush of office workers and hurrying shop girls. It was quiet now, easier to get a seat with just a few other passengers including a couple like him—prosperous, well-dressed middle-aged men who had lingered a little too long in a city tavern because they could think of no good reason to hurry home.

After seven stops, Good Mayor Krovic got off at the kiosk on the corner and turned into his street walking under overhanging cherry trees until, halfway down, on the right-hand side, he reached his gate. It seemed to cling to the wall for support, like a Saturday-night drunk against a lamp post. "I must do something about that," thought Tibo. "I really must." He ducked under the birch tree where the brass bell hung in case of visitors and noticed a butterfly clinging to it and stamping feet as fine as horsehair on the rim. At the other end of the path, as he fished in his pockets for the big black house key, Tibo was sure he could hear a tiny ringing.

A few minutes earlier, in the centre of town, above Dot's second-best butcher's, Peter Stavo walked into a flat where the kitchen was steamy with stew and dumplings and he kissed the fat wife who had stood in front of that same stove these thirty years. She shooed him off with a tea towel and an angry tut and complained, "You're in early tonight! And you've been drinking." But, when she was sure his back was turned and he had settled into the chair with the paper, she looked at him with a smile.

And, on the other side of Dot, as the tram pulled away from Green Bridge, Agathe made an effort to pull her shoulders back and walk straight and tall as a poplar, curvy as a skittle, round the corner into Aleksander Street, past Oktars' delicatessen and up the stairs to the flat where Hektor was standing on the landing, scraping a charred frying pan into the bin.

"Oh," he said. "Sorry. Me and Stopak . . . You were late coming home so we thought we'd make the tea."

Smoke wafted round the landing. It was even thicker inside the flat. "Have you called the fire brigade?" Agathe asked coldly.

"Aww, don't be like that," said Hektor. "Sorry, Agathe. Honest."

"Where's Stopak?"

"He's inside. He's having a little sleep." Hektor giggled stupidly. "A little sleep. That's all. Been a long day."

"So you were hanging paper in The Three Crowns all day, were you?"

And all Hektor could find to say was, "Aww, don't be like that. Sorry, Agathe. Honest."

She looked at him with his cigarette sticking out from under that ragged moustache, a blunted knife in one hand, a blackened pan scored with bright silver scars in the other and she almost laughed. This was what her life had become.

"Throw it away," she said. "Just drop it in the bin. It's ruined. Not worth saving. It's no good to me."

He was going to say, "Sorry, Agathe," again but he thought better of it. He dropped the pan and put the lid back on the bin.

"I'll make you a sandwich," Agathe said and, in the kitchen, she sliced bread and chopped ham and twisted the lid off pickle jars with all the cold fury of a harpy. Hektor said nothing. He ate his way through it and thanked her and left.

When Stopak woke on the sofa at 4 a.m. with a crick in his neck and a sick dryness in his mouth, his plate of sandwiches was still where Agathe had left it, balanced on his paunch.

And that's how things were for Tibo and Agathe—every day much the same. Ordinary. They would get up in the morning and take the tram to work at opposite ends of town and she would busy herself and be sad because there was no one in the world who cared for her or wanted her while, just through that door, just on the other side of that wall, Good Tibo Krovic was miserable because there was nothing and no one in the whole world that he wanted unless it was Mrs. Stopak.

They fooled each other. They fooled each other at the wedding when Agathe thought that Tibo had shed a sentimental tear, never considering that he might have been weeping with frustration because he wanted her and could not have her. And Agathe fooled him when she wept with jealousy for the fat baby growing in Kate's belly and he never realised. They fooled each other every day in a thousand ways, neither of them daring to admit their lack, neither of them daring to speak their pain, each unwilling to confess the truth about their lives. They almost, almost fooled themselves.

And yet they comforted each other. Agathe with her buxom cheerful beauty—she couldn't help being beautiful—and Tibo with his kindness. Tibo couldn't help being kind. They warmed each other with those little gifts—kindness and beauty. They are precious. They are always in short supply.

And, in days measured out by the chimes of the cathedral carillon and the clink of coffee cups and weeks measured out in new typewriter ribbons or sittings of the Parks and Recreation Committee, they clung together secretly, nursed each other unawares, dressed one another's wounds. When Agathe spent the morning looking at her blue enamel lunch box that sat on her desk in the place where once a little parcel from Braun's had nestled, when the high point of her day was taking it out to the fountain and feigning a surprised delight at discovering the sandwiches she had made for herself that morning, then that was the high point of Tibo's day too. See him there, up there on the secret balcony, by the flagpole, up in the sky, watching her, watching over her? It's the fulcrum of his life.

Or, when Tibo went home alone to the old house at the end of its blue-tiled path and sat in the kitchen as the cheese congealed in that evening's omelette and he burrowed in a briefcase full of council papers, hoping to find Agathe in it, hoping to drive her from his mind, she was in the flat in Aleksander Street, above Oktars' delicatessen, thinking about him.

When Stopak lay there silent and cold, snoring, not noticing the beautiful, plump, scented woman at his side or when Hektor stood in her kitchen, frying sausages on her stove and turning to spit in her sink with a cigarette burning runnels where it lay on her table as Stopak dozed on the sofa next door, then Agathe's first thought was always, "Mayor Krovic would never do that. I bet Mayor Krovic would never behave that way. I can't see Mayor Krovic doing that."

When she lay in bed stroking Achilles the kitten, who grew under her hand into a strong, sleek cat with claws like sabres, she always went to sleep wishing him well. "Goodnight, Achilles," she would say. "Goodnight, Achilles. Goodnight, Mayor Krovic. Goodnight."

And, alone, in the big house at the end of the blue-tiled path at the other end of town, Mayor Krovic would hear her and roll over in his bed under the quilted counterpane that his mother made when he was a boy, pull it up to his ears and say, half asleep, "Goodnight, Mrs. Stopak. God bless you and keep you."

See how they watched over each other?

B*ut the summers are short in Dot.* Cold winds began to blow over the Ampersand more often and, sometimes, there was no shelter to offer.

That was how it was the day the letter came—a great white snowflake of a thing that lay on Tibo's desk when he arrived at work, carrying winter in its folds. Agathe had dealt with all his other mail, sliced his letters open deftly, unfolded the pages, shaken them out, fixed each one to its envelope with a paperclip, laid them in a neat pile on his desk under that iron paperweight that looked like a squashed black doorknob. But not this one. It lay there screaming like a siren, boasting to the other envelopes about the quality of its paper, its high rag content, its deckle edging, its tissue lining and, written across the top left corner in a confident fountain-pen hand were the words "Strictly private and confidential."

Tibo picked the letter up. He weighed it in his hand. He balanced it, diagonal to diagonal between the tips of his fingers where the strong paper corners burrowed into his skin like tiny gimlets. He blew on it and watched it spin there. He threw it down on the desk. He was just pushing back his chair so he could rise and go to the door to ask Agathe for some coffee when she appeared there, carrying a cup and saucer.

"I'm not being nosy," she said but she sounded concerned.

"No, that's all right," said Tibo. "I've been expecting this for a while. I know what it is."

"Right," said Agathe. But she stayed where she was, hands folded together at the wrist, standing on the other side of his desk.

Tibo tucked the point of his little finger under the flap of the envelope and ripped it open. The ragged edge of the sky-blue tissue lining spilled out like a wound. He read it aloud to her. "Dear Krovic, As I'm sure you know, the lawyer Guillaume has seen fit to make a formal complaint to me about your conduct in a recent case. You are a good man, Tibo Krovic, doing a good job, and we need more like you.

"Everybody is entitled to a half hour of madness every now and again and no harm done and even Guillaume says his man deserved what happened. If matters are as he alleges, I don't have to tell you that it would be a very serious situation indeed but, if you can tell me now that the whole thing is a lot of bollocks, that'll be good enough for me. I am writing this to you by my own hand from my own chambers and I don't have to tell you that none of this will go any further. I know you can clear it all up very quickly, my boy."

It was signed with a flourish "Judge Pedric Gustav."

Tibo dropped the letter on his desk with a grim sigh. "So that's that, then."

"That's what, then? It's a lovely letter."

"Oh, Mrs. Stopak, read it! It's an invitation to resign."

Agathe snatched the letter from the desk. "Listen," she said. "Listen. 'Tell me it's bollocks and it's over, I know you can clear this up, none of this will go any further.' He wants you to stay on. He's asking you to stay on. It's not an invitation to resign."

"Mrs. Stopak, the very best you can say is it's an invitation to lie."

"Oh, don't be silly. Nobody's asking you to lie."

"Judge Gustav is. All that stuff about a mad half hour and how Yemko Guillaume knows his client deserves all he got. If Guillaume thought that for a minute, he would never have complained to the judge and, if Gustav believed I had a leg to stand on, he'd have had his secretary write this letter, not this hole-and-corner business, writing to me secretly from his locked chambers. It's a very kind, very generous, very pleasant invitation to resign."

Agathe pushed the letter around the desk with the rubber tip of her pencil. "Let me write to him. I can type something up in a minute. You don't have to do it."

"Mrs. Stopak, I'd have to put my name to it. I'd have to sign it."

"No, I could sign it. I could say you were out of the office."

"I know you're trying to be kind but no. It's ridiculous. No."

"Ridiculous! Now I'm ridiculous, am I?" She flicked Judge Gustav's letter across the desk. "Have it your own way, then. I might be ridiculous . . ."

"You're not ridiculous. I didn't mean you."

"Well, I might be ridiculous but at least I'm not . . ." She stopped to draw breath. "At least I'm not prissy!"

"Prissy?" said Tibo. "Prissy. You think I'm being prissy. Telling the truth is prissy, is it?"

Agathe stamped out of the office. "Oh, go ahead and resign if that's what you want to do," she said. "See if I care." And she slammed the door and sat at her desk and wept, dabbing hot tears from her eyes because she did care. She cared a great deal. She had to sit there and listen as Tibo banged about in his office looking for paper. She had to give it to him when he finally gave up the hunt and came out to ask for help. She sat listening for the scrape of his pen as he wrote, feeling the nib scoring against her flesh as it scored against the paper. She handed him an envelope and took a single red stamp from the tray in her drawer and, when he strode out of the office, heading for the postbox, she sat watching him go.

"I don't think you're ridiculous," he said, without turning round.

And, too soft for him to hear, Agathe said, "I don't think you're prissy." And then she had another little cry because she couldn't share this with him and she couldn't protect him from it or take it on herself.

She did what she could. She did her job well. She made him coffee. She told him funny stories about Achilles the cat and utterly, completely refused to pass on a word of gossip—oh, all right then, but you mustn't tell another soul—about what the Town Clerk's wife had got up to at the Sunday School picnic, she brought him the evening paper but she never, never mentioned life at home or Stopak or Hektor.

And Tibo did what he could for her. He was a kind and considerate employer. He was always polite, always asked nicely for whatever he wanted done, never made her work late, always made sure there were biscuits with her coffee and sometimes even a cake, never, never mentioned that he was crazed for her and wanted her past bearing. And, above all, he watched over her with devotion, whether that meant he had to get up from his desk a dozen times a day to open the door between their offices or run like a madman as soon as she left at lunchtime so he could stand on the tower of the Town Hall to look at her. Tibo did what he could. He sensed her pain. He recognised it as if it had been reflected from a mirror and, because of that, he watched over her.

And that's what he was doing that day at the end of summer when Agathe sat down at the edge of the fountain and accidentally knocked her lunch box into the water.

Look down now from the top of the Town Hall, as Good Tibo Krovic did that day, as he has done in memory so many days and nights since. Look at the square, full of people, some happy, some angry, some lonely, some loved, pretty girls and plain, that filthy old drunk with his broken, wheezing accordion hanging from one arm, the policeman coming to move him along, the dog on a string, the tram clanging past. Look at the day. It's a bright afternoon at the beginning of September, summer's last throw. The flowers in the window boxes are making one more brave effort, the hanging baskets are striving for one last surge of colour, one final glorious trumpet blast to outdo the municipal geraniums of Umlaut, the trees along the Ampersand are defying autumn, the geese among the islands have refused all arrangements for flying south. And all of them, flowers, trees, leaves, birds, dogs, drunks, shop girls, all of them chorus together, "It will never be winter!" because there, in the middle of the square, sits the proof of it. Mrs.

Agathe Stopak, tall and buxom and creamy pink, sitting on the edge of the fountain, permitting sunbeams to kiss her.

Look at her sitting there. Look at her through the eyes of Good Tibo Krovic. Look at the shape of her, the curve and the line. Look at her foot resting feather-light on that flagstone, toes point-peeping from her sandals, the round arc of her heel, the nip of her ankle, the swell of her calf, the bight of the back of her knee and on, up to where the polka-dot silk of her dress holds a promise of thigh and stocking-top and tense suspender clasp. Look at the slalom curve of her, hurtling downhill from her chin, round her throat, over breasts that would outdo the statuary of a Hindu temple, the sheer mathematical impossibility of her waist, the swell of her belly, the buttocks that spread and settle and accept the fountain's marble edge. Look at her as she moves, the grace of her, the joy of her, shaking out that chequered cloth over her knee, a sedentary Salome.

She turns to reach for a sandwich from her lunch box, every joint in motion, waist and shoulder and elbow and wrist and knuckle, curve and line and angle, down to the very tip of her finger which now, for just a moment, brushes the lid of the box and pushes and begins to tip. And this is the moment that lasts forever. This is the moment when Good Tibo Krovic stands outside time, as far above the ticking of the clock as he is far above the square. For Mrs. Stopak's lunch box is moving. It is slipping off the edge of the fountain. It is sliding into the water as slow as syrup in a winter kitchen and Tibo begins to run. Through the door beside the flag pole, a leap from the top of the four wooden steps, into the small white room beneath with its buckets and its ladders and its dust sheets and its mole-heaps of crumbling plaster, a struggle with the lock and out on to the back stair as the door bangs behind him, then crashing and leaping and falling like a rock, down three floors past Licensing and Entertainments, past the Town Clerk and the City Engineer, past the Planning Department, into the terrazzo corridor outside his office, through the glass door and, before it's had time to bounce on its hinges, across the thick blue carpet and down again, down the green marble stairs that lead to the front door and City Square where, just beside the fountain, Mrs. Stopak is turning with disgust to fish her sopping lunch box out of the water.

Good Mayor Krovic pauses before he steps out into the sunlight. He tugs firmly down on his waistcoat, he shoots his cuffs, he pushes his fingers through his hair, he exhales deeply through his mouth and sucks air in through his nose with a whistle until his lungs are full, his breathing calmed. And then, in the very instant that the heel of his shoe lands on the smooth grey flagstones of City Square, the mechanism of his watch moves on, tick turns to tock and time starts again.

"I would be honoured if you would let me buy you lunch," he said and, for some reason, God alone knows why, he felt himself compelled to fold in half, bowing like a hussar in some Viennese operetta.

"This is not the way to ask a woman out," thought Tibo. "Not a married woman—not a married woman who works for you! Good God, Krovic, what were you thinking?"

The big heart of Good Mayor Krovic sank because he knew the mistake he had made. She would reject him, mock him, accuse him in the middle of City Square, point at him for the townspeople to laugh at and that would be the end of it—he'd have to resign. He'd be hounded out of town. His life of service would end in disgrace when she exposed him as a pervert and a philanderer. But she didn't. She didn't. Mrs. Agathe Stopak turned to him, squinting in the sunlight and giggled like a girl and said, "I would be honoured to accept." And then she curtsied—a gesture just as foolish and mechanical and overblown as his had been but done with such a twinkle as to set the clumsiest suitor at ease. She tossed her dripping lunch box back into the fountain as if it meant nothing, as if it was no more than a tin box full of wet bread, and she took his arm and moulded her body to his as they walked out of the square and over White Bridge and Tibo melted.

But something changed in Agathe too. In that single instant when she saw Tibo standing there and reached out and took his hand, something changed. Her sadness lifted. She found herself suddenly wanted and desirable again.

Here was a man, not just any man, mind you, but the Mayor of Dot, Mayor Tibo Krovic himself, who had taken the trouble to ask her out to lunch. And why not? Why not? She was a good-looking woman, pleasant company, why not? What harm could there be? There was nothing in it. Nobody could possibly object or take exception. But, even so, Agathe felt a strange thrill in it. She felt almost mistressy. Not wifely or secretary-ish but almost mistressy and, if truth be told, even a little bit naughty and, above all, changed.

She pressed herself close to Tibo as they walked together up Castle Street—probably too close. For a moment, she found herself asking, "If it was Stopak who was asking you for lunch, would you walk this way with him?" But a little voice in her head answered quickly, as if it had been waiting for just such a question, "If Stopak ever asked you to lunch, would you be walking with the mayor?"

They walked together, side by side, through the square across White Bridge and up Castle Street, Agathe stepping out in her heels in a wide, comfortable hip-swinging roll. She jiggled deliciously beside him in a thin white dress with big black polka dots on it and wafts of scent rose up from her as the top of her head brushed his chin. When she walked, she wiggled and, when outraged conscience complained, "Stop that, Agathe Stopak! You are a respectable married woman!," it was all she could do to stop from purring and rubbing herself on Tibo like a cat against a table leg. She felt her hair brushing his chin as they walked. She wondered if, with him standing so close, he might not be looking down her dress. And then she realised she didn't care. She wanted him to look down her dress. In fact, she would be downright offended if he didn't. She glanced up quickly to see if she could catch him at it and turned her eyes down again, satisfied.

The heavy scrolled doors of The Golden Angel swung shut behind them and it was only then that Mrs. Stopak felt the brief squeeze of panic close round her heart. If this had been a Stanley Korek picture, this would have been the time when the piano player stopped playing, the room fell silent and all eyes would be on them. But that sort of thing doesn't happen in respectable cafes like The Golden Angel. They don't have piano players in The Golden Angel and, if, at any time, a valued and respected client like Mayor Tibo Krovic should choose to honour that establishment with his custom in the lunch hour, whether that be in the company of his secretary or anybody else, then he can be sure of only the most impeccable service.

Cesare was an obsidian statue behind the counter—black suit, black tie, a bramble-gleam of black hair, carefully shaped black eyebrows mirrored below his nose in a blue-black moustache but, for just a fraction of a portion of a moment, the iron cast of his face shifted. Agathe saw it. She spotted it as she came through the door—a tiny flash across the face, a microscopic hiking of those eyebrows, an all-but-invisible twitch of the lips, a look in the eye that said, "Mamma Mia, the mayor again, twice in one day and with a woman too. Unbelievable. Incredible!" before he regained his self-control and dispatched a waiter to greet them with nothing more than a swift-swivelled glance.

"For two, sir?" the waiter smarmed and urged them to a shadowed alcove against the back wall.

"I think I'd rather sit in the window, please," said Tibo, "if that's all right with you." He turned to Agathe with a questioning smile and she nodded.

The window seat—on full view to the whole of Dot. Now how could there possibly be anything scandalous about that?

The table was set for four and, as the waiter cleared away the extra places, Tibo and Agathe settled themselves.

"The menu, Madam, Sir. Sir, the wine list. I will bring some water." And the waiter withdrew.

They were suddenly awkward. Agathe asked, "Would you prefer this chair so you could look out the window?"

"No," said Tibo, "I'd rather look at you."

Agathe looked down at her twining fingers and resisted the temptation to fiddle pointlessly with the napkin.

"Would you like something to drink?" said Tibo, opening the cream-coloured folder that held the wine list.

"Better not. What will the boss say if we go back to work squiffy?"

It was such a stupid thing to say, such a lame joke, and she looked so girlish and naughty when she said it that Tibo couldn't help laughing at her.

"We'll stick to water, then," he said. And things went better after that.

They spoke about everything, starting with the outbreak of nits at the Western Girls' School. "They say the little devils only live on clean heads but that's not true. There's always one filthy head where they start. I was in the chemist's the other day and they told me there was not a jar of nit powder to be had in the whole of Dot. Makes me itch just to think of it."

Tibo promised he would contact the Sanitary Department and make sure that something was done.

Then they moved on to that scandalous performance with the hypnotist at the Opera House last week. "Well, I'm no prude," said Agathe.

"No more am I," said Tibo.

"Oh, good," she thought. "Oh, good!" But what she said was, "And I enjoy a laugh as much as anybody but you heard what happened when he got Mrs. Bekker up on stage?"

"I heard." Tibo nodded gravely.

"That poor woman teaches Latin at the Academy. How is she supposed to hold her head up after something like that? How is she supposed to keep order in a classroom when half the town has seen her drawers? I've heard," Agathe glanced over her shoulder to see who might be listening, "I've heard that the Licensing and Entertainments Department was about to step in but money changed hands. The Opera House is selling out every night and palms were greased."

Tibo's face clouded. "That had better not be true. Everybody in the Town Hall knows I'd have their jobs for something like that. This isn't Umlaut, you know!"

The waiter returned and hovered, smirking. "Ready to order?"

They held the menus in their hands, unopened, leaning close over the table, heads almost touching in an open incitement to nits and they looked at each other and, for some reason, they burst out laughing again.

"I'm sorry," said Tibo, "we haven't really chosen. What's good today?"

"It's all good every day, sir," said the waiter.

Tibo wondered why the man's face didn't bulge from the constant exercise of supercilious eyebrows. "Well, what's especially good today?"

The waiter gathered the menus up in expert hands. "The sole is fresh off the dock this morning, sir. Picked it up myself, so I did, and it was still flapping in the boxes. And sir will be wanting the Chablis with that."

"Oh, why not?" said Tibo. "You're only young once."

Agathe looked at him in feigned horror and pressed a fluttering hand to her chest as if she was about to swoon away.

"Stop fussing," Tibo grinned, "I'll square it with the boss."

The waiter brought a basket of bread. They ate it with a glass of wine.

The food came—soft, creamy, delicious fish and crisp vegetables. They ate it. They drank the second glass of wine. It sparkled on their tongues, it filled and refreshed them, lifted and restored them. They laughed a lot.

And then, over coffees, she told him about Sarah, the pretty girl who takes the money in a glass booth in Dot's second-best butcher's. "She has been unlucky in love," said Agathe.

"Sarah?" asked Good Mayor Krovic.

"Sarah," said Agathe. "I was in there on Saturday and she looked like death and I said to her, 'My dear, are you really quite well?' and she said, 'I feel terrible—I haven't had a wink of sleep and I have a broken heart and you are the only one who has even noticed. Thank you.' And she gave me my change."

"Sarah?" said Tibo in wonderment. "I was in there on Saturday and she sold me half a kilo of sausage. I didn't notice anything wrong."

"I noticed," Agathe said with a sigh. "I recognised the symptoms."

When she said those words "I recognised the symptoms," the great weight of sadness that Agathe had dumped in the fountain along with her lunch box suddenly came rushing up Castle Street and forced its way into the cafe to sit at the table beside her. "I recognised the symptoms"—what an admission. It was an acknowledgement of a broken heart, a damage report, but not yet a flag of surrender.

Tibo put out his hand to hers. It was only a small table. They were sitting close and, for a second or two his arm and hers lay together there, his fingers reaching almost into the crook of her elbow, hers brushing the sensible tweed of his jacket and then a kind of pressure down the length of her arm to where their hands met and clasped for a time, finger to finger, a reassurance, a touch from Tibo that said, "I recognise the symptoms. Me too. I recognise the symptoms."

But, more than that, it was a touch—the first time a man had touched Agathe with affection for . . . well, for a long time, and it felt good to be touched. A woman like Agathe needs to be touched. She drank in those few moments and stored them up. The joy of it disappeared into her like drops of rain on a parched field and, deep down, something that had seemed dead began to swell and blossom again.

"You and Stopak . . ." Tibo asked, "things are not happy?"

"No—things have not been happy for the longest time."

"The baby?"

"Yes, I suppose she was the start of it. I suppose. Little mite. Wee soul. God bless her. No day passes . . . you know."

"I know. I know. You'll see her again."

"Yes," said Agathe. "Yes." The empty "yes" of the bereaved. She was suddenly stricken with a runny nose and sniffed it away—rather more loudly than she would have hoped. "Not for the longest time," she sighed.

"Do you want to . . ." Tibo was having trouble finishing his sentences but, somehow, it didn't seem to matter. They understood each other.

"No." Agathe shook her head. "A trouble shared is a trouble

doubled, my old granny used to say. Thank you, Mayor Krovic, but it wouldn't do any good. There's nothing to be done for it and what cannot be cured must be endured."

"You are very brave," said Tibo.

"I'm not brave at all. Sometimes I just want to run away. I have read about the coast of Dalmatia. It's warm there."

"But it's warm here," said Tibo, who had never imagined that anybody, let alone Mrs. Agathe Stopak, could hanker for a life beyond Dot. What possible attraction could there be in that? Dot had a river as pretty as other rivers, nice ducks, beaches not far away, historic monuments—they were all in the pamphlets on the front desk at the Town Hall.

None of that seemed to have occurred to Agathe. "It's warm here now," she conceded. "Today it's warm. But it can't last. Nothing lasts—I've found that out—and, in a little while, it will be freezing cold again. Snow on the streets for weeks, dark by lunchtime."

"Oh, hardly," said Tibo.

"Well, nearly. And it goes on for months. On the coast of Dalmatia, it's warm all year long and they have castles and rocky beaches and lovely old towns where the Venetians used to sail."

The Venetians . . . Tibo went back in his mind to the exhibition at the Municipal Gallery and that image of the beautiful, naked Diana, with the forest pool unfolding in ripples at her feet.

"Sometimes," said Agathe, "I buy a lottery ticket and then, all month long, I carry the coast of Dalmatia round in my purse. My own little house, by the sea, on the coast of Dalmatia. For me. No Stopak. Me and a good man who loves me and reads me Homer and brings me glasses of wine and good bread and dishes of olives while I lie in a cool bath."

"Oh, God," thought Tibo Krovic. "Oh, God. Oh, St. Walpurnia. Mrs. Agathe Stopak lying in a cool bath. Oh, God." He suddenly recalled the postcards tucked in a paper bag at the back of his drawer. "Oh, God. Oh, St. Walpurnia."

"Do you like olives?" he squeaked.

"If I win the lottery, I will learn to love olives and I will learn to love Homer."

"Then I would bring you olives."

Agathe laughed. It seemed like the right time to pull her hand away from his, when there was a smile to cover the gesture so it would seem as ordinary not to be touching as it had seemed ordinary to touch.

"I would," Tibo insisted. "I would bring you olives."

"You are a good man, Mayor Krovic," she said.

"And I like Homer. I seem to fit."

She smiled at that and she was still smiling when Tibo went to pay the bill. He seemed to fit. A good man who liked Homer. But this was Tibo Krovic, the Mayor of Dot. Surely he wouldn't, he couldn't, he couldn't possibly mean . . .

"Ready?" asked Tibo at her shoulder.

"Yes, I'm ready," said Agathe. "I'm ready." She noticed that he left the bill lying in the saucer pinned down by a few coins. This was not an allowable expense to be claimed on the council's accounts.

They walked together down Castle Street in the sunshine, over the bridge across the Ampersand and into City Square, still arm in arm like before, still as close as ever, only, this time, going back, it felt different.

"I should leave you here," said Tibo.

"Here? Aren't you going back to work?"

"Yes. In a bit. Things to do. Just a couple of things first. I'll see you later." Tibo looked abashed.

"And well you might," thought Agathe. "Oh, I'm good enough to take out to lunch, good enough to hold hands with—'And a quick look down the front of your dress, that would be just lovely, Mrs. Stopak, but I'll be coming back to work on my own, Mrs. Stopak. Thanks a lot, Mrs. Stopak.'" But all she said was "Fine" and she clip-clipped angrily up the stairs to her office, cursing inwardly. "'I seem to fit.' I seem to fit, indeed! Well, you won't be trying me for size, Mr. High-and-Mighty Krovic, and I'll tell you that for nothing!" she fumed all the way up the stairs to her office where she thumped her handbag on her desk and shovelled angry scoops of coffee into the percolator.

Of course, if Mrs. Agathe Stopak had looked out her window about then, she would have seen Tibo Krovic down in the square, looking into the south-most fountain and scratching his head. The water was deeper than he had imagined and there, at the bottom, he could see Mrs. Stopak's blue enamel lunch box. A single bloated cracker was disintegrating on the surface of the pool. Tibo took off his jacket, folded it carefully inside out, as he had been taught to do at the age of eight, and laid it on a clean patch of pavement. He rolled up his sleeve until it tightened like a tourniquet well above his elbow, knelt on the edge of the fountain and began to grope for the tin. Mayor Tibo Krovic always had a keen sense of his own dignity and he was aware that this pose, head down, trouser seat in the air, leaning out at full stretch, was, perhaps, a little less than heroic. In fact, it brought to mind one of those desperately unfunny shorts they liked to show between the main features at the Palazz Kinema. "The man twirling the ladder should arrive just about now," thought Tibo, "but the terrier won't run off with my jacket until after I fall in the water."

He stretched a little further. The water reached his sleeve but he just managed to brush the tin box with his fingers. It scraped along the bottom of the pool, coming a little closer. This time, Tibo was able to hook a finger under the lid and he dragged it up and let the water drain out. Inside there was a mess of bread which he tipped into a trough of geraniums. He looked at the box. "It'll be fine," he thought. The few remaining doughy bits that stuck in the corners he wiped away with his vast green handkerchief. "But, if I buy her lunch, she won't be needing this again anyway."

Tibo picked up his jacket and walked across the square to the Town Hall where Mrs. Stopak seemed ridiculously pleased to get her lunch box back. "That's what you've been doing?" she gushed. "Thank you, Mayor Krovic. I thought that . . . No. Nothing."

"No. Tell me. You thought what?"

"Nothing. Nothing. I've made some coffee. Want one?"

"No thanks," he said. "Work to do." From that very moment, Tibo Krovic, a man who had never loved a woman before, knew beyond any shadow of a doubt, that he loved Agathe Stopak. He knew, in the way that he would have known if an elephant had entered his kitchen, not that he had ever seen an elephant but something so big and so grey and so wrinkled could be nothing but an elephant. So, as obviously as an elephant, this was love. He walked on into the inner office but he left the door open in the hope that Mrs. Stopak might drift by from time to time. She did not. But she did find herself breaking off from her work rather a lot. She did find herself stopping to look at the lunch box that sat atop her in-tray where the little box from Braun's had left its mark on memory just a short while before. She looked at it as if it were made of moon dust—a strange object from another world where men were kind and took a bit of trouble and, most of all, where they were not ashamed.

"He does seem to fit," she whispered to herself. "A good man who likes Homer. He seems to fit."

From her place at her desk, Mrs. Agathe Stopak turned to look at the open door to the mayor's office, hoping that he might appear to demand coffee or paper clips or to bark dictation at her. But she was frightened to go near in case she saw him and that was probably just as well because, just on the other side of the door, Good Tibo Krovic was sitting at his desk in silence, a pencil gripped between his teeth, holding his breath as he listened for the slightest sound of her, or raising his nose to the open door, hunting for her perfume.

At five o'clock, Mrs. Agathe Stopak tidied her desk, locked her drawer and left the office. Just on the other side of the door, Mayor Tibo Krovic heard her go. He heard her arranging her papers, sliding the drawer shut, locking it, heard her walking, quietly, across the room, imagined the perfect pink O of her mouth as she blew out the tiny flame warming the coffee pot, felt her leaving, trailing perfume in her wake, listened, straining, for her call of "Goodnight" and prayed that it would not come because he could not trust himself to respond, whispered his own silent "Goodnight" to her and sat, like a waiting hunter while the clock ticked through ten aching minutes, just to be sure she was gone, just to be sure she wasn't coming back.

And, all that time, he was sitting, waiting, watching, Mrs. Agathe Stopak was standing halfway down the stairs, one hand on the banister, breathing in whispers because, halfway down the stairs, she realised that, for the first time, she had forgotten to say "Goodnight" to the mayor and she knew why. She couldn't have managed it. Standing there on the green marble staircase, she felt a sudden strange warmth coiling inside her and she hurried away to escape it.

Up in his room, Mayor Tibo Krovic picked up his pen and began the work he should have done that afternoon—the contracts he should have approved, the letters he should have signed, the licensing applications and planning consents he should have "glanced over"—and, at the end of it all, when the bells in the cathedral struck seven, Tibo left his office and walked down the green marble steps of the Town Hall, out into the square and over White Bridge. The ducks paddling in the Ampersand quacked politely as he passed. Bats nestling under the arches flittered in wide swoops as they hunted the evening moths. Everything had changed. The colours were a little sharper, the birdsong a little sweeter, each individual quack of each individual duck swimming under the bridge across the Ampersand was that bit more "quacky" and cheerful and defiant. All the way up Castle Street, Tibo tried to catch sight of himself in shop windows as he passed. "Not bad," he thought. "Tall. Not fat. Not slim, but not too fat for a man who had been mayor for twenty years." He decided on a new suit. Two new suits. And some shoes. The mayor of a town like Dot should be well turned out. He deserved it. Dot deserved it.

And, as Tibo stepped smartly up Castle Street, admiring himself in the shop windows as he passed, Mrs. Agathe Stopak was standing by the stove in her flat in Aleksander Street, turning ham and eggs over in a shiny frying pan with a wooden spatula and looking out the scullery window over the darkling town and wondering about him as that strange new feeling which had found her on the stairs and followed her home on the tram curled about her shoulders and rubbed itself down her back.

"Are you going out tonight?" she asked, as she put the plate down in front of Stopak and his evening paper.

"Yes."

"With Hektor?"

"Yes. Any objections?"

"When's he coming?"

"'Bout eight. Maybe sooner."

"Better eat up then." And she made plans for a long hot bath.

A few minutes later, as Mrs. Agathe Stopak was standing at her sink, pouring away the greasy washing-up water and taking a last look out the window where there was nothing to see now but a steamy image of herself looking back from the glass, Good Tibo Krovic was sitting down in his kitchen with a plate of herring and fried potatoes and a notebook open on the table in front of him.

He made notes—a list of things he had decided he would like to buy for Agathe. Sweets, especially Turkish delight, soft and pink and yielding, the essence of hedonism, a symbol of the Fall, so sweet. And jellied fruits, for the tang. And chocolate gingers. And chocolate caramels. And books—a Homer, a new one. No, an old one, old and love-worn. Find one. Hunt it out. Perfume. "Tahiti," he remembered the name. He remembered it every day. In fact, he had added "Tahiti" to the list of beautiful words he liked to say to himself from time to time. Saying it brought to mind Mrs. Stopak's smell and, when he said it, he imagined himself in a naval uniform, lying on bone-white sands under a nodding palm with Mrs. Stopak nestled in the crook of his arm, bougainvilleas in her hair. Perfume. And knickers. Men bought knickers for the women they loved, didn't they? Would he dare? Go into a shop and buy knickers? Mayor Tibo Krovic? Buy women's underwear? He scored a heavy line through the word "knickers" and looked at it. It was a reproach and a challenge. On the next line, he wrote "lingerie" and left it there. There may come a time, after all. Well, there might. Tibo filled a whole page in his notebook but he found, when he read it again, that so many of the things he had written there were presents he would like to receive—the leather writing case he had seen in the window of Braun's, a silver pen, even the stockings he had listed were, he conceded, not really for her at all. Not really. "I can add more as they occur to me," he said and quickly put down "lottery tickets" on the very last line.

Tibo sat for a long time at the table, reading and rereading his list and watching and wondering at the images each word provoked in his mind. He was experiencing feelings now that he had never known before or had buried for so long that he believed himself immune to them. He astonished himself. Even reading the word "lingerie" made something hoist in his chest. He put down his pen and lifted his head from his notebook. "I am in love," he told the dark kitchen. "I love you, Mrs. Agathe Stopak. I love you." He said it again as he scraped his cold herring into the bin under the sink. How strange that, whether love comes or love goes, all thought of food disappears. Lucky that, sometimes, love stays else we would all starve to death. "I love you, Mrs. Agathe Stopak." He said it again climbing the stairs and again, several times more, as he lay down in his bed and went to sleep.

Across town in Aleksander Street, Mrs. Stopak was lying down in her own bed, fresh and warm and tingling after a long bath. The strange feeling that came to her at work had never left her. It had snuggled next to her on the tram home, it coiled itself around her at the stove and lashed its tail in the bath water and now it lay beside her in the bed, as warm and heavy and purring as Achilles. It made her feel guilty—guilty and delicious. She befriended it. And then it was morning.

The bed was still empty. Agathe was not alarmed. She folded the covers back and swung her feet down to the floor. It was cold. She ran to the bathroom, past Stopak where he lay in the sitting room, collapsed, face down on the settee, head tipped towards the floor, snoring and drooling. He was still there, unmoving, a lard statue, when she trotted back to the bedroom and let her nightgown fall to the floor with a whisper. She stepped from the crumpled ring of warm cotton, flicked it into the air on the point of her toe, caught it, balled it in two hands and flung it on to the bed. She moved part gymnast, part burlesque dancer, all poise and tease and unconscious buxom grace. She stood in front of the old bow-fronted chest and bent over easily, her body splitting, opening a little, as smoothly as the drawer where she kept her knickers and there, at the back, was the shiny red box from Braun's.

Standing there, like an ivory carving of Pandora, she held the box in the palm of her hand and looked at it, rewrapped, retied, put away as if it had never been opened and she hesitated. "Not for him," she told the mirror. "For me. Me." This time, when Agathe opened the box, she shredded it, tore through the cardboard, ripped the tissue paper, tugged the ribbon off in knots. In a second, it went from being the relic of a bloody martyrdom to so much rubbish—old used packaging, that was all. She tossed it to the floor and kicked it away with a painted toe. Agathe was nothing if not modest—modest in every sense—but she found herself studying the mirror on the dressing table again, watching herself as she put on the tiny, gauzy strips of lingerie and she acknowledged herself as beautiful, even desirable. She allowed her fingers to trace over her own curves, watched them as they passed and then, when she glanced back at the mirror again, she was astonished to find the woman there looking back with a curl of pink tongue peeping from between her lips. It was a hungry look. Agathe was blushing. She hurried to dress. A simple white blouse, a sensible wool skirt of charcoal grey, perhaps a little too shaped, a little too snug over the hips and narrow round the calf, but sensible and modest enough, the sort of thing that the mayor's secretary could wear without attracting a whisper of comment, even if it did force her into something of a wiggle as she walked. She smoothed it down over her bottom with the flats of her hands and, yes, there, managed to feel the hint of those special knickers, just. Just barely.

When Agathe left the flat that morning, pausing long enough to put a mug of coffee down on the floor next to Stopak's hand and shake him by the shoulder as she went, she walked with a strut and a shimmy in her step. When the conductor on the tram looked at her with one of those looks, the kind of look that said, "I am trying very hard not to whistle at you," she smiled back at him with the suggestion of a wink and let her fingers linger in the palm of his hand when she handed over her fare. The strange feeling from the night before was still with her—that breathlessness, the excitement that gave everything a new tang, an electric buzz that ran through her. It was still there. It was still there when Agathe hurried down Castle Street, catching glimpses of herself in the shop windows as she went—not that she was late for work, she simply felt the urge to run and fought it. At the corner, she saw Mamma Cesare wiping down tables in the big bay window of The Golden Angel, halted in her tracks for a moment and knocked on the glass with a knuckle until the old lady looked up, saw her and smiled.

"You look lovely," she mouthed.

Agathe pantomimed "Thank you!" back, blew her a kiss and hurried on. She moved through the crowds like a dragonfly over a pond, flashing colour and light as she went, with her bottle-green coat, her hair and shoes and handbag gleaming and her blue enamel lunch box glinting dully in her hand.

That same electric feeling lingered round Tibo too. It woke him early and sent him hurrying to work with no breakfast. Before anyone else came in to work, he placed an envelope on Agathe Stopak's desk, right in the centre, where it would be the first thing she saw when she sat down. Tibo took out his fountain pen and wrote "Mrs. Stopak" across the middle of the envelope and underlined it. He wanted it to look brisk and official and businesslike but not unfriendly, just the way he would always have written a note to any of his staff but love had changed everything, even his handwriting. Tibo felt that anybody looking at that envelope, seeing those two words, would know at once that they were written by a man to the woman he loved. It would be as if every letter he had ever written was to be read out in City Square, as if an inventory of his library was pinned up on the doors of the Town Hall and a biography, garnered by a lifetime's worth of government spies, was serialised in the pages of the *Evening Dottian*. Everything he was was in those two words.

Tibo picked up the envelope and looked at it again. Two words. There was nothing else there. He put the envelope back on

Agathe's desk and went into his office through the connecting door. But, a moment later, he returned, picked the envelope up and tossed it casually on to Mrs. Stopak's blotter. He looked at it lying there. Was it casual enough? He walked past the desk, as someone would if they were walking through the office to see the mayor and happened to glance at Agathe Stopak's desk. The envelope blared at him like a siren. He picked it up and threw it again. Still no good. Tibo grabbed the envelope and, this time, standing in the connecting door to his own office, he flicked it through the air towards Agathe's desk. It landed in her wastepaper basket. He retrieved it and dropped it on her blotter as he sprinted through the empty office. Miracle of miracles, it was standing bolt upright on its edge, propped against her stapler.

Tibo looked at his watch. There was still time, he reckoned, to take the envelope downstairs and slip it into the mail. He took out his pen again and added:

The Mayor's Office
Town Hall
City Square
Dot

Then he took the envelope, rushed down the back stairs and pushed it through the half-moon opening in the glass front of the concierge's office. Tibo was breathless. He pushed his fingers through his hair and tugged down on the front of his waistcoat. He composed himself. He was ready to walk back up the stairs looking like the Mayor of Dot.

But, just as he reached the first step, the door of the concierge's office opened and old Peter Stavo came out. "Oh, Mayor Krovic," he said. "Good to see you. I'm sorry to bother you but this letter has just arrived. It's for Agathe who works in your office. Since you're going that way yourself I wondered if . . . ?"

And, while Tibo was coping with Peter Stavo, Agathe was running up the green marble stairs with her coat flung over her arm. She walked into the office eagerly. "Good morning," she called but there was no reply. "Mayor Krovic?" She peeked round the door to his office. "Mayor Krovic?" It was empty. Disappointed, Agathe hung up her coat, checked her hair in her compact, decided that she would do and started the first pot of coffee of the day.

Sandor the message boy had already been on his rounds and the morning's post lay in a tray on her desk. While the coffee brewed in its pot, Agathe sat down and began work but she had barely sliced through the first envelope when she looked up from her desk again, staring at the door like a dog waiting for the key in the lock. Agathe stood up and took a napkin from the pile beside the coffee machine.

She hurried into Tibo's office, unfolded the napkin and placed it on her head as she bobbed a curtsey in front of the town shield.

Agathe told me, "What I said to you before—about Stopak? Well, no offence, but much good you did. And now there's this. This with Mayor Krovic. With Tibo Krovic. And it's supposed to be your job to speak up for the women of Dot and you know I'm not a bad girl but, sometimes . . . well, I just think you expect too much. You know how things are, I imagine. So, I don't expect miracles and I'm not asking you to go against any principles but, if you could, please, try to be kind and understanding and even, maybe, a little bit generous, that would be very nice." Then she said a polite "Thank you," bobbed again and took the napkin from her head as she left the room.

When Tibo walked in carrying a letter, Agathe was already back at her desk, sorting the post into the usual neat piles. Tibo stopped in the doorway and looked at her with the sort of awe and wonderment that he might have looked at a painting or a sunrise. She was breathtakingly beautiful, plump and pale and pink and womanly, the colours and curves of the inside of a shell. He bent over her desk as he passed, drinking deeply of her scent. "This came for you," he said.

"Oh, thank you," said Agathe. "I wonder why it wasn't in with the rest of the post."

"That would be because I sent it."

Agathe glanced down at the envelope and smiled, recognising

the mayor's familiar handwriting. She sliced the envelope open. Inside were ten lottery tickets and a note but when she looked up to thank him, Tibo was already walking away. He did not pause to turn or look back until the door of his office had shut safely behind him and he could stand, hands behind him, flat against the wood, and draw breath quietly until the hammering in his chest subsided. "Done it," he said. "See? That was easy enough. Just a letter. That's all it was. Nothing to it, really."

He took off his jacket and sat down at his desk to work while, just feet away, Agathe sat at her desk and looked from the envelope in her hands to his door and from his door to the envelope in her hands and back again, shaking her head with happiness and disbelief. "Lottery tickets," she whispered, "Lottery tickets—ten lottery tickets. He wants me to have my little place on the coast of Dalmatia. Lottery tickets."

She pulled them from the envelope to spread them across her desk and a folded sheet of notepaper fell out. "Dear Agathe," it said, not "Dear Mrs. Stopak." She noticed that. "I hope you enjoyed our little lunch yesterday as much as I did. If you'd like to join me again today, I would be delighted. My treat." And it was signed simply "Tibo."

Twenty minutes later, the longest twenty minutes of Tibo's life, Agathe was standing outside his office door holding a cup of coffee with two ginger biscuits in the saucer. With her free hand, the hand holding a folded slip of council-headed notepaper, she knocked and, without waiting for an answer, she walked into the room like Venus returning home to Olympus after a long afternoon spent driving shepherds crazy with love. The grey clouds cleared with her arrival. Sunlight streamed through the open shutters and kissed her perfect toes as they passed over the carpet and Tibo looked up from his papers at her with the sort of look that men sitting in the electric chair give to telegram boys who arrive unexpectedly in the execution chamber.

Leaning over his desk, Agathe placed the cup carefully on his blotter. Good Mayor Krovic made a heroic effort not to look down the front of her blouse as it gaped invitingly in front of him. He told himself that he had not noticed the unfeasibly tiny, the adorably transparent, underpinnings which he had most definitely glimpsed there and he forced himself to look her squarely in the eye when she said, "This came for you, Mayor Krovic," handed him the fold of notepaper and wiggled out of the room.

Sitting back in his chair, Tibo opened the note and read it. It said, "I would be delighted to join you for lunch." He was so astonished that he failed to notice Agathe's whispered "Thank you" as she passed the town arms on the wall.

FOR THE REST OF THE MORNING, THEY WERE too embarrassed to speak to one another. There was a declaration that had been made—whatever it meant—but each seemed to agree with the other that there was nothing more to be said until the cathedral bells declared it was time for lunch.

Agathe's typewriter clattered, her telephone jangled, the coffee pot emptied and filled again until, far off across the square, the pigeons rose like a widow's veil over the cathedral and, a second or two later, the burnished, mellow "gong" of the bell reached the Town Hall and Tibo appeared in the door of his room. "That sounds like one o'clock," he said. "Do you fancy . . . ?" Tibo almost said "me" but he didn't, he didn't.

"Yes, I'm ready," said Agathe. "I'll just get my coat."

Tibo was already waiting by the hatstand, her coat in his hands, holding it out to her, ready to ease it up her arms and over her shoulders. A whisper of "Tahiti" reached him as she shivered it into place.

"Colder today," she said.

"Yes. Much. Yes."

And there was another frightening moment when they wondered, each of them, if this was what lunch would be like—a string of foolish, empty comments about the weather, an embarrassed shuffle when they had hoped for a waltz and no escape from their shame for a whole painful hour.

Agathe took his arm or Tibo offered it; it hardly mattered now since it was what they both wanted.

"You bought me lottery tickets," she said as they walked over the bridge and into Castle Street.

"Yes, I did," said Tibo.

"That was very kind. Thank you."

"Just a silly nothing. Nothing at all."

"Why?"

"Why?"

"Yes, why did you buy me lottery tickets?"

"Don't you play the lottery? Yesterday. I thought you said. Didn't you? I thought you said you played the lottery every month."

"I did, yes. It was kind of you to remember."

"I remember," said Tibo. "You play the lottery and, when you win—note 'when' you win—you will buy yourself a villa on the coast of Dalmatia."

Agathe could have hugged him for that but he looked down at her with a brisk, businesslike "We're here" and swung open the big, gilded door of The Golden Angel.

This time, the flicker of recognition that flashed round the room was enough to send Cesare's dark Italian eyebrows shooting almost to the ceiling. His Honour the Mayor! Twice in one day for two days in a row! And with the same woman! Both days! The shock of their arrival sent the waiters into a spasm. From opposite sides of the room, from all corners, four of them started forward, rising on to the balls of their feet as light and poised as gigolos in an Argentine tango hall. But each one, as he moved, instinctively swept the cafe with his eyes, spotted a brother waiter in mid-tango, sank again to his heels, rose, stepped, glanced silently towards Cesare who stood, unmoving behind the counter, flashing his eyes, secretly semaphoring an eyebrow to this one and then that until each, in turn, stopped, halted, covered in confusion.

It was left to Mamma Cesare to save the honour of The Golden Angel. She stepped forward and, from somewhere below the level of Tibo's chest, she said, "Table for two? This is way, please." Small and brown, Mamma Cesare waddled in front of them like a magic toadstool leading two lost children through a fairy story.

"This is nice table," she said, inviting no discussion. "You like me to bring menu or you trust me to bring what's good?"

Tibo sat down and smiled across the table at Agathe. "Just bring what's good," he said.

"Is nice," said Mamma Cesare. "You two talk." And she left.

"So what will we talk about?" Tibo asked.

"Lottery tickets—I think we should talk about lottery tickets. You were going to tell me why you bought them for me."

Tibo rubbed a hand over his face in an embarrassed gesture. "You don't mind, do you? I wouldn't want to offend you."

"Silly. Of course you haven't offended me. It's all right. I'm sorry. It was a lovely present. It doesn't matter why you bought them for me." Agathe looked down at the tablecloth and traced the pattern of the weave with the tip of her fingernail until Tibo stopped her by laying his hand over hers.

They were touching again for the second time in two days, the second time in their lives.

"I got you lottery tickets because I want you to be happy. All I want is for you to be happy. I realised, well, some time ago, that I have wanted you to be happy for as long as I've known you. If I could buy you that house you want on the coast of Dalmatia I would, but I can't so I bought you lottery tickets instead. You deserve it. You deserve presents. You deserve everything."

There was a pause. A moment of silence when nothing was said and nothing happened apart from Tibo's thumb moving softly and slowly, backward and forward against the back of Agathe's hand. Pressing there, there, on the padded mound of flesh between her thumb and forefinger, rubbing so gently that Agathe felt as if her skin would shred away under his touch. The feeling came back to her from when she was a little girl, staying with her cousins on the farm and she fell ill. Her skin had felt just that way then, before it happened, before she got sick, all raw and sensitive and open, as if it wasn't even there and there was nothing to protect her from the world and every touch was like hot coals.

"They've given us the window seat again," he said, after a while.

"Yes. It'll be 'our table' before too long." And then she wondered if she had gone too far and added a hasty "Sorry."

"What are you sorry for now?" said Tibo. "Stop apologising. You have nothing to apologise for. Who has taught you to do this?"

"I just thought it sounded a bit presumptuous," she said. "As if I expected you to take me for lunch every day. As if this was going to be a regular thing."

"I think I'd like that," said the mayor. "I think I'd like this to be a regular thing. If you would."

"Yes. I think I would like that very much. If you would." And then, after as much time as it takes to swallow really quite hard, she finished with "Tibo."

The mayor noticed. "You called me 'Tibo,'" he said. "You've never done that before."

She squeezed his hand and smiled. "You started it. You called me 'Agathe.'"

"I wouldn't dare!"

"Yes, you did! That note you sent with the lottery tickets, it said, 'Dear Agathe.' I noticed. It's the first time you've ever called me anything but 'Mrs. Stopak.'"

Tibo cleared his throat and nodded. "Yes," he said, slowly, "and, would you believe I managed the whole thing in slightly less than a pad and a half of notepaper? Whole forests were cleared so I could write a dozen words inviting you out to lunch."

They were quiet for a moment, looking at one another across the table and then a door swung open at the back of the cafe and Mamma Cesare came out, carrying an armful of steaming plates. As she negotiated the tables, Tibo and Agathe unwrapped themselves from one another, uncoiling their fingers, drawing apart with a last, magnetic tug until, when Mamma Cesare arrived, they were sitting there, prim and respectable and decent and linked by nothing but their eyes.

"Spaghetti," Mamma Cesare announced obviously. "You come tomorrow, you get gnocchi."

"Today, I'm glad we're getting spaghetti," said Mayor Krovic but he never looked away from Agathe's face.

"Very nice." Mamma Cesare smiled. She put down a basket of crusty bread and pointed out, "Bread, good bread," and offered wine and water, salads, oil and vinegar and performed all the necessary sacramental rituals of the Italian cafe, dusting their plates with curls of Parmesan and wielding her pepper shaker like an unfeasibly phallic truncheon.

When she left again, Tibo said, "Tell me more about you."

"I told you too much about me yesterday. Tell me about you."

Tibo struggled with a mouthful of spaghetti for a moment until, when he felt it was possible to speak with some dignity, he said, "Nothing to tell. You know everything. The whole town knows everything. That is my great tragedy—to have nothing that is not known."

"I hardly know a thing about you," said Agathe.

"I find that hard to believe. From what I gather, there's nothing much happens in Dot that you don't know all about."

"Silly stuff. Trivial stuff. Nit powder and hypnotism. All nonsense. I know you are a good man, Tibo Krovic, and kind and handsome . . ."

"Handsome!"

"Yes. In your way, very handsome. Quiet and honest and trustworthy and calm and kind but I don't know the first thing about you."

Tibo looked at her across the bread basket, a forkful of spaghetti held halfway between her plate and her mouth and he saw things in Agathe that he had never, never seen in any woman before. There had been a time (was it ten years ago, twenty years ago, was it longer?) when days like this should have been a commonplace, when Tibo Krovic, a rising young man of Dot, should have been seen in the cafes of the town, in The Golden Angel or even The Green Monkey, laughing too loudly, drinking a little too much, surrounded by friends, holding hands with some lovely young girl in a shadowed alcove, pretending not to notice as she imagined curtains and wedding dresses, making plans to send her flowers in the morning, making plans to see her sister next week. He should have done that then. There should have been decades of young women, dozens of them, one after another, succeeding each other annually on his arm at the Christmas Charity Ball, a string of willing victims, tangled in his sheets or even, imagine it, one who came and stayed and never staled. Just one. The one. The one who thickened at wrist and waist and ankle, swelled at the hip, moulded the mattress into familiar curves and hollows and plumped and blossomed and fruited, again and again, a whole houseful of fat, pink, clever kids. It would have been right and natural then but not now. Now he had missed his chance. Not even the dedicated gardeners of the Municipal Parks and Recreation Department could produce daffodils in October.

Now, to be sitting here, in this place, like this, now, with a woman like Agathe Stopak, now it was wonderment and a miracle. And yet it was true. Now, with the first frosts just around the corner, after a long, empty summer when there had been no time for armfuls of women, no tumbled, tousled, sheet-tangled dozens but two or, perhaps, a brief three—which is far, far fewer than one—here he was with Agathe. There would have been something to boast about in the dozens, something saloon-bar-ish, something cigar-puff-ish, something moustache-twirl-ish and there might have been something downright heroic about the one, the one and only but there was something pitiful and pathetic and dull about the three—three who never stayed, never stuck, never clicked. Tibo thought of them and he felt ashamed because he knew now—he had known for twenty-four entire hours—what it was to love. He loved Agathe. He was in love with Agathe. The times before—they were a kind of sickness. He knew that. And now he had found the cure.

She leaned forward a little, putting her head above the plate and, as she parted her lips and took the soft strings of pasta into her mouth, he felt his heart rush.

"Sorry," she said and dabbed her mouth with her napkin.

"No. No. I was staring. Me. My fault. Sorry." He could not drag his eyes away.

"One thing," she said, to break the silence.

"Pardon?"

"Tell me one thing about you. Tell me your middle name."

"I don't have one. I am plain Tibo Krovic."

"No," Agathe said, decisively, "you are 'Good' Tibo Krovic. That's what they call you. Did you know?"

"Yes. Somebody told me once. It's quite a burden."

"Mimi," said Agathe.

"Your middle name? Your middle name is Mimi?"

"Would you believe it was my granny's name? I know. It's ridiculous."

"I think it's lovely," said Tibo.

"Good Tibo Krovic is not a very good liar. Now it's your turn. Ask away."

He stopped to consider, tearing a lump of crusty bread to crumbs while he looked intently at the ceiling. "All right," he said, "tell me what it would take to make you happy."

"That's not very fair, is it? I ask about middle names and you ask what it would take to make me happy!"

"Sorry," said Tibo. "Too much. You're right. I shouldn't have. Sorry."

Agathe put down her fork. "I'm not offended. It's a good question. It's a question I ask myself and you know, Tibo, I have no idea. I haven't got a clue. There must be something. There must be somebody."

"But you have Stopak," said Tibo. It came out sounding more like a question.

"No," said Agathe. That was all.

They looked at each other across the table then, so many messages, warnings, desires, pleadings and encouragements in that look, all unsaid, all understood, half believed and half imagined.

"No," said Tibo.

"No." She picked up her fork again. "Anyway, the rules of the game are clear, so now it's your turn. You tell me. What would it take to make you happy?"

"Me?" said Tibo. "I'm happy. I'm perfectly happy."

"Well, that's good," said Agathe. "That's fine. But I don't believe you. Oh, don't look all offended at me. When was the last time you laughed?"

"Just now. Just a minute ago. With you."

"Before that, when?"

Tibo was having trouble remembering. "It's difficult when you put it that way. I laugh all the time. I laugh. I do."

"I believe you do," said Agathe. "What about friends?"

"Lots."

"It's not healthy to have lots of friends—quality above quantity when it comes to friends. And I'm not talking about people who know the Mayor of Dot. I mean people who know Tibo Krovic, people who know how many sugars he takes in his coffee."

"I don't take sugar," said Tibo.

"I know that, I've made your coffee for years. Who else knows?"

Tibo made a resentful jab at the final knot of spaghetti on his plate. "I don't think I like this game anymore," he said. "You're too good at it."

Agathe reached across the table and offered her hand. She whispered, "I'm sorry. I'm sorry." And then, with their fingers locked again, she asked, "How many sugars do I take?"

Tibo looked ashamed. "I'm sorry, I don't know. You always make the coffee."

"See?" she laughed. "You're better off than I am. You've got one more on your list than I have."

Tibo said nothing.

"You can ask, you know. You have my permission to ask."

There were so many things Tibo wanted to ask but he decided to go slowly for a while. "Very well then, Mrs. Agathe Stopak, how many sugars do you take in your coffee?"

"Just the one. A flat one. Does that make us officially friends now?"

"I think it does, yes," he said and he leaned forward to kiss the tips of her fingers but, just then, at the other side of the room, he spotted Mamma Cesare heading towards their table and he released Agathe's hand with a bad-tempered sigh.

"Everything's good?" the old lady asked.

"Lovely," they chorused stiffly.

"Good, lovely, very nice. I bring you coffees now, very nice."

"I think," Tibo glanced at Agathe to check, "just the bill. We should be getting back to work. And we can get a coffee there."

Mamma Cesare snorted her disapproval. "You maybe gets coffee but it's not so good as mine. I am bringing bill. Tomorrow you are having gnocchi." And she waddled off.

Outside again on Castle Street, Tibo asked, "Do you like gnocchi?"

"I'm not entirely sure what gnocchi is," said Agathe. "Anyway, tomorrow's Saturday."

For a moment, Tibo was unsure why that mattered. Gnocchi—little potato dumplings—you could eat them any day of the week if you felt like it and then the full weight of Saturday hit him. Saturday. The weekend. Two whole days without coming in to work. Two whole days without any excuse to see Agathe. "Yes," he said. "Saturday. Have you anything planned?"

"Not really. No. In fact, no." She was hoping that Tibo might take that for an invitation but he said nothing in reply.

They walked on a little further and she tried again. "How about you? Have you anything planned?"

"Well, don't laugh but I thought I might go shopping. Maybe buy a suit. Or even two."

Agathe ooooooohed mockingly.

"Oh, don't! I said not to laugh."

"I'm not laughing. Yes, you could probably do with a new suit."

They carried on down Castle Street in silence, Agathe stepping out beside him with that wide, easy, rolling stride that made men turn and look after her when she passed, Tibo tall and straight and elegant, each of them wondering if the other could read their thoughts.

Tibo did not say, "Damn my suits. To hell with suits. Can you imagine all the things I would like to buy for you? Can you imagine all the things I'd shower you with, every day, if I could? New dresses, new shoes, furs and jewels and underwear, beautiful, beautiful underwear and sweets and pastries and flowers and champagne and knick-knacks and fripperies and trinkets and gewgaws and pointless, silly nothings."

And Mrs. Agathe Stopak did not reply, "Do you know what kind of knickers I am wearing. Can you see? Can you guess? Very, very naughty. Teeny. Ridiculous. Can you imagine what sort of woman would wear knickers like those? I hope I don't fall under a tram on the way home. What they'd make of knickers like those at the Infirmary, God alone knows."

"Yes, a new suit," said Tibo. "And I thought I might have a look at the brass band in Copernicus Park on Sunday."

"On Sunday?"

"Yes, Sunday at one o'clock."

"At one?"

"Copernicus Park, at one o'clock," said Tibo emphatically. "It's their last performance of the year. It always feels like the end of summer. The swallows go, the cranes fly south, the geese disappear from the Ampersand."

Agathe laughed. "And the Fire Brigade Band packs up its euphoniums! Come on, Mayor Tibo Krovic, you promised me a cup of coffee!" And she started to run, clattering over White Bridge and into City Square. Before she was halfway across, Tibo was running too.

Mayor Krovic looked back on that afternoon in his office as the first of his life. That's what love is like—it gives everything a new taste, paints everything in different colours, caresses the nerves with pin-sharp sensation, makes the tediously mundane bearable again. The coffee brewed that afternoon in the same old pot that had coughed and burped and spluttered on the table by the door for as long as anybody could remember was like no other coffee Tibo had ever drunk. For one thing, he made it himself—the first time he had made his own coffee in the Town Hall for a very long time—and Agathe sat at her desk and laughed out loud as he hunted for the coffee can and misplaced the spoon and scattered sugar across the floor. But she smiled graciously when he handed her the cup and let her fingers trail over his for far longer than was needful as the saucer passed from hand to hand between them.

And then they talked, but happily this time, about life as they wished it might be, not as it was—not in a cold little town in the north but on the shores of a warm, wine-dark sea; not surrounded by thousands of people and none of them knowing how much sugar to put in a cup but with just one person who knew but didn't care because there was wine to drink.

It came in sentences and half phrases, the little bits of truth and, in between, they spoke of that week's programme at the Palazz Kinema and how wonderful were the raisin cakes that Agathe's granny used to make and how you can't get them like that anymore, not for love nor money, and what it was like to be nine years old and fish from the end of the pier and put crabs in a box to scare your mother with their rattling and clawing in the middle of the night or how awful it is to be alone, without love, and how odd it is that pomegranates are never in the shops for more than a few weeks.

Outside, the bells of the cathedral tolled out again. And again. The sky began to bruise.

"We should work," said Tibo.

"Yes, we should," said Agathe.

"I have work to do," he said.

"Me too."

"Yes."

"Take that last cup of coffee with you, if you like."

"Yes. Thanks. I will."

Tibo walked backwards to his office, looking at Agathe all the while over the rim of the cup held at his lips like a toast, looking right in her eyes and walking backwards until he turned the corner into his own room, through the door to where the carpet was thick and he was, quite suddenly, alone. "I really must work," he called.

"And so must I," she said.

"No, but really." Tibo sat down at his desk and took out one of Agathe's red files, opened it and sat looking hopelessly at the papers. His mind was busy with thoughts of her—no room for municipal nonsense.

"Do we care about the regulation height of gravestones?" he asked, loudly.

"New rules on cemetery memorials and stuff. It's all coming up at the Parks Committee on Tuesday. I put the papers in your folder." Agathe was gasping and grunting from the other side of the door and there was a lot of noisy clattering, chairs scraping across the floor, the sound of furniture shifting.

Tibo got up to investigate. "What are you doing out there?" And he met her coming into his room, struggling with a small table. She held it wedged across her hips, trying to nudge it and nose it through the door and into the inner office.

"Surprise!" Agathe grinned like a fool. "I thought I could bring this in. Maybe we could work together for a bit. Get on faster. I brought the biscuits too." And there they were—a packet of ginger biscuits, teetering on the edge of the table she was carrying.

"Put that down," Tibo ordered.

"You don't want me to sit with you?"

"I don't want you to hurt yourself. Give it to me."

He took the table and put it close up against his desk, touching, right opposite his chair, a bit of alien territory annexed by his blotter. "I'll get your typewriter," he said.

Agathe trotted behind with her chair and a ream of council-headed paper. "This is fun," she said as she sat down and flicked through a notebook.

"This is lunacy," said Tibo and he glanced at her and smiled and shook his head. "Madness."

But they got the work done, passing the biscuits across the desk, crunching and munching and sweeping crumbs on to the carpet in gritty little heaps, sitting for long minutes, looking at one another, just looking and each careful never to be looking when the other was and piles of paper started to mount on their desks, moved from one side to the other and safely closed up in dull, proper, spinsterly folders.

And then Tibo reached across his desk and lit the lamp. Shadows leapt up in the corners of the room. "It's late," he said. "After five o'clock."

"I can stay," said Agathe.

"No. You mustn't. Better not." There was a kind of warning in his voice and a plea. "It's the weekend. You're entitled."

"Yes," she said. Agathe stood up and stretched, all line and curve and movement and beauty and sadness. The weekend. That word again. The long two days. The lonely time. And all that time, night and morning, the ferry would be sailing back and forth to Dash with couples standing along the rail or holding hands in the prow or laughing in the saloon and then, when it reached the islands, they would grab their bags and run up the pier and find an inn with a smoky fire and clanky plumbing and fall into bed with a bottle and laugh and roll around and love but Agathe wouldn't be among them and, on Sunday at one o'clock, Tibo would be sitting down in Copernicus Park with the Fire Brigade Band. "Yes. I suppose I'd better be going," she said.

Peter Stavo's bucket clanked out on the landing. His mop sploshed and swished like an escaping squid.

"I'll just put this table back."

"No," said Tibo. "Don't be silly. I'll do that. You run along."

"All right. Thanks. Goodnight," and she paused, "Tibo."

"Goodnight, Agathe. Goodnight, Mrs. Agathe 'one flat teaspoon' Stopak."

She smiled at him and, in a couple of swift paces, she was outside the door again. "This was fun, wasn't it? Lunch and everything. Nice."

"It was wonderful," said Tibo. "Lunch and coffee and this. Everything."

"Everything. Yes."

He heard the sound of the hatstand rocking and pictured her putting her coat on. Faintly, he heard her say "Bye" to Peter Stavo and then the place went quiet.

In just the way that every moment with Agathe had suddenly become that much more vivid and sharp, when she walked out of the office, the world turned sepia for Tibo. There was a tram ride home, an evening paper, a bowl of soup from the pan he had made three days before, a bath and bed and he recalled none of it. And then it was Saturday and the drumming, the heartbeat, the toothache started again. Agathe, Agathe, Agathe—her name, round and round in his head.

"Shops!" Tibo told himself as he tipped his half-full coffee cup into the sink. "Suits. Come on, Krovic, make an effort." He gave his pockets a hasty slap, just to check that wallet and keys were in their proper place, banged the door shut so the big, brass letter box jangled and stepped out along the blue-tiled path. Beads of dew were waiting in a fringe at the bottom edge of the bell that hung by the street and Tibo noticed a few yellow leaves from his birch tree clinging damply to the gate as it slouched across the step at the end of the path. "I must do something about that," he said. "I really must."

The trams that serve Dot on a Saturday are very different from those that roll through the streets the rest of the week. On Saturday, they are busy all day and not just when they carry people to work first thing in the morning or back again at the end of a long and trying afternoon. On Saturday, the trams are full of children—sour-faced brats dragged unwilling to the shops with their mothers, troops of them with rolled-up towels tucked under their arms heading for the Municipal Baths or coming home again, shivering, with their hair soaking and plastered down flat over their skulls, aunts and grandmothers dressed up for coffee and torte in Braun's or returning, each with seven large parcels held together with finger-slicing string, big sisters in giggling convocations preening over one another, tittering towards the Saturday dance, big brothers who like to travel in to town on the top deck, standing up against the taffrail with their mates, facing backwards and talking too loud so that half the passengers sit fretting about the *Evening Dottian*'s most recent article on the razor gangs that might be stalking the city and the other half sit hoping for an overhanging branch to appear unannounced and sweep the tram like a sabre.

Mayor Krovic did not mind. Heading into town, the conductor let him share the platform at the back of the tram and they clipped along, leaning over at the bends with a shriek of iron wheels while Tibo read the paper, one arm hooked round the white-painted pole, knees sagging, hips swaying as he soaked up the motion. "Insouciant," Tibo said to himself. He imagined the people on the pavement must think him vaguely piratical as he hung there. Nobody noticed.

The tram slowed for its final turn into Cathedral Avenue, slowed and wobbled and Mayor Krovic turned and stepped backwards off the platform, landing surely on the cobbles with balletic grace, tall and confident and he raised his folded paper to eye level and snapped it away in a courteous salute.

As the tram disappeared behind the houses, the conductor waved back and smiled. "Good day, Mayor Krovic," he yelled.

Tibo opened his wallet and took out a folded envelope. On one side it read, "Mayor T. Krovic, Town Hall, City Square, Dot" and, on the other side it said, "onions, sausage, chicken, lentils, carrots, book" and, underlined twice, "suits." Tibo liked to have a list. He ran his eye down it and planned the day.

"Book," he thought. "Knutson's."

Tibo waited until a coal lorry from Schmidt and Hodo lumbered past then he dodged into the traffic and ran across the street. There is a broad flight of stone steps that forms an alley leading from Cathedral Avenue towards where Commerz Plaz joins Albrecht Street and, about two thirds of the way down, on the right hand side, is Knutson's bookshop. The stairs leading down to the shop open out into the alley in a gentle fan with an iron rail up the middle for safety and, at the bottom, a double sweep of broad bow windows, filled with tiny panes of old green glass, all bubbles and ripples so that looking at the books inside is like trying to peer at a library at the bottom of a lost lagoon. The shop front is painted green, a dark dusty green, the colour of an aspidistra in a great aunt's parlour, and, if the paint looks thin, it is unbroken and unblistered. Written above the door in gold letters of a classical design are the words:

I. KNUTSON, DEALER IN MODERN,
ANTIQUE AND ANTIQUARIAN BOOKS

Tibo loved that place. He loved every moment he ever spent there and he counted them all out from the loud and confident "ping" of the bell as he opened the door until it rang behind him again when he left.

Tibo still had on his shelves the very first book he had bought from Knutson's—a boyhood purchase he made on a day of rain when the water dripped from the hem of his coat and ringed a puddle on to the dark wood floor like a forbidden, coaster-less glass on the table at home.

"Everything in that box is the same price," Mrs. Knutson had said. "Special offer—one each."

Tibo remembered standing there, considering what to buy. He fretted for so long that Mrs. Knutson left and her husband was standing at the till when Tibo handed over two old volumes.

"Now then, young man, what will we charge you for these?"

Tibo remembered the feelings of embarrassment and concern that flooded over him then. Money was short—so short that he could not afford to be dainty about it. He looked forward to the day when he might pretend not to count the pennies and there was a dry squeak in his voice when he said, "The lady told me they were all the same price—one each."

Mr. Knutson raised an eyebrow above the line of his spectacles. "Well, the lady should not have said this very foolish thing since the lady has not gone through the box like you have gone through the box." The shopkeeper stopped to consider. "At this price, you can buy only one. So which do you want?"

"Thank you," said Tibo. He knew he was being tested.

A big question was being asked of him, this young man—this boy—who dared to stand on his dignity, here, in Knutson's bookshop and demand his rights while he dripped marks on the floor. "Thank you," he said. "I'll take this one." And he laid a finger on the spine of an illustrated Dante.

"You're sure?" said Knutson. "Absolutely sure? You can still change your mind. You can have the other if you want."

"No, thank you, I will stick with that one."

"Then I will wrap it for you." Mr. Knutson spooled off a length of brown paper from the roll that hung at the end of his desk, tore it cleanly across and wrapped the book with an experienced grace. He held out his hand for the coin.

"I'm sorry," said Tibo. "I only have a five."

"So now I have to give you four back? Mister, you don't know what you're doing to me. You're killing me here." Mr. Knutson cranked the handle on his cash drawer and it opened with a metallic ring. He counted out four coins into Tibo's hand with a grudging and constipated gesture and he kept a hard eye fixed on him all the way to the door. "You made the right choice. It's worth four hundred," Mr. Knutson said.

Tibo was aghast. "I'm really very sorry. I'll put it back, of course."

But Knutson raised a forbidding palm. "You will, of course, not put it back, of course! You and me, we made a deal. A deal is a deal, Mister—you should learn this. Nobody got cheated here. Nobody ever gets cheated in Knutson's shop—not ever. It's a matter of honour. But please, for the love of God, carry it home under your jacket. It's raining out there." And he turned his hand from a raised stop sign to a wave of dismissal.

The cold, bright ping of the bell that sent Tibo out into the alley that day welcomed him back to the shop now. And, inside, everything was the same, except for the place where Mr. Knutson had once stood and where now Mrs. Knutson stood alone, a single bookend, an odd volume.

She greeted him warmly as "Mayor Krovic!" although, after so long, after knowing him from boyhood, she would be entitled to use his name.

But Mrs. Knutson seemed to feel that it did her shop credit to have the Mayor of Dot as a customer and she took a proprietorial, motherly pride in using his proper title—not just any book lover coming in to stand amongst the shelves and take down a volume and open it up and test the spine and examine the colophon and check, yes, there it is, the "e" on page forty-six when it should be an "a," not just any customer but Good Tibo Krovic, the Mayor of Dot himself, you know.

"Mayor Krovic," she announced to the whole shop, "always a pleasure to see you. Is there something particular we can find for you today?"

"Mrs. Knutson," Tibo offered his hand, "you look well and as lovely as ever. I'm just looking, thank you."

"Very good, Mayor Krovic. Take your time. A customer like you, Mayor Krovic, is always welcome at Knutson's—from a boy and now look. Look!"

Further back in the shop, heads were beginning to appear from between the alleys of shelves—the heads of less-favoured customers who looked over their scholarly spectacles or took them off altogether and allowed them to dangle, testily, from thin gold chains in the physical embodiment of a "Tsk!"

"And it is always a pleasure to be here," Tibo said in soft, hushing tones. He patted her hand, noticed the thick knuckles, the blue veins showing through pale, soft paper-thin skin. "I'll just have a look round."

"Yes, Mayor Krovic, that's what to do. You just have a look round. You'll always find something at Knutson's."

Tibo hid himself amongst the shelves, nodding apologetic greetings to the other customers as he passed—"Sorry," "Sorry," "Good morning," "Excuse me"—and navigating, as confidently as if he had been in the Town Hall, past Modern First Editions, past Drama, past Poetry, past Theology and Religion, a vast section as empty and unexplored as the Amazon where—all unknown to Tibo—generations of impatient lovers had blasphemously embraced and on, beyond Travel, Exploration and Ethnography to Classics.

"Good morning, Mayor Krovic." Yemko Guillaume filled the derelict leather sofa at the end of the aisle as a walrus fills an Arctic sandbank. His knees were forced apart by the sag of his huge belly, his arms were crucified along the back rail and his head lolled under that morning's *Daily Dottian* which peaked like the roof of a pagoda over his nose.

He pinched the paper between sausage fingers and lifted it clear. "It is Mayor Krovic, isn't it? I heard you announced."

"Hello, Guillaume. We keep running into one another."

"Alas, no longer in the courts. I heard what happened. I am genuinely sorry."

"No hard feelings on my side. You did entirely the right thing."

"But not, sadly, the 'good' thing," said Yemko, "not what you would have done. I regret it very much."

There was an awkward moment of silence between them until Yemko harrumphed a little and said, "Excuse my rudeness. Won't you sit down and join me?" He made a sort of lolloping motion sideways and cleared a gap at one end of the complaining sofa but, when Tibo looked at the scant sliver of bare cushion which Yemko had managed to expose, he thought back to their chat in the gallery and said, "Thanks. I think I'll stand."

Yemko smiled at him forgivingly and said, "I remember that day at the exhibition, when I told you about my letter to Judge Gustav."

"Honestly, there's no need to go on about it—I do understand."

"No, no," said the lawyer, "I have accepted your absolution. I was going to talk of other things. I remember we spoke of the ancient poets now all unread." He gestured round the walls at shelves stacked floor to ceiling. "Have you come to refresh your memory, Krovic? I do, from time to time. I'm afraid I abuse poor Mrs. Knutson's hospitality awfully."

"We do supply several Public Libraries in Dot, you know. They really are quite good."

Yemko was unable to suppress a shudder and he made the sort of face you see on a maître d' when somebody orders red wine to go with fish. "I'm sure any library with which you concern yourself is nothing short of lovely," he said. "I prefer not to use them. I prefer not to use anything with 'Public' at the front of it. There always seems to be the implied threat that one might bump into one's customers."

"I bump into my customers all the time," said Mayor Krovic.

"But only *most* of your customers are criminals and lowlifes—*all* of mine are."

Tibo sat down on a wing of the sofa and crossed his arms. He asked, "Did you never consider buying books of your own—books you could read in your home safe from the gaze of the hated customer?"

"Well, it seems an awful waste when all I could ever want is right here. I have enjoyed that same volume of Catullus for . . . well, for a very long time now and I have a kind of theological objection to buying books—seems unfair to take them away. I often wonder what the booksellers buy that is one half so precious as the goods they sell."

"Vintners," said Tibo. "It's vintners."

Yemko rolled forward a little in a suspicion of a bow. It was a physical acknowledgement of a worthy opponent, his way of noting, "You got it—well done." A gigantic yawn rippled through him and threatened to dislocate his jaw and he said, "Anyway, you still haven't told me—are you here to bone up on Diana and poor

Acteon? You'll find them over there." He gestured to a tall, thin column of shelves by the window. "Ovid. *Metamorphoses*—the only thing he wrote that's worth a damn but then which of us can light a candle that will burn for two thousand years? Which of us will be remembered a fortnight after we have gone?"

"There's old man Knutson," said Tibo. "He is remembered."

"I don't recall him."

"And I doubt if he would mind. But Mrs. Knutson remembers and it's been more than a fortnight."

Yemko looked as if he was having trouble staying awake. The tented pages of the *Daily Dottian* were an increasingly tempting retreat. "Forgive me, Krovic, but that's just a silly sentiment, not a lasting memorial. Mrs. Knutson will soon be swept away in Time's all-effacing stream and those of us who remember her will quickly follow. A few short heartbeats from now there will be nobody who remembers that the bookseller Knutson was ever even a memory for someone else."

"Love's like that. It's personal. If you love, a mausoleum is of no consequence."

Yemko looked at him from watery blue eyes for quite a long time and then he said, "Oh, dear. Oh, my dear, dear Krovic. This is worse than I thought." He opened his newspaper, spread it over his face and settled down to sleep again. The interview was clearly at an end.

Tibo rose to his feet and crossed to the other side of the room where he looked through shelf after shelf of Homer for a while. There were some beautiful books there, austere leather-bound editions, books lurid with flamboyant tooling, books in floppy paper covers, books that might have been bought by the yard to spend decades unopened on grimly respectable shelves. But he found the right one—the one he wanted to buy for Agathe. This was a book that had been loved but not too much, used but not too harshly. It rejoiced in soft suede covers the colour of red wine, the colour of a libation. It would sit nicely next to a bowl of olives in a sunny room. Tibo lifted it to his nose and drank in the smell of a hot beach, sand and rosemary. It filled his hand with the weight of a sword and the pull of an angry tide. This was the book.

Quietly, careful of waking Yemko, he turned to go but, from behind, from the sofa, he heard, half whispered, "Give me a thousand kisses, then a hundred—another thousand, a hundred to follow—still another thousand and a hundred more. And when we've squandered all those thousands, tear up the bill and never count—lest any think our kisses ill and grudge how many."

"Your friend Catullus?" Tibo asked.

"Catullus," Yemko agreed. "Have a care, Krovic. Some think kisses very ill indeed and, sometimes, the bill is terribly hard to pay."

There was nothing else to say. Tibo left.

Before long, after a final, fond, embarrassing yelled exchange with Mrs. Knutson—"Come again, Mayor Krovic. Always a pleasure to see you here, Mayor Krovic!"—Tibo was back in the alley with Agathe's book in his hand.

Mrs. Knutson was so warm, so enthusiastic, so proud of him and yet, as the shop bell rang out behind him, Tibo found himself muttering, "She has no idea if I take sugar—not a clue." Still shaking his head gently, Good Mayor Krovic followed the alley down to Commerz Plaz.

His first instinct was to go to Braun's for those suits he had promised himself but, after a little thought, he decided on Kupfer and Kemanezic instead. More expensive, possibly, a smaller place with a smaller stock but the sort of place where there would be only a few other customers, the sort of place where he could expect to try on a suit without a crowd of well-built matrons emerging from the tea room to stand, idly brushing cake crumbs from their bosoms for half an hour as they looked on, giving unspoken advice and fashion hints in nods and smiles and conspiratorial sucks of the teeth—the sort of place which, if not exactly private, was still something less than a freak show. And that mattered to Tibo.

Walking down to Commerz Plaz he shifted Agathe's book from hand to hand, letting the air waft over the damp and wrinkled marks his palms had made in the parcel. The fear of buying clothes had never left Tibo Krovic—the same tension he had felt as a boy, when he watched his mother scrabbling for the last few pennies for a pair of trousers or sighing all evening at the thought of next day's trip to the shoe shop, was still with him. The guilt was terrifying. It burned him and, even now, the prospect of stepping into a tailor's shop left him dry-mouthed and wet-palmed. Mayor Krovic would gladly have squandered his last penny on Agathe Stopak for the joy of seeing her smile, he couldn't pass the stinking accordion man down in City Square without dropping a coin in his greasy hat but he recoiled from the hedonistic indulgence of a new shirt and the thought of *two* new suits was beginning to feel like Babylonian excess. But, like everything else in his life—until these past few days—the trip to Kupfer and Kemanezic was planned and thought out.

It was part of a system, the design for living, which Tibo had invented for himself as a way of getting through life, if he but knew it, without living at all. And, now that he had set the plan in action, he could not change it or step back from it. Tibo Krovic was as firmly committed to buying two new suits from Kupfer and Kemanezic as the No. 17 tram was committed to running along Cathedral Avenue.

And, just as the No. 17 tram would have slammed to a halt if it found Mrs. Agathe Stopak in its path, so Tibo turned the corner into Albrecht Street and stopped. She was there.

Agathe had come into town early and killed time pressing her nose against the front window of the Fur and Feathers pet shop, swapping kisses with the puppies in sawdust-filled boxes on the other side of the glass. Agathe envied them. She envied their innocence, their lack of wanting, their contentment, their undefeated urge to love. To be a puppy must be a wonderful thing, she thought—just to wait there for the first person who wanted you and to go off with them and love them. Life was more complicated for ladies in Dot—even if they wanted nothing more than a puppy did. She pressed her fingers against the glass a little sadly and walked on.

When Tibo found her, she was looking in the window of the Ko-Operatif Shoe Shop and looking at her feet and looking back up at the window and Tibo wanted to rush up to her and grab her by the hand and drag her through the door and buy everything. He wanted to buy every shoe in the shop. He wanted to sit her down on one of those red leather benches in there and open his cheque-book and summon a shop girl and say, "Ladies' size five and a half. We'll take one of each! No! Two of each. That is, a pair of each!" He wanted to say, "Agathe, this is a pair of fur-lined boots and you can wear them every day of the winter and never come to work with cold toes again. And this is a pair of high-heeled slippers, all covered in spangles and you can wear them when we go dancing. And look at these! And these! And the handbags to match."

He said, "Hello, Agathe."

She looked up, pleased and surprised and delighted to see him and she took a step forward to greet him, her hand half raised, stopped herself and said, "Oh, Tibo. Hello!" And her hand carried on, upwards to brush her lips.

"Buying shoes?" he asked, stupidly.

"No, not really." She pointed through the glass at a pair of winter boots. "I was just wondering about those. The snow will be here soon. What do you think?"

"Go mad," said Tibo. "Treat yourself."

"Maybe I will, after pay day, but it seems a dreadful extravagance. I've got a perfectly good pair of galoshes, after all, but . . ."

"But your toes get cold," Tibo said.

"Oh, they do, they do. Don't yours? And when my feet are cold it takes me forever to warm up again."

Suddenly Tibo found the courage to say, "You could always warm your feet on me."

But Agathe kept talking. She said, "You know, I bet there isn't a single shop in Dalmatia that sells galoshes or winter boots. No demand. In Dalmatia everybody has warm toes. Sorry, what were you going to say?"

Tibo smiled and said, "Nothing."

The traffic went by in Albrecht Street, packed trams rattled past, a few cars and an old grey lorry, loaded up with barrels of butcher's waste, bony meaty bits sticking out, on its way to the fertiliser factory and, high above all that, way up at roof height where the flats are small and cheap and the window-sill marigolds are covered in soot, little birds flew by, like black dots against the sky, singing. Nobody heard them. And, at the corner of the alley where a bright gold dandelion had sent up yellow star bursts and paper-white pom-poms, one after another, all summer long like a month's slow firework display, a cat with blue eyes went past. Nobody saw it. But later, in memory, Tibo found them all engraved there, the sulphur bright flowers and the well-bred cat with its ribbon and its bell that only passing birdsong drowned out.

"Why are you here?" Agathe asked.

It sounded like a catechism and the answer should have been, "To know you and enjoy you forever." But Tibo said, "I came in to buy myself a suit."

"Oh, yes, I remember. Can I come?" she asked, in just the way she would ask if he wanted another cup of coffee. "Can I come?" to see this intimate humiliation, like a trip to the doctor, like being a spectator while he had his ears syringed or his corns shaved.

"Can I come?"

"Yes, of course," Tibo said, "of course." And he offered her his arm.

KUPFER AND KEMANEZIC WAS ONLY two shops away—a glazed door with a brown linen blind and a single broad window with a moustachioed mannequin who had stood in the same spot, impassive as a sentry, never altering his pose or his coiffure since he took up his post these fifty years since, not when the summer sun beat through the glass all day and threatened to melt his wax moustache, not in the winter when he was forced to endure the humiliation of facing Albrecht Street as he modelled the latest heavyweight combinations. He stood solid and steady through it all, the embodiment of the kind of service a Kupfer and Kemanezic customer could expect.

"Imperturbable," Tibo murmured to himself as he passed under the mannequin's gaze and opened the shop door for Agathe. "Imperturbable," a pleasant word—not so nice as "elbow" perhaps, but with a similar clarety roll-in-the-mouth flavour and, now, a kind of a spell about it.

Agathe looked up at him with a question.

"Nothing," Tibo said. "Sorry. Just . . . Nothing."

Inside, the shop was endless—a long canyon of soberly patterned carpet stretching away between towering walls of wooden shelves and drawers marked "socks blue" or "socks black" and numbered according to size and, far away at the other end, Tibo and Agathe saw themselves walking towards themselves, side by side, in a rank of mirrors. It was a suddenly startling image, disturbingly bridal. A man and a woman like that, so close, nervously comfortable, self-consciously at ease. They glanced at one another in the reflection and quickly turned away as if they had been caught in something furtive.

"Sir, Madam." It was Kemanezic himself, splendid in a gleaming white shirt with a scarlet handkerchief blazing from his breast pocket and a tiny pansy, almost hidden against the midnight blue of his lapel. And then, with a sudden recognition, he herded a tiny gilded chair towards Agathe and commanded her into it with a tiny nudge on the back of her leg. "Ah, Mayor Krovic. A delight to welcome you to Kupfer and Kemanezic. How can we be of service?"

"A suit, I thought." Tibo's voice sounded pipey and reedish.

"Sir." And like a magician producing a live snake, Kemanezic was suddenly holding his tape measure. It lashed and whipped round Tibo, marking off the size of his chest, his shoulders, the length of his arms, his waist and—"Would Madam care to look through this book of swatches?"—his inside leg.

Kemanezic conjured a tiny leather-bound pad from his inside pocket and made a few quick notes. "I think I have that, Mayor Krovic. If you would care to choose the cloth and come back in a fortnight, we can be ready for the fitting."

Tibo was defeated. "Yes," he said, "of course. In a fortnight." And, after quickly selecting two different materials from the swatch book, he turned towards the door.

"But, in the meantime, the mayor will be needing something to tide him over," Agathe said. "Something off the peg. You do have something. In this blue, I think." She held out the sample book, folded open at a soft herringbone cloth.

"Off the peg?" Kemanezic hesitated. "I'll check, Mrs. Krovic." And he retreated.

They were alone in the shop then, Tibo and Agathe, and he looked at her gratefully and said, "Thanks."

Agathe gave a sympathetic smile.

"I didn't know what to say," said Tibo.

"And he was relying on that. You mustn't let people boss you around."

"I'm all right with the Chief of Police or the Town Clerk—it's just," his voice faded to a shuddering whisper, "tailors."

Agathe looked down at her toes. "Did you notice?"

"Yes. He called you 'Mrs. Krovic'—I noticed."

"We should put him right."

"We should, really," Tibo agreed but there was something boyish and reluctant and just-five-minutes-more-ish in his voice.

They looked at each other, trying to hold back giggles, until Mr. Kemanezic returned, leading a milky-faced boy who staggered under armfuls of suits and calling them back to a fragile solemnity.

Mr. Kemanezic flicked back the curtains of a cubicle so the rings rattled. "If you would care to try these, Mayor Krovic."

Kemanezic had the gift—you find it in mothers, really good teachers and villainous butlers in Inspektor Voythek movies—of making the simplest, friendliest request sound like a bloodcurdling threat. He could put an arm-twisting compulsion into a breath and he said, "If you would care to try these, Mayor Krovic," the way prison governors walk on to death row and say, "It's time now, son."

Tibo looked nervously at Agathe but she shooed him on with a slight flap of the hand.

The curtains rattled on their pole again and Tibo was alone in a tiny wooden room. There was a dim lamp in a ground-glass shade overhead, a mirror screwed to the left-hand wall, two coat hooks side by side on the right-hand wall and a small brown bentwood chair jammed in the corner. He sat down and undid his shoes, stood up and prised them off, toe to heel. He took off his jacket and hung it on a coat hook, undid his trousers, held them carefully by the cuffs, gripping them under his chin until the creases were properly lined up and hung them on the back of the chair. They slid off with a sigh and concertinaed on the floor. Tibo picked them up and laid them across the seat. They stayed.

He looked in the mirror glumly. Black socks, white legs, shirt tails hanging down. "I look like a turkey," he whispered to himself and he bubbled his cheeks out. He wondered how any woman, let alone the pink and plump and "Tahiti"-fragrant Mrs. Agathe Stopak, could ever look at him and want him. "But you wouldn't normally start with the trousers," he told himself. "You'd start at the top and work down." But that left the socks. Tibo imagined himself standing naked in just his black socks and he moaned, "Oh, Walpurnia!"

"Everything all right in there, sir?" said Kemanezic.

The curtain gave a suspicion of a twitch but Tibo's fist shot out to grip a bunched and decisive knot of fabric. "Fine!" he barked. "Thank you. I'll just be a moment." He released the curtain warily. It made no sign of suddenly flying open.

After a moment's watchfulness, Tibo tugged a pair of trousers from the first of the hangers provided by Mr. Kemanezic. Sensible blue cloth, deep pockets, half-lined to the knees, adjustable straps at the sides with black buttons to keep them in place. These were trousers. And they fit. He slipped his shoes back on. They actually fit! Tibo was admiring himself in the mirror when CHIIIIIIING! the curtain whipped back and there was Mr. Kemanezic, knuckles white as he gripped the ends of the tape measure that hung from his neck. "Is everything all right, Mayor Krovic? If I might be permitted to assist."

With another magician's gesture, Mr. Kemanezic swirled the jacket off its hanger and moulded it to Tibo's body with sweeps of his hands. "Single-breasted, Mayor Krovic. Very flattering style. Four-button cuff. Single vent. Very modern."

"I thought . . ." said Tibo.

"Very wise, sir, and I agree with you. The double-breasted style is really suitable only for the slimmer gentleman."

Kemanezic poked two fingers down Tibo's waistband and ran them round his body. "Good fit here, sir, not too snug." Then he gave an eye-popping tug on the back seam. "Enough room in the seat, is there? We pride ourselves on our generous cut."

"Thank you," Tibo gasped. "I was just thinking that or something very like it."

"I am so pleased to hear that, Mayor Krovic. Why don't we give the excellent Mrs. Krovic a chance to pass her eye over our efforts?" And, with a single swinging waltzing move, he twirled Tibo through the curtain and back out into the shop.

Agathe stood up and welcomed them with a smile. "Oh, yes," she said. "Oh, yes. Well, come here then—let me see." There was a chivvying pride in her voice that was more than friendly. She had the sort of tone that is reserved for wives and Tibo noticed it and wondered if he liked it and decided that, yes, he did like it. He felt she was entitled to it.

It was the voice "the one" would have used, if she had ever come, if he had ever found her, and, now, hearing Agathe speak, Tibo knew that she *had* come, he had found her. Agathe was the one.

She had been at his finger ends for years and now, in Kupfer and Kemanezic, here under the gaze of drawers marked "socks blue" and "socks black" and standing in front of glazed cabinets full of underpants and nightshirts, with racks of glowing, garish ties standing round like spectators at a road accident, he saw that she had been the one all that time. But she was Mrs. Agathe Stopak and, though she walked out of Kupfer and Kemanezic with him, she would leave him. She would leave him at the next tram stop and go back to Aleksander Street and Stopak, the paperhanger. He saw everything as clearly as if he had been looking down on the whole of Dot from the crown of my cathedral, he saw it all and he said, "So, what do you think?"

"Oh, I like it. Very smart." She turned to Mr. Kemanezic. "Do you have another one like it in black?"

"Yes, Madam."

"Exactly like it?"

Kemanezic was icily polite. "Exactly alike, Madam. In every respect. Exactly."

Agathe gave a winsome smile. "Then I think," she exchanged a quick glance with Tibo, "we'll take one. Black. Would you bag them both, please? We'll be wanting the hangers."

Mr. Kemanezic made a little bow, like the little bow Yemko

had made in the bookseller's, in recognition of a worthy opponent and he withdrew.

And, after that, there was no more than a moment of embarrassment at the counter—the commercial equivalent of biting down on a wad of cotton wool once the tooth is out. Tibo opened his chequebook on the scratched glass top of a cabinet containing endless rows of folded white vests, filled out a jaw-droppingly huge amount and took possession of two bulging brown paper bags, each printed with "Kupfer and Kemanezic" in dusty red letters, diagonally across the front.

Kemanezic hurried from the till to open the door and stood like a half-closed penknife as they passed.

"Those suits are absolutely wonderful," Agathe said breathily.

"Thank you, Madam. Thank you. We can assure you of years of satisfaction."

"So wonderful, in fact, that Mayor Krovic will not, after all, be requiring the made-to-measure ones, but thank you for your trouble."

The door closed so firmly behind them that the wax mannequin rocked against the glass of his window as if, finally, he had decided on a fretful bid for freedom.

Tibo grinned. "You are so clever. Thank you." He turned back and saw Kemanezic glowering from a corner of the brown linen blind which quickly twitched back into place over the door. "Come on," he said, "before they set the dogs on us."

In a gesture befitting the Mayor of Dot, he offered his arm and, in a gesture befitting the one, she gripped it with two hands and pressed her face close against his shoulder.

They were walking together like that—like a man carrying suits, walking with the woman who loves him, along Albrecht Street, past the Ko-Operatif Shoe Shop and towards Commerz Plaz—when Tibo noticed a taxi, moving very slowly, coming towards them, banking heavily to the pavement like a schooner rounding Cape Horn in the teeth of a gale and, inside, holding on to the leather strap that hung down beside the rear window, was the lawyer Yemko Guillaume. As the taxi laboured past, he turned his head slowly, as an unassailable turtle would turn its head to observe some harmless log that floated by. He did not smile. He did not nod. He did not wave. There was no gesture of recognition as he drove past but his eyes met those of Tibo and held them blankly as if he did not see. But he saw and then the taxi passed and Tibo stood looking after it and the back of Yemko's head, facing directly away, straight ahead, through the windscreen.

That evening, sitting alone in the house at the end of the blue-tiled path, looking into a fire that whispered and sighed and settled, Tibo saw himself in Albrecht Street suddenly stiffen, suddenly chill. He saw himself straighten, lifting his head away from where it had rested against Agathe's, suddenly becoming formal and correct, arriving at the stop for the Aleksander Street tram like a bank messenger arriving with a parcel to be signed for and saying, "I think this is where you catch the tram, isn't it?"

He said it over and over again as he beat the iron poker into the embers—"I think this is where you catch the tram, isn't it? I think this is where you catch the tram, isn't it?"—mocking himself. "You couldn't invite her for a drink, could you? You couldn't ask her for a coffee. You couldn't just walk with her." Tibo thought of walking with her, all the way through Dot, from one end to the other, her body pressed against his until they found themselves out in the country in the dark and Agathe suddenly came to her senses—or not—and they spread their coats under a tree like blankets and lay down together. "But, oh, no! You couldn't do that, could you, Mayor Tibo Bloedig Krovic? Not after the lawyer Guillaume looked at you, not after he spotted you. Oh, no, that wouldn't be at all right, you bloedig idiot!" He dropped the poker in the hearth with a clatter and went to bed.

But he couldn't rest. Some time later—it was too dark to see the clock—Tibo threw back the covers and dressed. He put on his new black suit and the polished shoes he had left standing at attention under his bed and he went out into the darkened streets. All the trams had stopped running. There was nobody about and he began to walk back to the centre of town but, when he turned the corner at the top of the street, Tibo saw the lights of a taxi coming towards him. He would have hailed it but it was moving very, very slowly and canted over to one side so it almost scraped the pavement. Tibo was nearly sick with fear and shame. He knew that, although he could not see him, Yemko Guillaume was in the cab and he knew that, when it caught him, the doors would fly open and he would be dragged inside and then the cab would roll onwards forever, at a snail's pace, with Yemko in there laughing at him until he was dead. He began to run and he ran and he ran but, every time he stopped for breath, head down, leaning on a lamp post, sweat falling in hot drops to sizzle on the pavement between the toes of his polished shoes, the taxi would trundle round the corner and he had to run again with the air scorching into his mouth and down his throat and burning his lungs.

"If I could only find a policeman," Tibo said. "Why are there no policemen? What do I pay my rates for? I'm the Mayor of Bloedig Dot, you know!"

But he ran on and on, past all nine tram stops on the way to town and always with the terrible black cab rolling along all lopsided just a few yards behind, sometimes so close that he felt its tyres rubbing at the heel of his shoes, and he never saw a soul except for Sarah, who was sitting at the window of the second-best butcher's in Dot holding a packet of sausages marked "Krovic" and crying her eyes out. "Here's your sausages, Mayor Krovic," she said, between blubs.

"Thank you, Sarah," said Tibo. "Why are you crying?"

"It's onion sausages and you've been a long time."

So Tibo apologised and promised to come back and pay later but now he would have to go because the taxi was coming and he hoped she would understand and just then, when he looked back to the corner of the street, the slanting yellow lights of the cab appeared.

Tibo ran on again, turning into Cathedral Avenue and, as he ran, he tugged at the packet of sausages which Sarah had given him, ripping it open as he went and scattering sausages, one by one, on the road. Naturally the taxi had to swerve to avoid them—or sway slowly and lopsidedly across the road to dodge them where they lay—but, as Tibo's aim improved, he found he was able to hit the wheels with his sausages and send the taxi skidding in a pool of grease and meat. That meant it was miles behind when he reached the doors of the cathedral and ran inside and there was still no sign of it when he pulled open the door to the bell tower and started to climb the stairs. "You'll never get me now," he said, but he hadn't gone very far before he turned a corner and found himself at the top.

And there was Mrs. Agathe Stopak, wearing the mayoral robes and she said, "I hope you don't mind." But, just then, she let them fall away and she was completely naked and pink and buxom, except for her stockings.

"Don't look so shocked," she said and then she jumped off the wall of the bell tower and grabbed the biggest bell in the cathedral and held on to it with her legs wrapped round it and she started to rock and sway, like kids do when they want to get a swing started in the park. "Come on!" she said. "Come on! Help me."

So Tibo took a flying leap off his side of the wall and grabbed on to the bell and he sat on the edge of it, opposite Agathe with his legs all tangled up with hers and he rocked and he swung and, every time she pushed forward, he leaned back and, every time he pushed forward, she leaned back, rocking and laughing and yelling encouragement at each other. "Yes, yes, like that! That's the way! Yes!" And, as Tibo looked down, down the middle of the bell tower, past Mrs. Stopak's beautiful creamy thighs, down to the bottom where the floor was a tiny, shrunken square at the end of a long tunnel of perspective, he heard her say, "Isn't this where you catch the tram?" and he screamed but nobody could hear him because, just then, the bell swung right over and rang with a terrifying "BONG!"

*NOW, IT'S WELL KNOWN THAT THE DOC*tors say the dreams we think last the whole night long really last no more than a heartbeat or two. We fly for hours through clouds or stand all day, stark naked in the High Street or collapse into a laughing embrace with a mother who is not, after all, dead these thirty years or flee for miles pursued by phantom taxis, gasping and exhausted but, in the strange world this side of sleep, it's all over in the flicker of an eyelid.

And so, when Tibo woke himself with the sound of his own yelling, tangled in the blankets and clutching his pillow for dear life, the Sunday carillon that started the whole thing was still ringing over Dot and into his bedroom.

Tibo was not a churchgoer. He enjoyed leading the council procession on its annual pilgrimage up the hill to the cathedral and, in moments of desperation, he would cry out—as all good Dottians are taught to do from infancy—to invoke the name of Walpurnia. Sometimes, he might even look up from his desk and talk to the bearded nun on the town arms as he would to an old and trusted friend. He regarded prayer as an opportunity to calm himself and to gather his thoughts in a quiet place but he did not believe anybody heard—not really. When he said the words, he meant them sincerely. They rumbled in his heart the way snow rumbles when it falls off the roof in a thaw but, in a little while, the snow is gone. It turns to mist or it trickles away in the gutter and there is nothing at all to show that it has ever been there. When

Tibo prayed, he knew he was talking to himself, not to me and certainly not to God and he knew that meant it wasn't really prayer at all so, since he could talk to himself as well in his own kitchen as in the cathedral, he didn't bother.

There were worse men than Mayor Tibo Krovic making their way to church that morning and maybe they needed it more but what Tibo needed was coffee and not going to church gave him time to make it. He shuffled to the kitchen by way of the bathroom. His body ached as if he had been sleeping on a mattress full of rocks. He was still tired, unrefreshed and troubled by odd, embarrassing, shaming bits of dream that lingered in his brain like cigar smoke lingers in curtains. He groaned and shook his head to chase them out but it didn't work.

The image of Agathe's stocking-tops and her white thighs and that deep, plunging, rocking sensation stayed with him strangely, the way the motion of the Dash ferry would stay in his legs long after he reached the quayside. But this wasn't in his legs.

In the kitchen, Tibo measured four scoops into the coffee pot, put it on the stove and hurried to the front door to pick up the Sunday paper. There was nothing in it. The usual front-page story, the same one they seemed to have every week, hinting darkly at some failure in the provincial government that might or might not involve corruption or, at the very least, a serious dose of nepotism, possibly. That and the second female lead in the latest Horace Dukas picture caught up in some scandal with her chauffeur and a picture of a strangely shaped tomato discovered in a market garden near Umlaut. "That's Umlaut for you," Tibo said. "Home of the deformed tomato." He threw the paper down on the table and got on with the business of making toast.

The rest of the morning was much as you would expect for a prosperous man living alone with nothing to do and too much time to do it. He finished eating. He found, despite propping the paper carefully against a square green tin of jam and examining it carefully, page by page, that there was not a single thing in it worth reading. He rinsed the dishes and left them standing on the draining board. He washed. He shaved. He went to his bedroom to dress, holding the sleeve of his new black suit against his cheek, smelling it for that new suit flavour and, perhaps just to check that it was not stained with the sweat of a nightmare race through the streets before he put it on.

And then he put on his coat and found, in the pocket, the brown-paper parcel, tied with string, which he had placed there the night before. Agathe's book. It was meant for Monday and Tibo reasoned that, if he took it with him now, it would mean he expected to meet her today, on Sunday at one o'clock, by the bandstand in Copernicus Park, which, of course, was absolutely untrue. If Agathe happened to be there, that would be nothing more than a happy accident so it would be pointless taking the book now. Silly and pointless and, in fact, it might even act as some kind of bad-luck charm to ensure that, if anything, she did not turn up at all.

He slid the package out of his pocket and laid it on the hallstand. The front door closed with a bang, the brass letter box rattled, Tibo's heels rapped like gunfire down the blue-tiled path and he passed under the damp and dripping birch tree, through the complaining, slouching gate and out to the street but this time he turned downhill, not up, heading for the park.

Already it was past noon and the sun was tipping in the sky behind half-hearted clouds, like a blurred lemon. The wind was coming in from the Ampersand, blowing slowly straight from the east over endless miles of steppe and a few extra miles of sea that couldn't quite be bothered to freeze yet but, in spite of that, half of Dot seemed to be heading towards the park, mostly the nice half, the half Tibo was proud to represent, the half with rosy cheeks and polite, scrubbed children in knitted hats and polished shoes, the half that Tibo envied and the half that looked up to him and smiled and waved and nodded and said, "Mayor Krovic," briskly in a cosy symbiosis of smugness.

Tibo was proud of the park too with its big arched gates of stone, almost like a little castle, and its fancy iron railings and that broad sweep of gently sloping grass that fell away under an avenue of trees to flatten and spread round an ornate and substantial bandstand with its bell-shaped roof of real slate.

He approached through the sunken Italian garden, an annual triumph by the staff of the Parks Department who defied the cartographers and the evidence of their own eyes to produce, every year in Dot, a little bit of Tuscany or Umbria—something warm and dry and basil-scented that reindeer might choose to nibble if only they could be bothered to walk a little further east. See, here he comes now, between the tall columns of cypress, self-conscious in his new suit, wondering if this is quite the right way to walk and if it was the way he walked yesterday and if he might not try to walk rather differently, in a way befitting the Mayor of Dot which yet did justice to his new Kupfer and Kemanezic suit. And walking this way brings him, from the north side, towards the bandstand, that strange octagonal structure, all red, white and blue cast-iron confectionery with gilded bits, like icing, towards the top. He is looking round now for a suitable chair.

The Fire Brigade Band concert is always popular and the last of the year is a gala event for the people of Dot. It's a place for new hats—a place to be seen. Obviously Mayor Krovic would be quite entitled to take a seat anywhere in the front row surrounding the bandstand but that might be regarded as ostentatious. And to take a seat away at the back, in the sort of place where, really, nobody would know whether the Mayor of Dot had bothered to come at all, would be rather too modest. It might even be regarded, in its way, as showing off—as ostentation disguised as humility.

Good Tibo Krovic had been Mayor of Dot long enough to know that these things mattered and, even when he found a suitable chair, he could not sit down until he had been seen, until he had smiled and nodded at a few people whose names he could not quite, at that moment, recall exactly and certainly not until he had shaken hands with one or two local figures in the crowd: Tomazek the President of the Licensed Victuallers' Association—"And this must be your sister. How do you do? Your mother? Oh, Mrs. Tomazek, I can't believe it"; Gorvic, the Town Clerk, "and Mrs. Gorvic, a pleasure, always"; and, of course, Svennson, the Fire Chief, "Fine body of men you've got there, Svennson. Always do the town proud, they do." And it was only when he turned away from that sort of nonsense, turned round, ready to sit down in the slatted chair with its folding iron frame, two rows in from the front, that he had decided was just about the right one for the Mayor of Dot to be seen in, it was only then that he saw Agathe standing on the gravel path that circles the bandstand, out there, in front of everybody, in her bottle-green coat, holding her handbag modestly in two hands in front of her and waiting, politely, for him to be finished.

"Agathe." When he said her name there was a smile in it. "I never thought . . . Well . . . This is nice." And he started to edge out from the row of seats, apologising as he went, until he reached the meandering gap which the park staff had left as an aisle and he could walk forward to meet her on the gravel. He took her hand, not the way he had taken Svennson's hand or even the way he had taken Mrs. Gorvic's hand, palm open, thumb up, firm, dry, manly grip. He held his hand out to her with the fingers pointed down to the path and she took it, slipping her hand into his, her hand facing forward, his facing back and they stood, side by side like that, holding hands.

"We have to find somewhere to sit," he said. "The band is about to begin."

"It's a bit busy," said Agathe. "Maybe you should just go back to where you were and sit down. I don't think we'll find two seats together. I'm sorry. I'm very late. I couldn't get away and then the tram took forever and, when I got here, the place was so busy that I couldn't see you at first."

"Oh, don't be silly. We'll find something. Let's look round the other side."

The Mayor Krovic of the day before, the one who stiffened and bristled in Albrecht Street, might not have said that or, if he had, he might not have walked, holding her hand like that, round the gravel path around the bandstand but this was a different Mayor Krovic—one who had spent the previous evening staring into the fire and cursing himself for a fool and most of the previous night fleeing from a demon taxi or tangled in Agathe Stopak's invitingly milky thighs. Yet, despite that, Tibo felt like a bull in a show ring.

Every seat in the park was turned to face the bandstand and, for the hundreds in the crowd, there was nothing else to look at but Mayor Tibo Krovic walking hand in hand with—who was that woman? Quite a pretty woman. You don't think? No. Surely not. Tibo felt Agathe tighten her grip and she gave a little skip as she hurried to match his stride.

They arrived at the south side of the bandstand and there, filling most of the front row, was Yemko Guillaume. Tibo's heels skidded in the gravel of the path as he came to a halt and he might have turned to run but, when he looked back, the first of the Fire Brigade bandsmen was already taking his place on the platform.

And then, when he glanced in panic at Yemko, he knew it was too late to flee. The lawyer was sitting on a thick polished plank which he had laid across the whole of the front row of seats—not that he was quite huge enough to require all seven seats but he was heavy enough to need all twenty-eight chair legs. Even with the plank to spread his weight, the row of seats sagged and splayed beneath him. As Yemko raised his hat in greeting, Tibo noticed, over his shoulder and beyond the crowd, a waiting taxi purring menacingly by the park gate.

"It appears the whole town has turned out," said Yemko. "And we are about to start. Please, won't you and your companion join me? For some reason I seem to have a number of chairs to myself."

Tibo and Agathe looked at one another in resignation. Sitting next to Yemko would be less embarrassing than standing alone in front of the crowd for the next hour and they would, at least, be together. So, although she blamed the lawyer Guillaume for forcing Tibo from the bench and hated him for it, Agathe was gracious. She said simply, "Thank you," and took the chair at the end of the row, leaving Tibo to squeeze in to the last empty place—the place next to Yemko Guillaume.

Before he sat down, Tibo observed the polite pleasantries. "Mr. Guillaume," he said, "permit me to introduce my friend and colleague, Mrs. Agathe Stopak. Agathe, this is the learned Mr. Yemko Guillaume."

In an act of gallantry that clearly cost him some pain, Yemko leaned forward on his cane, half rising, half bowing, and extended a hand which Agathe politely shook by the fingers. "How do you do, Mrs. Stopak? The pleasure is all mine."

"How do you do," she said.

And Tibo sat down between them.

With a flamenco dancer's flick of the wrist, Yemko produced a thick white printed card. "Perhaps Mrs. Stopak would care to have this, Krovic."

Tibo passed it on and Agathe leaned forward with a brief smile of thanks. She was unfailingly polite.

"It's a disappointing selection," Yemko continued, "rather heavy on military music—lots of very brisk oom-pah-ing. Still."

"Still?" Tibo sounded rather more tetchy than he would have wished.

"Still, I suppose one must give the public what they expect. You and I have had this discussion before, I think. People like to know where they stand. They don't like it when their neighbours fail to live up to expectations. They prefer their Sunday School teachers not to be tango-dancers in their spare time. They like their mayors to be nicely hidebound. They would be disappointed to the point of actual distress if some clownishly fat lawyer turned out to be anything less than a gourmand. And they would be downright embittered if the Fire Brigade Band dared a little Mozart. There is nothing worse than a disappointed mob—nothing uglier." Guillaume turned to look Mayor Krovic in the face and he added, "And I speak as one who is intimately acquainted with ugliness."

Good Mayor Krovic felt suddenly moved. He clapped his hand down on the straining cloth that covered the lawyer's thigh just as he might have reassured a worried dog. "Guillaume . . ." he said in a "Come along now—what's brought this on?" kind of voice. But then he seemed to realise the meaning of what Yemko had said and, without thinking, he began a justification. "You know I am as hidebound a mayor as any town could hope for," he said.

Yemko looked him straight in the eye for a moment and said, "Quiet."

Tibo never learned what that meant. The music was beginning.

And it turned out that Guillaume was right. The programme was dire. No finesse, no emotion, just thumping, blasting marching tunes—a lot of warmongering Mittel-Europaische nonsense. Under the cover of the music, when she thought everybody in the rows behind would be looking straight ahead at the bandstand and not at her, about halfway through the second piece—"My Saucy Pomeranian Maid," the programme said—Agathe slipped her hand to her side. It was an invitation and Tibo accepted. He slid his hand down to where their thighs were jammed together and folded his fingers in hers. "I brought sweets," she said and, with her free hand, she passed him one. Tibo took it left-handed and held one end of the wrapper in his teeth to tug it open.

"I like a nice caramel," he said. "Are there nuts in this?"

"No. You'd better see if *he* wants one."

"Would you like a sweet?" Tibo whispered.

"Thank you, no." Guillaume held up a pink palm in rejection.

"He's such a sourpuss," said Agathe.

Tibo squeezed her hand. "Shh. You've never met the man. He's all right. Really, he is."

"After what he did?" Agathe hissed.

"That was nothing. He didn't mean it. It's all forgotten."

"You're too soft for your own good," she said. "But I like you soft." And she squeezed his arm with her free hand and cuddled in and buried her face in his coat sleeve, the way she had done when they were walking together down Albrecht Street, before the taxi passed. "Oh, I got powder on your coat. Sorry," she said and brushed it off.

*NOW, OF COURSE, IT NEVER, EVER HAP*pens, except in stories but if, say, a seagull, passing over Dot on his way home from a hard day spent swooping around the funnel of the Dash ferry and considering a trip to the docks or a rummage in the bins of the fish market, if such a seagull, flying sufficiently high, had chanced to look down just about then, he might have seen, at one end of Dot, Agathe pressed close up against Tibo for warmth and Tibo pressed close against Yemko for lack of space and, if he turned his bright black eye towards the other end of Dot, he might have seen, just possibly, through the scullery window, in a flat on Aleksander Street, two men having lunch. But, of course, he could never have heard what they were saying, being so high up and the wind from Dash blowing so fiercely about his ears and since the best stories—including this one—are built from words the way that houses are built from bricks or beaches are built from little bits of sand, it is probably best not to waste too much time on that particular seagull.

But, if, say, Achilles the cat had been sitting by the stove in the kitchen of the flat in Aleksander Street, he would have heard every word. In fact, Achilles had just finished rubbing his paw over his ear and he was about to devote the next few minutes to licking his private parts when the clang of Agathe's new frying pan falling into the sink sent him leaping under the sofa.

"Any more bread?" asked Stopak.

"Just this," said Hektor and he wiped a thick slice through the bacon fat on his plate and ate it with a wolfish snap.

"Any eggs left, then?"

"You ate the whole box. No wonder you're the size of a horse."

"Gotta keep my strength up."

"I'll bet," said Hektor. "That Agathe making demands on your body again? Eh? Eh? Is she?"

Stopak feigned outraged modesty. "She's a beast. Can't keep her hands off me. It's constant. Non-stop. Not a minute's peace."

He tore a horseshoe-shaped chunk out of a thick slice of bread and left golden teeth marks shining from a pavement of butter.

"Any more beer?"

"It's in the corner cupboard."

Hektor got up to look. "You're down to your last couple of bottles," he said. "But the Crowns will be open soon. Since you're a mate, I'll let you buy me a real drink."

They sat in silence for a while, Stopak shovelling at piles of refried potatoes, Hektor leaning back in his chair to blow smoke rings at the ceiling.

"So, that Agathe, eh?"

"Yeah, that Agathe—she's some woman, I can tell you."

"I'll bet. You're a lucky man, cousin."

Stopak couldn't speak for a bit. He was struggling with an unfeasibly huge lump of bacon but, eventually, he managed to say, "Listen, Hektor, it's not all it's cracked up to be, you know. I'm telling you, good looks like mine—it's a curse, mate. It's a curse. She's like a wild animal."

"It must be hellish."

"Hellish."

"Bet you could tell some stories."

"You wouldn't believe the half of it, pal."

"If that mattress could talk, eh?"

Stopak grunted through a mouthful of food but he said nothing. Even when Hektor sat silent, willing him to say something, filling the air with a great conversational gap that cried out for a story of Agathe naked and voracious, even then Stopak said nothing.

He took another swig from his bottle. "Whatcha doin'?"

"I'm drawing you."

"Can't blame you."

"You're a good subject. I've got sketchbooks full of you."

"I'm paying you to be a paperhanger now, not a portrait painter. Anyway, I thought you'd given all that up—that artist stuff."

"Can't," said Hektor, "it gets in the blood. Sit still."

Stopak turned back slightly towards the window. "Better? You sold any of these pictures of yours yet?"

"Any day now."

"You should stick to painting gutters and window frames. That's what puts bread on the table."

"There's more to life than that," said Hektor. "Time is it?"

Stopak checked his watch. "They're open. C'mon, you can buy me a drink."

"I'll just wash up first."

"Leave it," said Stopak. "We're wasting good drinking time. Agathe can do it when she gets in."

"Where is she anyway?"

"Church. Church again. She's always at church."

"Asking St. Walpurnia for the gift of chastity, I'll bet."

"Too late for that, pal. That wife of mine, I tell you, she's like a bitch in heat. Never a moment's rest. She just can't stay off me. I'll tell you what you should do—you should paint her! Paint Agathe. Nice big nude for over the fireplace."

Hektor closed his sketchbook and put it in his jacket pocket, jammed in down there next to a little brown copy of Omar Khayyám. "I couldn't do that," he said. "Paint Agathe? Naked? Wouldn't be right. Couldn't think of it . . ."

They closed the door and Achilles went back to the stove to lick his balls.

And, just about the time he settled down to work, the men of the Fire Brigade Band were getting ready for a break. With cheeks puffed out like apples and sweat lashing from beneath their polished brass helmets, they galloped together over the last few bars of something stirring towards the crate of beer that was lying in a zinc bath, next to the lawn roller at the back of the park-keeper's lodge. Eyes on the conductor, everybody. Keep up, that means you Mr. Glockenspiel, all together now, big finish aaand . . . Applause!

"I'm afraid we're only halfway through," said Yemko in a voice of doom.

"I can't think why you come if you hate it so much, Mr. Guillaume," Agathe replied.

"Perhaps less for the music and rather more for the company. Do you think perhaps that's why we come, Mrs. Stopak?"

In a quieter setting, had she not been surrounded by happy, noisy people, Agathe's little "Hmmph" might have been noticeable but nobody noticed it and, since she was sitting in the front row and everybody was, more or less, facing forward, nobody but Tibo noticed that she took her hand away and crossed her arms with an angry little pout. But even that was spoiled when Yemko upstaged her by taking off his hat and raising it, like a flag, on the top of his cane.

"What on earth are you doing now?" she asked.

"Yes," said Tibo, "what *are* you doing?"

"You will find," said Yemko, "that I am a constant source of amazement and amusement." And he smiled with the appealing, engaging, unrefusable smile of a baby and, in spite of herself, Agathe found she was smiling back.

Yemko waggled his cane up and down and started humming—"Oompah, oompah, pom, pom, pom"—that silly tune the band had been playing earlier, but the amazing thing was that nobody else in the crowd even seemed to notice or think it the least bit strange, even when he twirled the cane and started spinning his hat like those Chinese jugglers who were such a hit at the Opera House two seasons ago with their plates on sticks. "This is exhausting," he wheezed. "I don't know how much longer I can keep it up."

"Well, if it's a matter of the sky falling on our heads or something," Agathe giggled, "I think I could take over for a bit. Oompah, oompah, pom, pom, pom."

"I am under an obligement to you for that kind thought, Mrs. Stopak, but it seems that, after all, there will be no need." And then, instead of saying "Oompah," Yemko lowered his cane and said "Ta-daaah" with a kind of fanfare flourish.

There at Agathe's elbow was a skinny man, wearing a taxi driver's badge and carrying a large bamboo table with folding legs and a picnic hamper.

"You were signalling," said Tibo.

"Of course I was signalling, Krovic. Did you think I'd lost my mind? How on earth was the poor chap to find us?" But his voice sank to an exhausted whisper as he turned to Agathe and said, "Mrs. Stopak, would you be gracious enough to act as hostess? 'Bliged."

The taxi driver disappeared into the crowd again, pressing his fists into the small of his back with a groan and leaving Agathe to tackle the picnic hamper on the table. She opened it with the sort of look on her face that Hester Roskova had when she opened the treasure chest in the final scene of *Pirate Queen of Jamaica*.

"This is packed," she said. "There's everything in here!" And then she looked up at Yemko, sagging on his cane like a big top the day the circus leaves town. "Are you all right?" she asked kindly.

"See if there's anything to drink in there," Tibo said. He laid a hand on the lawyer's shoulder. "Overdid things a bit, I think. You'll soon be right."

"There's wine," said Agathe. She passed a dark green bottle and a corkscrew to Tibo. "I'm never any good with these." That was a lie. Agathe was perfectly able to use a corkscrew but she wanted to defer a little—to make the point that, like taking the rubbish out or bringing in the coal, this was a job for a big, strong man.

Tibo held the bottle down between his knees, drew the cork and poured a little wine into the glass which Agathe held out to him. "Take some of this," he said and, holding the glass by its foot, Yemko drank a sip. It left his lips stained purple where, before, they had been an interesting shade of blue.

"Thank you," he said. "I think you'll find some iced biscuits in there. Might I have one, please?"

"Iced biscuit!" said Tibo.

"Iced biscuit!" said Agathe, passing him one the way a nurse would pass a scalpel to a surgeon at the crucial point of a tricky operation.

Yemko took a dainty bite and chewed politely with his front teeth, like a rabbit. "Don't mind me, children," he said. "I'll be fine in a moment. Go ahead. Eat up. Enjoy."

"There's enough here to feed an army," said Agathe.

"Were you expecting us?" Tibo asked. "Surely you weren't planning on eating all this alone."

"It's as I said, my dear Krovic, one must never disappoint one's public. I planned to nibble on a dry biscuit but, by tonight, my legend would walk abroad on Cathedral Avenue. Blameless accountants and ministers of religion would swear they saw me eat an entire cow. Now, you must help me." He turned to Agathe with a wheeze. "I think you'll find a bottle of champagne in there, Mrs. Stopak. You and Mayor Krovic must help yourselves."

So they did. Tibo popped another cork and they drank champagne and ate cold chicken and ham and beef cooked pink and sliced thin and there was a big jar of preserved peaches and a pot of cream as thick as custard. They ate it all and laughed but, while they ate, Agathe would turn to Yemko from time to time with a look of gentle concern.

She leaned close to Tibo. "Swap seats, would you? Let me sit beside him."

So, all through the second half of the concert, all the way up to "Radetsky March," Tibo sat on the end of the row, by the aisle, picking marzipan fruits out of the picnic basket and feeding them to her because both her hands were occupied, one holding his hand and one laid gently over Yemko's, patting it softly from time to time, reassuring him.

Heaven alone knows what the tuba player made of it but, by the time the Fire Brigade Band got to the national anthem, Yemko had completely recovered from the strain of juggling his hat. Along with the rest of the crowd, he managed to drag himself to his feet but, unlike Tibo and Agathe, he didn't bother with singing along.

Tibo said, "Well, that's that for another year. Time to get ready for winter again."

"It was a lovely picnic," said Agathe. "Can we help with clearing it up?"

But Yemko shook his great head. "The driver will do that. It's been a pleasure."

"Then I'll take Agathe to the tram."

"Yes," said Yemko. That was all he said but he managed to put so much into it, the way that geese flying south from the Ampersand never say anything more than "honk" but manage to fill the whole sky with melancholy and longing just the same.

Tibo recognised it and decided that now would be an excellent time to make his goodbyes and set off through the park with Agathe towards an afternoon of who knew what.

But Agathe recognised it too and it very nearly broke her heart. From hating the lawyer Guillaume with a cold fury, she had gone, in the space of an hour, to loving him as only a mother can love. She looked at him and, for some reason that she could not explain, she wanted to help. So, when Good Mayor Krovic said, "I think we might catch a tram by the main gate, if we hurry," she only said, "Yes. Why don't you go ahead? I'll catch up in a minute," and turned back to Yemko.

Tibo would never have admitted it, of course, but he was a little offended. "Yes," he said, "of course. I'll wait for you at the gate." And he began to shuffle down the choked path, between the toppled rows of folding chairs, jostled through the crowd like a cork, looking back over his shoulder at where she stood, face to face with Yemko, a pace apart and holding his hand. As he went, Tibo noticed, far out to sea, the dark pencil-line of cloud along the horizon that always signified a coming storm. There was a sudden gust of wind that made the people burrow down into their collars and laugh about "winter coming."

Agathe was almost the last to leave Copernicus Park that day.

The crowds cleared quickly once they were through the bottleneck of the park gate, some walking home, some heading for the tram stops arranged on either side of the road and serving routes that led to every corner of Dot with a more than municipal efficiency.

Standing alone by the big stone pillar, Tibo noticed a sweet wrapper stuck to his shoe. He bent down to pick it off and dropped it in the bin that hung from the green iron lamp post nearby and, when he looked back, Agathe was there. She started beating him on the back and shoulders with a gloved hand. "You've been leaning on something," she said.

But he shooed her off. "You'll be spitting on your hankie to give my face a wash next."

Agathe was standing there, just as she had been with Yemko, face to face but close to him, the buttons of her coat brushing his, her face turned up to him, chin raised, nose in the air, eyes closed, smiling faintly. She was happy, she was amused by his silly protests, she was confident, like a woman who knew she had the right to brush dust off a man's shoulder.

Her body and Tibo's were touching, belly and breast and thigh, as naked as a wedding night with nothing to separate them but the layers of warm wool cloth that wrapped them. Her hair moved in the wind. The scent of her filled him. She was waiting to be kissed.

Tibo did not kiss her. He pulled away, stepped back by the length of a shoe and said, "What did Guillaume want?"

Agathe's shoulders slumped. She opened her eyes. It was as if a sigh of disappointment ran silently through her whole body and she said, "He wanted to offer me his friendship. He says that he is my friend. Tibo, are you my friend?"

Good Mayor Krovic looked briefly at his feet, then back into the park and the empty bandstand and then at Agathe again. "I'll take you to the tram," he said.

While they waited at the tram stop, they did not speak. When the No. 36 came round the corner with "Green Bridge" written in big white letters on its signboard, Agathe only said, "Bye, then." And, when it stopped and she climbed on to the back platform, her coat tight over her hips, the curve of her calf taut, heel and ankle curved and carved like a statue, she did not look back and, when the tram slid away again, Mayor Krovic looked up and down the street and found himself completely alone. He began to walk. There was nothing else to do. Before long, it began to rain but he kept on walking. After about an hour, he was on Foundry Street and, from there, it was only another mile to the docks. It was quiet there. No work to do on a Sunday. Old newspapers lay flattened like starfish in the rain. The cobbles were black and greasy and coal dust choked the gaps between them. Cigarette stubs lay in piles by the warehouse doors, marking the spots where the dockers had gathered to slouch around and talk and spit. There were rainbow pools of petrol shining on the dark water. It puckered like orange peel where the rain hit it.

Depressed seagulls with button-black eyes would glare at Tibo as he passed or rise up briefly, screeching like old machinery. They had already picked the fish boxes clean of scraps. They were bored. The rain grew heavier. Tibo walked on, through the docks and out the other side to where the cobbles vanished into a wild path that wandered among sand dunes for a bit and down to a long spit of gravel beach that led towards a tall grey lighthouse, appearing and disappearing through the squalls. Tibo found himself stumbling now as the pebbles crunched and shifted under his feet until, at the very end of the land, he reached the smooth stone wall at the foot of the lighthouse. He climbed up and walked round the flat parapet, standing with his back to the tower, looking out to where the islands were hidden by the weather and he yelled so the gulls rose off the water and cackled, "What the bloedig hell are you doing, Krovic? What are you doing? Is this what your life is? Is this the man you are—too frightened or too stupid to kiss a woman." He put his face in his hands. "What are you doing?" he asked himself again.

Far behind him in the town, where the lights of evening were beginning to sparkle from street to street, Agathe was standing at the sink, her coat and her handbag dumped on the kitchen table, her shoes kicked off and lying sideways on the floor as she washed the last of the dishes that Hektor and Stopak had abandoned. She had one of those little mops, the kind that's held on to a stick with thick copper wire, and, every time she plunged it into the tired suds, she asked angrily, "What are you doing, Agathe? What are you doing? How can you make such a bloedig fool of yourself, woman? Is this what your life is?" She scrubbed her frying pan until it gleamed.

And just round the corner, in The Three Crowns, where the wind was blowing straight off Green Bridge and battering rain off the window, two men sat at the corner table. One of them was asleep, holding a bottle barely propped upright on his enormous belly and the other sat squinting through the smoke of the cigarette he held between his lips, drawing, scoring out and drawing again in the sketchbook open on his knees and asking himself, "What the bloedig hell are you doing? Drawing her all day long. Drawing her every day. Imagining what she looks like naked when you could go there now and find out. What the hell are you doing? Is this what your life is?"

OUT AT THE LIGHTHOUSE, AT THE VERY FARthest bit of ground that could still call itself "Dot," Tibo turned his back on the storm and began to walk for home, crunching his way over the beach and back through the dunes, into the docks where the whores had come out for their night's work. They yelled "Hello!" at him as he passed and asked him if he was lonely. Tibo almost laughed at that. He tramped on, saying nothing, sticking to the middle of the road, not looking at the men in the shadows. They did not look at him. Along Canal Street and, finally, back on to the avenue along the Ampersand, the elms dripped on him as he passed. Already most of their leaves had fallen and the rain had knocked almost the last of them off. They lay in a greasy carpet on the path.

Tibo reached City Square. He dug in his pocket for his keys and opened the side door that led to the back stair. When it closed behind him the whole Town Hall seemed to shake. Tibo put his hand out in the dark and found the bottom of the banister. He slid his foot forward over the tiled floor until it collided with the first step and he began to count, "One, two, three. Landing. Turn." Then he counted fifteen more steps, then another landing and fifteen more, all the way to the corridor that led to his office. Tibo shuffled and stumbled his way through the dark, fingering his way past Agathe's desk and into his own office where he groped across the table hunting for his lamp. He felt better with some light in the room—less like a burglar, more at home.

He took off his dripping coat, shook it, hung it on the stand in the corner of the room and sat down at his desk. It was the first time Tibo had looked inside that drawer for some time. It slid open easily. There at the back, at fingertip reach, he found a paper bag printed with "Municipal Galleries, Dot" and, inside, just as he had left them, two picture postcards. He took the one printed with the Venus of Velázquez, the rich, creamy, pink and scarlet woman lying on her couch, gazing in the mirror with a look of longing and welcome, the one he had bought because—he could admit it now—it reminded him of Agathe. The other, whatever it was, he stuck back in the drawer without even looking at it.

Tibo glanced up at the town arms that hung opposite his desk and huffed a long sigh which he hoped I might recognise as a cry for help. He flicked his wet hair back over his head to ensure that it did not drip on the postcard, rubbed his hand on his trouser leg to dry it off and picked up his pen. He wrote, "Mrs. Agathe Stopak, Office of the Mayor, Town Hall, City Square, Dot" in rows on the side marked "This side for address" and sighed again. Such a tiny square of white cardboard—half the size of an envelope—that was all there was left to write on, all the space there was to tell her. Tell her what? Another sigh. Another glance up at me in my place on the shield and he began to write again. "You are more beautiful than this. More precious. More to be desired. More to be worshipped than any goddess. Yes, I AM your friend." The card was full. He jammed "K" into the bottom corner and went to look for a stamp in the light that spilled from his room on to Agathe's desk and, when he found one, he dropped a coin into petty cash.

It would take too long to explain how Tibo put his coat on again and crashed about in the dark back down the stairs to City Square. Just hurry through that part and imagine him there, standing at the double-fronted postbox on the corner of White Bridge, with its enamel signs marked "City" on one side and "Country or Foreign" on the other. Tibo pushed the card into the "City" slot and held it there until the very last moment. There was still time to pull it out and think about this again. It was just a postcard. But even so. It was evidence. It was something in writing. Dammit, what did that matter? Evidence of what? But was it even the right words? Was it enough? The card slipped from his fingers and nestled deep in the locked iron box and Tibo turned away for the tram, breathless, his heart racing. "You've done it now," he said, all the way up Castle Street. "You've done it now."

The enamel sign on the posting box promised, "A final collection will be made from this box at midnight" and the postal authorities were true to their word. The postman came at midnight. Not at five minutes to midnight, when he was at the top of Castle Street, not at ten past midnight when he was outside the Opera House. Midnight. The midnight postman was not an art lover. He did not notice Tibo's card and, anyway, although he had the ordinary human curiosity about other people's business, postmen do not have the time to snoop at every card or speculate about every scented envelope or every bill printed in red. They have sacks to fill, they have mail to dump down the big brass hoppers outside the main Post Office with its statues over the door, really quite beautiful statues that reminded some people of angels—one holding out a bronze letter and the other holding a lightning flash. "That's for telegrams," the postmaster explained to every new recruit.

Tibo was long ago in his bed, washed warm again in a hot bath, suit hanging from the kitchen ceiling and drying in the warm air rising from the stove, when his card arrived under their care. It slid down the wooden chute that led from the brass hopper and spilled on to a broad table in the middle of the hall where Antonin Gamillio, who was not really a postman at all but a writer who worked nights at the Central Post Office to keep himself in paper and ink until his novel of working life in the main post office of a medium-sized provincial town was finally accepted by a publisher, glanced at the address and flicked it deftly towards a sack marked "Central" which hung open against the wall. Antonin was rightly confident of his flicking skills. So confident, in fact, that he had already begun to read the address on the next letter he picked up before Tibo's card had even landed in the sack. It was a matter of pride to the mail sorters in the Central Post Office that they did not have to watch the mail as it glided towards its sack, which is a pity because, seven years before, a letter addressed to Mr.

A. Gamillio from one of the biggest publishing houses in the capital had missed the sack marked "Parkside," hit the wall behind and slid to the floor to stand upright against a table leg, where it remained to that very night, clouded in grey dust.

Fortunately, although such tricks of fate are popular in novels as a means of provoking misunderstandings and unhappiness between lovers, nothing of the kind happened to Tibo's card. After a while, the bag marked "Central" was taken from its place on the wall and carried to a bank of wooden pigeon holes, each row labelled with a street name, each individual box labelled with a number, except for the very end of the very bottom row where four boxes had been knocked into one and marked "Town Hall." Shortly before 3 a.m., Tibo's card landed in that box, tied with a red rubber band between a letter complaining about a broken pavement on the corner of Commerz Plaz and another in a brown envelope with a cheque inside for the Licensing Department. Imagine it—a naked goddess sandwiched between stuff like that! But that was how she travelled—not wafted on wave tops or carried by cupids but bound in rubber bands and dropped in a sack and swung through the door of the Town Hall post room by half past eight in the morning. And, when Agathe arrived for work forty minutes later—she was late mostly because she could think of no good reason to hurry to work—the card was waiting on her desk.

Look at her now. Look at her, slicing her way through the morning's post and then she finds the card. "That's odd," she thinks, "that's odd, that's strange, that's unusual." She picks it up. She turns it over. She reads, "more beautiful than this, more precious, more to be desired, more to be worshipped" and she reads "K." Who is "K"? But it says, "I am your friend." No. No. It says, "AM your friend." It says, "I AM your friend." See that? It's the answer to a question and "K" is for Krovic. "K" is Tibo.

Do you know the word for this? It's "glee."

Look at her. Look at that smile. A bit of cardboard and a few words, that's all it took. So little. And look at her now, turning the card over, looking at the naked goddess lying there and thinking,

"More beautiful than this? Am I more beautiful than this? More desirable?"

Of course! Of course, because the woman in the painting is just blobs of colour on a bit of card but Agathe Stopak is warm pink flesh—the real thing. The woman in the painting was shovelled into a whore's grave in Madrid centuries ago but Agathe Stopak is here now, blood in her veins and breath in her lungs. Look at her. Look at her now, hurrying into Tibo's empty office, to stand in front of the town shield and hold up the card as if to say, "Look what I did at school today!" And she's bobbing that pretty curtsey of hers and saying, "Thank you!" with a smile because she's a good girl and polite.

And now she's hunting in her drawer for a tack and she's pinning the card to the wall above her desk and she's sitting there, just looking at it and that's exactly what she was still doing when Mayor Krovic came into the office looking like a man who thinks he's in a lot of trouble.

But Agathe smiled at him with a twinkle and, with the tip of a shaped and polished fingernail she tapped the bottom corner of the postcard, not so much to straighten it as to draw attention to it.

"Good morning," Tibo said. There was a quaver in his voice. "Lunch? I mean later. Would you like to go for lunch? Later? With me?"

"That would be lovely, Mr. Mayor."

"Good," said Tibo. "Good. Look, I have to go out now so would it be all right if I saw you there—at The Golden Angel—about one?"

"That would be lovely, Mr. Mayor," she said.

"Right. And I'm sorry about the other thing. About before. The friend thing. Sorry."

"I know," she said. "All forgotten." And she gave the postcard another little adjustment with the tip of her finger.

Agathe was already sitting in the window seat of The Golden Angel by the time Tibo came hurrying up Castle Street just after one. He saw her smiling at him through the glass and he pushed through the lunchtime customers to join her.

Agathe lifted her handbag from the seat it had been protecting on the opposite side of the table. "I ordered for you," she said. "I'm getting daring in my old age."

"Good," said Tibo. "What are we having?"

"Same as usual—whatever Mamma Cesare decides is good today."

They laughed and Tibo said, "I brought you a present." He put the brown paper parcel down on the table and slid it towards her. "It's a book."

Agathe gave him a look that said, "I guessed that," and picked up the parcel.

There was a way about Agathe Stopak, a way she had of doing things that made people look at her. She didn't mean to do it—in fact she had no idea she was doing it and, if she had, it would never have captured people the way it did. But, sometimes, she would move or look or just be and she would move or look or be more perfectly, more beautifully than anybody else had ever thought of doing any of those things before. She did it then, lifting the parcel to her mouth as if to kiss the knots that held it closed, gripping the string in her teeth and tugging it open. She brushed her fingertips over the worn gold letters on the front of the book. "Homer." It was half a question.

"You said you wanted one for your house in Dalmatia. When you win the lottery."

"I'm not much of a reader, Tibo."

"That doesn't matter—you're not the one doing the reading, remember. You'll be lying in a cool bath, drinking red wine while I feed you olives."

She smiled and raised the book to her nose and drank in its scent. "It smells like the beach—the beach on a sunny day. Thank you. It's lovely. I will keep it safe until you want to read it to me."

"Now's a good time," said Tibo.

"Not quite now—not with our pasta on its way. But I've got something to show you."

"My turn for presents," Tibo said hopefully.

"Sorry. I haven't got you anything, but you can share this if you like." Agathe opened her bag and brought out a notebook. It bulged, the pages splayed fatly as if there were a thick bookmark between each one. "Look," she said, "this is my house on the coast of Dalmatia. I carry it round with me all the time. This is where you can read me Homer."

Agathe flicked through the pages and showed him the pictures she had torn out of magazines and saved there. "Look, I want big flowerpots like this standing by the front door with lavender and rosemary growing in them and thyme down among the cobbles."

Tibo thought of the coal dust between the cobbles on the road through the docks and the whores and the men in the shadows.

She said, "I used to keep paper scraps like these when I was a girl and swap them with my friends in the playground. You could buy them from the newsagent. I used to like the ones with pictures of fat angels, leaning their elbows on clouds and looking grumpy—like Mr. Guillaume."

Tibo opened the book and pointed. "Tell me about this," he said but, just then, the waiter arrived and put down two huge bowls of pasta.

"Penne picante," he announced and he waved his magician's passes with the pepper shaker and the Parmesan shaver and hurried off.

"That's how I want the fireplace," said Agathe, "big enough to sit in, out of the draughts in the wintertime. When I move to Dalmatia, I'm never going to be cold again."

"I won't allow it," said Tibo.

Agathe almost purred at that. She wriggled a little in her seat and said, "I'll bet" with a wicked smile and then Tibo felt stupid and awkward because she had out-brazened him. He had tried to be louche and dangerous and man-of-the-worldly and she had seen through him in a couple of words.

Tibo looked into his plate. "Eat up," he said and then, after a bit, "It's very good, isn't it?"

"Yes, it's always good here but I could do just as well."

"You like to cook?"

"And I'm very good at it. Not that anybody notices these days." She stabbed at her pasta.

"Tell me what you like to make."

Agathe was enthused and smiling again. "Granny taught me," she said. "I make man food."

Tibo groaned inwardly. "Yes, you do," he thought. "You'd make perfect man food. You are man food." But he had learned enough to say nothing and he just nodded an encouragement.

"Men like something meaty, something they can get their teeth into."

Tibo almost whimpered.

"Are you laughing at me?" she asked. "Food's a serious business. It's how you show somebody that you love them. Well," she looked into her plate again, "one of the ways. Finding just the right ingredients, choosing a nice bit of meat and cooking it right and serving it up nicely on a nice table. That's a nice thing to do for somebody. It shows you care. It's kind."

Tibo knew that you can be cruel to someone without doing anything at all, without hitting them or shouting at them but simply by denying them the chance to be kind. He put his hand on Agathe's. "What would you cook me?"

She thought for a moment and said, "I would cook you fish soup—no, beef soup. Beef, and I'd cook you my rabbit in cream and mustard sauce and I'd make you a big creamy rice pudding with plenty of nutmeg and loads of fat raisins."

"I'll get fat as a raisin myself."

"Not if I had my way," Agathe thought. "I'd keep you fit. I'd work it off you, Tibo Krovic, you lovely, lovely man." But what she said was, "Well, you could do with building up and, anyway, you've got a long way to go before you catch up with Mr. Guillaume."

"Quite a long way," said Tibo, "but I don't think I'll bother with pudding. I'm sure Mamma Cesare gives us bigger portions to let us know that we're favoured customers. But you have something if you like."

"No, I'm fine," said Agathe. "I'll make you a coffee at the office."

Mamma Cesare came out from behind the polished coffee organ when Tibo went to pay, smiling and nodding enthusiastically and assuring them how nice it was to see them both and how nice they were to come in and how nice they were looking. "All verra nice. Always verra, verra nice." She beckoned confidentially to Agathe who bowed close as Tibo waited politely out of earshot by the door. "You come see me soon," she said. "Come tonight."

"I can't come tonight," Agathe said. It was a lie. She could easily have gone. After all, she had no reason to stay at home but there was something about Mamma Cesare's insistence that made her reluctant, made her want to rebel.

"Come soon, then," said Mamma Cesare. "Please come soon."

It made Agathe feel sad and ashamed. "I will. Soon," she said.

Tibo and Agathe walked arm in arm down Castle Street through the crowds of shoppers and the office workers trudging back to their desks after sandwiches by the Ampersand or a pie in the Dot Arms.

"I hope you like your book," said Tibo.

"I love my book."

That word. It jangled over the noise of the street like the sound of coins falling from a pocket or a baby crying. It was just a word, spoken on a busy street but it deserved more coming after it than "my book." It deserved less coming after it. One word, not two. "I love my book," Agathe said again. It was the only way to drown out the noise of it.

"I love your book too."

She looked at him, wondering, waiting for him to say something else.

"You know," he said, "your book—the one with your house in it."

"Oh," she said.

"I think it's lovely—your book."

"Yes, I like it." She sounded disappointed somehow. "I can

carry my whole house around with me and my lottery tickets inside. I take them out and look at them. Warm my hands on them. It's a little glow of hope folded up in my handbag."

If Tibo felt the sadness of that, he showed no sign. He said, "You offered to let me share it. I'd like to, if I may. I'd like to find things that you like and help to build your house for you—until you win the lottery and the real one comes along. If you'd like that."

"I'd like that," she said and they were back in City Square.

LIFE WAS LUNCHES AFTER THAT. THEY spent their mornings looking forward to lunchtime and, all afternoon, they laughed about what they had laughed about at the table. They went for lunch and laughed and talked about everything. They talked about books and Tibo was an expert on books. He had read everything and he shared what he knew with her. They talked about food and Agathe was an expert on food. Whatever they ate at The Golden Angel, she could make better at home. Soon she was filling her blue enamel lunch box with good things for Tibo to heat up in his own kitchen. No more herring and potatoes for him. They talked about life and sadness and loneliness and each found that the other was an expert. But each was expert in a different field. Tibo knew the loneliness of being alone, Agathe knew the loneliness of being with another.

Tibo brought her gifts—stupid, silly things that he thought would please her—books that he thought she would like, boxes of Turkish delight—she held the firm pink pieces between two fingers and enveloped them with her lips for his entertainment—treasures from the dusty back rooms of the junk shops of Dot, meaningless nothings that meant everything. Almost every day, Tibo had some little present for her.

Every month he bought her another strip of lottery tickets and, every month, she failed to win a penny. But that didn't matter. They sat together in The Golden Angel at lunchtime and made plans anyway. They pondered over maps of the coast of Dalmatia from an old Baedeker which Tibo had dug out of a box in a bookshop on Walpurnia Street. They squandered endless napkins on drawing and redrawing plans of the house which Agathe would build with her lottery winnings. Here would be the bathroom, no, here, opening on to a loggia with a view down to the bay and the cliffs in the background. The kitchen should be so and the sitting room here with a fireplace big enough to sit in, in case of a hard winter, and a store for the olives and a library for the Homer. Sometimes Tibo arrived at The Golden Angel with pictures torn from catalogues and they would discuss how to furnish the house. It grew in their minds into a low range of white buildings under red clay tiles with broad, shaded eaves over a verandah facing south.

Inside there were huge comfortable leather sofas, imported at great expense from the gentlemen's clubs of London where they had been seasoned for a century with good cigar smoke and brandy spills. Bright Afghan rugs littered the floors. Double doors of etched glass in gilded rococo frames—stolen from The Golden Angel—led from the sitting room directly into a bedroom furnished with a sleigh bed, where the walls were hung with cabbage rose paper and layers of muslin, swagged over the window, softened the glare of the summer sun. Lingering over creamy ravioli, they chose white cotton bedlinen and they selected a range of simple napery for the table, but they rejected crystal. Agathe picked up one of the thick pressed-glass tumblers from the cafe table. The sun shone through it with a greenish tinge. After twenty years of use and washing, the tumbler was scratched and roughened like a bit of bottle-glass ground smooth by the waves. "This is what the sea will be like in Dalmatia," she said. "We should have glasses like this. We don't need fancy glasses. We need glasses that will bounce if we drop them—only bigger, to hold more wine. I intend to be in the bath for a long, long time."

The thought of Agathe in the bath, water coiling and folding over her hips, her belly, her breasts, gave Tibo a delicious shiver. That afternoon he stopped at the chemist's and bought her a box of clear scented soap.

In the evenings in Aleksander Street, Agathe cooked things,

wonderful things, man food, and she brought them to work in the morning in her lunch box or in pots or dishes which she balanced on her knees as she rode on the tram. And, when she gave them to Tibo, she would say, "Eat this," or "Good soup," or "Eat this. It's a pie. I worry that you don't look after yourself."

In the evenings, when Agathe was standing at her stove cooking and thinking about him, Tibo was sitting in his kitchen, eating and thinking about her. In the evenings, as he sat down to eat the food she had prepared, Tibo would ask himself, "I wonder if she remembers what she said about food and loving somebody." And he would open the *Evening Dottian*.

In the evenings, when she ladled the stew she had made into the clean dish which Tibo had returned to her that morning, Agathe would ask herself, "I wonder if he remembers what I said about food and loving somebody." And she put the leftovers on a plate for Stopak.

In a strange way, it meant they were together all the time, at work or at home and, all the time, they were thinking, "It's going to happen."

When they walked up Castle Street together to The Golden Angel, they walked arm in arm thinking, "Today, it's going to happen."

When they hurried back through chilly City Square to an empty office, they thought, "Now, it's going to happen."

Agathe, standing alone by her sink, washing the pots, said to herself every night, "It's going to happen tomorrow."

Tibo in his kitchen, wrapping Agathe's newly washed pie dish in a tea towel, ready to hand back to her, would whisper to himself, "I know it will happen tomorrow."

All through the long weekends, when there were no lunches at The Golden Angel, when they lingered long in the fish market or gazed endlessly in the windows of Braun's or wandered pointlessly in Copernicus Park, just on the off chance, you understand, that maybe, purely by chance, they might meet, then each of them said over and over, "It's going to happen."

When Tibo brought her jars of olives—which she did not

like—when he brought her that old torn Baedeker with its maps of Dalmatia, when he sat with her in The Golden Angel, making plans for her house, when he brought her windows and curtains and ornaments to put in her book, when he walked into the room, when their hands touched on the tablecloth, Agathe knew, "It is going to happen."

When Agathe came to work smelling of the special soap he had bought for her, when she opened the box of Turkish delight he gave her and she held a piece between finger and thumb and folded her lips round it and took it into her mouth and looked at him from under eyelids that drooped with pleasure and said nothing at all, when a waft of "Tahiti" drifted through the office, when she walked into the room, when their hands touched on the tablecloth, Tibo knew, "It's going to happen."

And Tibo, in his empty house, where the bell at the end of the path rang softly in the autumn gales and Agathe, lying in a cold bed alone and touching herself with hands she pretended were not her own, both of them said, "It's going to happen. Now."

But neither of them, not Good Mayor Krovic or Mrs. Agathe Stopak, ever said, "Today I will!" Not for more than two months. Not in the fag end of September, not in October, not in November when the decorations went up in Braun's and the mechanical birds were set twittering in its near-legendary Christmas tree, not until December when Agathe began to lose patience.

To tell the truth, Mrs. Stopak was getting annoyed—annoyed and even a bit angry. It probably had something to do with the time of year. It was cold and Agathe always hated to be cold and she hated clumping to work in galoshes instead of the pretty shoes she liked to wear—shoes that would show off her legs—and, of course, December is the end of the year. That upset her. It would mean another year with Stopak, another year with nobody in that bed but Achilles and no baby and no love.

As she walked flat-footed, in cold rubber shoes down Castle Street that morning, Agathe had worked up quite a fury. When she awoke in the flat in Aleksander Street, she had noticed just a small and bitter cinder nestled near her heart but it was alive and glowing and she blew on it all the way into town on the tram. By the time she got to the Castle Street stop, she had added a few torn scraps of "What's wrong with him?" and some thoroughly dried "Is it me?" to the heap and fanned it with a little "Can't he see?" Just before she climbed the green marble staircase in the Town Hall, it started to take light and, when she sat down at her desk, the whole heap was blazing merrily.

Agathe sat down at her desk and threw off her galoshes, letting them thump to the floor across the room and stand there pigeon-toed against the wall, as if an invisible schoolgirl had been sent to the naughty corner as a punishment. And, when Tibo came in and said, "Good morning" in the same cheery way that he always did, she said nothing. Tibo made it all the way into his office before he realised, then he stopped halfway through the door, leaned backwards and asked, "Are you all right?"

"Fine," she said icily.

He came out of his office and stood by her desk. "Sure?"

"I am absolutely fine. What could be wrong? I'm fine."

"Right," said Tibo and he went back into his office and sat down at his desk.

Agathe arrived a few minutes later. She dumped a pile of letters on the blotter in front of him and, with her free hand, she presented a china bowl. "Fish pie," she said.

Tibo took it with a smile. "Thank you. You spoil me, Agathe."

"Yes, I do," she said. "Are we going for lunch today?"

"Of course."

"Of course. Why 'of course'? Were you going to ask me?" And she stamped out of the office.

Tibo got up from his desk with a sigh and followed her out.

She was already sitting down in her chair, thumping a stack of papers into line on her desk.

"I'm sorry," he said. "You are quite right. I have no business taking you for granted."

Agathe "hmmphed" at that.

"Agathe, if you are free at lunchtime, I would be very happy to take you to lunch."

"Right. Yes. That would be lovely."

"Agathe, have I done something?"

She almost had to bite her tongue. She wanted to leap out of her chair and grab him by his lapels and say, "Tibo, you haven't done a damned thing. More than three bloedig months of lunches and you haven't done a single damned thing. Am I invisible? Don't you see me?" But, instead, she said, "No, Tibo. Nothing."

"You're sure?"

"Sure."

"You'd tell me?"

"Yes."

"I have to go to the Libraries Committee now. I'll be there all morning."

"Yes." That was all she said and she didn't look at him as she loaded another sheet of council-headed paper into her typewriter.

"Right, then. I'll look forward to seeing you about one."

ALL THE WAY THROUGH THE LIBRARIES Committee, when the councillors were talking about the number of books that should be replaced that year and what to do with the old ones and which new ones they should buy and whether or not schoolchildren should have to pay a fine if they kept a book out for too long, he was listening with only half an ear. He was worrying about Agathe and thinking about the evening before when he had found, in a magazine, a picture of a pair of china cats with shiny green marbles for eyes and floppy roses painted all over them. Now they were in his wallet, torn out as neatly as he could manage and ready to go in Agathe's book. It would be all right, he decided. Whatever it was that had upset her so much, he would sort it out. He would make it right again.

When, at last, the Libraries Committee was over, Tibo hurried back to his office. Agathe was already gone. He ran down the stairs, pulling his coat on as he went but there was no sign of her in City Square or amongst the crowds on the bridge and he was more than halfway along Castle Street, almost at The Golden Angel, before he caught sight of her, just going through the door.

By the time Tibo hurried into the cafe, Agathe was sitting at the window seat. She saw Mamma Cesare smile as soon as the mayor came through the big swing doors, smile and wave and point to where Agathe was sitting with her chin cupped in her hand.

Agathe found herself resenting that—the way that everybody

noticed Tibo, the way that everybody welcomed him and went out of their way for him, the way everybody brightened if he bothered with them in return. And yet he took it all for granted. He accepted it all. He never noticed that he was wonderful. He never noticed that she thought he was wonderful. He never noticed that she loved him.

She watched him dancing between the tables towards her, bouncing along like a cheerful puppy and so, so stupid. Tibo sat down and she welcomed him with a huffy sigh. He pretended not to notice. She noticed that he had pretended not to notice.

"What's good today?" He smiled. "What's tasty and delicious, apart from you, my favourite mayoral secretary in the whole world?"

"'Tasty and delicious'? If I'm so 'tasty and delicious,' why don't you take me away and eat me, you idiot?" But she said only, "Soup. It's soup. When I arrived, Mamma Cesare said it was soup today."

"Good. What kind?"

"How would I know what kind?"

"Sorry. I just asked."

"Look. I came in. She said, 'Hello.' She said it was soup today. I sat down and you arrived. That's all I know."

Tibo looked hurt. He put on his "wounded" face and shut up. She could see him working things out behind his eyes. "What do I say to that? Better just say nothing at all."

She wanted to grab a breadstick and stab him in the eye with it. She wanted to stand up on the table and yell, "Bloedig hell, Tibo, say something! Notice me." But there he was leaning on his elbow, looking over her shoulder and out into Castle Street. She tutted and rolled her eyes to the ceiling.

After a little time, the waiter arrived with two huge bowls of minestrone, one in each hand, and baskets of bread decorating his forearms and, by some miracle, he managed to put everything on the table without spilling a drop.

Tibo nodded thanks at him and smiled politely and picked up his spoon. "This looks good," he said. It was a plea for an armistice.

Agathe ignored it and bent over her steaming bowl, saying nothing. In the silence, their spoons dragged with a noise like anchor chains.

"Oh, I almost forgot," said Tibo. He leaned back in his chair and reached into his pocket for his wallet. "I brought you a present."

"I hope it's money."

"No, it's not money. Do you need money? I can get you money if you need it."

Agathe shook her head and let her tongue mop up some stray soup in the corner of her mouth. She reached across the table with an impatient gesture as if to say, "Come on, come on," and took the scrap of paper from Tibo's fingers.

"For the house in Dalmatia," Tibo said. "They are ornaments. Cats. China cats with marbles for eyes."

"Yes, I see that." Agathe reached into her handbag and brought out the notebook where she kept her clippings. She tucked the cats between the pages and dropped the whole thing on the table with a thump.

He looked wounded and baffled again, like Achilles when he turned up at the flat with a nice fat mouse to play with and she was less than delighted. It was a bit of paper, just a bit of paper. Why was she expected to ooh and ahh over every little thing?

"We have imagined you a beautiful house," said Tibo, patting the book. He sounded nervous.

"Yes, we have. Do you think we'll ever go there?"

Tibo smiled. Almost everything Agathe said could make him smile these days. "I am doing my best. All those lottery tickets and you haven't won a thing. Not one single jackpot."

"It's not my fault," she said. "You always buy faulty ones. You should take them back to the shop and demand a refund. Anyway . . ." she looked deep into her soup, "anyway I'd be just as happy with a damp little flat by the canal. It doesn't have to be on the coast of Dalmatia."

"You deserve the coast of Dalmatia."

Agathe dipped her spoon again. "I deserve the very best of everything but I'm prepared to settle for something ordinary if it can be mine. Good isn't so bad, is it?"

She looked at him, wondering why he could not see this was the time. "I will settle for something ordinary if it can be mine"—that's what she'd said and, now, if he would only offer that little bit of something ordinary, he could make it wonderful.

But he said nothing and that made her see him differently.

Agathe looked round the cafe at the waiters running from table to table, the businessmen hurrying over their lunches, the people out in the street looking up at the thick grey sky and wondering about snow and she knew that, if she had asked any of them who was sitting there at the middle table of three right in the front window of The Golden Angel, they would have said, "Good Tibo Krovic." But today they would have been wrong. Today they should have said, "Right Tibo Krovic."

Good isn't so bad. Agathe would have settled for "good" and, if he had chosen to do the good thing, Tibo could have stood up right there and then, he could have knocked the table over if need be and he could have picked her up in his arms and run out with her as if he had been rescuing her from a blazing building. He could have saved her. He could have taken her back to the big iron bed in his house at the end of the blue-tiled path with its broken gate and its brass bell and he could have spent all the rest of the afternoon saving her. He could have saved her all night. He could have saved her until he was too exhausted to save her any more. He could have saved her again and again like no woman has been saved before or since, saved her in every way he could imagine and some he'd never thought of until that very minute and then she would have come up with some ideas of her own. But he did not. Tibo Krovic was the Mayor of Dot and the Mayor of Dot had never been known to carry another man's wife down the street, not even if she was his secretary, not even if she was in love with him, not even if she had loved him, it seemed, for as long as she could remember.

The moment passed. She saw it disappearing away from the

tiny point where "When" becomes "Now" and starts streaming backwards to "Then." It only takes a second.

Embarrassed, he lifted the notebook that held her imaginary house and began to flick through it. "What do you think of that?" he said, pointing to a magazine clipping of a huge bath.

"I think it's colourful," said Agathe.

"Colourful? But it's white."

"I think it's colourful," she said, looking straight at him.

And she said it again, so softly that it made almost no sound. "Colourful, colourful, colourful."

Good Tibo Krovic was baffled. He wondered if, perhaps, Agathe was having a breakdown.

"Are you all right?" he asked.

"I'm fine, Tibo." And she spooned up some more soup but she held it a little away from her mouth, not trusting herself to eat it without spilling it. Her hand shook. Her body was shaking. Looking at her, Tibo thought she was about to burst out laughing. In fact, she was a breath or two away from a sob.

"How's the soup?" he asked, pointlessly.

"Mmmmm. Minestrone." Her voice had a sarcastic edge. "You know, of all soups it is the most . . ." There was a pleading in her eyes and, inside her head, she was saying over and over again, "For God's sake, Tibo, look at me. Look at me. Look at me. See me."

"Colourful?" Tibo said.

"Exactly, Tibo, colourful." And she moved her mouth silently again. "Co-lour-ful, co-lour-ful. I wonder why we never invented soup like that in Dot. Why did it have to come from Italy where it's already hot and bright and life is so . . ." She looked him full in the face and said the word again, "Co-lour-ful."

Tibo was reluctant to admit that he didn't understand this game. He concentrated on soup. "We have borscht," he said. "It's good soup. As good as anything the Italians make."

"It tastes like the cold earth. It's like eating a grave. But I am prepared to admit that borscht is at least . . ." She paused long enough to make Tibo look up from his plate. "Co-lour-ful."

"Colourful?"

"Co-lour-ful," she replied, silently.

"I don't understand what's got into you."

"No, Tibo, that's the worst part!"

She said, "Co-lour-ful" silently again, as tears gathered in her eyes, threw down her napkin, fumbled for the handbag at her feet and hurried out of the restaurant.

Tibo had spent enough rainy afternoons in the Palazz Kinema on George Street to know that that, whether he called after her or ran out into the street or sat straight-faced and finished his soup, he was in danger of becoming a cliché. In the seconds that it took to consider which particular humiliation would be preferable, he saw Agathe run past the window and away.

Tibo decided to finish his soup. With the waiter looking on from behind at his reddening ears, Good Mayor Krovic found it took a very long time indeed. He did not order anything else. In fact, without even turning round, he raised his hand and, staring straight ahead through the window, he gestured to the waiter standing against the back wall. "Bring me the bill, please," he said and, when it came, he left it under a little pile of notes and coins—far more than was needed—and walked quickly outside.

It was cold. The first snow flurries of winter were whirling down Castle Street and over White Bridge. They followed him into City Square where workmen were turning off the fountains until spring. Tibo tightened the belt on his thick overcoat and jammed his hat down as he looked across the river to where the dome of the cathedral was disappearing into an angry fist of grey cloud. Although it wasn't two o'clock yet, most of the lights in the Town Hall were already burning. Inside the building, Tibo climbed the stairs to his office. Next door, Agathe was not in her chair. The clock ticked. The wind threw handfuls of frozen nails against the windows. Darkness came on. Tibo left the connecting door to his room open but Agathe did not return to work and, at six o'clock, Good Mayor Krovic cleared his desk, locked his drawer and left for the night. From somewhere down the brown corridor came the clunk and rattle of Peter Stavo's mop bucket. It sounded as far away and lonely as the last crane flying south from the Ampersand in autumn.

At the tram stop, nobody spoke. People in the queue stood wrapped in their coats, tipping their hats into the oncoming snow, ignoring each other as the wind tugged around them until the tram sailed up out of the dark, glowing like a liner in the middle of a night ocean. The tram pulled up, the queue moved forward and the people jammed themselves inside, all except Tibo. He stood at the back of the queue and then climbed the stair to sit alone on the upper deck. Tibo took the bench at the front of the tram and slouched in the seat with his legs flung out, his collar turned up and his hands stuffed in his coat pockets. The wind was at his back all the way home as the tram nudged through the streets of Dot.

Downstairs, the people in the bright tram could see nothing beyond the dark windows but Tibo watched the houses going by, street lamps passing close enough for him to reach out and brush away the little piles of snow that were gathering there, fathers returning home from work, front doors opening into rooms where children played, warm kitchens where bowls of soup had steamed the windows blind.

At the sixth stop, Tibo stood up. A thin ridge of snow had formed across the shoulders of his coat in a line marked by the edge of the tram bench. Good Mayor Krovic clumped down the slippery stairs and stepped backwards off the tram as it slowed and swung past the corner of his street. At his gate, the wind was rocking the bell in the birch tree so that it almost—almost—rang.

Tibo saw it swinging in the light of a street lamp and, for some reason, the word "plangent" came into his head. "Plangent," said Tibo and he swung the bright edge of the bell with the tips of his gloved fingers. It rang gently against the clapper. "Plangent," said Tibo again. He lifted the broken gate and swung it back on its slumped hinges. The blue-tiled path was beginning to disappear under a thin slime of wet snow and Tibo walked carefully, stiff-legged, to the front door. The prints of his heels showed like black bites in the snow.

Tibo did not bother with the lights. He walked down the hall in darkness to the kitchen where he took his coat off and shook it so the wet snow scattered across the floor and immediately began to melt. He put his gloves inside his hat and left them close to the big iron stove where they would be dry and warm in the morning. And then he sat down at the table with a lump of black bread on a wooden board and a plate of yellow cheese. Tibo ate. He read the paper. He decided to go to bed. He lay there, listening as the noise of the wind died away to be replaced by the deep, dark-white quiet that comes with heavy snow. What did it mean? What could it mean? And then it was morning.

Tibo wiped the steam from the mirror above the sink and stared at himself. He seemed suddenly a little greyer. He plunged his shaving brush into the scalding water, shook it and rubbed it on the soap. The mirror was steamy again. Tibo took the towel from his shoulder and rubbed the glass.

"Colourful," he said. "Colourful! Colourful! Colourful!" Then, just as Agathe had said it, Tibo said, "Co-lour-ful." Then, silently, gently "Co-lour-ful, co-lour-ful." The razor slipped from his fingers and rattled into the china basin. "Co-lour-ful." Tibo stared in astonishment as the man in the mirror looked back and mouthed, "I love you."

W*HEN SHE LEFT THE GOLDEN ANGEL,* Agathe ran down Castle Street, faster than any respectable woman of Dot above the age of twelve has ever been seen to run—running like she was on fire and crying and sobbing so her make-up ran in oily streaks down her face. And people who turned to look heard her saying, "Eeeee-uh! Eeeee-uh!" over and over, like a cow with a broken leg. She ran like that, her shoes slipping over the frost-slimy pavement, her throat scorching with sobs, her face a gorgon's mask of tears and snot, all the way down Castle Street, across White Bridge, past the pillar box where Tibo posted her card and right into Hektor who greeted her with an "Oof!" and something cursed. Agathe didn't even see him. She bounced away from him as if she had collided with a wall or run into the side of a tram. She never even looked at him, just staggered a little, sidestepped and carried on running but she had only gone a pace—not even a pace, one foot still high in the air—when Hektor recognised her and hooked her by the elbow.

Agathe spun round like a bead on a string, spun round and collided with him again, her face in his shirt, her head folded between the lapels of his flapping coat, his arms wrapping her, stopping her, holding her up but still she was making that noise.

"Agathe!" There was fear in his voice. "Agathe. Stop it! It's me. It's Hektor. What's wrong with you? What's happened? Are you hurt?"

She rubbed her wet face across his shirt.

"Agathe, are you all right?"

"I'm fine," she said and sniffed with a noise like a choked drain.

"You're not fine."

"I'm fine. Let me go."

"I'm not letting you go."

"Hektor, you don't have to hold me up."

"I'm not letting you go."

Hektor stood there, rocking slowly and gently like an elm in a cornfield, breathing calmly and easily until her breath fell into step with his, until her fists unclenched and her arms unstiffened and wrapped themselves around him, holding him under his coat. "It's snowing," he said. "We should go."

"We should go," she said. And they walked off together, holding each other, saying nothing.

The tram route that links City Square with Green Bridge and comes back in a circular route along Cathedral Avenue to the top of Castle Street is one of the best served in Dot. If they had wanted a tram, they could have found one easily enough, but they walked together through the snow as it fell about them, muffling the noise of the city, sending the people of Dot indoors, drawing down a swirling curtain at every street corner and sweeping the town with frozen feathers that fell into the Ampersand with a hot hiss. They walked like that, hugging each other like sleepwalkers, until they reached the corner of Aleksander Street and the jangle of a broken piano in The Three Crowns woke them up.

"I should go in," Agathe said but she kept her arms around him.

"Should you?"

"I should go in."

"Is there anybody there?"

"I don't know. Maybe. Probably not. Not usually."

"You can come home with me."

There was a groan in her voice. "Hektor, I can't."

He said nothing. The snow fell. The sky was white.

"I can't, Hektor. I can't."

"It's snowing," he said. "Still snowing. It's snowing worse. I should go home."

Agathe was standing there face to face with him, the buttons of her coat brushing his shirt, her face turned up to him, chin raised, nose in the air, eyes closed, snowflakes melting on her open lips, landing briefly on her pale skin and dying there.

Her body and Hektor's were touching, belly and breast and thigh as he tried to wrap her in his coat, holding the flaps of it around her, warming her and protecting her. The scent of her filled him. She was waiting to be kissed. Hektor kissed her. Not hesitantly. Not brushing her lips with his. Not giving her the chance to draw back with indignation. Not hinting. Not fearing. Not asking if this was the thing she wanted to do because he knew it was. He kissed her and he kept on kissing her with the snow swirling about them now and the piano jangling and the smell of the stale beer and the noise of the bar.

"Is there anybody there? At your house?" she asked.

"No. Nobody. Never."

She held him closer, laying her hands flat on his back, under his coat, against his shirt, feeling the heat of him, pressing her face into him, his neck, his chest, his throat.

"Never?"

"No, Agathe. Never." He planted small kisses on her snowy hair, over her forehead, across her eyes, back to her mouth.

"Take me there," she said.

Hektor's flat was close by, just a little further along the river and round the corner in Canal Street. Now, when they walked, they walked quickly, not like people who wanted to linger together, not like people who went unwillingly towards a reluctant parting, but like people hurrying to something they had waited for and longed for, dreamed of for ages. The trees along the black canal held up bare arms to the sky. Snow was piling in the dips between their branches. It had already hidden the cobbles that ran in front of the tenements and smoothed itself over the rusty railings between the pavement and the water's edge and the cascade of downy snowflakes falling all around made the street lamps sparkle like the glitter ball that hangs from the ceiling of the Empress Ballroom in Ampersand Street.

Agathe and Stopak used to go dancing there and, just for a second, she had a memory of a handsome man in a blue suit, holding her in his arms and smiling at her. She drove it from her mind. "Come on," she said and held Hektor a little tighter. "Is it far now?"

"We're here. The green door. Number 15. Soon get you warm."

She pressed her mouth on his again. He tasted of cigarettes. "I'm warm. I'm warm. It's only my face that's cold."

"I believe it." He grabbed her to him and stood for long minutes kissing her and kissing her, dragging his hands over her, skating over her curves, enjoying her. Even through the thick cloth of her coat, the feel of her was something wonderful and the smell of her perfume was filling him. The kissing went on and on, his hands grew more and more insistent until she was pressed against him and moaning deep in her chest, rubbing herself on him, grinding against him with his hands on her as her coat rose up over her hips and her skirt followed it, sliding over her thighs.

Agathe broke away. "No! Not here. Not in the street. Let's get in the house. Come on, for God's sake."

Hektor patted his pockets, searching for his house keys.

"Come on! Come on!" Agathe was shuffling from foot to foot in an eager little dance behind him.

He searched every pocket twice—his trousers, his coat, his jacket inside and out and then he found them, jammed down under his sketchbook and his Omar Khayyám. The books strained the cloth as he tugged them out. "Hold these," he said, passing them to Agathe and stooping to the keyhole. "I can't see what I'm doing." His hands were shaking. "I'm so cold." And there was a tremble in his voice.

And then the door swung open and he turned round, ready to welcome her but she almost ran past him, out of the snow and into the darkened flat, her hand brushing his as she passed. "Show me the way," she said. She had already taken off her coat.

Is it really necessary to say more of what took place then? Is this the kind of story that requires details like that—a record of every last sigh and whimper and groan? "Show me the way," that was what Agathe said. But that's not what he did. Hektor didn't show her the way. Hektor reminded her of the way.

All that he could give she soaked up like a sponge that's been left to dry out on the bathroom shelf all summer long and then, when it finds itself in water again, it absorbs everything, it softens and it swells and it drinks in every drop and then it gives everything back again, willingly. Agathe was like that. Hektor reminded her how to be like that. Hektor reminded her that she had never really forgotten.

All afternoon, they made love in the old brass bed that stood in one corner of Hektor's room and, when they were too tired to make love any more, he went to the cupboard under the sink and brought out a bottle of vodka that shone blue in the snow-light from the window and they sipped it until it was dark, holding the covers up to their chins and talking. And then they made love again.

At midnight, when Good Tibo Krovic was asleep, alone in the house at the end of the blue-tiled path, when Stopak was lying face-down on the sofa with an empty beer crate beside him and the front door swinging open to the landing, when Achilles the cat was trampling a nice, flat circle on Agathe's bed and settling down for the night, Hektor was standing naked at his stove, making a six-egg omelette as Agathe leaned on one elbow, naked in bed, and watched him, smiling.

And, after they ate the omelette and after they drank a little more vodka, while the snow squandered itself silently all night long and the stove creaked and rattled and cooled, they made love.

THEN IT WAS MORNING. AGATHE LAY ON HER back, awake, as she once lay in another life, naked, pinned under a snoring man who half covered her, half embraced her.

The curtains were closed but they were thin and unlined. They fitted none too well. The winter dawn was approaching, the street lamps were still burning outside and every scrap of light was dancing back from the snowy street and through the gaps at the edges of the curtains, through the gap at the middle where they didn't quite fit, through the scalloped bite marks at the top where they sagged on the pole, filling the room with a mouse-grey light.

"A man did that," Agathe thought. "I could fix those. I could make some nice curtains for this place."

She lay in bed, her left arm pinned under Hektor and crooked around him, pillowing him against her breast, her right hand free and twisting his hair in curls around her finger. From time to time, she bent forward, awkwardly, and kissed him on the top of his head and lay down again on the pillow, smiling and whispering, "You are just gorgeous," or "Thank you. Thank you," and, once, "What have I done?"

She looked round the room. Things were appearing in the gathering light, stepping out of the shadows and taking shape—the stove, probably not the cleanest, a large china sink below the window with a cupboard underneath and dishes piled on the draining board, another cupboard (or a wardrobe?), a table in the middle of the room and three chairs round it.

The fourth was at her elbow, pretending to be a bedside table. The dirty vodka glasses stood there and a pack of cigarettes and a box of matches and two books—the books Hektor had taken from his pocket and handed to her at the door. Agathe picked them up and put them on top of the blankets in front of her, one large and black and plain, one small and greenish brown with worn suede covers, all bent and stained and faded. There were gold letters stamped on the spine and on the front—"Omar Khayyám." A nice name. Carefully, so as not to move too much and wake Hektor, she opened the book, holding it in her one free hand and turning the pages with her nose. Agathe was surprised to find poems. Small poems. Lots of them. Some happy ones. Some about love. Quite a few about drink but mostly sad ones. Still, she liked them and decided to read some more a bit later.

She put the book down and trailed her fingers over the blankets, looking for the other one. It was plain and black like a Bible but, where a Bible is thick and squat, this was elegantly proportioned, slim, stylish. Where a Bible has pages that are cigarette-paper thin, these were thick and creamy white. With the book lying flat on the bed, she opened it and picked it up, one handed, and held it overhead, as if to read the ceiling and there, spread over two pages of plain paper, she saw herself, naked. Agathe gasped. She almost cried out. She nearly jumped from the bed but there was a naked man lying asleep on her. Quickly she turned the page. Another naked Agathe. And another and another. Pictures of Agathe, beautifully drawn pictures of Agathe sitting, walking, standing, stretching, running, lying down, all beautiful and all of them, every one of them, naked. Her mind flew to the postcard still pinned up over her desk. "More beautiful than this, more to be desired," that was what it said.

And she realised, "I am more beautiful. I am more desired."

"Do you like them?" Hektor spoke without moving his face from her breast, without even opening his eyes. She felt his moustache moving against her skin and the bristles of his morning chin.

"Oh, God, they are lovely," she said. "Hektor, I had no idea. I never knew."

"Well, now you know. But you don't know the half of it yet."

Hektor made to roll out of bed, putting his knees and elbows down carefully on either side of her so as not to squash her. For a second or two, they were touching again along their whole lengths and she felt him stir. He looked at her and smiled and kissed her nose, then he rolled on, out of bed and on to the floor.

"You hungry?" he asked.

"No. I'm fine." Looking at him Agathe couldn't help grinning.

"Coffee?"

"That would be nice, yes. Thanks."

"I'll make some in a minute. Something to show you first."

Hektor went to the sink and tugged the flimsy cotton curtains off the window. "Need some light," he said.

But Agathe had dived under the covers with a shriek.

"Hektor! I've got no clothes on!" She peeked out from the blankets. "You've got no clothes on! The whole street will see you."

"Don't worry. There's nobody about. People in Canal Street don't get up much before opening time at the Crowns. And it's my house. If I want to go about with no clothes on, that's my business. Now, look at this."

From the gap at the side of the sink Hektor pulled out a large oblong canvas, covered in a torn sheet. "No, I'm standing in the light," he said, "that won't do." He brought the painting to the foot of the bed and held it up. "Don't say anything. Feel," he said and he let the sheet fall to the floor.

Agathe had half expected to see another image of herself but she was unprepared for this. The picture glowed with colour and life and animal heat. It warmed the room with a kind of lust. She could feel it in every brush stroke, a dark longing that Hektor had carried with him for days or weeks or months and caressed and pounded into the canvas. She lay, the painted Agathe, on her right side, her back turned to the room, hair piled high on her head and a few loose curls falling temptingly from her neck. She was stretched on a couch of plump cushions, nestled in velvets and rich silks and putting them to shame with the soft, pale simplicity of her skin. But there was more, for the whole of the background was taken up with a giant mirror in a gilded frame and she lay there, smiling, completely exposed, front and back, every rose-pink cello curve of her wantonly on show.

"It's based on a famous picture," said Hektor. "It's called *The Rokeby Venus* by a man called Velázquez. What they call an Old Master. You probably haven't heard of him."

"Oh, no. I recognise it." Agathe had thrown back the covers and she was crawling along the mattress like a tigress confronting a rival. The painting fascinated her and appalled her. That look, that knowing smile, reflected in the mirror, the hunger in her eyes. How could he have known that? How could he have painted that?

Hektor gestured over the canvas with a finger. "I made the mirror bigger. In the old days they only had little ones and I wanted . . ."

"I know what you wanted—you wanted all of me." Agathe was kneeling at the end of the bed, gazing at the picture, forgetting the morning cold and the drawn curtain and the window on the street. "You wanted all of me." She reached out to brush the painting with her fingers but Hektor danced it away.

"Don't touch," he said.

With the picture gone, Agathe collapsed back on the bed like someone released from a spell. She stretched out on her back and writhed slowly, pouting, dancing to the music of words only she could hear—more beautiful than this, more to be desired. "Hektor wanted all of me," she said, "and Hektor can touch me if Hektor wants."

"Hektor wants."

"Draw the curtains," she said.

Draw the curtains. That's probably very wise advice. With the curtains closed, even those thin and skimpy curtains, there would be nothing to draw attention to No. 15 Canal Street, nothing to startle the pale children with their thin trousers and leaking shoes as they pelted each other with snowballs on the way to the Eastern Elementary School and, if a barge full of coal should happen to be passing along the canal, there would be no reason for the captain to gawp and run backwards along the deck so he could stay level with the window for as long as possible, not the slightest clue that a beautiful young woman was in there, making love with her husband's cousin for, what, the fifth time since lunch yesterday. Draw the curtains. It's sensible advice for the people who read stories, as much as for the people in them. Draw the curtains and wait outside in the snow for a bit until Agathe opens them again, just as she did that morning, all washed and dressed with her hair brushed and her make-up done. And, when she opened the curtains again that morning, the omelette pan was washed and the vodka glasses were rinsed and sparkling and the coffee pot was hot on the stove.

Agathe put it on a tray with a bottle of milk she had found outside on the bathroom window sill, two blue cups and a green sugar bowl. Wet spoons had set the sugar into a solid lump but a few pokes with a fork had broken it up again, more or less. She carried the whole lot to the table in the middle of the room, where Hektor was seated, in his shirtsleeves, reading yesterday's early edition of the *Evening Dottian*.

And then a strange thing happened. That sob which had been hanging around the corner of her mouth as she ate her soup in The Golden Angel only the day before, hanging round and pretending to be a laugh, suddenly came back. Agathe sat down at the table and began to pour the coffee and, just as she did, she started to laugh. And she laughed until she cried, laughed and laughed with two hands over her face, hiding her eyes until she sobbed and choked and wept, until she was doubled over, wailing and beating the table with bunched little fists and letting the tears roll off her face on to the striped oilcloth.

Stopak would have been frightened by something like that. Tibo too, for that matter, but he would have touched her, put an arm on her shoulder, patted her hand and cooed soothing noises until it passed. But neither of them would have understood it or known how to react. Hektor was wiser. He sat at the other end of the table, sipping hot coffee and reading the racing tips, snatching a glance at her from time to time but saying nothing, not touching her.

Even when the sobbing was past, he said nothing. When she lay, rolling her face on the table and moaning, he never said a word.

When she was still and sniffling softly, Hektor made no sound. He kept reading the paper until Agathe dragged herself up from the table, ran the cold tap in the sink and washed her face and took a dish towel from the rail on the front of the stove and balled it into her eyes. Even then, he said nothing. Even then, he waited until the alarm clock on the window sill had ticked out twenty tiny, tinny ticks and only then he put down his paper and set his cup back down on the tray and said, “It had to come out.”

“Yes,” she said. “Oh, God. What have we done? Hektor, what have we done?”

“We’ve made each other very happy—that’s what we’ve done. Well,” he looked modestly at the tablecloth, “at least you have made me very happy.”

She flapped the dish towel at him. “You made me happy too. A lot.”

“I didn’t mean that way,” he said. “Look, I really mean this. If you regret last night, then it never happened. Go to work and say you slept in. Stopak won’t even notice you weren’t home. He’s probably still sleeping it off as usual. Go round the corner, give him his cup of coffee and he’ll never be any the wiser. He won’t hear it from me.”

“Is that what you want?”

“Is that what you want?”

“Tell me what to do,” she said.

“I’ll never do that. Promise.”

“Then tell me what you want to do. Tell me.”

“I want you to move in with me.”

“Oh, God.” She buried her face in the dish towel again.

Hektor left the table and came to stand beside her, holding her by the shoulders and cradling her face against his chest. He said, “Agathe, listen to me and, if there’s a word I say that isn’t the truth, you’ll hear it and know it. I love you. I have loved you from the day you married Stopak and I danced at your wedding. I love you. And Stopak is killing you. Day by day, he is killing you and it makes me want to kill him. If you want to stay with him, you can. If you want to come to me sometimes for things that Stopak doesn’t give you, I won't deny you but I love you and I want us to be together. Come to me."

Agathe said nothing for the longest time and then she sniffed. "I love you too, Hektor. I love you. Oh, I love you."

"So it's settled, then?"

"You want me to come and live here?"

"I thought we'd go to Aleksander Street. Swap with Stopak."

She pulled away from him. "Hektor! No! You're not serious."

"I've worked it all out. He's a reasonable bloke. I'll just explain the situation and he'll see right off that two need more room than one and I'll get him packed up and bring him round here. You don't have to see him."

Agathe covered her face with the dish towel. Shame was burning in her chest like bile. "Hektor, he's my husband. You can't do that to him."

"Look, it'll be simple."

"It's not simple. You'll lose your job for one thing."

"I won't."

"You will. He's not going to keep paying the man who stole his wife."

Hektor took her by the hand and led her back to the table. "Sit down," he said. "You should know some things. Things you know but won't admit you know. You're a widow, Agathe. Stopak is dead. The man you married is dead. He's been dead for ages. It's just the drink that keeps him alive. He lives on beer and vodka like a vampire lives on blood and, as long as he gets that, he doesn't want anything else. I didn't steal you. He threw you away. If I went round there now, I could buy you for a crate of vodka. Your conscience is clear."

But her conscience was far from clear. Yesterday she had been at the middle table of three, right in the front window of The Golden Angel, whispering "co-lour-ful" at Tibo. Today she was in a flat in Canal Street, telling her husband's cousin that she loved him. "There's more. Things you should know," she said.

"I don't want to know a damned thing. What's past is past. My mum told me, 'It doesn't matter who was first as long as you're the last.' That's all that counts. So I'll go round there and tell Stopak what's what and we'll go off and paint some houses and, tonight, you come home as usual."

"Oh, God, Hektor, I can't. I can't. I can't. Let me come home here to you. I can't go back there. There's the neighbours and Mrs. Oktar in the shop. I can't. I can't. But I love you. I do love you. I love you. Let me come here. Please."

He nodded and held her hand and kissed the tips of her fingers. "If that's what you want, come here—if that's what you want."

She was happy then and smiled and kissed him some more—little kisses over his eyes and his nose and long ones on the mouth. "I love you," she said. "You know. You'll laugh. Don't laugh. You'll think this is silly but it's not. A long time ago—I was thinking about this in bed last night when you were snoring . . ."

"I don't snore."

"Yes, you do." And she kissed him again. "While you were snoring, I was thinking and I remembered, a long time ago, this old lady I know told my fortune and she"—kiss—"told"—kiss—"me"—kiss—"that I would"—kiss—"journey over water"—kiss—"and meet the love of my life"—kiss. "And when I ran over White Bridge yesterday"—kiss—"I met you."

Hektor laughed.

Of course he laughed and of course Agathe did not love Hektor. She loved Tibo. She even loved Stopak a little, in a sad, pitying, regretful, nostalgic kind of way. She didn't love Hektor, but Agathe was not the kind of woman who could spend the best part of a day rolling around in a hot bed with a man if she did not love him. Agathe was a good woman. The other kind can do that sort of thing and just accept it for what it is—a bit of harmless fun, an amusement, a release, the answering of a bodily need like eating a sandwich or going to the lavatory—but a good woman like Agathe would shrink from something like that with a black-burning shame, the way that a slug shrinks from salt. It was an impossibility. It was literally unthinkable for her. She simply could not have formed that idea in her head so, out of gentleness and kindness and to protect her from the agony of madness, her mind embraced another, equally impossible impossibility—Hektor was the love of her life.

It's not so unbelievable. Each of us makes up stories to help us make sense of the way things are. From the strange process in our brains that turns the world right-side up although everybody knows our eyes see it upside down, to the charming belief that "everything will work out fine in the end," from the hopeful phantoms that linger round lottery kiosks to the lasting conviction that, if only our fathers had been a little nicer or if only we had studied a little harder for that exam or if only we had worn the other tie to that interview, everything would be all right now—everybody does it.

Human beings have an almost limitless capacity to delude themselves—a tenacious ability to deny the blindingly obvious, a heartbreakingly lovely talent for believing in something rather nicer than whatever it is that is staring them, baldly, in the face, right the way up to the clanging doors of "the shower block." And what a great blessing that is. It's what makes us write poems. It's what makes us sing songs and paint pictures and build cathedrals. It's the reason that Doric columns exist when a tree trunk would do the job just as well. It is a glorious, beautiful, agonising gift and it makes us human.

WHEN AGATHE LEFT THE FLAT IN Canal Street that morning—already over an hour late for work—and waddled, stiff-legged for fear of falling, through the snow to the Foundry Street tram stop, she knew she loved Hektor. She knew it. She knew it the way she knew her name and her shoe size, the way she could point to Dot on the map or bake a cherry cake without looking at the recipe or weighing things out. It was just something she knew, something pointless to deny.

And, when she sat on the tram on the way to City Square, the warm, churning glow of love that she felt rising in her chest and boiling up through her smile was every bit as real as the waves of shame and trepidation that now and then washed over her too. Tibo. What could she say to Tibo?

Tibo, for his part, had already decided what he was going to say to Agathe. Tibo was going to say, "Co-lour-ful." He would say it and keep saying it—"Co-lour-ful, co-lour-ful, co-lour-ful . . ." slowly and distinctly, looking her right in the face. That would let her see that he got it. He had finally understood what it was she was trying to tell him and he wanted to say it back to her. "Co-lour-ful! Co-lour-ful! Co-lour-ful!" over and over again, every day of his life, over and over for the rest of his life. No—for the rest of *her* life, that was the important thing. He was determined that Agathe should know that she was loved, and loved more and loved better than any other woman in Dot—any woman in the world—and know it every day of her life.

"I love you, Mrs. Agathe Stopak," he shouted. "Colourful! I love you colourful." Nobody heard when he said those things because, when he said them, Tibo was standing in the kitchen of his house all alone but he was determined that, soon, the whole of Dot would know it. He had known for ages, of course, for weeks since that very first day when her lunch box fell in the fountain but only now was he free to admit it.

It would be difficult. He recognised that. There would be a scandal. Tongues would wag and fingers too but Tibo was ready for that and, when the man in the bathroom mirror asked him, "What about the mayor's job? Are you ready to give that up too?" Tibo had answered, honestly, "Yes, even that."

"What will you do? How will you live? How will you feed her?"

"I'll find something."

"Not in Dot," said the mirror mayor. "Who would hire you? What can you do? You have risen too high, Mr. Uppity Krovic. No one will catch you when you fall."

"Then we will move. Move to Umlaut."

"It'll be even worse there. You'd be a laughing stock. Front-page news in Umlaut. Don't kid yourself. You'd be lucky to get a job playing the piccolo in a pissoir and, if you did, the city authorities would bring parties of schoolchildren along on educational outings just so they could hold you up as a dreadful example."

"I'll move to Dash and open up a bait stall on the quayside."

"Not exactly the coast of Dalmatia, is it?" said the mirror mayor.

"She doesn't care about the coast of Dalmatia. She'd be just as happy with a damp flat in Canal Street with me. She told me that. She loves me and I love her. I love Agathe Stopak."

Tibo was still saying that when he walked out of the house a few minutes later. "I love you, Agathe. I love YOU, Agathe," trying it out for the sound of it, for the newness of it in his mouth until, when he got to the end of the path and walked out of the slouching gate on to the street, he raised his head from the slip-slidy path and the sky was over him like a blessing—white-bright and pearl-pink in the east, still dove-grey and rat-black behind him in the west.

"Nacreous," said Tibo and he turned left, up the hill towards the tram stop.

At the top of the street, Tibo was pleased to see that the depot night staff had spent their time profitably in fixing snowploughs to Dot's trams. Frozen snow lay in rubbled heaps in the middle of the road but here, and all across Dot, the rails were clear, trams glided smoothly and efficiently, people went to work as usual.

Tibo sat on the top deck again, just as he had on the way home the night before but this time it was a pleasure, not a penance. Wrapped in his scarf with his coat collar buttoned up, the chill wind off the islands meant nothing to Tibo. He looked down from the tram, smiling, swaying through Dot, bright, clean, snow-shiny Dot, the town where Agathe Stopak lived, nodding like a maharajah atop a stately, gilded elephant.

"Howdah," he whispered to himself.

That morning, for the first time in a very long time, Mamma Cesare and the staff of The Golden Angel were surprised, and not a little disappointed, to see Mayor Tibo Krovic striding right past their door without coming in for his usual Viennese coffee with plenty of figs. Instead, he walked a little further down Castle Street and crossed to the florist's shop that Rikard Margolis had run for thirty years, since his mother died under an unfortunate avalanche of tulip bulbs. They still speak of that day in the dockyards of Dot. In exchange for every bloom in the shop—except those urgently required for that day's funeral orders—Tibo wrote a cheque for an impossible sum and gave directions for everything, baskets and bouquets and posies, to be delivered directly to his office as soon as possible.

The flowers arrived in relays, carried down snowy Castle Street in procession by three hurrying shop girls and Mr. Margolis himself. They trotted over White Bridge like dairymaids, a bucket in each hand and each bucket bursting with flowers except for the two runs that the florist made alone when he came, shivering, into the Town Hall in his shirtsleeves with his coat folded gently around rare stems of orchids. "They are very delicate," he said, cupping his hands round the cup of coffee Mayor Krovic offered.

And then, standing in the mayor's office with almost his entire stock filling the room, Mr. Margolis sent his three shop girls back to work with orders to get busy on the wreaths for the milkman Nevic, whose funeral was that afternoon, and he began to build a bower of flowers, just as Mayor Krovic ordered, around Agathe's desk. Before long, there were mountains of blooms covering every surface, jostling round her typewriter, camouflaging the coffee pot, marching in every direction across the floor, standing to attention like a guard of honour to guide her to her seat. And Tibo, poor, stupid Tibo, was so caught up in the thrill of it, rushing from one side of the room to another, handing individual blooms to Mr. Margolis as he snapped off leaves and twisted little bits of soft wire, so entranced by the whole thing, so lost in the sheer delight of the fairy grotto he was helping to create, so eager to share Agathe's happiness when she saw it, so desperate to present it to her "colourfully," that he never even noticed she was late for work.

In fact, Mr. Margolis was just walking down the green marble staircase, slipping his coat on with an exhausted sigh and shuffling towards City Square with four tin buckets in each hand when Agathe arrived at the Town Hall. She held the door open for him as he passed, unfeasibly overburdened with buckets, red in the face and grumbling as he went, but Agathe barely even noticed he was there. And, when he'd gone and she stood inside, just over the threshold, it took the door bumping shut against her bottom on its automatic closer to nudge her forward.

Poor Agathe. She took a deep breath, bit her lip, set her shoulders and climbed those stairs just the way Constanz O'Keefe had done on her way to the guillotine in the final reel of *Passion in Paris* but, at the top, there was no jeering mob baying for her blood, no brutal executioner waiting to bind her hands and force her into the dreadful embrace of the guillotine with a sneer on his lips and ice in his heart. There was something much worse. There was the perfume of a thousand flowers—hothouse roses skilfully forced into bloom in December and chrysanthemums and freesias and big-eyed daisies and dozens and dozens of others, flowers she could not name, flowers she had never seen before, flowers piled everywhere till they filled the room and clotted the air with their scent. And, in the middle of it all, standing alone on her chair, in a simple blue glass bud vase, was a perfect white rose. She bent to pick it up and a plain card, tied on with stiff gold thread, rattled against the glass. It said, "Colourful. Tibo" and there were three kisses.

Agathe sat down in her seat with a bump so the castors squeaked and the chair rolled back a little. She sat there, her handbag hooked over her arm, one hand holding the rose in its vase and she jammed her fist in her mouth and sobbed.

Behind her, the door to the landing closed quietly and Tibo came out from his hiding place there, out from that dead triangle of space where he had been waiting to surprise her and walked quickly to her and put his hands on her shoulders and bent and kissed the top of her head and said, "Shhh, shhh. It's all right now—everything will be all right now. Colourful, colourful, colourful. I understand now. No tears. No more tears. Shhh. Shhh. Oh, Agathe. Oh, my darling Agathe. Colourful, colourful, colourful."

Agathe took her knuckles out of her mouth and let her handbag drop to the floor and put the rose in its vase carefully on the desk. It looked very prim and chaste alongside a stem of violent red lilies draped there, along the carriage of her typewriter. She reached across herself and, without turning round, without lifting her head to be kissed, without saying anything, without making any sound at all beyond a few little sniffs, she patted Tibo's hand where it lay on her shoulder. Just kind and gentle pats, a gesture of quiet and comfort and sympathy.

"Colourful," said Tibo. "Colourful."

Agathe said nothing. She rubbed the back of his hand softly.

"Colourful, Agathe. Colourful."

She said nothing.

"Agathe? Colourful?" He expected her to reply. Hadn't he cracked the code? Didn't he deserve the reward? Still holding her shoulders, he spun her round in her chair to face him. "Don't cry now. You don't have to cry any more. You can be happy forever now—as happy as you've made me." He took her hand and kissed it. "Do you like the flowers? They're all for you. I thought they would be," he paused for half a second to let quotation marks form in the air, "colourful."

Agathe gave a little "snitch" and she felt her eyes brim with tears again.

"Don't cry, don't cry," he said. "It's all right. I know now. Colourful. I know what it means."

"Yes, Tibo, I know what it means too."

"Colourful."

She put her hand up and laid her fingers across his lips to quiet him but he kissed her away like an idiot and he said, "I love you."

There's really only one thing to say when somebody says that and there really isn't too long to say it in. It doesn't take too long before a beguiling shyness or a thrilled dumbfoundedness or a dramatic pause lengthens. And lengthens. Into an embarrassed silence.

Agathe had to look away, shaking her head slowly and closing her eyes and not opening them again until she was staring down at the floor. "There's something I think you should know," she said.

"No."

"Yes. You have to."

"No. Look, it's just silly. There's nothing I need to know. It doesn't matter."

"You should."

"No. Look. Look at these flowers." He trailed his hand pointlessly over a spray of orchids on her desk, suddenly fascinated with them.

She said nothing.

Tibo became engrossed in a pot of daisies. He moved to the other side of her desk and buried his head amongst foliage. "So, you and Stopak," he said, "you're going to give it another go. That's nice. That's . . . Well, I'm glad for you. Really."

"No, Tibo," she said. "I'm leaving Stopak. I've left. I'm leaving. There's somebody else."

"Since yesterday? But yesterday you said . . . Yesterday you told me . . . Yesterday? There's somebody else."

"It's not like that. I've known him for ages."

"And all this time! All these lunches!" Now there was anger in his voice as well as hurt and Agathe resented that. He was entitled to the hurt but she grudged his anger.

"All what time?" she sneered. "All those lunches? Do you want your money back?" She opened up her handbag, emptied it over the flowers that clogged her desk and shook everything out and waved her purse at him like a weapon. "Is it the money that bothers you?"

"Agathe."

"Is it?"

"Agathe. No."

She let her arms fall and slumped into her chair, defeated. "In all this time . . . All this time . . . And after all these lunches . . . What? You never even kissed me."

"I couldn't."

"Today was the first time you kissed me. I was yours for the taking. I wanted you so bad and you could've had me and I wouldn't have said a word to anybody if there was just a chance I could have had one little bit of you to call my own but you never even kissed me until today."

"Today was the first day I knew. I never knew. You never said. It was only today."

"Oh, Tibo, stop it. Not today. Today is a day too late. I'm sorry. I am so, so sorry."

Tibo ducked amongst the foliage again. She saw the top of his head nodding there, appearing through a wall of leaves like a wounded animal, half seen in the jungle. "Can I ask who it is?" he said.

"Tibo, does it matter?"

"Is it a secret?"

"No, not a secret. We're going to be together. You don't know him. His name is Hektor. Actually, he's Stopak's cousin."

"You're not serious!" Tibo hurried round the desk to stand in front of her again. "Agathe, you're not serious. Not Hektor Stopak? Of course I know him. Do you know the kind of man he is? He's got a record an inch thick. He's a waster, a violent criminal."

"Stop it!" She put her hand up as if she was trying to halt a runaway train. "He's not like that. I know what he is. He's not. I know he's not the tenth part of the man you are but he wanted me when you didn't. He was there and you weren't. He's real and you weren't and it's him I love."

"For God's sake, Agathe."

"Tibo, please be happy for me. Please."

"Has he even got a job?"

"Of course, and a house, and he's a great, great artist."

"Good. I'd like to buy his pictures. Where should I go? Where can I get one?"

"You can buy one soon enough. Everybody will want them. I'm going to help him. He'll be world famous soon."

"Soon. Any day. Very soon. Just not yet!"

"Tibo, please. Please stop this. Please, Tibo."

They were tilted towards one another, leaning close, not shouting, speaking cold pain at one another, pleading for the pain to stop, throwing more pain and then, with that last "please," their bodies seemed to spring apart like classroom magnets, like animals fighting in a forest where fear and pain outweigh adrenaline, when they realise that neither of them will survive this, when they skulk away.

Tibo stood and looked out the window. "A day too late," he said.

"Please understand," she said.

"I understand. Believe me, I understand. Agathe, it's the story of my life. I understand. Who could understand it better? All I have ever wanted was for you to be happy. If this makes you happy then it makes me happy. That's what love is, Agathe."

There was very little left to say after that and they sat for a while, crying out to one another in silence, Tibo looking out the window towards City Square, seeing the spot where she sat on the day she dropped her sandwiches in the fountain, looking up to the dome of the cathedral which he was now, more than ever, convinced was empty and hollow in every way, and Agathe looking from her shoes to her hands to the flowers on her desk to Tibo's sad shoulders and back again to her shoes.

Eventually she said, "Tibo, I need you to believe that I was telling the truth. When I said it yesterday, I was telling the truth. You are the same man I fell in love with, the same wonderful man, the same good, kind, clever man, and I will never stop loving you. I will always, always love you."

"Oh, for the love of God," he said. "For the love of God, Agathe, shut up!" And then, walking quickly and carefully in a kind of dance step so he kept his back to her all the way, he managed to reach his office and slam the door.

Now, it may have been because the whole of Dot and everything in it had been poised, on the edge of its seat, for months, shredding at its handkerchief, waiting for Mayor Krovic to say, "I love you," and waiting to see what would happen when he did, or it may have been because a lump of pigeon guano, two centuries in the making, shaped like a bomb and hard as concrete, had somehow fallen off the roof and into the workings of the clock but, whatever the reason, the bells of the cathedral had missed the last two quarters of the hour. And, whether the tension of the moment had passed and somehow released the frozen workings of the clock or whether the clock's massive spring had succeeded in crushing the guano to something like talcum powder by the time they arrived, the team of engineers who hurried, gasping, up the clock-tower steps when the carillon failed to sound, found nothing whatever wrong. A few minutes after Mayor Krovic hurried away to hide in his office, the bells of my cathedral struck eleven, right on time and Agathe pushed aside an arrangement of chrysanthemums that was crowding round the coffee pot, retrieved a packet of ginger biscuits and took them down the back stair to Peter Stavo's glass-fronted booth.

When they had drunk a mug of coffee together and eaten almost the entire packet of biscuits without saying a word, Agathe stood up and said, "Mayor Krovic wants you to take those flowers in his office up to the hospital. Order a taxi. In fact, order two. Order several. There's a lot of flowers. I'm going home. I'm not feeling so good."

The glass door rattled in its frame as it shut behind her and Peter ate the last three biscuits alone. "Poor kid," he said.

PEOPLE ARE CREATURES OF HABIT. WE run along in familiar tracks like the trams of Dot, sometimes leaning over a bit on the bends, sometimes screeching a little or sending up a shower of sparks but, for the most part, sticking to the same routine. And, although Agathe had left the rails she had run in for years and years, she was surprised to find that she kept rolling. She didn't topple over, she didn't shudder to a halt. No injuries, no fatalities, no damage, just a new route, away from the usual tracks, free of any track at all, in fact.

She was not naturally a poetic person but all those things occurred to her when she got off the tram at Green Bridge, just as she had always done. It was only after she had waited dutifully at the side of the road for the traffic to clear, after she had let the tram pull away safely, that she remembered about Hektor and the two extra stops to Foundry Street. "I don't live here," she said and she began to trudge along the snowy pavement, past The Three Crowns and on, towards Canal Street.

She was sad. She couldn't help it. Not even the glow of new love could change that. Agathe could never have walked away from a scene like that with Tibo and not be sad. She thought of him running away, with his back to her. She thought of him closing his office door—a thing he never did—and she knew why. She knew he had been hiding his tears and the thought of it hurt her. "I can't go back," she said. "At least Hektor still has a job and two can live almost as cheaply as one. Cheaper probably, once I get a grip on things. And he won't be wasting all his money in The Three Crowns any more—especially if he can't go drinking with Stopak."

She was still congratulating herself on Hektor's employment prospects when she turned right into Canal Street and spotted him there, carrying boxes into the flat.

Agathe made a face like a trout and said, "Why aren't you at work? It's the middle of the day."

"Oh, that's nice," he said. "Here I am, lugging all your stuff around town and that's the thanks I get. Didn't take long, did it?"

"What didn't take long?"

"For the hot little girlfriend to disappear and the nagging wife to come back."

"Hektor!" She was outraged. After months of use, she found the words "Tibo Krovic would never have said such a thing" ready to fly from her mouth but she swallowed them back like bile. "Hektor, just tell me why you're here."

He picked up a red cardboard suitcase with leather corner bumpers and carried it into the flat. From the darkness inside he yelled back, "Well, it turns out Stopak wasn't as reasonable as I thought he'd be. Told me to get lost—or words to that effect."

"What?" she hurried into the flat after him.

"Yeah. I am now, officially, unemployed."

"No. No. Tell me what happened."

"Nothing happened. I went round there as usual. I made some coffee. I put him in the picture."

"What did you say? Oh, God, I should never have let you do this. I should have done it. It was up to me."

"I wasn't horrible about it. I'm not an idiot. There's no reason to rub the guy's face in it. But there's not a nice way to do it, is there? What should I say? I told him you spent the night here and you weren't coming back. He's not stupid. He didn't need a diagram."

"And he was angry?"

"Let's see, was he angry? Well, he emptied his coffee in my face and punched me in the guts."

"Oh, no. Oh, Hektor, you didn't fight!"

"Sorry, kid, he's a big man. It took me a bit to make him see sense."

"Is he hurt?" Agathe was having trouble revising her loyalties.

"Hey, it's me who got the coffee in the face. It's me who got the punch in the guts."

She rushed forward and started dabbing his face with pouty kisses. "Yes, yes, I know," she said. "My poor baby. But he's such a big strong baby."

Hektor wasn't in the mood. He brushed her away with one hand and grabbed her plump arse with the other. "Look, nobody's hurt. It made a bit of a show for the neighbours . . ."

"Oh, God!"

"And I'm out of a job but that doesn't matter. It'll give me more chance to paint, so it will. And you've still got a good job at the Town Hall. That'll keep us going for a bit . . ."

"But, Hektor . . ."

"And, anyway," he kissed her hard, "I should be saving my energy for seeing to your womanly needs." Hektor kicked the door closed and dragged her to the bed.

That's how things are with lovers—at the start at any rate—and, because Hektor made her remember that, he made her forget that it had once been that way with Stopak too. And, when she groaned under him or on him or beside him, when she touched him, when they whispered, when they screamed, she forgot everything else.

She forgot her job and the awful dread of facing Tibo again, she forgot about going in to work every day to keep them both, she forgot about everything except making Hektor a great artist. She would make him great. She would make him famous and she would do anything that needed to be done, sacrifice anything, fill his table and warm his bed, cook for him, work for him, strip for him, pose for him, lie for him, anything that it took because she loved him and that's how things are with lovers—at the start at any rate.

IT WAS DIFFERENT FOR TIBO. HE WENT FROM place to place, from his home to his office, from his bed to his bathroom, the way that the clockwork apostles moved around the cathedral. He had a route to follow, a job to do, actions to perform but he had no idea why. He had no control and he had no direction, he simply did.

Overnight, Tibo's mind became a numb shriek. He found himself standing on the stairs at four in the morning, unsure whether he had risen unaccountably early or if he had yet to finish climbing the stairs to bed. He stopped eating. What would be the point in eating? Everything tasted like old wood, there could be no joy in it and, anyway, anything that he ate would only be a reminder of other things he had eaten in the past—things that she had made.

With winter deepening, Tibo found himself out of doors more and more. Every day—sometimes twice a day—he walked out to the lighthouse to stand under its sabre beam, letting the storms scour him. Mostly, since the days were so short and there was work still to be done, he found himself there in the dark, the sea roaring invisibly round the jumbled rocks at his feet and clawing its way viciously towards him in mountains of yellow spume where the lighthouse beam passed. But, sometimes, he found himself there in the daytime, fitting his breathing to the turning of the huge lenses he could hear grinding round on their mechanism at the top of the tower or fighting to match his heartbeat to the crash and suck of the waves. Everything became a reminder of Agathe.

Everything was a metaphor for her. The lamp of the lighthouse suddenly extinguished or moved a few yards to one side would leave poor mariners helpless or guide them blindly straight to destruction. The Pole Star shifted. Everything that had been true was a lie, everything that had been solid was a phantom. Standing there, for hours at a time, Tibo tore and shredded at himself. The same anger, the same hurt beat through his veins again and again, driven round by his broken heart. "How could she do this to me when she said she loved me? She does love me—she said that again—she cares. So how could she hurt me this way? So she lied. She's a liar and a whore. But how could I fall for a liar and a whore? What kind of idiot does that make me? If I can't spot a liar and a whore like that, what good am I? Maybe I've stuffed the accounts department with crooks and thieves. If Agathe is a liar and a whore, then nothing is real, nothing makes sense, nothing is certain. So she isn't. She can't be. Agathe is a good woman. So how could she do this to me?" On and on, over and over, in time with the angry waves that gasped a tempting invitation at his feet. Tibo stepped back from the edge, walked slowly backwards until he was pressed against the solid bulk of the lighthouse and waited there, in the rain, until the rhythm in his blood subsided.

"I will not," he said. "I will not. I am Tibo Krovic, the Mayor of Dot. I will not go mad. I will not go mad." Again and again he said it, louder and louder until he roared down the waves and the gulls rose up in terror and yackled at him and then, with his hair soaked flat on his head and his coat flapping in the wind, he stumbled back along the shingle spit towards the docks and home. "I will not go mad." He kept repeating it, like a charm against lunacy. It protected him from the women in the shadows along the dock road and they drew back into the deep doorways of the warehouses as he passed. They are used to dealing with the crippled but they avoid madmen. Sometimes the mad hear the voice of God and it never seems to have a good word for whores and, from time to time, the madman has a knife to help him with God's work. They listened to his muttered promise and let him pass, wondering if they could ever be as certain. "I will not go mad? I will not go mad? Another winter of this and I might."

His daily walks to the lighthouse taught Tibo to love the gulls. In order not to go mad, he resolved to be like them. The key was not to panic, he decided, to be at home, now, in the place where he found himself, like a gull. If a fisherman of Dot found himself alone and adrift at sea, he would suffer and probably die because he felt himself in the wrong place, but a gull was as happy on land as on sea, as much at home on this bit of sea or that bit. If you have no home, it doesn't matter where you stay. It doesn't matter if the waves come in black walls. Just float. Just survive. Be a gull.

At work, where he did not dare to look out the window in case he saw a fountain and where she was, just on the other side of the door, working, smelling beautiful, being Agathe, it was there he began his morning with that insane business of standing just inside the door, listening for the "clump" of Agathe's galoshes when she came in to work and rushing to fling himself on the carpet, squinting through the crack beneath the door for a glimpse of her plump little toes as they wormed into her shoes. A few seconds of undignified wriggling and then poor, good, mad Tibo would sigh and stand up and brush the carpet fluff from his suit and go and sit down at his desk with his head on the blotter and listen to Agathe Stopak, clip-clip-clipping across the tiled floor of the office next door, putting something in a filing cabinet or brewing coffee or simply being soft and scented and beautiful and on the other side of the door and he would sigh and groan and cry.

He tried to be a gull. He tried to make himself float and be at ease in whatever place he was in. Just float. And then the picture came to him of a seagull waking after a storm, waking far out to sea with no sign of land, flapping, rising from the water and beginning to fly. "I have flown the wrong way," said Tibo, "deeper into the ocean and now I'll never get home. All this time, I was flying the wrong way." He put his head in his hands and he began to weep.

Weeping was something Tibo did a lot. At the lighthouse, at home in the big old house at the end of the blue-tiled path or in his office, alone, with the door closed. He developed a facility for it. He found he could weep the way some people can catnap. With a ten-minute gap in his diary between appointments, he could give himself up to grief, let the tears roll down on to his blotter, stop, compose himself and go on with the business of the day. Agathe knew, of course, and it wounded her but there was nothing she could do.

One day, not long after she moved to Canal Street, she tried. She tapped gently on his office door, waited, heard nothing, knocked again and, after a moment, when Tibo said, "Yes. Come in," in a choked voice, she entered with a folder of mail. Tibo kept his head down, apparently engrossed in some report or other, too busy to look up or acknowledge her, not when she put the folder on his desk or even when she took his hand. He froze. His pen halted mid-line.

Agathe knew she had made a dreadful mistake but she seemed unable to prevent herself from making it worse. It was as if there were two Agathes, one standing by the desk holding Tibo's unwilling hand, one hanging from the ceiling and looking on in horror as she said, "Tibo, please, I want you to understand. This isn't about you. You are the same wonderful, lovely man and you always will be and I will always, always love you but I have to do this. I have to. Please, Tibo, try to be happy for me. Try to understand."

He never moved his gaze from the page in front of him. He left his hand lying in hers like a dead fish. He said, "I understand. I understand perfectly. How many times? How often must I absolve you? How many times do you want me to bleed? All I ever wanted was for you to be happy. And now you're happy so I'm happy too. I'm happy for you and these . . ." he swirled angry circles of ink round the pale blobs on his blotter, "these are tears of joy."

Agathe left. There was nothing more to say and she wanted to hurry away before her tears started falling on the blotter alongside Tibo's. There was a pigeon dancing on the window ledge of Rents and Commercial, over on the other side of the square and Agathe stared hard at it through the window, gripping the edges of her desk almost as if she were afraid of falling off. Behind her, she heard Tibo close his office door with a click.

Tibo preyed on her mind. That evening, sprawled across the bed while Hektor sat at the table and drew her, saying nothing, she raged over him. "He has no right," she thought. "It's none of his business. He had his chance. He had plenty of chances. I won't let him spoil this with his snivel, snivel, snivel. Not now I've got a real man." She tilted her head to look at Hektor.

"For God's sake be still," he said.

"Sorry." Agathe moved back to where she had been. "Can't you talk to me?"

"No. I'm working. You think I'm playing at this or something? Look, just shut up."

Agathe sighed and went back to a respectful silence.

There was a spider's web in the corner of the ceiling and three tarry-coloured blobs, two large and one small. How could they have got there? And what about that Tibo Krovic? It offended her that he was so upset. It offended her more that he refused to show it. He should rage and scream and call her horrible names, plead to win her back—hit her even—but he wouldn't. He just persisted in pretending that he wished her well when anybody could see that he was broken up inside. He was doing it to get at her.

"You moved your leg. Put it back. No, the other leg. Now you've moved both of them. Wider. Good."

But it was Tibo's obvious suffering that upset Agathe most. It offended her womanly instincts, all the motherly, nurturing, nourishing, healing urges that she had in abundance. He needed fed. She could feed him. "I could, I suppose. I could. I mean I was ready to before. It wouldn't mean anything. It would be an act of kindness. I could. Once."

Hektor snapped his sketchbook shut. "Keep still," he said. "Stay absolutely still. Hold it. I want you exactly like that with just that look on your face." He tossed his trousers over the bed and leapt on her.

THE NEXT MORNING—IT WAS A THURSDAY and the last Thursday morning of Mamma Cesare's life—Mayor Tibo Krovic went to The Golden Angel as usual, drank his Viennese coffee with plenty of figs, taking his time, then he left a packet of mints by his saucer and walked out into Castle Street.

As usual, Mamma Cesare hurried towards the Mayor's table as soon as he was finished but this time, instead of clearing things away carefully, she took the mints, tucked them into a pocket of her apron, rushed through the swing doors and left Tibo's cup and saucer abandoned on the table behind her.

Outside on the street, Mamma Cesare had to hurry to keep Tibo in sight. She ducked between the passers-by, weaving through the morning crowds on short legs, amongst people she had never seen before, people who were always outside, on their way to work, when she was inside, serving coffee and torte. Their breath hung in the air above her head, whispering, twisting rope-wraiths of steam all the way down Castle Street like the chill reflection of moisture that hangs over a quiet river on summer mornings and marks it out in the middle of still fields or hidden at the bottom of a valley. It was a very cold day. People remarked on it to one another as they went to work and later, in The Golden Angel, they wondered whether perhaps, if Mamma Cesare had stopped to put on her coat, instead of rushing down Castle Street wrapped only in a brown cotton apron, she might not have lived a few years longer.

But Mamma Cesare did not feel the cold when she was running. It tugged at her sleeve to slow her as she hurried down the street, it forced burning fingers into her lungs as she ran, but she did not notice. She concentrated on Tibo, watching to make certain that he followed his usual route, down Castle Street, over the icy Ampersand across the efficiently gritted square and into the Town Hall. Only when she was standing under the broad arcade of square, granite pillars at the front of the building, peeking out, sweeping her eye across the square, up Castle Street, both ways along Ampersand Avenue and back again, watching, only then did she begin to feel the cold winding itself around her, gripping her, piercing her and dragging her down like prey.

She danced a shuffling dance behind the pillar, hugging herself, muttering dark curses in her old mountain dialect, beating clenched fists around her body, blowing on her bent brown fingers until, when Agathe came past, she shot out an icy claw and grabbed her by the wrist.

Agathe clutched at her chest. "Good God, you terrified me!"

"Is a good thing." There was a shiver in Mamma Cesare's voice. "You should be plenty scared. You come tonight."

"I don't know," said Agathe. "I'll try. Look, are you all right? You look frozen. Come in and warm up for a bit."

"Never mind that stuff and never mind 'I don't know.' You come. Long time I'm waiting. You keep saying you're going to come. Tonight. Come tonight. You just better."

Even through the cuff of her winter coat, Agathe felt the little woman's grip like a talon.

"Long time I'm waiting," she said again. "You come."

Agathe looked down at her wrist and tried to twist away. "All right. Yes, if it's that important, I'll come."

"Promise me now. You promise."

"Yes, I promise."

"Ten o'clock. Same as before. You promise."

"Yes. I promise. Ten o'clock."

Only then did Mamma Cesare release her grasp and she turned away and began shuffling on bent legs towards White Bridge without another word.

The icy cold that was already worming its way towards Mamma Cesare's heart had penetrated Agathe too. She felt it as she climbed the green marble staircase, rubbing her wrist and scowling. It hung about her in the office and deepened. The place was chill. The place was frosty. The lamp under the coffee pot was out. Tibo was grey. She saw him hurry into his room as she approached. When she reached his door, it was closing quietly in her face. She raised a hand to knock, thought better of it and went to hang up her coat.

Agathe was still determined to make her offer to Tibo. Not for her own sake. Not that she wanted it but she felt it would be a resolution for him, a full stop, the drawing of a line which she would generously make possible for him. It would free him and, after it, they would both move on. She sat at her desk, behind a mountain of papers ready for typing, clackety-clacking her fingers mechanically over the keys and perfecting the words she would use. "Tibo, I was thinking . . . No. Tibo, I've been thinking . . . No. Have you ever wondered, Tibo? Look, if, just once, we . . . Oh, God."

After two hours, the pile of papers on one side of Agathe's desk had dwindled considerably and the pile of papers on the other side was mounting higher. She was getting ready to tidy up and go downstairs to Peter Stavo's little office for a coffee when the door opened and Peter came in.

"There's a man downstairs asking for you," he said. "Don't like the look of him much. Rough looking. Says his name's Hektor. What do you want me to do with him?"

Agathe sighed and tapped a bundle of typed papers together on the edge of her desk. "It's all right. I know him. I'll come."

He was waiting in the tiled space at the bottom of the stairs, shuffling about with his hands in his pockets, looking untidy and glancing up eagerly as if to hurry her on. When she saw him there, shambling and messy, the thought of Tibo, so neat and quiet up in his office, flashed into her head but, in spite of it, Agathe brightened when she saw him anyway. She couldn't help it and she hurried down the last few steps towards him. Peter Stavo shut the door of his booth without saying a word and made a great show of reading the paper.

"You got any money?" Hektor said.

She was crestfallen. "Yes. A bit."

"Give it to me, then."

"It's in my purse. It's up in the office."

Hektor just stared at her as if she was an idiot. "Well?"

"Yes. Right. Hang on a minute. Sorry." Agathe hurried back up the stairs, asking herself, "What am I apologising about?" but she said nothing.

Hektor was anxious and jumpy when she returned. She opened her purse and said, "How much do you need?" but his hand snaked out and dipped away with every note she had.

"Is that it?" he asked. "It'll do, I suppose."

"Hektor, that's all the money I've got."

He snatched the purse from her and looked inside. "There's the tram fare in there still. You can get home. Whaddya need it for anyway?"

"What do *you* need it for?"

He suddenly chilled. His eyebrows knitted and his mouth formed into a hard line. There was a movement, just a slight twist of his hand that made her gasp and draw back and, inside his glass booth, Peter Stavo dropped his newspaper and stood up.

"So that's how it is, is it? You grudge it. I'm grudged a few coppers. I'm like a little kid, waiting for pocket money from Mummy, is that the story? Have it back. Have the bloedig lot!" And he flicked the money at her with his thumb so it exploded against her chest like a bullet wound and the notes fluttered to the floor.

"No," she said, "I didn't mean that. Hektor, I just asked." Agathe crouched on the floor, picking up the cash but, by the time she had gathered it together, the door to City Square was banging and Hektor was gone. She hurried after him and he had slowed down enough to let her catch him at the corner, by the letter box, just where she had run into him that first day. "Hektor, Hektor," she tugged at his thin black coat. "Hektor, I'm sorry. Of course you can have it if you want it."

He wouldn't look at her.

"Hektor, please, take it."

She made the notes into a bundle and pushed them into his coat pocket. She felt his fingers close around them. She felt his hand make a fist.

"Well, so long as you're asking," he said. "Just don't do me any favours."

"No. No. It's not a favour. We share. It's your money too. I want you to have it." Agathe put her face up to be kissed.

He did not kiss her. "Right, then. So long as we're clear. So long as it's sorted out. I'll be late. Don't wait up."

"Where are you going?"

"Oh, for Chrissakes, Agathe! I'm not a bloedig puppy. I'm not on a string. Is that what you think, is it? That what you think of me? You want another Stopak, is that it? Is that what you want?"

"No, Hektor. No. I want you. I just asked. Hektor, don't be like this. I'm sorry."

"I can't come and go? It's like you think you own me or something. I'm some bloedig toy."

"No. It's not that way."

"I'm not clocking in and clocking out for you."

"No. I'm sorry. I'm really, really sorry. I'll see you tonight."

"Right." That was all he said and he turned away towards the tram stop with his head down and never looked back but, before he was out of the square, she saw him reach into his pocket and hunch over the bundle of notes and spread them flat and count them and shake his head and walk on.

Agathe turned back towards the Town Hall where Peter Stavo was waiting at his open door. "Coffee's about ready," he said.

"Thanks. I'd better get back to work."

"Everything all right?" he asked.

"Fine. I'm fine."

"He's a wrong'un, that one."

"He's not. He's all right." She plodded up the stairs.

At the door to the mayor's office, she met Tibo hurrying out. He had taken the chance to leave when she was away from her desk and, meeting her like that, he was suddenly dry-mouthed and awkward. He pushed a hand through his hair. He spun on his heel to go back to his desk, realised he was trapped, spun round again to face her. He said, "Good morning, Mrs. Stopak."

"You're going to sack me." Agathe's lip trembled.

"Should I sack you? Have you done something that deserves sacking?" He might have said something kinder, something gentler, something a bit reassuring like, "Don't be silly. Why should I sack you? Of course I won't sack you. I love you." But that sort of thing had been beaten out of him—she had beaten it out of him—and now he was more inclined to come out fighting and save himself from more beatings.

"I don't know," she said. "Do you think I've done something?"

Tibo tightened his tie into a pea-sized knot and said, "I'm not going to sack you."

"You called me 'Mrs. Stopak.' You haven't called me 'Mrs. Stopak' for a long time. I thought you were working up to something. I thought you were going to sack me."

Tibo looked over her shoulder at a spot on the wall just on the other side of the passage. "Yes," he said. "Mrs. Stopak, I've been meaning to . . . Well . . . After some thought, I decided that it would probably be for the best if, in the light of the circumstances, we reverted to a more formal style of address. If it's all right with you, I will call you 'Mrs. Stopak' and I'd prefer it if, from now on, you were to call me 'Mayor Krovic' or just 'Mayor.'"

"So you're not going to sack me?" Her shoulders slumped. "Mayor Krovic."

"No, I'm not going to sack you."

"Or transfer me?"

"No."

"I like this job." That was a lie. She hated it. She hated the atmosphere that had hung about the office for weeks, the embarrassment, the pain, the coldness.

Tibo said, "You are an extremely competent and efficient secretary. I can't think of anybody who knows the job better or who could do it as well. Things have been difficult this past while—

there's no point pretending otherwise—but we are both adults and we can find a way to . . . Yes . . . Quite."

His eyes were hurting from staring at the same bit of wall. He might have said, "I have no reason for getting up in the morning except for the thought that I can be near you all day and it's killing me but being away from you would kill me quicker," but he didn't.

"Thank you, Mayor Krovic," Agathe said and she walked on slowly towards her desk. "School party visiting the Town Hall at three o'clock," she said. "Don't forget. You wanted to greet them personally."

"I won't forget. Thank you, Mrs. Stopak." Tibo stumbled down the stairs as if he had been shot and had not yet plucked up the courage to die.

And Agathe, when she sat down at her desk, empty and exhausted, was astonished to see that *The Rokeby Venus* was still pinned up there, a little dusty and lopsided, forgotten. She pulled it down and read it once more. "More beautiful than this. More precious. More to be desired. More to be worshipped than any goddess. Yes, I AM your friend." Then she tore it into pieces and dropped them in the bin. The drawing pin stayed stuck in the wall but it wasn't worth gambling a nail on and she decided to leave it there.

Strangely, though the postcard had hung there, unnoticed, for weeks, that drawing pin seemed to catch her eye all the time and, when it did, the torn picture came back to life—the postcard, the message Tibo had written on it, what it meant, Hektor's version of it, what that meant, what she thought it meant. It was there when she came back from eating her sandwiches in Peter Stavo's glass booth—too cold to eat them in the square now. It was there just before three when she looked up from her work and went to the door of Tibo's office to knock a reminder of the visiting school party, it was there when she sat down again and there at five when she cleared her desk and turned out the lamp.

"Dammit," she said and left.

AGATHE BOUGHT A PAPER FROM THE ONE-legged vendor who stood at his usual spot, on the corner next to the bank, roaring slurred and unintelligible headlines at the passing crowds. He was dirty and a bit smelly, standing there in the same thick coat he wore, winter and summer and wearing a cap that gave off fumes of creosote as she dropped a coin into his hand. "Somebody's baby," she thought. "Somebody's baby. Like my baby. Poor baby."

Waiting in the queue for the tram, Agathe saw Tibo leave the Town Hall, heading for Castle Street and home. She watched him for a moment until he turned his head and looked towards her. Quickly, she glanced down at her paper and buried herself in an article on record-breaking cabbage exports at the docks. She read the headline and then, without moving her head, she flicked her eye back to where Tibo had been standing a moment before. He was still there, still looking towards her. She turned her back and bored into the evening paper again, hating him. "Mr. High-and-Bloedig-Mighty Call-Me-'Mayor' Krovic. My baby, my poor baby."

Her eye caught on "sauerkraut" and she read it, that same word, over and over again until the tram came and the queue shuffled forward.

Spring was still a long way off and the six dim bulbs that lit the inside of the tram turned the windows to blank sheets. The passengers sat ignoring one another, reading their papers, looking out the impenetrable, steamy windows, studying their gloves or pretending to read, over and over again, the coloured cardboard adverts for Bora-Bora Cola stuck along the edge of the ceiling. At the back of the tram, face-to-face across the aisle, there were two bench seats lengthways, along the sides of the tram. Agathe hated sitting there, forced into confrontation with whoever was sitting opposite. She looked down at the floor, she riffled pointlessly through the contents of her handbag and then, at the second stop along Ampersand Avenue, when the conductor yelled, "Ash Street! This is Ash Street!," the tram filled up.

Almost a dozen passengers squeezed in from the cold and damp of the riverside and seven of them had to stand. They shuffled along the aisle, reaching up for the red leather straps hanging from the brass rail that ran the length of the tram and there, right in front of Agathe, looking right at her, was Mrs. Oktar from the delicatessen.

They each did exactly the same thing at exactly the same time. They each looked at one another, they each recognised a nice woman they knew and liked, a neighbour from Aleksander Street, somebody they hadn't seen for a while and they each smiled and they each said, "Oh, hello" happily and then they remembered why they no longer saw one another and embarrassment fell across their faces.

"Mrs. Stopak," said Mrs. Oktar.

"Mrs. Oktar," said Mrs. Stopak.

"Keeping well?" said Mrs. Oktar.

"Fine, thanks." Agathe nodded. "You? Keeping well?"

Mrs. Oktar managed to move her lips a little but, beyond a faint "Hmmph," nothing came out.

There was nothing left to say. Mrs. Oktar pretended to look out the window. Agathe unfolded her newspaper and pretended to read.

"Sauerkraut, sauerkraut, sauerkraut," she read and the tram wobbled slowly onwards as she fumed silently. "She has no business judging me. I haven't done anything wrong. I haven't. I am not ashamed. She doesn't know a thing about it."

Mrs. Oktar's hip was pressed against Agathe's knee. The coarse weave of her winter coat was making Agathe's skin hot and itchy. She imagined the raised pattern forming there, like the mark of a waffle iron, and it made her angry. She tried to make little jerking movements with her knee, enough to annoy Mrs. Oktar or perhaps even dislodge her but not so much as to appear rude or difficult and she fumed.

The conductor was squeezing through the tram, demanding fares, churning change around in a horseshoe-shaped leather satchel that hung from his neck. Mrs. Oktar needed two hands to open her purse and pay him. She let go of her strap and leaned forward for balance, nudging Agathe's paper aside as she picked out a few coins. They exchanged frosty smiles and they arched eyebrows at one another. Agathe noticed, tucked inside Mrs. Oktar's purse, was a coloured card with an image of me on it and she felt a little pang.

"Green Bridge! This is Green Bridge!" the conductor called and he clanged the iron bell.

"This is mine," said Mrs. Oktar.

"Yes," said Agathe.

"You go on a bit further," said Mrs. Oktar.

"Yes," said Agathe.

"Well, bye, then," said Mrs. Oktar.

"Yes. Bye," said Agathe.

Mrs. Oktar gave another of her icicle-thin smiles and walked down the tram for the pace or two that took her to the back platform. And then, just before she stepped off into the darkness and disappeared towards her neat, bright flat above the delicatessen, all smelling of cinnamon and good bacon, she glanced back and found Agathe looking right at her.

"What you did," said Mrs. Oktar, "I wish I'd done it years ago." And she walked away.

The rest of the way to Foundry Street, Agathe sat, slack-jawed, looking at the place where Mrs. Oktar had been standing, wondering at the amazing, unknown strangeness of other people's lives. She was so astonished that she forgot to brace herself for the horrid walk round the corner and through the tunnel to the flat in Canal Street.

Agathe hated walking down Canal Street. Without the coating of snowflakes it wore on her first night there, it had lost its romance. The cobbles were old and broken and dirty, the railings along the canal-side were chipped and rusty and, although she had reported the broken street lamp to the Department of Works, nothing had been done. Somehow, Canal Street never seemed to get to the top of anybody's list and she could hardly go to the mayor to demand action.

Achilles recognised her tread in the darkness and jumped from the window sill of the flat, silent as dusk, to purr round her ankles. She reached down and tugged his ears. "I know, I know. I love you too," she said. He coiled about her feet, running a little ahead and rushing back to her again, making happy "meyowrrs," keeping her company.

Agathe walked hesitantly towards the flat, not trusting her heels on the gritty cobbles and clutching her keys like a knuckle-duster, claws of steel and brass poking from between her fingers, ready for the first drunk who stepped out of the shadows.

Achilles, on the other hand, loved Canal Street. When at last, after a week in the flat, sleeping in the box which Hektor had used to kidnap him from Aleksander Street, he had been allowed out to explore, Achilles had felt instantly at home. Everything that Agathe hated about the place, he loved. He loved its dirt and its wildness, its shadow and its threat. He loved the way nobody—except Agathe—ever bothered to put the lids properly on the bins, he loved the rats that skulked near the drains, the broken-down sheds with their flat roofs—ideal for summer sunbathing—the beautiful lady cats with their question-mark tails lifted invitingly high, the midnight fights and, above all, he loved Agathe. Out on the street, he rolled along with a boxer's liquid stride, walking with swivelling shoulders and easy hips, always ready to spring a flick-knife claw but, with Agathe, he was a kitten looking for cuddles and tummy rubs.

He caressed himself across her calves as she bent to tackle the lock on the door. "Yes, yes, I know. You're hungry. Soon have you inside. It's just so dark here I can't see what I'm . . . gottit!"

The door swung open and Achilles hurried inside, brushing past her the way she had brushed past Hektor as he fiddled with the lock on their first night. But tonight, apart from Achilles, the flat was empty. When Agathe went to shut the door, only shadows squeezed through the gap to join her. She was cold and she was lonely and there was a horrible question forming at the back of her mind that she chose to ignore.

"Come on, you. Let's get you fed."

Achilles lashed his tail approvingly as she reached under the sink for a tin of fish, opened it and tipped it into his dish. He purred a clanking purr, like the distant Dash ferry heading for port, and bent to eat.

"What about me," Agathe wondered. She looked in the cupboard. There was a lump of stale bread lying on its wooden board and a lone egg. "Fried-bread omelette. A very small fried-bread omelette. Nobody ever died of it."

She rubbed the bread with garlic, chopped it into lumps and fried it golden and crispy and, all the time she was doing it and while she beat the egg and peppered it and poured it into the pan, she told Achilles what she was doing, explained every step, as her granny had done, so that one day Achilles might make a fried-bread omelette for himself—if he felt like it.

Agathe slid her omelette on to a blue plate and sat down at the table with the newspaper spread open in front of her. There was nothing to read. Someone had set fire to a sofa dumped outside a block of flats and there was a dire warning from Fire Chief Svennson about the dreadful consequences.

"Small fire, none dead," she told Achilles. "You know, in some ways, I quite like living in the sort of town where something like that can make the paper. If that's all they've got to talk about, we're safe in our beds."

Achilles lay on his back and said nothing. He let his paws flop loosely from the wrist and offered his belly for tickling.

"Yes, yes. I see you, bad cat." Agathe decided to ignore him.

She tried to make her omelette last but, after four quick forkfuls, it was gone. "It's going to take me longer to wash up than it did to eat. You know," she said, "it's a marvel to me that I never found myself in the *Dottian*. The scandal! But then, that's not what Mrs. Oktar thought, is it, little cat? I didn't tell you I'd met Mrs. Oktar, did I? She was asking for you."

Then, because she wasn't in the mood to get up and go to the sink, Agathe turned the page and, in just the way that she would have heard her name spoken across the babble of a party, she saw the words "Hektor Stopak" in the middle of a grey page of print. It was there, inside a black box with "Round the Courts" in big letters at the top and a silly picture of a set of scales at one side.

"Oh, God! Oh, Walpurnia! Oh, Hektor, no!" Agathe slapped a hand down flat over the page and folded the paper shut and then, when Hektor's name and whatever he had done were safely hidden away, she drew her hand out again.

At her feet, Achilles was bunching himself for a spring into her lap. He danced about, shifting his paws a shade forward, a whisper left, judging just the right angle for a leap through the narrow gap under the table, changed his mind and, instead, stood with his paws on her knees, like a baby demanding to be lifted.

Agathe laid him over her shoulder like a stole, stroking the purrs out of him as she stared blankly at the *Evening Dottian* with its front-page advert for the winter sale at Braun's and, inside, tales of abandoned furniture on fire and sauerkraut and something worse. She sat like that for a time, staring ahead at nothing while Achilles, eyes closed and smiling in an ecstasy of relaxation, lay draped over her shoulder until, at seven thirty, the mechanism of the alarm clock ticking on the window sill fell into place with a sharp click. "Time's getting on," she said and she stood up to wash the dishes.

While the kettle boiled and Achilles paced about looking huffy and offended, Agathe counted out the change left in her purse. There wasn't much—tram fare into work tomorrow and that was about all—certainly not enough for a trip to The Golden Angel and back as well.

"I won't go," said Agathe. "I have to go. I said I'd go. I promised."

She tipped the money out on to the draining board and started to count, flicking the coins off the counter and into her palm. There was enough for two tram fares.

"Go there, come back, walk to work? Walk there, tram back, tram to work? Go there, walk back?"

The kettle was boiling. Agathe gathered up the coins and put them back in her purse. "Hektor's bound to have some money left. He can't have spent it all."

She washed the dishes. She dried the dishes. She put them away in the cupboard without even once looking at the newspaper on the table.

She rolled down the sleeves of her blouse and buttoned them and smoothed down her skirt and checked her hair in the mirror and then there was nothing to do until her meeting with Mamma Cesare—and that was a couple of hours away. Nothing to do but read the paper. Nothing.

Agathe went and sat on the bed. She could see the paper, lying, closed, in the middle of the table. She lay down and looked at the marks on the ceiling again. She sat up. The newspaper was still there. She went back and sat at the table again, not touching the paper, hands flat on either side of it, just looking at it. She looked at it for quite a while and then she clapped her hands together and screwed the paper into a ball. The noise of it startled poor Achilles who broke off from licking his bottom and looked round the room with a surprised expression.

"Right, that's it! I can't stay here. Walk. Come on, Achilles, we're going out." And, before the alarm clock had ticked many more ticks, she had put on her coat and hurried Achilles out to the street. But, before the alarm clock had ticked even another ten ticks, she had come back to snatch the balled-up newspaper from the table.

There was a secret in it, something Hektor did not want her to know about, something he was ashamed and heartbroken about and so, Agathe decided, he must never know that she had even bought a paper. It didn't matter that she had refused to read it—who would believe that? Hektor must simply never know. Walking along Canal Street, Agathe wandered close to the railings and let the paper fall into the water. She saw it in the weak light of the street lamps, floating white against the black of the canal and then slowly unfolding like a rose and spreading and collapsing until it sank.

Agathe walked on. She was pleased with herself. She was proud of her resolve. She had made a decision not to pry and she had stuck to it. And she allowed herself a little "holier-than-thou" glow too. Hektor had done a bad thing. She forgave him. Worse, he had tried to deceive her about it. She forgave him. In fact, to protect him and love him the better, she would deceive him and pretend that she had been deceived. Poor Agathe, how little she knew about lies.

IT WOULD BE TOO TIRESOME TO WALK ALL THE way into town with Agathe, too painful to watch her lingering outside The Three Crowns, talking kindly to the cold children told to "wait there for ten minutes," listening for the sound of Hektor's voice at the window, standing with a hand on the door, hesitating and hurrying away when it swung suddenly open. Too painful. Never mind that she crossed the road before she got to Aleksander Street. Too private. Don't linger there on Green Bridge as she stands watching the river passing, lumps of black water throwing back random sparkles from the street lights. Too cold. Try not to notice as she throws a glance up at the warm light of the Oktars' flat on the corner. That's her business.

Don't pester her as she walks along Cathedral Avenue, going the long way to town, from street lamp glow to shadow to street lamp glow. She has her own thoughts and don't intrude when she climbs the stairs up to the cathedral, to stand for a few minutes outside the doors that are locked against her. If she has something to say, it is not for you to hear. Why not walk ahead a little? Wait for her down Castle Street, outside The Golden Angel.

Now, nobody could say that Agathe had hurried to her appointment with Mamma Cesare but, when she arrived, it was barely nine o'clock and she was already cold. She put a hand on the bright, polished handle of the door—so different from the door of The Three Crowns—and pushed into a warm world of light and quiet and steam and almonds and coffee.

It was still busy with couples sharing a late supper after a visit to the Opera House and kids out to impress their new girlfriends with espresso coffees and cigarettes and single men with frayed shirt cuffs who would rather pay for someone else to cook a risotto than risk burning down their own kitchens, but Agathe found an empty table in the corner, far away from the big bay window and she waited there, quietly, with her gloves laid out flat on the table in front of her until Mamma Cesare came over.

"You're early," she said and not in a welcoming way.

"I'm sorry. Does it matter? I've nothing else to do. I thought I'd just wait."

"What would you like?" Mamma Cesare asked.

"Thank you. Just a coffee would be lovely."

"I come back. But we stay open till ten. You want maybe the paper to read?"

"No!" It came out a little more urgently than Agathe had meant. "No. Thank you. Just the coffee is fine."

Mamma Cesare went to the coffee organ and pulled some levers and gushed some steam and squirted some hot water and rattled an old tin jug and returned to Agathe's table with a beautiful, quivering, puffy cappuccino—a cumulonimbus of a coffee—but this time with no chocolate in the saucer.

Mamma Cesare dug into the pocket of her apron, pulled out a little notebook with a leaf of carbon paper tucked under the top sheet and wrote out a bill.

"Oh," said Agathe, "I didn't bring any money."

Mamma Cesare made gimlet eyes and picked up the bill again. "You are guest. Is no charge for guests."

But Agathe noticed, when the old lady went back to the till, she jammed the bill down on a copper spike and dropped a few coins in the cash drawer.

Agathe knew how to make a cup of coffee last an hour. She looked up at the clock hanging high on the back wall behind the counter and she promised herself one sip every four minutes. Between times she would watch the people in the cafe, make up stories about them, imagine their lives, what they did when they weren't watching a lonely evening drip away in The Golden Angel.

It was a game she had played before but somehow, tonight, she could find only sad stories to tell. That man sitting alone had been coming to The Golden Angel every evening since his wife passed away. That woman had decided to treat herself to a night out and, tomorrow, she would go to the Post Office on Commerz Plaz and ask again why there was no letter from her husband telling her to join him in America. That couple holding hands was married—but not to each other—and tonight they would part for the last time and forever.

After a dozen sips Agathe had managed to make herself miserable and then, with ten minutes to go until closing time, the hands of the clock stuttered into place and, like the mechanical apostles up on the tower of my cathedral, the waiters of The Golden Angel glided into action. One stepped briskly to the door, shot the bolts and produced a large brass key which he turned in the lock with a noise like a pistol. The customers looked up from their coffee cups and saw him standing there, barring the door against latecomers, ready to show them out. And, before they had time to feel offended, ashtrays were vanished from their tables, picked-over plates were cleared away with a curt "Finished, sir?" that didn't really require a question mark and tablecloths were brushed decisively. It was an expert operation—efficient, proficient, practised and just a pencil-moustache width this side of actual rudeness. The customers started to leave—the lonely widower, the star-crossed lovers, the deserted wife. As she stood at the door, tying a scarf over her head, Mamma Cesare called out to her, "Tomorrow, that letter comes. You see. Tomorrow."

"I hope so," the woman said and she stepped out into the dark with a brave smile.

At the end of a day of surprises, Agathe took this last surprise in her stride. "I wonder how I knew that," she thought as the door closed, leaving her the last outsider in The Golden Angel.

The waiters went to work, tipping chairs on to tables ready for the morning mop, filling sugar bowls and salt cellars, ferrying the last of the dishes to the sink. Before the cathedral bells struck ten, the cafe had been scoured of every trace of customer, wiped clean, sparkled up and made ready for another day.

"Turn your chair up," Mamma Cesare told Agathe. "We go." And she led the way through that little swing door Agathe had seen on her first visit, into the dark side passage that burrowed into the back of the building. "Keep up," said Mamma Cesare as she bustled ahead.

Agathe turned a corner in the twisting passage and saw her standing there in the yellow light of her bedroom door, beckoning. "Come quick. Come quick," she said and disappeared inside.

When Agathe arrived and closed the door, Mamma Cesare was sitting on her bed, shoulders slumped, looking ashen and exhausted. "Come in. Sit," she said. "Sit here." She patted the mattress at her side and, when Agathe sat beside her on the complaining bed, she took her hand. "Very, very sorry," said Mamma Cesare. "A bad, nasty old woman is what I am."

"No, you're not," said Agathe.

Mamma Cesare patted her hand. "Yes, I am. Not nice to you but it's only because I worry for you."

"Oh, shush," said Agathe. "You don't have to worry about me. You're just feeling a bit low. It'll be better when the summer comes."

Mamma Cesare made a watery smile that said, "When summer comes, it won't find me waiting." But she swung her feet to the floor without saying anything and picked up a big key from a dish on her dressing table. She gave a watery sniff. "Listen, you remember a long time ago, I told you that people tell me things and I listen?"

"I remember, yes," said Agathe.

"I want you to meet some friends of mine. Help me move this." Mamma Cesare's dressing table stood where it had always stood, jammed into the only spare corner of the room, half across a plain pine door. She bumped at it with her hip, rattling the pins in the pin tray, jingling her potion bottles together, knocking over her wedding photo in its worn frame, until it moved away from the wall a little. "Come, come! Help me. I'm an old woman."

"In the cupboard?" asked Agathe. "You want to look in the cupboard?"

"Not a cupboard, silly girl—it's a stair."

Agathe gripped one corner of the table and tugged it forward. It moved quite easily, the way it would for a strong young woman in good health.

"Good. Enough. Now we can go in."

Agathe expected a creak. She was looking forward to a passage hung with cobwebs and squeaking with bats but Mamma Cesare would never have put up with that nonsense. The light from her bedroom spilled through the half-open door and fell on a broad passage, hung with faded red brocade and a flight of curved stone steps rising into the shadows.

Mamma Cesare took Agathe's hand and led the way. "You come and see," she said.

Agathe brushed against a velvet rope that hung, like a handrail, at the wall and, higher up, golden shapes glinted as she passed, tridents and lion masks supporting the glass globes of old gas lamps. Then, as the dim light from Mamma Cesare's bedroom faded to nothing behind her, a rainbow glow grew up ahead—golds and reds and blues and greens, pouring out on to the dark staircase through a stained-glass doorway alive with roses and lilies, swirling with foliage and, at the centre of it all, two faces side by side, one sobbing and one laughing.

"It's a theatre!" said Agathe.

"Of course," said Mamma Cesare. "You were expecting maybe a fish market?"

"But I've lived here all of my life and I've never heard of this place."

Mamma Cesare snorted. "All your life. How long is that? Since the day before yesterday—and you never heard. The day after tomorrow and you forget."

"Can we go in?"

"Can you think of any more silly questions?" Mamma Cesare leaned against the door and pushed her way through.

It was like walking into a jewel box two rooms high and dripping with golden flowers and bunches of fruit. All around the stage, fat little golden cupids were skewered to the walls like butterflies in a case, frozen in attitudes of amazement at the astounding things about to happen on stage, surely, any moment now. Half a dozen rows of red velvet seats reflected back from foggy silver mirrors that hung on the walls, all misty and crackled like a glass snowstorm, and lamps glowed from a rococo octopus of a chandelier high in the roof.

"It is beautiful," said Agathe.

"Beautiful," Mamma Cesare agreed.

"A beautiful, tiny, secret theatre. Who else knows about this place?"

"You, me, Cesare. He pretends he has forgotten."

"How could you forget this? It's wonderful."

"He does. When he is just a little boy, it frightens him so much that he never comes back. Shut the door, lock it up, put the table in the way, pretend it's not here. People do that, you know. People, sometimes, they lock the door and pretend."

If Agathe recognised herself in that, she refused to admit it. She said, "But it's lovely here. Why doesn't he like it?"

Mamma Cesare took a deep breath and looked up at the ceiling. "That first day, when we open that door, everything is black. Everywhere, cobwebs and dust, lying like fur on the floor and hanging down, here, here, here, everywhere old boxes and paper and rubbish. Little Cesare, he runs away and doesn't come back. He doesn't like it. He doesn't like the theatre people."

"Theatre people?"

Mamma Cesare took Agathe by the hand and led her down to the front row. "Here," she said. "Sit here beside me and tell me what you hear."

Agathe listened. The place was silent. "Nothing," she said. She cocked her head and listened again. "Still nothing."

"Maybe later," said Mamma Cesare.

"What am I listening for?"

"You listen. I talk. Me and my Cesare, when we leave the old country, you think we want to come to Dot? What's a Dot? Who heard of Dot? We only know America! You go to America, you work hard, you make lots of money and, one day, little Cesare is President of the whole States American. So we walk. We walk for days and days, my Cesare and me, and we come to the sea and we find a boat for America." Mamma Cesare raised a stern little finger. "No questions. Don't talk. Listen. What do you hear?"

"Only you," said Agathe.

"Use your other ear! Two weeks we are on that boat, rolling round and bouncing up and down, but at least we have calm weather—that Cesare, such a man!" Mamma Cesare laughed until she coughed and coughed until she choked and pulled herself up with a wheeze.

Agathe looked worried. "You're not well. We should get you to bed. I'll make some tea."

"It doesn't matter. Listen. Keep listening."

Agathe nodded and held the old lady's hand. She was concerned. "I'm listening, I'm listening."

"Two weeks on the boat, then, one night, the captain pulls back the covers on the hold and he shows us America. But the police are everywhere, he says. So we go down into his little boat and we row to the beach and my Cesare, he carries me through the waves and everybody is kissing and shaking hands and saying goodbye and then, in the morning, here we are in Dot."

"Not America?"

"Not America."

"Oh, God. What did you do?"

"We work. We work and we work and we work. I wash every floor in Dot, every shirt in Dot, every turnip in Dot and, for three weeks, we are so happy to be in America and then, a little bit at a time, we find out that we are not. What do you hear now?"

Agathe was frowning a little. "I thought I could hear a band."

"I see it in your face."

"Go on with the story."

"One day I wake up and I know the truth but this is what people do. They know things and do not believe them. I say nothing to Cesare but Cesare knows and he says nothing to me. Then, when we are lying in bed, so tired from turnips, he tells. And we cry."

"There it is again," said Agathe. "The band. Can you hear it? They must be out in the street."

"Maybe," said Mamma Cesare. She turned her head to listen and her fingers began to move, as if in time to the music.

"You hear it too," said Agathe.

"Maybe. So you want to dance or hear my story?"

"Story," said Agathe.

"After that, we are so angry that we work even harder. We got a nice room over a little shop. Then the shop gets empty. We rent the shop and we start to make coffee and it's like nobody in Dot ever tasted coffee before. Everybody loves us. And then, one night, late at night, after work, I go for a walk and here is The Golden Angel, all empty and broken and dirty, with its windows all boarded up and the theatre people, they come out and they tell me I can buy this place for nothing because nobody wants it and nobody comes near but I can have it if I clean up the theatre."

"I'd have told them to clean their own theatre."

"They can't. They need me. They know everybody in Dot. They know everything about everybody and they pick me. You know why?"

"Why?"

"Because we are the same. You ever hear of a pogrom? One day, a long time ago, the theatre people hear there is a pogrom coming so they pack everything up, the band and the menagerie and the fire-eater and the singers, all the wigs and the costumes and the furniture and they leave. But they never get to America and they come back."

"They should make their minds up."

Mamma Cesare said, "And you should maybe be a bit respectful."

The glow of the theatre was shifting like a sunset. Overhead, the chandelier was dimming and there was an expectant flutter of golden wings as shadows crept across the walls. It seemed to Agathe that most of the light in the theatre was coming now from the stage, as if the footlights had sighed into life but, towards the back, there remained a murmur of shadows. "They came back," she whispered.

Mamma Cesare took her hand and held her down into the chair. "Nothing to be scared about. I am strega from long line of strega. I have the gift. My boy Cesare has the gift. And you. They like you. They look out for you. They worry for you, that's all."

"They came back!" It was all Agathe could say. She could hear the band quite clearly now, there, on the stage, not far off in the street but right there.

"Shh," said Mamma Cesare. "Same thing happens with them. Bad captain. One day, he puts them down on a beach and says, 'This way for America. With your drums and your performing dogs and your tambourines, you walk a little way and here is America.' It's a sandbank. And he sails away and the tide comes back and everybody drowns—all except for one little girl. This little girl they wrap up in a velvet blanket with red and gold stripes which is belonging to Mimi the Wonder Dog and they put her in a drum and she floats away. Now they come back here to wait for her."

"But she must be dead."

"Don't tell them. It would make them sad."

Agathe was squirming in her seat.

"Sit still before you wet yourself," Mamma Cesare advised. "Look. Just watch. Look."

Mamma Cesare knew the theatre people well. She knew their names and their stories. She could see them clearly but, for Agathe, it was like watching a photograph slipping into a bath of chemicals. Slowly, little by little, the image of them formed on stage, the beautiful dancers with their long legs and spangled tights, the strongman in his leopard skin, the dogs leaping through paper drum skins, the jugglers with their Indian clubs but she looked too long, left them too long in the developing fluid and the image thickened and darkened and disappeared.

"They've gone," she said.

"No. Stop looking, then you see."

"I can't see."

"Well, they see you. They want to meet you for a long time. And they tell me that man, the painter, is never going to make you happy."

Agathe looked down at the floor and said, "I know. I left the painter."

"No, you left the paperhanger. You went to the painter. You think I don't know? You think they don't know?"

On the stage, Agathe noticed the theatre people standing still, no dancing, no juggling, looking out at her. A blue blur, like a moving flame was flitting amongst them, the way a bird shifts from twig to twig and Agathe felt a heat of love and sympathy as it passed.

Mamma Cesare pointed angrily at the stage. "They know. You had a good man and you got rid of him."

"Stopak was no good!"

"Who's talking about Stopak? Look at them. Look at the stage. You think they don't know? You think your granny doesn't know?"

"Granny!" Agathe gawped at the blue light on the stage. "Granny, is that you?"

Mamma Cesare was exasperated. "Stupid girl! That's not your granny. That's my Cesare. You don't see his moustache? Oh, you make me tired. Bed now. Bed. You go now. And remember."

Agathe whispered, "But my granny had a moustache."

AGATHE RODE HOME ON TOP OF THE TRAM, letting the cold wind batter at her as she went and trying hard to make sense of all that she had seen and heard. "But my granny had a moustache," she said, time after time. "My granny had a moustache," until it sounded so ridiculous that she started to laugh and, by the time the tram reached Green Bridge, she had realised that the whole thing was nonsense. It was obviously nonsense. It couldn't be anything but nonsense. She was tired—that was all. Overwrought. A haunted theatre! A spooky strongman with pink tights and iron barbells! Nonsense.

What was so wonderful about lifting the ghost of a heavy weight and, anyway, where would the ghost of barbells come from? Or the ghost of Granny's moustache? The thought of it was so ridiculous that she burst out laughing again but she stopped when the tram turned along Ampersand Avenue and there, coming out of The Three Crowns, she saw Hektor. He was drunk, shambling like an ape with his hands in his pockets, almost bent double to the pavement as he waltzed from wall to gutter and back again. Agathe looked at him with horror and disgust, just as she would have looked at any shabby drunk but then she remembered that she loved him and how ashamed he was for whatever it was that he had done and she remembered how it felt to kiss him and she felt sorry for him. Poor Hektor.

Agathe hurried from the tram at Foundry Street and ran, clippity-clip, through the tunnel, over the cobbles, down Canal

Street and back to the flat. She lay in bed against the wall when Hektor came in, plump and pale and feigning sleep, while he blundered round as only a drunk trying to be silent can.

Even when he knocked over the chair, she pretended not to notice and, when he threw back the covers and came to bed like a falling tree and passed out on his back, Agathe only waited for a moment to tuck the blankets around him and wrap a leg over him and kiss him. The bristles round his mouth had a familiar prickle about them.

"My granny had a moustache," she said and she kissed him again and fell asleep.

She was still there, tangled in him, legs and arms jumbled together as if they had gone to sleep in a paupers' grave, when the alarm clock went off.

Agathe rolled to the floor. Hektor did not stir. She washed and dressed and, when she returned, he had curled into the empty warmth she had left behind, his body filling the shadow of hers pressed in the mattress.

There was nothing to eat, no breakfast to make, nothing to do but go to work, but she needed money and the only money was in Hektor's trousers. He had managed to fling them over the hook on the back of the door before he went to bed and, when Agathe reached stealthily into the pockets, the heavy buckle of his belt rattled against the wood.

"What are you doing?"

"Nothing. Shhhhh. Go back to sleep."

But he didn't go back to sleep. He half sat up in bed, looking angry and sick. "Are you going through my pockets?"

"No. I'm sorry. I just need some money for the tram. I have to go to work."

"Get your own bloedig money."

"What?"

"You don't go through my pockets. You don't do that to a man. Have a bit of respect."

Now she was getting angry. Now she was beginning to feel a little afraid so she calmed herself. "Hektor, I'm not going through your pockets. I just need the tram fare."

"I don't have it."

"But I gave you all my money yesterday."

"Well, it's gone and you're going to have to get some more. A lot more."

There was a dark edge in his voice now, enough to make her worry about how she answered him. "I don't understand," she said.

Hektor rolled down into the bed again, turned away from her so the curl of his lip was magnified through his whole body. "I don't understand. I don't understand," he mocked her in a stupid, whiny singsong. "Look, I'll make this so simple even you can get it."

He threw back the covers and walked towards her.

Even yet, months after the first time, Agathe felt something gush through her when she saw him move that way but, this time, it was different and she found herself shrinking back into the corner by the sink as he drew near, flinching as his hand shot out past her head to grab his trousers from the hook.

Hektor's pockets were sagging and swollen with loose change after a night in The Three Crowns. He jabbed an angry fist and brought up a handful of coins and forced them on her. "Here, take it! Want more?" And he did the same again so that Agathe was left standing there with money spilling out of her fingers and bouncing on to the floor.

She cradled her hands over the table and put the money down in a rough heap. She said, "Hektor, just enough for the tram—that's all I need." And she began picking a few coins out.

"Well, I need more. I need money for paints and canvas and a man's got to be able to buy his mates a beer or is that not allowed any more or something?"

"No, Hektor. It's allowed. Of course it's allowed."

"Right, then."

He was still standing in front of the door, naked, holding his trousers in his hand and Agathe would have stayed all day waiting by the table rather than try to push past him and go.

•

Finally, after a few moments of silence, he put his trousers on.

"I'd better go," she said.

"Yes." She imagined pages of embarrassed apology in that one word—as if he had come to his senses after a drunken party burdened with hazy memory of some shameful incident. He stood aside and even opened the door for her, looking at the floor like a little boy standing in the naughty corner.

Agathe picked up her coat and bag and hurried past him.

"Wait a minute!"

Her heart sank.

"Don't I get a kiss?"

She turned back. "'Course you get a kiss." She kissed him.

"A proper kiss."

She kissed him again, right there on the doorstep and he tasted of bile and dry morning-mouth and unbrushed teeth and he smelled of beer and old cigarettes and sweat and man and she wanted more and more of him until he had to push her off and say, "Go. Go to work or come back to bed."

"Work," she said. "Money for paints."

All the way to work, running up Canal Street, waiting at the tram stop, jostling along Ampersand Avenue on the top deck, Agathe had the taste of him in her mouth. She searched it out on the tip of her tongue, tracing every fragment of it and wondering what it was that made her afraid of Hektor and yet more afraid to pull away. She had never been afraid of Stopak—not once in all those years—and she could think of nothing about Mayor Tibo Krovic that would ever make her frightened. But Hektor did. There was something. Maybe because he was a man, a real man, a man's man, the kind of man she'd never known before. But such a boy too. A little boy ashamed to tell her the truth about what he had done and why he needed the money. "Silly boy," she thought. She would pay his fines and be glad to do it and he need never even say, "Thank you." Just knowing—that would be her reward.

Agathe was smiling when she stepped off the tram and walked into the Town Hall. The morning mail was waiting on her desk ready for sorting—a heap of ordinary-looking letters for Mayor

Krovic, a grey cardboard file from the Town Clerk, a couple of tender documents to do with roof repairs at the abattoir and, underneath it all, placed in the middle of her desk before the mail boy arrived, a sheet of paper with the Mayor's handwriting. It said, "There is a note on the door of The Golden Angel saying 'Closed due to bereavement.' Please find out what's happened and if there is anything we can do." And it was signed "K."

THREE YEARS HAVE CHANGED A LOT OF things in The Golden Angel. The little wedding photo in its finger-worn frame, the one that used to stand on Mamma Cesare's dressing table, hangs now in a place of honour in the parlour. And above it is a larger one in an ornate frame of gold showing a middle-aged man with suspiciously black hair and a dark-eyed woman in a jelly mould of a dress. It is Cesare and Maria, his much younger wife who feeds him pasta every day and tells him every night that she likes Dot, even if it is cold and far from the old country.

Maria has not come alone. There is little Cesare now—he can almost climb out of his cot already, which is good since little Maria will be needing it when she arrives soon. And there are the "uncles," Luigi and Beppo, Maria's brothers, who looked down a dried-out well on a two-goat farm and decided that waiting tables in their new brother-in-law's faraway cafe might not be such a bad thing.

Cesare was astonished at how quickly his reputation as a millionaire businessman had spread in the old country but, he reasoned, family was family and, if it made Maria happy, it would make him happy.

It made him miserable. Luigi and Beppo hated each other and they were fiery—not at all the sort of men Cesare would have hired to stand like Swiss Guards around the Vatican of his cafe. They jabbered at each other from one side of the room to the other and no amount of eyebrow flashing from Cesare could persuade them to stop. Sometimes—thank God Mamma hadn't lived to see it—

he had been forced to step out from behind the coffee organ and speak to them—actually speak to them—before they would shut up. But it never lasted. Before long, they were hissing and spitting like cats or jabbing fingers and jutting chins and biting thumbs in vile gestures which, happily, meant nothing to the quiet, untravelled customers of Dot.

"This won't do," he told Maria.

"Put one of them in the kitchen with me. Tell them it's a promotion. That'll sort it out." And she kissed him.

So, first thing next morning, Cesare tapped Luigi on the shoulder and said, "Good news—you're being promoted. Report to Maria in the kitchen. There's no pay rise."

But it was a mistake. Maria had always liked Luigi better and Beppo knew it. From the time they were little children, when Beppo went out to catch lizards or to watch the men killing a pig or to throw stones at little birds, Luigi was always at home with Maria, making dolls out of a bit of knotted cloth or picking flowers in the orchard and giggling. Now Beppo saw this imagined promotion as another rejection, just one more chance for the two of them to huddle together in the kitchen and talk about him.

Beppo fumed. He started to take a perverse delight in ordering the wrong things from the kitchen only to bring them back and say, "They changed their minds," or, "They say the minestrone tastes like sewage. Luigi must have made it." And then there would be another explosion of babbling and a crashing of plates and a banging of shutters.

"This can't go on," said Cesare. "Our beautiful home has turned into a battlefield."

But Maria just kissed him some more and said, "They are brothers. It'll sort itself out."

She didn't help. She worked hard on the menu and when, one day, she invented a new pizza, she called it "Pizza Luigi."

"What about me?" Beppo asked. "When are you going to make a Pizza Beppo?"

"I will, I will," Maria said, "just as soon as I get enough arseholes for the topping!"

That cost The Golden Angel another cup and half a dozen plates.

"Take them out for a drink," Maria advised. "If they could just sit down over a few beers, they could sort this out."

Beppo was eager to go, even if it meant cutting into his own, private drinking time but Luigi never would. Every night after work, he hung up his apron and hurried back to the little flat he shared with Zoltan, a whey-faced waiter with a thick moustache who looked out at the world from beneath a long lick of dark hair. They never invited anybody round. They never went out.

Cesare wondered what they found to do with their time.

"They play mummies and daddies," Beppo snorted and Maria smashed another cup on the wall behind his head.

"Many a true word," Cesare thought.

And it wasn't very many days afterwards that he came in to the cafe and found Zoltan slouched at a corner table with the mop bucket steaming, unused beside him.

"What's wrong with you?" Cesare said.

"I got a letter. My parents are coming on a visit."

"Why is this a bad thing and why does it stop you mopping my floors?"

Zoltan stood up and leaned on the mop. "My parents hate me."

"And you're upset because it's your job to hate them, is that it?"

"They hate me because I wrote home and told them I was living with a girl. Now they are coming to meet her."

"And you'll look foolish because there's no girl. Serves you right. Why on earth would you tell them such a stupid, cruel lie?"

"So I wouldn't have to tell them something even worse," said Zoltan and he slopped the mop on the floor and began to scrub.

"Get on with your work," Cesare said. He went and stood by the coffee organ and pretended that he hadn't understood.

But there was no pretending when the door swung open a few minutes later and Luigi walked in. To be fair, he looked wonderful and Cesare found himself watching, swivel-eyed, as this dark-eyed beauty, all curls and heels, swayed into the cafe but, when she spoke—"I am Louisa and I'll be working here from now on."—Cesare gaped in astonishment. In fact, he was so astonished that he never even moved from his spot by the coffee organ and "Louisa" walked on, through to the kitchen, with no more than a wave at the smiling Zoltan.

The pigeons on the cathedral dome rose up in a cloud when they heard Maria's scream and she came running from the kitchen, her apron thrown up over her face, crashing blindly into the tables and howling as she went.

Only Beppo was calm. "I knew it all along," he said. "How could you not know?" He went to the kitchen and said, "Welcome, sister—I love you."

Come away from there now. Come away from The Golden Angel and down Castle Street and across White Bridge and through City Square, up the green marble staircase of the Town Hall and into the office of Good Tibo Krovic. See him now, just as you saw him on that first day, flat out on the floor of his office, lying on the carpet, squinting through the gap under the door and hoping for a glimpse of Mrs. Agathe Stopak.

And then, after he has seen her passing by, after he has gazed with love on her little pink-painted toes, after he has reassured himself that she is at her desk and well and close to him, Mayor Krovic can get on with his day.

That day began as all his days began—with standing up and brushing the carpet fluff from his suit and sighing. And then Good Tibo Krovic sat down at his desk and sighed some more. Sighing was an improvement for Tibo—an advance. These days, he merely sighed. He was no longer a slave to helpless, broken sobs. Tibo had learned to adapt, the way that a dog with three legs learns to more or less run, learns always to lean against the lamp post before it pees. He no longer lost himself in unexpected fits of crying. He found that he no longer had to leave notes for Agathe, giving her orders or asking for her help with this or that. He could bring himself to talk to her and his voice stayed calm and level. He could even look her in the face unless, by some chance, she turned those deep, dark eyes on him and he had to look away. But, like the three-legged dog, Tibo was an amputee. Something had been wrenched out of him and it would never grow back.

It was a weakness. He blamed himself for it. He blamed Agathe for it. He blamed himself because, in spite of all his stern resolutions—"I will be happy by New Year," or "I will be over this by my birthday" or "September marks two years and two years is enough"—he found that he still loved her and he hated himself for that. He found himself ridiculous, mourning for years over something which had lasted for months and which he had acknowledged for only moments before it ended. But, he reasoned, that would be like denying a life simply because it was brief. A baby dead in the cradle, a baby stillborn, was still a baby, still to be valued and treasured, and this was still a love, however short.

So the pendulum swung back and he gave himself a pat on the back, applauded his unchanging, steadfast love, recognised it as proof of his own nobility and her weak faithlessness. It was Agathe's fault that he had never healed—her fault that he was forced to endure the daily wounds of her beauty, her scent, her great dark, sad eyes.

And every day, when he was with her and never mentioned his pain, never gave her the slightest clue, never breathed the tiniest recrimination in all those three years, he knew, in his heart, that she took for indifference what was a constant, day by day, act of love. It pained him that she failed to notice everything he did for her but it made his martyrdom all the sweeter, except on the occasional days when he noticed himself glorying in the lash of her coldness. Then he would hold his head in his hands and mutter, "Pitiful," at himself. It was pitiful to find the courage to say nothing now when, three years ago, he had lacked the courage to speak until it was far, far too late.

Tibo endured the usual fantasies of the abandoned lover. He imagined himself dead and yet, somehow, still able to watch and enjoy the delicious, bittersweet sensation of Agathe kneeling by his grave and soaking it with her repentant tears. He imagined, again and again, the day when she would come to her senses and appear on his doorstep, pleading for forgiveness, admitting her mistake, acknowledging him as the master of her heart. And then the joy, the bliss of that moment when he could snatch her up in his arms and kiss away her tears and lead her to his big old bed. Even after three years, Tibo had yet to decide whether the thrill of it could ever rival the sheer delight of slamming the door in her face.

But Agathe was not repentant. She never once begged forgiveness and, though Tibo was sure he read a certain pained sympathy in her eyes, she never spoke a word of concern to him. That was her gift to him when, every day, she longed to pet him and mother him and reassure him but didn't and, instead, stayed distant and aloof because she hoped it would cure him. That was what she did for him and he took it for unkindness.

It wasn't unkindness. Agathe was incapable of unkindness. She meant it as a courtesy. She was offering him the same comfortable, protective blanket of secrecy that she had drawn about herself.

Agathe never said a word about her life outside the office to anyone—least of all to Tibo. She never mentioned the flat in Canal Street, never discussed Hektor or what he had done, never said a word about the last picture he had abandoned, unfinished, or the next he was about to begin, soon, because these things can't be forced and it's not like laying bricks or delivering milk bottles. If Hektor got a job, she said nothing. She said nothing when he kept the money for himself and spent all of hers too. She said nothing when he was out of work again—and he was always out of work again, before too long. She never admitted to the gnaw of disappointment that had settled in her chest quite early on and stayed there, quietly, unless she looked at it, when it would show its teeth and turn into something like fear. She never admitted that—especially not to herself—and she said nothing of the nights and the days and the nights she spent in Hektor's bed, whole Earth turns when she refused to get up for even as long as it took to eat, in case she missed a moment of him. She never spoke of that—especially not to Tibo. She was quiet and private and discreet. It was a protection for her and, from politeness, she offered it to Tibo too, never asking anything, pretending not to know. She was calm and brisk and businesslike, as cold and beautiful and unchanging as marble.

And Agathe was looking particularly beautiful that morning when she knocked on the door of Tibo's office.

"Come in, Mrs. Stopak," he said.

She arrived, bringing drifts of "Tahiti" and echoes of distant angel choirs in her wake and, when she spoke, Tibo concentrated very hard on the tiny mole just above her top lip, a little full stop to her sumptuousness. But it didn't help. His mind was flooded with so many things. Agathe eating lunch with him as she used to do. Agathe naked. Agathe by the fountain. Two snails in tiger-stripe shells he discovered on the lighthouse path, aching their way from one grass fringe to another which they could neither see nor imagine, crawling on over an endless, infinite, horizon-bending vista of gravel, a jagged Pacific of dust which they had three quarters crossed before he picked them up and placed them at their destination. Agathe naked. Agathe walking down Castle Street. Agathe naked. The smell of her, the sound of her, the way she had fitted against him as they stood by the gate of Copernicus Park. Agathe naked. And why? What did it mean? What did any of it mean? Two snails crossing a path and his life without Agathe—which was more meaningless? And why did it matter?

"This morning's post," she said and placed a leather folder carefully on his desk.

Tibo said, "Thank you." But it was automatic—he wasn't aware of having said it and, had he been on oath and facing the lawyer Guillaume, he could not have sworn that he said it. "Just close your eyes and think lovely thoughts," he told himself. But his eyes were open. It didn't work. "To die will be an awfully big adventure"—one silly observation seemed to follow another and Tibo found himself cursing the Library Committee of a generation before. If they had never bought that copy of *Peter Pan*, if he had never read it, maybe life would be better now. Or maybe not.

"There's nothing remarkable about it," she said.

"No."

"The post, I mean."

"Yes, I know. No."

"It was just, I thought. Well, I didn't know if you were . . ."

"Well, I was," he said. It annoyed him that, even now, they could read one another's minds, finish one another's sentences.

"Right. Of course you were. Sorry."

She put another folder on the desk. "Today's diary. Planning Committee at eleven. Lunch is clear . . ."

"It always is," Tibo thought.

"You're opening the new gym hall at the Western Girls' School at 3 p.m."

"Ribbon cutting?"

"And a gymnastic display. Not you. Just the girls. Then there's nothing until the full council meeting this evening. The agenda's in there."

"Thank you, Mrs. Stopak," he said, looking firmly at his blotter and, when she stood still at the other side of the desk, he said, "Thank you," again. Without moving his head, Tibo raised his eyes from the desk and let them linger on her as she left. "Oh, dear God," he whispered. "Oh, Walpurnia."

Tibo busied himself at his desk. There were bits of paper to read, bits of paper to write on, bits of paper to look at for a long time or move round on the desk from here to there, from this folder to that. He reached for a paperclip but the little dish where they were supposed to be was suddenly, unaccountably empty. He opened his drawer. Long experience of desks had taught him that every drawer in every desk in every office in the world contained at least one dusty mint, a blunt pencil, an out-of-date railway timetable and a paperclip. He reached into the back of the drawer and, under two of last year's promotional calendars from Weltz's garage, his hand found a dry crinkle of paper. He had forgotten the postcards from the museum, of course, but touching the bag made the memory come alive again.

There was no reason not to take the bag out, no reason not to look at the card he knew would be inside, no reason not to think whatever thoughts looking at that picture again might bring. But Tibo somehow felt that would be wrong—a self-indulgent picking of the scab which he had resolved to leave alone so he lied to himself and pretended not to recognise the bag's autumn-dry rustle for what it was.

"Well, now, I wonder," he said and stopped. There was no point, no audience to fool but himself and he was not fooled. With the tips of two fingers he slid the postcard from the bag and let it fall on the blotter. The beautiful woman beside a gushing fountain. Diana. The baleful goddess flashing fire and ice from her eyes. Agathe. Three years had not altered her. She was unchanged, unfaded. Tibo sighed. He tore the card in two, then tore it again and dropped it in the wastepaper basket beside his chair. There should be nothing left, he decided, no scrap of evidence that survived, nothing. But even nothing was something. The fact that he had destroyed that postcard was proof of something and it existed now—like the other one, the one he had sent—as much by its absence as it ever had at the back of his drawer. Like the soap he had bought for her, now long ago washed down the sink, like the Turkish delight long since eaten, like the disappointing lottery tickets long since thrown away. After three years, there was still a gap where they used to be, like the shape of a picture faded into wallpaper, the indelible sign of something that wasn't there.

AN HOUR OR SO LATER, MAYOR TIBO KROVIC was saying, "Odalisque," to himself at the very moment when Agathe knocked on the door of his office.

"Mr. Cesare from The Golden Angel is here," she said. "He doesn't have an appointment. I said I'd see if you were in."

"Yes, I'm in," said Tibo.

He stood up and came to the door thinking, "Odalisque, odalisque" silently inside his head, enjoying the plump, fruity "O" and the jagged tang of the "isk" and revelling in how well they fitted her. "Would you get us some coffee, please, Mrs. Stopak?"

"There's no need—he brought his own."

Cesare's head, brilliantined black and bluebottle-sheeny, appeared round the corner of the door. "I hope you don't mind," he said and he offered a square basket which held a stoppered jug, wrapped in cloths, and about a dozen pastries.

"Why should I mind?" The mayor spread his hands in a gesture of welcome. "Come in. Mrs. Stopak, we'll need cups and saucers, I think."

Agathe retreated and returned again with two cups as Tibo settled Cesare into the chair opposite his own.

"You're not joining us?" said Cesare but there was a note of relief in his voice and Agathe made a pretty smile of refusal with a sad glance at Tibo.

Cesare proffered his basket. "Take a pastry. Take two. For your coffee break."

She hesitated.

"Yes, do," said Tibo. "Take a pastry."

His encouragement seemed to make up her mind. "No thanks," she said and left.

They sat there together, Good Mayor Krovic and Cesare, for a few seconds, Cesare half twisted round, holding up a basket of unwanted pastries, both of them looking at the door, neither of them saying anything until "Well," said Tibo.

"Very, very lovely," said Cesare and he gave an appreciative sigh.

And then they seemed to have run out of things to say again.

"Well," said Tibo. "Well, well." And he clapped his hands together and rubbed them, trying to look jolly and unawkward.

"Coffee?" said Cesare.

"That would be lovely."

"Just as you like it, Mayor Krovic, Viennese style."

"Lovely. Yes."

Cesare unstoppered the jug, poured out two cups and raised his in a toast. "Enjoy," he said and then, "Oh, I forgot. Pastry, Mayor Krovic?" He offered the basket. "Some kind of waiter I am."

Tibo tutted generously and picked out a pain au chocolat. "Here, you are a guest, Mr. Cesare. As you are a citizen of Dot, it is my pleasure to wait on you."

Silence again. Munching. Sipping of hot coffee. Mayor Krovic found himself studying Cesare's moustache, the tiny crumb of icing that had attached itself to it, its sleek blackness, the thread-thin line of grey where it had outpaced the dye brush.

They smiled and nodded at one another and munched and sipped and said nothing. The point of Cesare's visit, if there was one, seemed elusive and distant but Tibo was ready to wait. "Business good?" he asked.

"Can't complain. Always plenty to do. But we don't see enough of you these days, Mayor Krovic."

"No, I . . ." Tibo hesitated. "No, I must look in more often. Yes." He bit a lump out of his pastry. It gave him an excuse for not saying more but it took an age to chew and he swallowed it like half a brick.

"And you, Mayor Krovic," Cesare gestured with a stub of cake, "business good with you?"

"Oh, just the same," said Tibo. "Like yourself—always enough to do."

Another pause.

"Anyway," said Tibo. "How can I help?"

Cesare passed his tongue over his front teeth lest any stray pastry should be lurking there. "Yes," he said. "Yes, indeed. More coffee, Mayor Krovic?" He held out the jug. "Still hot."

Cesare shared out the last of the coffee but he left his own cup steaming on the desk and went to look out the window, hands in pockets, rocking on his heels. "Have you seen the new picture at the Palazz?" he said after a time.

"No. Any good?"

"I liked it so much I think I'll go again. Spy story. Elmo Rital, he's the hero."

"He's always very good."

"Yes. Always good."

Tibo put his cup down in its saucer. "Mr. Cesare, if there is something I can do for you then you must, please, feel free to speak."

"It's difficult," said Cesare. "Delicate."

"You can talk to me in complete confidence. Nothing will leave this room." And then, shamefully fearful that Cesare might be about to offer him a bribe, he added, "Nothing legal at any rate."

Cesare sat down again, knees wide apart, head in his hands. "It's nothing like that. Not business. A family matter. I need advice, Mr. Mayor."

"Then we'll talk like friends. Tell me. Start at the start."

Cesare puffed a deep sigh and slumped in his seat. "Mamma—you know she is three years dead."

Tibo shook his head. "Really? So long. It's like yesterday."

"Like yesterday," Cesare agreed. "We miss her every day."

"Everybody does. Dot will never be the same. But you have your wife now. She must be a great help."

"Yes," said Cesare and he said nothing more.

Tibo decided that this was one of those occasions when the silence should be allowed to develop and he reached for a Danish pastry.

When half the pastry was gone and while Mayor Krovic was flicking crumbs from his lapels, Cesare said, "I never, you know, felt happy about marrying while Mamma was alive."

Tibo nodded slowly.

"But when she was gone and I went back to the old country . . ."

"Oh, come on—you've lived here longer than I have."

"I know, I know but, still, I think of it that way. And there was Maria. So young and so beautiful and I brought her home."

Tibo leaned forward on his elbows. "Problems?"

"Me and Maria? No, never. But not long after she came, her brother Luigi arrived and, not long after him, comes Beppo." Cesare began to tell his story, starting with the brothers' feud and the quarrel over the pizza, everything, until he got to, "It's Luigi. He's been sharing a flat with one of the waiters. This morning, Luigi—my own brother-in-law—he came to work . . . My own brother-in-law . . . Maria—she loves him so much." Cesare passed a limp hand over his face.

"Go on," said Tibo. "He came to work and?"

With a great sigh, Cesare said, "And he was dressed as a girl. He says we are to call him Louisa." In the chair on the other side of the desk, Cesare sat with his head in his hands, close to tears. "Mayor Krovic," he said, "I don't know what to do."

"I'm the mayor," Tibo said helplessly. "I'm just the mayor. I'm not a doctor or a priest. What do you want me to do—have him arrested?"

"Could you have him arrested?" asked Cesare hopefully.

"Do you want him arrested? Is that what Maria wants? You came to me for that?"

Cesare was silent. He looked hard at the carpet between his shoes. He said, "Mayor Krovic, I came to you because you are a good man and you made something of your life. You know about life. Tell me what to do."

Tibo felt ashamed and embarrassed. A good man—how often had he heard that? Good Mayor Krovic. Could there be a more terrible burden to bear for any man? He was Good Mayor Krovic when he worked for three days without sleep after the Ampersand broke its banks. He was a good mayor. But a good man? A good man would have stopped working and gone to his old Aunt Clara to save her things from the flood.

The mayor found time for everybody but not for that old lady and when she died of it, died of the pain of losing all her things, Tibo knew he had killed her. Killer Krovic—*that* was what they should have called him. And yet here was Cesare asking for advice because he had made something of his life, because he knew about life. Tibo had had long enough to consider. He knew he had made his own life empty and pointless. He had done it alone and made himself alone and his reward for that was that people called him "good" and asked him what to do. Tibo was affronted. He knew himself to be a fraud and he covered his face with his hands and almost wept. They sat there together, Tibo and Cesare, two disappointed men, both of them ashamed, both of them sad, both of them saying nothing until, finally, Tibo said, "Mr. Cesare, you have paid me a great honour by putting your confidence in me this way."

Cesare wiped his eyes and blew a great, rasping honk into a vast red handkerchief.

Mayor Krovic waited for the echoes to subside and said, "I can't advise you as the mayor. Let me advise you as a friend and I'll tell you this. This is what I know about life. I have learned there is not so much love in the world that we can afford to waste it. Not so much as a drop of it. If we find it at all, no matter where we find it, we should store it up and enjoy it as much as we can, for as long as we can, down to the very last kiss and, if I were you . . ."

There was a knock at the door and Agathe stuck her head into the office. "Just to remind you about the Planning Committee at eleven," she said.

Cesare snuffled loudly. "You're a busy man. I should go."

"No. Stay," said Tibo. "Mrs. Stopak, please send my apologies to the committee. Councillor Brelo can take the chair."

"It'll make his day," she said and vanished behind the door again.

"If I were you," Tibo went on, "I would throw a party to welcome my new sister-in-law."

"It will be a scandal. He'll be a laughing stock. Think of it—the shame, the suffering."

"Are you thinking of his suffering or yours? If he can bear it, I think you can bear it. Life is short."

Cesare used his handkerchief noisily again and dabbed at his eyes. He said, "I knew I was right to come to you, Mayor Krovic. You are a man who knows about life but I never knew it had cost you so much to study."

Tibo suddenly found his blotter deeply engrossing again.

"No, no. Listen to me," Cesare said. "A moment ago we spoke as friends. Let me speak now, as your friend. I am an ordinary man and I'm getting old. But I am strega from a long line of strega. Why should a beautiful girl like Maria marry a man like me? Because I made a love charm, that's why. I can do the same for you. Just a few hairs from a comb, that's all it needs. So easy."

Still looking down at his blotter, Tibo snorted. It was a ludicrous notion. Maria loved Cesare for the man he was or, maybe, for the life he could give her—not for some stupid spell and, anyway, he didn't want a love potion. Tibo wanted a curse—some vicious, vitriolic, vengeful curse, something to make her suffer as he had suffered, something that would hurt and gnaw and never, ever go away.

"I can do that too," said Cesare.

"Do what?"

"What you said."

"Mr. Cesare, I didn't say anything."

"No, Mayor Krovic, as you said—nothing. Anyway, I should be going. You are a busy man and I have a business to run and a party to organise, thanks to you."

They walked together down the green marble staircase and shook hands in City Square, saying their goodbyes politely with no mention of spells.

But, when Tibo came back to his office and passed Agathe's empty desk, his eye was drawn to her handbag sitting on the floor by her chair and there, sticking out of it, was her hairbrush. Good Tibo Krovic, who denied God and the power of the saints—even St. Walpurnia—bent and tugged a few dark strands free. It was a desecration. He knew it. Tibo Krovic was not the man to rifle a woman's handbag—least of all the handbag of Mrs. Agathe Stopak. And he had done it with the promise of Cesare's spell still fresh in his mind. It was inexcusable. He hated himself for the poor shrivelled creature he had become. He hated her for making him that way.

Tibo wound her hair around his finger and kissed it, pretending to himself that he could find her smell amongst it. It was the first time in three years he had ever touched her and even then it was distant and disembodied, the ghost of a touch.

He heard the unmistakable scrape of her heels on the terrazzo of the back stair. By the time Mrs. Stopak returned to her desk, the door to the mayor's office had clicked into place.

Agathe sat down. She turned to look at the door of Tibo's room. She saw the two coffee cups left, one stacked on top of the other, beside the coffee machine. She resented the unspoken, take-it-for-granted command they contained. "Just wash these up, would you, Mrs. Stopak?" She rolled her eyes to the ceiling and tutted. She leaned her elbows on the desk and slouched forward. She noticed again, for the thousand thousandth time, the drawing pin, rusted into the wood there and remembered the picture it had once held.

"Ploink." With the very tip of a polished fingernail hooked under its cymbal-lid, she coaxed a tiny note from the pin. She sighed a bored sigh and swivelled in her chair. Her foot collided with her handbag, open on the floor beneath her desk. She looked down, saw the hairbrush poking out and pressed it a little further in. She closed the bag. Something was not right.

Like a bird that will abandon her nest if she returns and finds it disturbed, Agathe knew that something was out of place. She looked in the drawers of her desk. She lifted her handbag from the floor, opened it again, checked her purse. Nothing.

"Ploink." It had become a habit with her, flicking away at that drawing pin. It made her remember. Sometimes she could go for days without remembering even when, night and morning, she had sat at her desk, looking at the drawing pin and never seeing it. And then, for no reason she could imagine, all the old thoughts would come back and she would realise that she had forgotten to remember.

"Ploink." She remembered lying on her bed—Hektor's bed—as he painted her, the first of many nudes he had started and never finished. She remembered lying there and looking at the marks on the ceiling and wondering about Tibo and that question. She had never asked that question. She had never said, "Tibo, if, just once, you and I, we made love, knowing it was just that once, would that make things better for you? Would that be enough? Would that heal you?"

"Ploink." She stood up quickly and walked to the door of Tibo's room and, for the first time in three years, she walked in without knocking, just flung the door open and walked in and there he was, sitting at his desk, stuffing something into a brown envelope, and he looked up and smiled because she hadn't knocked and he had had no time to put on a scowl and his natural reaction was to smile at the very thought of her so he smiled, just as he used to do in the old days whenever she came into his room.

And she said, "Mayor Krovic . . ." and stopped. She stopped because it was impossible to go on. No sentence that began with "Mayor Krovic" could ever end with an invitation to come to bed. Agathe shut her pretty mouth so hard that her teeth rattled and she turned and went out. A moment or two later, Tibo got up from his desk and shut the door again.

THE NEXT MORNING, WHEN GOOD MAYOR Krovic got off the tram two stops early and walked down Castle Street to The Golden Angel, he had with him that same brown envelope which Agathe had seen when she burst into his office. As he walked, his hand went repeatedly to the inside pocket of his jacket and, with a flick of the finger, he assured himself that, yes, the envelope was still there, held safely behind his big black wallet.

Inside The Golden Angel, Tibo stood at his usual place at the high table by the door, sipping his usual Viennese coffee with plenty of figs and pretending to read the paper. The envelope itched in his pocket, just as the postcards had done years before. His ears burned with the shame of it but, today of all days, today when he most wished to be invisible and anonymous, there was no peace for Tibo in The Golden Angel. Every waiter in the place brushed past him apologetically where he stood.

Each one in turn wished him, "Good morning, Mayor Krovic," so he was forced to say, "Good morning," in return and then, as they flitted soundlessly across the cafe, every waiter he had already greeted would smile and nod again. Tibo folded his paper and buried himself in an article about Dot's oldest goldfish until the last of his coffee was gone. He looked at his watch. Ten to nine. He took a mint from the bag he had bought at the kiosk by the tram stop and rolled it, stuttering, along his teeth as he laid the envelope on the table in front of him. His fountain pen was loaded with black ink. He wrote "Mr. Cesare" in a big, angry hand, put the bag of mints on top of the envelope as if to stop it from blowing away, piled his saucer with change and walked out of the cafe.

Tibo made a point of arriving at the office a little before nine every day and Agathe always made it her business to arrive a little late. They had never made the arrangement formal—it was just something they had fallen into. It suited them. It meant fewer painful meetings on the stairs, fewer awkward silences or odd glances that might be taken as resentful or longing or reproachful. It was easier, that's all. And, knowing that he was in the office first let Tibo perform his silly ritual of listening for her step and rushing to the door and flopping to the carpet and squinting.

So that's exactly where he was, that's exactly what he was doing when Agathe came in to work a few minutes later. Poor, good, love-struck Mayor Krovic was lying in his usual place on the carpet, watching Mrs. Stopak's beautiful pink toes when they did an amazing thing and turned towards him. It took Tibo a second or two to realise what was happening and scramble to his feet. By that time, it was too late and, as the door swung open, it hit him in the side of the face. It made a noise like the time that coal lorry reversed into the statue of Admiral Count Gromyko but Agathe was brisk and unapologetic. "Tibo, stop carrying on like a baby and sit down!" She pointed him at the chair Mr. Cesare had used the day before and watched him as he nursed his jaw and probed for broken teeth with his tongue. "Tibo, I don't have time for this," she said.

Mayor Krovic felt his lip beginning to swell outrageously but he managed to say, "That's the second time you've called me 'Tibo.'"

"I should never have stopped."

"And the second time you've come in here without knocking."

"I don't have time to waste on formalities," she said. "This is urgent. This is an emergency."

Tibo was suddenly concerned. He stopped rubbing his jaw and said, "Tell me. Whatever it is, tell me and I'll help."

So she asked him the question. "This can't go on," she said. "You think I don't know but I know. You think I don't see but I see. I have to help you finish this." She took his hand. "So once, Tibo, just once and then never again. To end it. To bring the curtain down."

Good Mayor Krovic sat there for a long time, not saying anything, looking a bit angry, a little shocked, listening to the thumping pulse in the side of his head until, eventually, Agathe said, "Say something. Talk to me."

"Get out," he said. "Get out of my bloedig office right now."

Agathe stood up quickly. There was something glinting in the corner of Tibo's eye that she recognised. Hektor had it and, when it showed, Agathe had learned to stay away. She hurried out of the room and back to her desk.

"And shut the bloedig door!" Tibo screamed. It was fortunate that she was already sitting back at her desk and typing furiously when he whispered, "Bitch."

Tibo said a lot more when Agathe was out of earshot. He got out of the visitors' chair so angrily that it tipped over and rolled on the floor. He ignored it and fought his way round the desk to his own chair, growling like a bear. He kicked the tin wastepaper basket. He didn't mean to but it was in the way and it collided against his foot with a noise like a bursting drum so his fury exploded and he kicked it again so it bounced off the wall and again and again until it ricocheted off his shins and made him stop. He fell into his chair and raged some more. "That bitch! That bitch! Dear God, if she came in here again, I'd strangle her with her own stinking knickers. They couldn't find a bloedig jury to convict! Bloedig little tart! After all this time, just to dangle it in my face like that. That's what she thinks. She thinks I'm safe. Thinks I'm some bloedig poodle. Pick me up and put me down. Bitch!"

Tibo sat there, gritting his teeth and gripping the arms of his chair so hard his hands hurt. The breath came down his nostrils in hot snorts until, little by little, it slowed and calmed, his jaw worked less furiously, the pain in his hands forced him to loosen his grip and, quite soon, there was nothing left of his anger but a sore hotness in the back of his throat and a kind of shamefaced hurt.

All across the floor of his office Tibo noticed a trail of torn envelopes and crumpled papers and cedar-scented pencil sharpenings. He decided he had better tidy them up. He looked round for the tin wastepaper basket, picked it up and began to squeeze and haul and punch it back into shape. He found it calming but it was less than successful. Where the bin had been round and smooth and regular, now it was distorted and pineapple-ish. Tibo put it down on the desk. It tilted and rocked. It made him smile. He took it and went down on his hands and knees, pinching up little bits of spice-scented pencil-shavings, tossing in balls of paper with a heartening "clunk."

And it was when he finished picking rubbish off the floor and stood up, grunting, one hand pressing down hard on his desk to support himself, that Tibo started to wonder about the spell. How long did it take to cast a spell, after all? How long did they take to work? Could it happen in ten minutes? Was there time? The envelope he left for Cesare must have been in his hands within moments. The doors of The Golden Angel would still have been swinging on their hinges when Cesare opened it and, when he saw Agathe's dark hair nestled inside, he would have known at once what to do. Could such things be done straight away with just a few words, a few mystical passes, or did it need a full moon and an unsuspecting kitten? No, it was suddenly obvious to Tibo, Cesare had cast his love-spell in the time it took to walk down Castle Street and it was starting to work. Agathe was starting to fall in love with him again. She was fighting it but she couldn't help it. That was the only possible explanation for her stupid, clumsy offer and Tibo generously forgave her. "Poor kid," he said and he hurried out of his office, calling to her, "It's all right. I'm sorry. It's all my fault." But she was gone. He stood for a moment, holding his battered waste bin under his arm and looking at her empty chair until Peter Stavo arrived in the doorway, snapping a pair of pliers like castanets.

"Agathe said to tell you that she's not well and she's gone home for the day." He gave another flick of his pliers. "Mentioned something about a drawing pin that's been annoying her. I'm supposed to take care of it—and you look as if you could use a new bin, boss."

OF COURSE, AGATHE WAS NOT SICK AND SHE hadn't gone home. She left the Town Hall by the back stair, making her excuses at Peter Stavo's glass booth and she hurried through City Square to Braun's department store where she sat in the mirrored cafe and ordered coffee for one and cakes for three. They came piled high in a spectacular, silver-plated ziggurat of confectionery, scones on the bottom, sensible slabs of fruit cake in the middle and a ridiculous, impossible fanfare of cream cakes and meringues on top. Agathe ate them all and as she ate, she glared out of the window, across the street at my statue on top of the Ampersand Banking Company and commanded more coffee with wide, rolling waves of the hand.

Agathe abandoned her dainty silver pastry fork. It was too slow. She let it clatter on her plate and she began pulling at the mountain of cakes with her hands and forcing them into her mouth and, all the while, she stared at me, at poor, warty, hairy Walpurnia, unloved Walpurnia, left all alone to stand in all weathers on top of the bank, and cursed me. "You fraud! You phoney! Liar! Cheat!" And then, out loud, she shouted, "Moe aw-hee!" through a mouthful of eclair and waved her empty cup at a passing waitress.

The nice ladies who take their morning coffee at Braun's were not sorry to see her go and, to tell the truth, Agathe was not sorry to leave. The fit which had seized her had passed. She felt bloated and, when the girl at the cash desk made little, twittery, half-hearted gestures of disgust, fanning her weakly with a paper napkin, Agathe was ashamed to see a huge blob of cream on her nose, endlessly reflected in the coffee room's mirrored walls. She wiped it off with the back of her hand, the way the kids in Canal Street wipe their snotty noses, and fled, rattling down the stairs, through haberdashery, through cosmetics and perfumery and out, into the sunny street.

She was hot and breathless and sick. She might have gone home. She might even have enjoyed the sunshine and walked along the Ampersand. She glanced in that direction, thought about it and walked the other way.

Agathe knew enough about sadness to recognise all its shapes and colours. There was a particular kind of sadness waiting in Canal Street, one that she rubbed out every night with heat and shame and sleep but, standing in the street outside Braun's with the shadow of my statue falling on her like a blessing, she could feel something different. She almost recognised it, like the face of someone she used to know a long time ago, a pleasantly painful kind of melancholy like the tingle of pins and needles that only comes in a limb which is telling us it is not, after all, dead. There was just a glow of it, enough to notice and Agathe wanted more. She wanted to enjoy it for a little longer. She wanted to blow on it without blowing it out. She began to walk. She walked a little faster as she passed City Square, sticking close under the windows of the Town Hall in case Mayor Krovic might be looking out to catch her malingering.

She turned right into Radetzky Street and came out on the corner opposite the Palazz Kinema where they were showing *The Weeping Violin* with Jacob Maurer, and *The Weeping Violin* looked like just the sort of thing to feed the little gnaw of misery she was cradling inside. But the picture was almost over and the next show wasn't due to start for half an hour so she walked on to the end of George Street and the Municipal Art Gallery and Museum.

Now, Agathe was not much of an art lover, not a regular customer at the Municipal Art Gallery, but she had worked for Tibo Krovic long enough, seen enough minutes of the Arts and Libraries Committee, to know the sort of thing they contained—

repentant harlots about to throw themselves off a midnight bridge; sad children and sympathetic puppies; old ladies waving goodbye from cottage windows—acres and acres of gloomy canvas, the perfect place to wait for the second show at the Palazz.

The uniformed doormen were there to greet her—still in their jobs mostly because the doormen of Umlaut were still in theirs. They smiled and nodded, "Morning, Miss," one on each side of the double doors and they snapped to attention in perfect time, each reflecting the other in a row of polished brass buttons.

Agathe stepped into the cool shadows of the gallery but she never reached the sad paintings she had come to see. There was a lovely marble statue of a naked lady, lying on her back and making half-hearted efforts to fend off a beautiful, butterfly-winged boy angel. She stood in front of that for a bit, wondering about her own fending-off technique and whether she would bother to use it if ever she woke and found a butterfly-boy hovering over her bed. Agathe wandered casually round the statue and admired him from the rear and decided, no, she probably wouldn't.

She looked up guiltily and saw, across the hall, the gallery shop and, shining out at her, small and distant but unmistakable, unforgettable, Tibo's postcard. It drew her. It called her. She looked at it in puzzlement, almost unable to believe that such a thing existed—as if Tibo's card, her card, the card she had destroyed, had been the only one in the world and this was some miraculous resurrection.

Agathe counted the coins from her purse, took the card in its paper bag and hurried from the gallery, checking her watch as she went.

Along the road at the Palazz there was another shower of coins, rattled into the egg-shaped wooden bowl set in the counter of the box-office and another change from sunshine to shade as she plunged into the deeper darkness of the cinema. A girl with a tray of sweets and cigarettes hung round her neck, carrying a torch shrouded under a red hood, led Agathe down the sloping aisle to a seat in the front stalls. She sat down and looked around. The place was almost empty. Agathe had the whole row to herself. She slipped her coat off her shoulders and settled in the chair with her handbag on her knee. The postcard was sighing to her. She took it out and slipped it from its paper bag, tipping it forward to look at it in the silver-blue of the flickering newsreel. "More beautiful than this, more . . ." It was all so long ago yet Agathe found herself smiling. She was warm and tired and replete with cake. Before the main feature started, she was sound asleep.

IN THE MORNING, FOR THE FIRST TIME SINCE the day he bought the entire stock of Rikard Margolis's flower shop, Good Mayor Krovic did not go to The Golden Angel for coffee. He got off the tram two stops early as usual but, when he walked down Castle Street, he hurried past the cafe, slapping his folded copy of the *Daily Dottian* against his thigh as he went, like a jockey urging speed from his horse. Tibo was embarrassed. He knew he could not stand there at the high table by the door, sipping coffee and pretending to read the paper while Cesare smiled at him like a plotter. He hurried on to work. "I'm busy," he told himself. "Tomorrow."

As he crossed White Bridge, the swallows were screeching low over the Ampersand, tipping and shifting between the piers and snatching flies from the air as they passed. They would be leaving soon, gathering their children on telegraph wires and roof ridges and leading them back, through thousands of miles of empty sky, to Africa. It was wonderful, almost incredible—like the idea of Cesare's spell. You could believe that swallows slept the winter away, buried in mud at the bottom of the Ampersand or you could believe they found their way back from Africa every summer. You could believe Agathe Stopak had spent three years wondering what it would be like to sleep with you or you could believe she had been bewitched by a love spell. It was obvious really. You simply had to choose which was the more incredible.

Tibo crossed City Square, he said "Good morning" to Peter Stavo, who had just finished mopping the vestibule, he nodded gravely at the picture of Mayor Anker Skolvig and he stood aside for Sandor, the boy who delivers the mail, as he ran up the stairs towards the Planning Department.

It was just an ordinary day and Tibo was determined to keep it ordinary. He wouldn't make a fuss about that business the day before but he wouldn't ignore it either. It was said and couldn't be unsaid. And, anyway, Cesare's spell had ripened by another day. It would be stronger by another day. Whatever it was that had driven Agathe before would be driving her all the harder now—like a drug, like alcohol, flooding her by drips until she gave in. Tibo was prepared to wait.

He had waited and waited so he would wait a little longer as if he were waiting for some especially gorgeous peach to ripen and fall off the branch. He pretended to himself that it didn't matter that the peach was not his own or that he lacked the courage even to steal it; it was close to falling and the pocket it fell into would be his. That was enough.

On an ordinary day—a day a little more ordinary than this one—Tibo would have spent at least twenty minutes in The Golden Angel. Twenty minutes took a long time to pass alone in his office with nothing to do. He stood at the window in the corner. From there, he could see Castle Street and the bridge and a long way down Ampersand Avenue. It didn't matter from which direction she came, he would see her. Tibo stood still there for a long time, looking down at the opposite corner of City Square where a peculiar bunch of people had caught his eye—a circus strongman dressed in a leopard-skin rug, a girl with a white terrier which leapt and bounced through the hoops she held out as if it had been drawn on strings and two girls who stood a few yards apart, juggling Indian clubs. Tibo thought it strange that nobody paid them any attention. They seemed to be simply passing the time doing circus tricks the way that other people might stand looking at the clouds, jingling the change in their pockets. But then, when Agathe turned the corner into the square, the strongman stuck his fingers in his mouth and whistled, the girls snatched their clubs out of the air the way the swallows snatch the flies and the dog stopped in mid-jump, folded his legs under himself and fell straight down to the pavement.

Across the square and behind the windows of his office, Tibo felt the shriek of that whistle stabbing in his ears but Agathe seemed not to notice. It was as if she didn't hear and she gave no sign when the circus people formed up in a knot behind her and came hurrying across City Square with the little dog running round in yappy circles as they went.

Tibo was alarmed. He didn't like those people. They had the look of a gang of pickpockets or bag-snatchers or white slavers and Tibo was prepared to bet they couldn't produce a licence for that little dog either. He hurried out of his office and down the stairs but, when he reached the square, Agathe was alone.

"Were those people bothering you?" Tibo asked.

"What people?" she said and she pushed past him and on, up the stairs.

Tibo looked round. They had gone. There was a leprous-looking pigeon with one foot, limping along beside the fountains and two old women sharing a bag of cherries on a bench in the sunshine but, apart from that, the square was empty. No strongman, no yappy little dog, nothing. Tibo went back into the Town Hall and followed Agathe up the stairs to his office. At the door, he put on his "kind and generous" face, a stupid "There, there, I understand—kiss it all better" look that only a woman as wonderful as Agathe could ever forgive without slapping him first.

She was already sitting at her desk, pale and miserable and sad-eyed and, when Tibo came in, she looked up and read that look on his face and looked away again quickly.

Tibo had planned something bright and chirpy. Sitting in his kitchen in the old house at the end of the blue-tiled path, he had plotted the moment of their meeting that day—him perched on the edge of her desk as she arrived for work, legs flung out in front of himself, looking cheeky and relaxed, murmuring a confident "Hello" but it had all gone wrong again. She couldn't look at him for more than a moment and, when she did, it was with something like pain in her eyes.

"Everything all right?" he asked.

"Yes, thanks. Fine." Agathe busied herself with her paperclip tray.

"Fine?"

"Yes. Fine, thanks. Feeling much better."

"Fine." That was what she had said on the day she ran out of The Golden Angel. "Fine." Everything was "fine." She wasn't upset. He hadn't done anything wrong. And then she had left him.

"Fine," said Tibo. "Glad to hear it." And, in a couple of long paces, he was inside his office and closing the door.

But he was still there, still standing with his back to the door, cursing himself for making such a hash of things when he heard her there, behind him, her shoes on the hard floor, her fingers brushing over the wood at his back.

He held his breath until she said, "Tibo?" It was just a whisper. "Tibo, can you hear me?"

He let his breath out slowly.

"Tibo?" Still just a whisper. If he had been sitting at his desk on the other side of the room he would never have heard it.

"Tibo, can I talk to you, please?"

"You are talking to me." He passed his hand gently over the wood of the door, sure that his fingers and hers were barely separated, almost touching.

"Tibo."

"I'm listening."

"Tibo, please. I'm in trouble."

"I'll help you."

"You said that yesterday."

"Yesterday was different. Yesterday you hit me in the face with a doorknob."

Agathe was quiet. With his ear pressed against the door, Tibo could hear the snakeskin whisper of her hands as they passed.

"I hurt you," she said.

"Don't worry about it."

"No. The other thing. I really hurt you."

Tibo said nothing.

"I need you to help me."

"I'll help you. You've always known that."

She was quiet again.

"Tell me," he said.

"Hektor."

That was all she said but, when she said that word, it came up from her heart and filled her mouth and Tibo's hands balled into fists when he heard it.

"Tibo, he's in trouble."

"Yes."

"Please. It's all been a mistake. Tibo. Please, Tibo. He's been to court and, Tibo . . ."

"Stop saying my name."

But she said "Tibo" again anyway.

"Just tell me!" he said.

"Eighteen hundred."

Tibo said nothing.

"Eighteen hundred or he goes to jail." And then she said: "Tibo."

"You were ready to whore yourself for him."

"No, Tibo. No. I didn't know anything about it until yesterday. Last night. Not until last night. I swear."

"Yesterday. Just once. You and me. For eighteen hundred. You whore. Come for a walk with me and I'll show you girls who do it for twenty."

"Don't say that."

It made Tibo ashamed and, after a little, he said, "What do you want me to do?"

"I thought . . . maybe . . . I thought you could just write it off. I thought you could just tell the court. Have a word with somebody. Maybe."

"That's what you thought. You thought I could just break the law. You thought I could just bend the rules a bit, twist things a bit, call in a few favours because that's what happens. That's how it works. Everybody's a crook. Everybody's a thief. Everybody's on the take. Everybody's the same and I'm like everybody. You thought that."

She didn't say anything.

Tibo said, "Go away from me." He pushed himself away from the door and went and sat down, leaning back in his chair with his feet on the desk.

There was a dusty-smelling breeze coming in at the window and it blew the thin net curtains in and out in lazy billows as he sat, thinking of nothing, watching the dome of my cathedral as it appeared and disappeared between the breathing curtains. And then, at one o'clock, when a grey mist of pigeons rose up from the cathedral and, a moment later, the sound of the bell arrived at his office, Tibo went to look out the window and down into City Square. Before long, Agathe arrived, carrying her sandwiches wrapped in newspaper and sat on the edge of a fountain.

Tibo turned quickly away, took his chequebook from the drawer of his desk and walked out of his office on to the back stair. It took a few minutes to reach the Court Clerk's Department, up one floor to Planning and then into the corridor that ran, like a bit of gristle through a chop, linking this building and that, weaving through attics and down fire escapes until it died out against a pile of folding chairs and cans of green paint in the Municipal Buildings on the other side of the square. Tibo pushed through the last door and came out next to an office marked "G. Ångström, Clerk to the Court." He did not knock. It seemed that knocking had become suddenly unfashionable.

Mr. Ångström was eating a boiled egg sandwich and reading the paper when the mayor pushed into his office. It was not a large office, oddly shaped and jammed in under the roof with a sloping window that looked out into a dark courtyard where competing drainpipes pushed up towards the light like creepers, and, when Tibo flung the door open, it bounced off Mr. Ångström's desk.

"Oh," said Tibo, "sorry." And, when Mr. Ångström didn't say anything, he said, "Look, I've got this friend—he's in a bit of bother. Got a fine. I want to take care of it."

Mr. Ångström swallowed a large mouthful of egg sandwich. Then he said, "Name."

"Stopak. Hektor Stopak."

"Canal Street?"

"That would be him."

"I'll take care of it, Mayor Krovic."

"It's eighteen hundred."

"Don't worry about it, Mayor Krovic."

"What do you mean?"

Ångström winked confidentially. "It's taken care of."

Tibo slapped his chequebook down on the desk so it made a sound like a starting pistol and he began writing furiously. The noise made Ångström sit up nervously.

"I am making this out to the Town Council of Dot," said Mayor Krovic. "I expect it to be cashed." He glowered from the other side of the desk as Ångström wrote out a receipt and, when it was ready, he folded it and put it in his wallet. He said, "Look for another job, Mr. Ångström," and he banged out of the office.

Three times that afternoon, as Tibo watched the shadows fattening around the cathedral dome, Agathe came and knocked at his door. Each time he said, "Go away from me." The last time he heard her crying.

TIBO DID NOT MOVE FROM HIS CHAIR. WITH his feet on the desk and his hands cupped behind his head, he sat there, until his joints set like concrete, thinking about what he had done and what it had cost him. He might have bought Agathe, used her in ways only a customer could demand—but he loved her and the price of that was that he could never have her. He might even have left Hektor's fine unpaid, gone round to wait at the end of Canal Street, good suit on, shoes polished, nicely shaved and scented, to watch the constables take him away, but that would have made Agathe sad. So he had the worst of all worlds—the money gone and nothing to show for it but Hektor Stopak free to love her again tonight and the next night and the night after that while she believed that he had "fixed it," that he was the same as everybody else, the same as Ångström. "Not everybody is the same. I am not like everybody else." It was his only comfort.

And while Tibo sat on one side of the door muttering, Agathe sat on the other with hot eyes. "Home is where they have to let you in," she said. They were the same words Granny had said as a comfort with the reassuring promise that she would never be turned away, the same words she had said to herself like a prison sentence when she thought of another night in the flat in Aleksander Street with Stopak. And now they sounded like a threat. Home is where they have to let you in. She could not keep Hektor out and she realised suddenly that, more than anything, that was what she wanted to do.

At five o'clock Agathe was still sitting at her desk. She was still there at 5:30. When the cathedral bells struck six, she had managed to put on her coat but she lingered by the door of the office, sitting on the edge of the table beside the coffee machine, unwilling to move. "Home is where they have to let you in," she said. "But it's not even my home. It's his. I can't keep him out. I can't stop him coming in."

She left and all the way home on the tram, sitting on the chilly top deck with her hands in her pockets and her coat drawn around her, Agathe thought of things to say to him, things she might say to keep him from thinking about the money, things she might do. There were things she could do but, after that, he would still want the money and there was none and he would be angry and that would be her fault. Her fault and he would be angry.

The tram slouched towards the end of Ampersand Avenue. The bell clanged. The conductor swung from the back step and yelled, "Green Bridge, this is Green Bridge!" Up ahead, on the right, the lights of The Three Crowns were shining out into the street like the lamps of a fever ward, dismal and yellow and foggy. The music of a broken piano jangled into the street as the door bounced open and Hektor came out. The tram passed slowly. Agathe turned her neck to watch him cupping his hands round a match and lighting a cigarette. A loose bit of tobacco flared up in the flame and he knocked it away. There was a woman at his side, a skinny woman with short hair and too much make-up. She flung her head back. Agathe saw her mouth open in a laugh and fix on Hektor's in a parody of a kiss. The tram passed so slowly. Hektor reached in his pocket. He gave her something. He gave her money. She laughed again. Agathe saw them running together to the stone steps that lead to the path under Green Bridge, down to the arch where it was dark and out of the drizzle. The tram turned into Foundry Street.

*AGATHE STEPPED OFF THE TRAM, SUD*denly old and stiff and tired, and walked towards the tunnel that leads to Canal Street. The last lamp post in Foundry Street was out, the first lamp post in Canal Street was very far away and she kept her eyes fixed on it as she stepped into the gloom of the tunnel. On a sunny day in summer, when she was happy—and she had been happy, even in Canal Street—Agathe could walk quickly through the tunnel and enjoy the lap of canal water just beyond the narrow pavement and the crocodile-skin sparkles it sent dancing over the arched roof. But not tonight—tonight the pavement disappeared into an ink blot that flowed darkly to faraway Canal Street and the pale flame of that first gaslight. As she walked towards it, the wind blew up startling rustles, dead leaves and abandoned newspapers looking for a place to die, tiny black piles of whispering coal dust that had escaped from passing barges, small animal flitterings which she pretended not to have noticed and, over it all, the cold, final invitation of the canal, sucking just beyond the railings. She hurried on.

In Canal Street, the light of the gas lamp seemed to make the shadows beyond it even deeper. "There is nobody there. There is nobody there," Agathe told herself, but she stopped anyway and listened when the sound of her heels scraping on the cracked pavement echoed in the tunnel behind her, just to make sure that it was true, that there was nobody there, nobody who walked in time with her, stopped when she stopped, listened when she listened, peered out of the dirty shadows as she peered in, matched their breath to hers, waited until she walked again and walked on with her, trying not to laugh. "There is nobody there," she said.

The echoes pursued her all the way to No. 15 where she hurried with the lock and banged the door shut again and stood in the tiny square hall and said, "There is nobody here now!" with a little note of triumph in her voice. "Nobody here." But then the breath came out of her with a sigh and her shoulders slumped and she remembered that she had no money to pay the fine and she thought of that woman and of Hektor and remembered he would soon be home.

Agathe went to the cupboard in the corner by the sink and reached inside to hang her coat on the hook. Her hand brushed against something on the shelf and, when it fell to the floor, she saw it was her scrapbook with all its pictures of the house she and Tibo had built while they sat at the middle table of three, right in the front window of The Golden Angel.

The book was dusty now, its pages dry and fanned open like the petals of a blowsy rose. Holding it in her hand, Agathe could hardly believe that she had forgotten about it, that she had stayed for three long years in Canal Street and never once, in all that time, had she visited Dalmatia.

She sat down on the floor and began to turn the pages, stopping to look at the things that had once been so familiar to her, that bed, those ormolu doors, the thick wine glasses as green and swirled as seawater—things that seemed to come from another life, things that somebody else had once imagined and forgotten utterly.

Agathe was still sitting there on the floor beside the cold stove when Hektor came home and found her there. He looked at her and gave a kind of laugh, to let her know how pathetic she was. He asked her for the money and, when he did, Agathe forgot all about the things she had planned to say and the things she had planned to do. She simply told him that she didn't have it but that it didn't really matter because he had enough to spend on whores. And then terrible things happened.

That's the price I pay for my twelve hundred years in Dot—I see terrible things and I can do nothing. I can't help. I can't divert the falling brick as it tumbles from the rotten chimney into the street; I can't catch the runaway pram as it hurtles down the hill towards the junction; I can't stop the woman who makes a pie of rat-poison and feeds it to her children at supper or the pretty girl who kisses the lonely old man as if she loves him. I can only watch or look away—which is much the same thing. And my only comfort is that nothing lasts and nothing in Dot is ever just quite what it seems. Nothing.

In my golden tomb there is an angel feather, laid beside me by some returning crusader—an angel feather which fell from Heaven and landed on his helmet when he was liberating the Holy Places. Or so he said. Actually, it's a peacock plume which he took from the headdress of an Arab merchant's wife after he raped her. His version is much nicer. Nothing is as it seems.

Even my legendary beard, lying there long and lustrous in my tomb, is a fake. They took it off a carthorse who died behind the convent I don't know how long ago. The horse just coughed and collapsed, each leg in a different direction and sent a load of logs rolling back down the hill—and those nuns, how they could swear! Not much of an ending but now his tail is venerated every day. Surely, after so many years in a daily rain of prayer, it must be a holy thing too, like my bones. Nothing is as it seems. Not me, not the beautiful new sister-in-law at The Golden Angel, not the woman in the flat in Canal Street who seems as if she is alone, who seems as if she has nobody to love her or protect her while terrible things happen to her. Look away. Don't watch. Hide your eyes and remember that nothing is as it seems.

ABOUT THE TIME THAT AGATHE STEPPED off the tram in Foundry Street, Tibo was getting out of his chair in the office. He was frozen in position but the ache in his joints had turned into a scream and, anyway, he was tired of watching the dome of the cathedral with its clockwork exhalations of pigeons. He forced himself to get up and walked, stiff-legged as a scarecrow, out of the Town Hall, through the square and into the Dot Arms. He sat there until closing time, piling up a pyramid of glasses on the table in front of him, speaking to no one until they flung him into the empty street at midnight.

It was quiet. Tibo looked up at the sky. He saw Orion disappearing in a swirl of cauldron-black cloud that was boiling up from the edge of the world and whipping, like torn silk, across the stars. The cloud thickened and darkened. It spread over the sky like ink in water. The stars went out. Tibo tightened the belt on his coat and began to walk and, as he walked, the whole of Dot sighed like a sleeper in the night, drew its blankets over its head and stilled—the whole of Dot except for The Golden Angel. Black clouds filled the sky, piling up, layer on layer from the invisible horizon, behind the houses, above the rooftops, over the chimneys, clotting Heaven until there was nothing left of the sky but a single small velvet O like a surprised kiss, ringed with moonlight and turning slowly, slowly right overhead, as if Castle Street and The Golden Angel had been the centre of the world. And then, when there was nothing to hear but the darkness coiling itself under window sills and the sound of cats looking, the whole building breathed in. The walls seemed to sag, droop towards the pavement a little. Behind the windows, the blinds fluttered and drew back into the room as if on a breeze and the little acorn-shaped buttons on the ends of their white string pulls tapped against the glass. Up on the roof, the slates pulsed and rattled like dragon scales and, for a moment, nothing happened. Then there came a fluttering of gilded feathers, fingers of coloured lights that beamed out of forgotten windows high up on the side of the building, the sound of drums and organ chords and a faraway band. Downstairs in the cafe, piles of coffee cups danced, plates rattled their way to the edge of the shelf and fell to the floor.

In the parlour, Mamma Cesare's wedding picture dropped off the wall. In the best bedroom, beautiful dark-haired Maria rolled over in her sleep and said, "It's just a train passing in the night." Then she pulled her crisp white nightgown over her head and added, "Make love to me." And then, while Cesare pretended to have forgotten that there is no railway station in Dot, the whole house breathed out again, a long, whooshing finger of wind that blew out from under every door, that whistled from every keyhole and from the cracks round every window and howled down Castle Street towards the river. Wherever it passed, it sent rubbish bins rolling and tin cans and bits of newspaper swirled before it. It tore at the municipal flower pots, it shredded leaves from the trees, it set gates creaking and doors banging and lamp posts nodding and it shrieked out of town, over the bridge and along the Ampersand towards the sea until it reached Canal Street where it swirled through the tunnel with a noise like a wolf pack and battered at the windows until it reached No. 15. The street was quiet except for the sound of a woman crying in a voice that went from a scream to a howl and sank to a terrified whimper.

The wind blew again, flinging itself against the door, filling the keyhole, tearing at the lock forcing its way into the house, wrenching its way inside until the door bounced on its hinges and, a moment later, Hektor came running out of the flat, his face moon-white, struggling with his jacket as the wind tugged at it like a torn sail and he ran and he ran, past the last street lamp in Canal Street and into shadow. Far behind him, inside the tiny flat, there was the sound of someone saying soothing things, saying that everything would be all right now and that it was time for bed and things would be different in the morning and changed but, of course, there was no one in the flat—only Agathe. It must have been the wind.

Tibo did not notice the wind. It was just behind him, snapping at his back as he began to walk out through the darkened docks where the women waited. They grabbed him by the arms as he passed and staggered with him from lamp post to lamp post until his silence defeated them and they left him to walk on alone to the lighthouse that had been his friend. As he reached it, the last of the storm from The Golden Angel died away against the heel of his shoe with a gasp that hardly even stirred the sand. All through the night, Tibo stood under the lighthouse. Its pulse calmed him and the sound of the waves healed him and their spray blessed him. In the morning he was sober.

His watch had stopped because he kept it on his wrist all night long instead of winding it up and putting it carefully on the dresser by his bed but, when the first Dash ferry wallowed past the lighthouse, he knew it was seven thirty again.

And, an hour later, when the brown linen blinds shot up in the windows of Kupfer and Kemanezic, Tibo was waiting to buy a clean shirt and some socks and new underpants. He carried them to work in a brown paper parcel.

TIBO HAD NO IDEA HOW TO WORK WITHOUT Agathe. Without Agathe, he had nobody to open his mail, nobody to fill out his diary, nobody to read it to him. He had wasted a whole day, sitting with his feet on the desk because he refused to let her into the room and tell him what to do. Without Agathe, there was nothing to do.

And now, after he had washed himself in the bleach-smelling Gents at the end of the corridor, after he had unwrapped his parcel and changed his underwear, after he had picked a dozen pins from his new shirt and put it on and confirmed—beyond any possible doubt—that it did not go with his tie, he sat down in his office and went to sleep.

But, in the flat in Canal Street, Agathe was just getting out of bed. She was alone and she moved about the room, confident and naked although she could not shake the feeling that she had forgotten something, something that had happened or something she was supposed to do. It hung about her like a half-remembered dream until she dismissed it with a shake of the head. Agathe noticed the door to the street was standing open and the curtains had fallen from the window to lie in a pile at its left-hand side while the rail which had held them hung by a single nail at the right. She pushed them out of the way and washed herself in the sink, looking out at Canal Street as she did it, just as anybody in Canal Street might have looked in at her.

And while she was doing that, Achilles came home, tail up, shoulders swinging, wearing a smug "Boy, oh, boy, just don't ask" look after a festive night of rats and fights and lady cats. Because he loved Agathe, he came to wind himself around her legs as he always did but he had barely begun, he had just nudged her with the top of his head, when all his weary contentment disappeared and he recoiled with a panicked yowl. Achilles found himself trapped, with Agathe between him and the door and fear gripping him. His tail exploded into a terrified brush and he broke away from her, bounding across the table and on to the bed, running so fast he actually clawed his way around the wall for a couple of paces until he fell off and smacked his nose against the door which began to swing shut.

Achilles scratched and scrabbled pitifully against it for a second or two, screaming like a fire siren but, when Agathe moved to comfort him, he leapt for the collapsed curtains and dragged himself up the pole to the top where he squatted, spitting and fizzing like a Catherine wheel.

"Bad cat," said Agathe. "It's me. It's just me. There's nothing to be afraid of." And then she gave the most delicious shimmy that started at her heels and went up to her neck so her calves flicked one way and her thighs another, so her bottom flicked one way and her tummy another, her breasts flicked one way and her shoulders another and surprised beads of soapy water flew away from her body in a cloak of sparkles.

Achilles was unimpressed. He coiled and spat at the top of the pole and said, "Nerrryauummrrrrr," a lot.

"Be quiet," said Agathe. "It's a perfectly sensible way to dry yourself." And she wondered, "Now, do I still need clothes for going to work?"

She decided that, yes, she did and she took her blue dress from the cupboard in the corner. Her shoes were hiding under one of the upturned chairs. She picked them up, let the chair fall back where it lay and left for work. From his place at the top of the curtain pole, poor Achilles watched her go. When she did not return, he leapt to the floor and streaked out of the open door, hugging the cobbles.

Of course Agathe had no wish to harm Achilles and, anyway,

by the time he fled from the flat, she was already far away. She had decided to walk to work but it seemed to be taking much longer than usual. Dot was suddenly so much more vivid, so much more interesting and full of so many things to be investigated. As she walked, Agathe crossed and recrossed the pavement, entranced by the mysterious smears and stains outside The Three Crowns, fascinated by the sausages left hanging outside Mrs. Oktar's delicatessen, drawn from one glorious lamp post to another, stopping to explore each of them, hurrying on to the next. "Fantastic! Incredible! They are like iron orchid stems. Why did I never notice?"

When, at last, she arrived in City Square, Agathe was very late for work but, since the mayor was sleeping across his desk and quite unaware of the time, that hardly mattered. She sat down and looked at her typewriter. Nothing happened.

Then, at eleven o'clock, a barrage of bell notes through the open window woke Tibo and sent him shambling out of his office, looking for coffee. And Agathe was sitting there at her desk and Tibo saw her and his voice broke in a sob and he said, "Oh, Agathe. Oh, dear God. He hit you."

She waved him away saying, "Don't be silly, Tibo. Nobody hit me."

But Tibo was on his knees in front of her, grasping her by the legs with tears in his eyes as he reached up to brush her face with his fingers.

"He did this. The bastard. He did this. Oh, my poor Agathe, I'm so sorry. So, so sorry."

She smiled down at him with the indulgent look she would have given an idiot child. "Tibo, stop being so silly. Nobody did this. Nobody hurt me."

"But your face. Your poor face. My poor darling, look what he did. The bruise on your face. Oh, Agathe."

Very gently she brushed his hand away and held it between her own two hands and said, "Tibo, you have to understand. You have to be my big, brave mayor and try to understand. Hektor did not hit me. How could Hektor have hit me? Why would he hit me?"

"Because you went home without the money, without the eighteen hundred, and he hit you and it's all my fault."

"No, Tibo, that's just silly. Only a very bad man could hit a woman and I've been with Hektor for a long time and, if he was a bad man, I would have known. I turned my whole life upside down to be with Hektor. There was you and me, for example, and Stopak—everything. How could I have done that for a bad man, for a man who wasn't nice and didn't love me? That's ridiculous. Tibo, listen. This isn't a black eye. It's part of my skin. I am turning into a dog."

Tibo slumped on the floor in front of her. "A dog? You are turning into a dog?"

"Yes. It's a bit strange and a bit wonderful but you're not to be afraid."

"Where is he?"

"Who? Hektor?"

"Where is he? I have to kill him."

"Now you really are being silly," she said, "so it's just as well I don't know where he is."

"He hit you and ran away."

Agathe sighed impatiently. "Tibo, I've explained all this. Nobody hit me. I'm turning into a dog—a Dalmatian, I think. Remember how I always dreamed of going there—to Dalmatia?"

"A Dalmatian," Tibo said. He sounded defeated.

"Yes. I've got this black patch across my eye—which I think is very attractive—and there are some more on my legs already. I expect there will be others soon—as it goes on, as I change more."

"As you change more. Agathe, you are not a dog. You are not about to become a dog. You're just a little upset."

She shook her head. "Tibo, I've never felt better. Except, obviously, it's going to change things for us. I'm handing in my notice. I can't really work for you any longer. Dogs can't type."

"Or talk."

"Silly."

Tibo looked at her for a little and decided there was still room to appeal to her rational nature. "Agathe," he said, "have you thought how you'll live? You can't just wander the streets. Dot has quite a good dog catcher. He'll put you in the pound and then, if nobody claims you after ten days—and nobody will since you don't belong to anybody . . ." Tibo gripped himself by the ears and made a noise like electricity. "Dzzzzzztttt!"

Agathe looked wounded but she said, "Yes. I've thought of that and I was hoping that I could come and stay with you."

"With me."

"Yes, Tibo. Come on, tell me the truth—when you were a little boy, didn't you wish, sometimes, that a puppy would follow you home and you could keep it? Didn't you? You did, I know you did! Well, now it's happened."

Hearing her say that, Tibo could see himself, as a boy, standing on a street corner in a not very nice part of Dot, looking at a little dog with yellow feet, waiting, willing it to cross the road so it would be with him, so it would choose him and be his. But the dog went home. The dog always went home. And now here was Agathe, wagging her tail.

"All right," said Tibo, "you can stay with me. When the time comes."

"When the time comes," said Agathe.

"Yes, you can stay."

"Stay!" she said, firmly, with an upraised finger.

"I didn't mean that! Agathe, you are not turning into a dog. I won't allow it. I won't hear it spoken of. You are simply a little overwrought, that's all."

She made a solemn face.

"Agathe, please. Listen to me. I have to go out. Some things I need to do. Will you come? But, if you do, I need you to promise that you'll be good. None of this 'turning into a dog' nonsense."

"Tibo, it's not nonsense. Please try to understand. It's just the way things are and I'm not embarrassed about it and I'm not about to shut up about it."

Good Mayor Krovic brushed his hand across her face, just as he had dreamed of doing for years—except he had always seen it as a prelude to a kiss and never imagined he might be soothing a black eye. He said, "Oh, Agathe, my poor darling. I'm so sorry." Then, going quickly to the door, he said, "Wait here," and locked her in.

Tibo took the back stairs to Peter Stavo's booth and gave firm instructions that nobody was to go anywhere near the mayor's office for the next half hour—"not even if it goes on fire"—then he left.

*TIBO WAS NOT WELL KNOWN FOR HIS ATH*letic prowess. The people of Dot were unlikely to turn to one another over a glass of something in the evening and say, "I saw Mayor Krovic running along Castle Street again this morning." But he ran that day and he hit the doors of The Golden Angel like a runaway train and didn't stop.

Behind the coffee organ, Cesare's eyebrows shot so far up his face they almost vanished into his brilliantined hair but he managed a thin smile of welcome. It turned to a look of alarm when Mayor Krovic defied protocol and crossed behind the counter. "Cesare, a word." That was all he said.

The situation was so grave that Cesare was unable to communicate by eyebrows alone. He raised a finger and summoned Beppo from his place at the other side of the cafe. "Brother, you are in charge," he said. "Do not fail me." And then, in the moment or two that it took for Beppo to grow another six inches in height and become solemn as an undertaker, while the other waiters looked on and sighed like the wind moving through the reeds at the mouth of the Ampersand, Cesare led Tibo into his parlour.

He said, "There seems to be some misunderstanding. I serve—that does not make me your servant."

And Tibo, who knew he had behaved abominably and was too embarrassed to apologise, simply clenched his teeth and said, "Make it stop."

Cesare flashed his eyebrows again. A student of such things would have seen the gesture and read, "So, just the other day I came to you bringing coffee and cakes, talking to you as a friend, showing respect to your office and to you as a man. Today you humiliate me in front of my staff and my customers and you refuse to make any apology. Who are you, little man? Don't you know, in the old country, I could cut your throat for this?" But the only thing that Cesare said was, "Stop what?"

"Stop the curse. The curse I asked you to put on somebody. Make it stop."

"I never heard you ask for a curse," said Cesare.

He took an enormous bunch of keys from his pocket, selected the smallest, a tiny sliver of golden metal, and, with that, he opened the marquetry escritoire by the window and rolled back the lid.

"This is yours, I think." And he handed Tibo a familiar brown envelope. "Take it. It's just as it was. I never touched it. And you never asked for a curse."

Tibo looked inside the envelope. The twist of dark hair was still there as he had left it, fresh from her brush, still covered in his kisses. He said, "I am very sorry."

And Cesare responded with an eyebrow flash which might have meant "Too late," or "Well, that's all right, then." At that angle and with the light falling from the window that way, it was difficult to tell.

Cesare said, "Tell me about the curse," as if he had been a doctor from a long line of doctors and he was asking for a list of symptoms.

Tibo told him. "But it's not true, of course. She is not really becoming a dog."

"Foolish man, of course she is. This is bad," said Cesare, "very bad."

"What do I do?"

"You could find the person who has done this thing and make them stop. Of course, that person might be you."

"It's not me!" Tibo protested.

"Even so, there is probably no cure—except love, perhaps even unto death. That cures most things."

"I have not found it so," said Tibo and excused himself.

OUT IN CASTLE STREET AGAIN, TIBO HAILED A cab. The run to The Golden Angel had left him hot and sticky, the interview with Cesare had left him clammy. He took off his jacket as the cab nudged through Dot's lunchtime traffic, undid his top button, loosened his tie.

"Canal Street," said the driver. "This is as far as I go. Can't get the cab through the tunnel and I'm not sorry. They'd have the wheels off before I could turn her round."

Tibo got out and paid.

"D'you want me to wait?"

"No," said Tibo.

"Thank God for that." The cab reversed hastily away.

Tibo had never gone to Canal Street. It was the one indulgence of the jilted lover which he had denied himself. He'd never crept around at night, never listened at windows, never concocted fantasies from the contents of rubbish bins or washing lines, never hammered on the door in the middle of the night, never made a drunken, pleading declaration of love or issued a challenge to fight, never stood at the other side of the canal, just watching for hours on end until the snow settled on his hat as thick and stiff as wedding-cake icing. But he had wondered. And now it was real—the dirty cobbles, the rusty railings, the broken street lamps and No. 15 with its door swinging open. Hektor would be there. The man who hit Agathe. The man who took Agathe and hit her every night for three years. His house. And he would be in it and now Tibo would go inside and kill him.

He knocked on the door. He knocked again. He pushed the door open wider. He went in.

There were two doors off the tiny hall. He opened the first—a lavatory with a window to the back. He opened the second and found the single room where Agathe had lived and slept all this time, the curtains collapsed on the floor—"She made those," Tibo thought—the chairs overturned, the bed in the corner unmade. Tibo turned away. He couldn't bear the sight of it.

But there was no sign of Hektor. "He's not coming back," said Tibo, "and neither is she."

He looked round the room for Agathe's clothes but, apart from her coat hanging on the back of the door, there was nothing to show that anybody in particular lived there. He opened the corner cupboard and found her dresses on hooks, her seven pairs of shoes in a soldierly row and her underwear, serene on the top shelf.

Tibo gathered her dresses in one arm and, with his free hand, he began stacking her underwear. He needed a suitcase. He came out of the cupboard and looked around. The bed. If there was a suitcase, it would be under the bed. He draped Agathe's things across the rumpled sheets and fell to his knees, groping round in the dusty dark below the bed. That was when he found the paintings—pictures of Agathe standing, sitting, lying, mostly lying, displayed like cut fruit on the bed, this bed, that very bed.

He looked at them all, hating himself for enjoying them, sickened by the way they made him feel, slicing himself with jealousy again because Hektor had seen her like this, because Hektor had made these beautiful things and she had helped him. He was there for quite some time before he smashed the first of the pictures. He held it between two hands and drove it down on to one of the brass balls on the foot of the bed so the paint cracked and the canvas bowed and bellied but it didn't tear so he swung it sideways until the stretcher splintered and the whole thing collapsed. That was enough. Tibo looked at what he had done. He looked at the rest of the pictures, piled on the mattress, and covered them over with a flick of the bedspread. And then he took a fallen curtain, spread it on the table, piled her clothes on it and knotted it into a sack.

When Tibo left that place, he closed the door as if he had been closing the door of a tomb.

Nobody in Canal Street paid any attention to the strange man with the large bundle. Canal Street is the sort of place where unexplained bundles are quite often seen but almost never noticed, the sort of place where it's thought impolite to take too much of an interest in what the neighbours might be carrying around.

Tibo walked as far as Green Bridge before he found a tram and he tossed his parcel into the luggage compartment under the stairs as soon as he got on. By an effort of will, he ignored it all the way into town and he was downright casual about it when he got off. At the Town Hall, he held it below the level of Peter Stavo's window when he knocked and said, "Sorry, took a bit longer than I thought." And he wore it like a paunch when he turned his back and climbed the stairs.

"I've brought your things," he announced when he unlocked the office door but there was no sign of Agathe. It took a moment or two of going round the office, calling her name in urgent whispers before he found her, lying curled on the floor under his desk.

"It seemed appropriate," she said.

Tibo only humphed.

"I have been to Canal Street," he said.

Agathe lay, open mouthed, with her tongue out, head cocked to one side.

Tibo ignored it. "I have been to Canal Street and you are not going back. You're coming to stay with me."

"That's just what I've always wanted, Tibo," she said.

But there was a lot to do before he could take her home—a vital meeting of the Planning Committee that took up most of the afternoon, discussing a big new sewer project, a budget meeting to talk about next year's schools spending and all of that before the full council.

Tibo came back to the office as often as possible but he could only stay for moments and, at each visit, he found Agathe worse, her dogginess more pronounced.

She sat with her head on his knee while he went over the

school finance papers until he found himself absently playing with her ears. It seemed so natural and easy but—"No! This is insane!"—Tibo recoiled from it.

He fled from the room, locking it carefully behind him as he went, to where the major-domo of the Town Council of Dot was waiting on the landing, buttons gleaming, the silver mace with the statue of me at a military angle over his shoulder. "Ready when you are, Mr. Mayor," he said.

Tibo stopped to take his mayoral chain from its shagreen case on the table under the picture of Anker Skolvig's last stand and adjusted it nervously. "Look all right?" he asked.

"Just as always, sir."

"Then lead the way."

The huge double doors of the council chamber were flung open and the major-domo boomed, "Councillors and citizens of Dot, please be upstanding for his honour Mayor Tibo Krovic."

There was a noise like a cavalry charge as a room full of chair legs scraped backwards on the wooden floor but it could not drown out the lonely howl of an abandoned animal that filled the room and lingered, echoing, in the rafters.

"Close the doors," said Mayor Krovic.

AFTER THE MEETING, TIBO DID NOT JOIN his colleagues while they dawdled over coffee and biscuits in the councillors' lounge. He locked himself away in his office and when, at last, Peter Stavo came knocking, Tibo said, "I'll let myself out. Goodnight." He sat in the dark with Agathe, glaring at her, forbidding her to make a sound. And then the bells of the cathedral struck midnight and Tibo knew the last tram would be leaving the depot. And then it was one and Tibo knew the whole of Dot would be asleep.

"Come along," he said. "We're going home. I have your things in this bundle."

"That was kind," said Agathe, "but I won't be needing them much longer."

"Shut up," he said.

"I see you're picking up the tone of voice."

They went down the back stairs together, past Peter Stavo's cubicle and out into City Square. No one saw them leave. No one saw them walk up Castle Street and follow the route of all nine tram stops back to Tibo's house.

"Will you take me this way with you afterwards," asked Agathe, "when I am a dog? Will you give up the tram and walk? Dogs need exercise, particularly Dalmatians like me. We are carriage dogs—meant to run at the wheels of a gentleman's phaeton and see off footpads."

Tibo grunted the slouching garden gate out of the way and

stood aside to let Agathe past. "Somnambulist, somnambulist," he muttered. There was a still a space inside his head where he was able to hope that this might be a hideous nightmare.

At the end of the blue-tiled path, Tibo opened the door. "I'll show you to your room," he said.

"The kitchen floor will be fine," said Agathe and she walked confidently down the hall.

"Naturally. The kitchen floor. I had planned to show you the bathroom but I suppose if I leave the back door open to the garden, that will be sufficient."

"I'd prefer to use the bathroom for now, if that's all right with you, Tibo."

"That's fine, Agathe. I'll trust you to follow your nose. Goodnight."

And Tibo went to bed, too angry to cry, too exhausted to dream.

He woke up five short hours later to find Agathe sitting on his bed, that morning's copy of the *Daily Dottian* gripped in her teeth. Tibo snatched it away.

"It came through the door."

"Thank you for not tearing it to shreds," he said.

"Some do, some don't. I think I will be a 'don't.'"

Tibo noticed that she was wearing the same white and black spotted dress she wore on the day her lunch fell in the fountain—the day they began. But it was different, for now there were six pink buttons, stitched on in rows of three down the front.

She followed his glare. "I got up early," she said, "and made a few little alterations, just to try it for size. I've always suited spots and I've always had pretty nipples. Eight will be delicious!"

"You are not changing into a Dalmatian! I won't hear of it any more."

"Tibo, I am. Why can't you just accept it? Look what happened last night." She swung round on the bed and pointed her toes. "See? Black. My pink little toenails are turning into black doggy claws."

He grabbed her foot. "You painted this on!" And he started to rub with his thumb.

"Tibo, I did not! You're tickling me!" And she wriggled and twisted and writhed away.

They found themselves laughing—as they should—a beautiful woman and the man who loves her, rolling about in his bed first thing in the morning—of course they should laugh. But then, as her skirt rode up over her creamy thighs and Tibo saw those bruise-black blotches and he looked at her face and the way she smiled from behind that dark patch across her eye, suddenly it wasn't funny any more. All the fun vanished and he let go of her ankle.

"I have to get dressed," he said.

"I'll make you some toast."

As Tibo threw back the covers and stood up, the *Daily Dottian* fell to the floor so it wasn't until after he had washed and shaved—which took rather longer than usual because of all the time he wasted saying "Co-lour-ful" into the mirror—it wasn't until then that he picked it up again and read the headline:

DOT MAN FOUND DEAD IN CANAL

And then, on a second deck:

GRIM DISCOVERY AT LOCK GATE

It was Hektor, the "promising young artist and leading figure of the Ampersand school." Tibo folded the paper so the sports section was outermost and went down to the kitchen where Agathe was waiting with a pot of coffee and toast standing on the stove to keep warm. Tibo looked at the pile of blankets curled into a nest on the floor.

"You slept there?" he said.

"Yes. It was surprisingly comfortable. Here, have some toast."

It sounded like gravel in his head and he swallowed cup after cup of coffee to force it down.

"When Hektor left," he said casually, "did he mention where he was going?"

"No."

Tibo struggled to peel back the layers of meaning in that word. "Did he say when he might be back?"

"No. More toast?"

"No, thanks. So he just left? No reason? Just went?"

"Some friends came for him."

Tibo was suddenly hopeful. Friends. For a man like Hektor Stopak "friends" could mean only one thing—criminal associates. Some underworld deal gone sour, a smack on the head and over the railings into the canal.

"So, were these men he knew from The Three Crowns, perhaps?"

"I don't think so, Tibo. Coffee?"

"Yes, a little. Would you know them again?"

"Oh, absolutely. There were four of them—a strongman with a big handlebar moustache, two juggling girls and a girl with a performing dog."

Tibo was delighted. The gang of vagabonds he saw in City Square. "And those people are friends of Hektor?"

"No, Tibo, friends of mine. Sort of. From Mamma Cesare's haunted theatre, upstairs in The Golden Angel." And she told him the whole story.

At the end of it, Tibo couldn't think of anything to say except, "I see. I don't think you should bother coming to work today." And he left the house and walked up the hill towards the tram stop, swinging the bell as he passed. "Ambergris," he said.

As usual, people spoke to him while they waited for the tram. They spoke to him on the way into town. Tibo ignored them. At the Town Hall, he ducked into the side door and found Peter Stavo waiting to meet him.

"There are two policemen in your office," he said.

"I see," said Tibo again. He walked slowly up the stairs.

GOOD MAYOR KROVIC ALMOST BURST OUT laughing when he saw his visitors. They stood up to greet him like caricatures of detectives, great lumpy men, not long off the farm. One of them had trousers that flapped well above his ankles. The other wore his far too long so they flopped down over his boots.

Long trousers said, "I'm Welter—this is Detective Sergeant Levant."

Tibo shook hands. "What can I do for you, gentlemen?"

Welter nodded at the newspaper under Tibo's arm. "It's about the dead bloke—Stopak."

"Ah, yes. I've been reading about it. But I'm afraid I don't know any more than I read in the paper."

"And what about your secretary?" said Levant.

"What about her?"

"Mayor Krovic, you must know that Stopak and her, they were shacked up—had been for years."

Tibo felt himself make a face of disgust. "You must ask her about that," he said.

"That's why we're here," Levant said, in a sneery sing-song.

"Do you know where we can find her?" Welter asked.

"I'm afraid she hasn't been at work for a time," said Tibo, which was true but not an answer to the question.

"That's a worry," said Welter. "All her stuff's gone from the flat—not that that says much. Everything's gone. Canal Street, you know what they're like, Mayor Krovic. Picked the whole place clean right down to the plaster, so they did."

"Nothing left for you, then," said Tibo. "I mean by way of clues, of course."

"I know what you meant, sir," said Welter. He took a card from his top pocket and held it out. "If she shows up, sir, we need to talk to her."

When they left, with another handshake, Tibo fell into his chair. Any last shred of hope that this might be a bad dream had disappeared when he saw the policemen in his office.

There is nothing more ordinary than a policeman, nothing more calculated to blow away any lingering wisps of self-delusion. A policeman in the office is a bucket of cold water for the soul.

And now he had lied to them—or, at the very least, withheld information—all so he could protect the woman he loved, who might very well be a murderer but who was, anyway, almost certainly mad and who was intent on dragging him into her fantasies with lunatic talk of haunted theatres and a ghostly strongman! Except that he had seen the strongman. And the juggling girls. And the girl with the performing dog. He had even seen the dog—and yet he had said nothing to the police. The one real clue, the one thing that might have taken suspicion off Agathe and he had said nothing. And now he couldn't. There was no going back now, no way he could walk into Welter's office and say, "Oh, I forgot to mention the circus strongman and, of course, I only know about him because Agathe told me but she seems to think he might be a bit of a ghost, and I may also have forgotten to mention that she's staying at my house because I've loved her for years but I wouldn't bother talking to her because she's turning into a dog."

The more that he thought about it, the worse it looked—ruin, ridicule, disgrace, all the things he had feared, all the things which had made him hold back before, all the things which had cost him Agathe were looming now and, behind them all, he heard the squeak and clang of the prison door.

Tibo suffered the hunted, panicked feeling that only comes in nightmares, when "they" are just behind the door, when flight is compulsory and escape impossible, when capture would be almost a blessing if only as a release from the fear. He left his desk and stood at the window, watching the street, nervously combing his hair with his fingers. He paced the room. He left to make coffee. He changed his mind and came back. He noticed, for the first time, the new wastepaper basket Peter Stavo had found for him and thought it touching.

He blew his nose and tugged at his lapels and then, before he even knew he was going to do it, he fell on his knees in front of the town arms on the wall, covered his face with his hands and said, "Walpurnia, help me!" He said, "Help me. I have tried. I have really tried. I've tried to do the right thing for Dot and much good it has done me. And, if you won't help me, at least help her. Walpurnia, show me what to do."

That was all he said. It was all he could find to say. If a man is beaten and broken there are few words but, as little as he had left to say, he remembered Agathe and, as little as he said, it was enough.

It's hard to say what happened. A "tearing"—that might be the best way to describe it. Something that was torn or shifted or moved aside and, from the other side of it, I stepped through. It was a magnificent manifestation. When I stepped down off that shield, I was absolutely radiant. My robes shone, my skin glowed, my eyes sparkled, my long blonde hair whipped about in an orchid-scented breeze straight from the gates of Heaven. I was gorgeous. Of course, Tibo Krovic saw me as a warty old nun with a long black beard but, when he took his hands away from his face and found his whole office twinkling with starlight, the effect was much the same. Poor Tibo. A tiny bit of heavenly endorsement, the thought that somebody had noticed all his hard work—that was all it took to make him happy.

It was all so lovely that, when I spoke, it didn't matter that the words came out from under a big, bristly moustache. I said, "Good Tibo Krovic, this is what you must do—love. Love. Love. And, more than that, be loved and ready to accept the gifts of love in return."

Then, because it's more or less obligatory to end with something gnomic on these occasions, I told him, "You are better loved than you know, Tibo Krovic, and there is a friend who will help you when the dogs are running. Seek him out." I said that bit a few times more as the last of the stardust settled into the carpet and the gossamer curtain came back down and I stepped into the town shield again. "Seek him out. Seek him out," I said. I may have overplayed that part a little.

But, when the room was quiet again and Tibo found his breathing calm and even, when he hauled himself to his feet and ran his hands across the shield to make sure that it was really nothing more than wood and paint, he felt happy and he knew what to do.

"I am the Mayor of Dot!" he said and he strode off to Agathe's desk and took out a sheet of notepaper with the town arms on it. He wrote something briefly, in quick strokes of his fountain pen, and all but ran out of the Town Hall. In Ampersand Avenue, he hailed another cab and seven minutes later—because of the lorry-load of newsprint blocking the road outside the *Dottian* offices—Tibo arrived at the District Court. He nodded his way through the familiar staff and, outside No. 1 Court, he folded his bit of notepaper in half and handed it to a man in blue uniform standing by the door.

"Give this to the lawyer Guillaume, please," he said.

"Certainly, Mayor Krovic. Nice to see you back."

"Thank you. I'll wait for the reply."

The doors of the court swung shut against Tibo's nose and he stood, hands in pockets, whistling "The Boy I Love" until, a few moments later, they opened again.

"There we go, sir," said the court attendant and he held out the same folded sheet of paper.

Tibo opened it. There, under his own scrawled note, was another, just as brief, in a still larger and more flamboyant hand. It said, "My dear Krovic, I hope I may be of some assistance. Feel free to call at my home, 43 Loyola Street, any time after 9 this evening." And then, "I trust you are not allergic to pangolins. YG."

THE SUMMER DUSK WAS FALLING ON LOYOLA Street and fat little bats were tumbling between the popping street lamps when Tibo arrived for his appointment. He came under the arch at the back of Copernicus Park and into a world of shadowed laurel hedges and iron gates set between mossy pillars. Stained-glass windows with images of overflowing fruit baskets or ample girls in inadequate clothing made of whiplash traceries of foliage glowed out above every door except for No. 43. There the glass was quite plain but for the letters XLIII marked out in black. At the end of the path, the front door was standing open and a sheet of notepaper was trapped under the huge iron knocker with the invitation "Come in, Krovic."

Tibo gave a single, thunderous rap with the knocker, caught the sheet of paper as it fell and walked into the echoing building, announcing himself with hellos as he went.

The house was illimitable in the darkness—a vast, unplumbable thing of shadows and echoes and hinted vistas of closed doors. Tibo stood at the foot of a gigantic staircase, something stolen from the wreck of a foundered ocean liner, and called up into the dark, "Hello? Yemko? Yemko Guillaume? It's me—Tibo Krovic," until a door opened behind him and an oblong of butter-yellow light fell across the floor.

"You needn't look for me up there," said Yemko. "The top of my own stairs has been terra incognita to me these many years. There are seventeen rooms, I think. Sometimes I see them in dreams." He held out a hand. "I apologise for the lack of a welcome, Krovic. I heard your knock and raced to answer it with all the fleetness of foot at my disposal. Come in."

But, before they began the long, slow walk back into the room, Yemko raised a questioning eyebrow. "Did I ask? Are you allergic to pangolins?"

"Yes, you did," said Tibo, "and, as far as I know, having never met a pangolin, I am not."

"Never met a pangolin? My word, what a strangely sheltered life you have led. We must remedy that."

Up on the shelf at the back of the darkened room there was a posed taxidermy of a stuffed and mounted mongoose locked in battle with a pallid cobra. As his eyes adjusted to the gloom, Tibo saw another dancing round a dry branch and another where the cobra lunged at its feet. Half a dozen in all—a dusty gavotte of death and venom, a frozen forest of twisting, writhing, fang-bared poisonous combat.

"Unusual," said Tibo.

"Most," said Yemko. "In settlement of a debt, you know."

Yemko made a sucking, tweeting noise with his mouth and, just as he promised, a pangolin shuffled out from the gloom at the back of the shelf, rocking his head, brushing past the frozen cobras with a rattle of his bony body.

"Allow me to introduce Leonidas." And, with a slight bow to each, he said, "Mr. Mayor, Leonidas the pangolin; Leonidas, Mayor Tibo Krovic."

Leonidas looked up expectantly and Yemko scratched the tips of his pink piggy ears. "Yeeeees, you like that, don't you?" he cooed affectionately. "The scales of the pangolin are smoked as a cure for syphilis, you know," he told the mayor.

"In a pipe?"

"No, like fish. I don't know what you do with them after that. Chew them? Make tea with them? Rub them on the affected part? Who knows?"

Yemko turned away to coo at his companion, tweaking the

plump little ears lovingly. "But we won't let the baaaad men do that to little Leonidas, will we now? No, we won't. Bad men with their nasty stinky bits. No."

In a corner of the room, there stood a desk—the desk that Yemko had risen from in order to answer the door. Most of the room was deep in shadow but Yemko's desk was lit by two poseable lamps and there was a huge magnifying glass on a stand fixed over a tiny vice—the sort of thing that fishermen hunch over in winter as they prepare artificial flies for the coming season. A glass inkwell shone with violet ink and the rest of the desk was lost under a snowdrift of rice grains.

Yemko waved at it vaguely. "A hobby, you know. Would you like to see?" He motioned Tibo towards the chair with a gesture of invitation and moved the magnifying glass into position. "I'm a mere beginner," he said modestly. But there, quite distinctly, were the opening words of some strange poem written on a grain of rice—"'What a place for a snark,' the Bellman cried"—with all the punctuation properly in place.

Amazing. Tibo took his eye from the glass. Without it, he could barely see the ink marks on the rice.

"I once got as far as 'Forgive us our' when I was doing the Lord's Prayer but I ran out of rice. I'll try again. That's pretty much the standard text for those who share my silly obsession. I can't see why. Or why it must be a complete piece. Why not entire books of broken sentences in a pocket of grains? Reconstituted poetry in tiny snatches? A risotto of love letters, a paella of sagas, a pilaf of sonnets, a jumbled jambalaya of dictionaries? Everything so small, except the ideas. Small. I think that's what I like. I buy a packet of rice and lay it on the table, examine each grain in the hope it may be the one that has defied the ordinary bounds of rice-dom, expanded a little beyond the ordinary, left a tiny gap for one more idea, but I do not find it. Nature is remarkably uniform. She has set a limit on everything from diatoms to the blue whale. Everything except for me. I defy her border controls. Forgive me. I must sit."

Tibo hurriedly rose from the chair and helped Yemko into it. He deflated with an exhausted sigh.

"Think at what labour and expense these tiny grains are achieved. How many hours of toil in flooded fields buzzing with gnats, the exhausting, sucking plod behind the buffalo, the slap of his tail, the burning sun, the leeches, the back-breaking stoop, a lakh of times repeated, and all to produce this." He pushed a few grains around with his finger.

"Even once it has been brought round the world to the food hall of Braun's Department Store, it sells for pennies—so cheap is human sweat. And look at it, how white it is—a by-word for whiteness and yet not white at all. Look at this one." He held up an individual grain. "Pearly grey. Some are almost translucent, like ground glass, some have that deep white eye trapped in the middle—see? It reminds me of the insects stuck in those bits of amber that roll up on our beach sometimes but this is like a tiny piece of snow trapped in ice. Why, I wonder. What can possibly cause that? There is a book to be written about rice, I think. It lingers in someone's typewriter. Not mine, I fear. At my back, I always hear Time's wingèd chariot. There would even be room for a paragraph about that hideous, cheap yellow long grain they import from America and perhaps a chapter for Arborio, a discursive chapter following the slow wander of the Po and skating, like a mosquito on a pond, over its malarial swamps past Turin to end in a puddle of squid-ink risotto. And there must be page after page for Basmati. Basmati is the prince of rice, you know. That scented, aromatic, almost floral flavour. I could eat it alone, just as it is, with a little salt for the savour. Thousands do, millions, I suppose, every day.

"Many millions more content themselves with something less or with nothing at all. The Indians, when they cook it, they have a proverb. They say the grains should be like brothers—close but not stuck together. Basmati is the rice of choice for those who follow my strange calling. It's the flat-sided grains, you know—the ideal surface upon which to write. And regular, as regular as anything in nature, yet all different—no two of them just exactly the same, never quite the same size, never quite the same shape, always slightly chipped or slightly curved or slightly misshapen. Very like us, Mayor Krovic. Very like we Dottians for whom you care so deeply, each of us slightly chipped or slightly curved or slightly misshapen. Perhaps that applies even to you, Good Tibo Krovic. Is that why you have come to my house at dead of night?"

Tibo said, "Once, long ago, you offered me your help. As I recall, we met in the gallery and you told me . . ."

Yemko raised a single finger to silence him. "Of course, knowing you as I do," he said, "there can be no possibility that a man of your background and reputation could ever be involved in anything which would require my professional assistance or advice."

Tibo said, "But . . ."

Yemko lifted an eyebrow. "There can be no buts," he warned. "It goes without saying that you are entirely innocent of any wrongdoing and you have come here to ask my advice on behalf of an unfortunate friend." Yemko tugged gently at the ears of the pangolin which lay curled on his vast belly. "Tell me all about it. In fact, better yet, tell Leonidas all about it. Your next words should be 'Leonidas, I have a friend . . . ,' I think."

Yemko sank back in his chair and his huge head disappeared into the shadows which seemed drawn to him the way the moon pulls the seas. Light glowed from the grains of rice sparkling on the desk, everything else was velvet.

Tibo said, "Leonidas, I have a friend and, for some time, this friend has been in love with Mrs. Agathe Stopak, the secretary of the Mayor of Dot." Tibo could not have imagined a more astounding admission. In a few words he had acknowledged to Yemko Guillaume the most amazing secret of creation, a truth he had hidden from everyone, the reason the stars hang in the sky, the secret engine that drives the seasons, and Yemko's only reply was a polite little cough which may have been intended to mask a titter.

"Forgive me, Mayor Krovic, but Leonidas has known that for years. I think he had it first from Sarah, the girl who gives out the change in the second-best butcher's in town. La toute Dot has known it for years. Please tell Leonidas something a little more startling."

If Tibo had been merely astonished, he would probably have been unable to go on but the sudden realisation that his secret was known, that he was the only man in Dot who did not find it ordinary and commonplace—boring even—was far beyond astonishing. His mouth flapped uselessly for a second or two and then, grateful for the confessional blackness that filled the room, he told his story.

At the end of it Yemko gave a sigh, as travellers in the far north say they have heard the great whales make in the midst of an ocean of ice, and he said, "This is almost too much to believe. Transmogrification is one thing—after all, Leonidas used to be a dancing master at a private academy for young ladies until things became too much for him and, I suppose, a phantom circus operating all unknown at the heart of our city is believable, more or less. Yes." He twiddled his thumbs. "Yes, I could convince a jury of that but the idea that the Mayor of Dot, Good Tibo Krovic—or, at any rate, his close personal friend—could knowingly harbour a fugitive in a murder case? Well, it's preposterous, it's ridiculous, it's utterly fantastical." He turned to Tibo with delight and said, "You know what this means?"

"It means nobody will believe it and I have worried myself needlessly about nothing?"

"Good God, no, Krovic! It means ruin, disgrace, loss of reputation. It means prison and, above all, total extinguishment of pension rights! Krovic, they would hang you for it if they could and small children and old ladies would be trampled in the rush. You are the same as them, Krovic. How can you possibly expect them to forgive that?"

Tibo sat down quietly in a shadowed corner. He knew it was the truth. "You told me, if the hounds were in pursuit, you would help me."

"And I meant it. Are you willing to put yourself completely in my hands?"

"Of course."

"Then I will call on you tomorrow evening. Go to work as

usual. Behave normally. Remain calm. Now, be a good fellow and let yourself out."

Tibo rose to go but, before the door clicked shut on the room, Yemko spoke out of the shadows again. "You are not exactly like them, you know. After all this time, Tibo Krovic, I think I may have found my odd grain of rice."

THE HONEYSUCKLE WAS SPENDING ITSELF ON the night air and drunken moths were beating themselves senseless against the street lamps as Tibo walked home through Copernicus Park, his black brogues crunching on the well-kept paths. When he reached the old house at the end of the blue-tiled path, he was careful not to touch the bell beside the gate and he had left the front door unlocked so he could come in quietly without disturbing Agathe. But she was waiting for him anyway and she came running to the door to meet him and danced round in happy circles in the hall. Her transformation was complete.

In the hours that Tibo had been gone, Agathe had abandoned clothes just as she said she would and she was now utterly Dalmatian. She wagged at him joyously and said, "I knew it was you, I knew it was you. I could hear you at the end of the street."

"No, you couldn't."

"Yes, I could and the bell on the path gave you away."

"I didn't touch the bell."

"It sings with happiness when you pass, Tibo. Didn't you know?"

"I didn't know," he said. He could not keep the grief from his voice. "I'm going to bed now."

At the bottom of the stairs, watching him go, she said, "I love you, Tibo Krovic."

"I love you too, Agathe."

"Ah, but I love you as you deserve to be loved, as a dog loves, without asking anything in return but the chance to love you more."

Tibo said, "I have loved you like a dog for as long as I can remember. Now will you sleep on the kitchen floor again or will you come to bed?"

Agathe said nothing and Tibo lay down alone, on top of the counterpane his mother had stitched long ago. He left the curtains open so the sun would wake him gently in the morning and he looked down the bed at the mirrored wardrobe and the reflection of the soles of his feet. He was wakeful.

After a while, Tibo heard the sound of Agathe climbing the stairs, the click of her black toenails against the parquet. She stopped in the doorway and sat down, watching him silently. He looked at her, saying nothing. He patted the mattress encouragingly. Agathe came forward, head low, to where his hand hung over the side of the bed and licked at his fingers. She climbed on the bed and curled over his feet. The moonlight through the window made her white skin silver, made the black marks that dotted it inky. He stroked her gently. "I am very glad," he said, "that becoming a dog has not robbed you of the gift of speech."

"Oh, Tibo, don't be silly. All dogs can speak. We simply choose not to. We listen more than we talk. It's a way of loving."

"Are there other ways?"

"Yes, Tibo." And then it was morning.

I*N SPITE OF EVERYTHING THAT YEMKO HAD* told him—"Go to work as usual. Behave normally. Remain calm"—for Tibo, the day was not usual. He could not behave normally. He was not calm.

For one thing, he woke, exhausted, in a tangle of sheets, too late for the tram to work, with Agathe beside him. Her mouth was open, her tongue visible between strong white teeth as she breathed. He left her sleeping and made breakfast which he fed to her by finger-fuls as she lay across him in bed and he kissed her on the nose between bites.

"I must go to work," he said at last.

"Why must you go to work?" she asked and, since Dalmatians see things so much more clearly and Tibo could not think of any reasonable answer, he stayed a little longer.

"I must go to work," he said at last.

"Yes, I suppose you must," said Agathe. "Would you like me to come with you?"

"No, I don't think so. I don't think Peter Stavo would understand."

"He's never liked dogs," said Agathe.

So Tibo went into town alone and, although it was almost noon when he arrived outside The Golden Angel, he decided to stop for coffee anyway. The morning rush was over, the lunchtime rush had not yet begun and Tibo took his usual place at the high table near the door.

A moment or two later, a waiter began his slow glissando, stepping forward, napkin over his arm, ready to take the mayor's usual order. But he stopped in his tracks, frozen to the spot by a flash of Morse from Cesare's eyebrows and then—wonder of wonders—il patrone himself stepped out from behind the coffee organ and said, "What can I get you, Mr. Mayor?"

Tibo held out his hand and Cesare took it and they looked into one another's eyes for a bit and Tibo said, "The usual please, Mr. Cesare."

Cesare snapped his fingers above his head like castanets and, without letting go of Tibo's hand, he shouted, "The usual for my friend Mayor Krovic." And then, in a confidential tone, he asked, "How are things?"

"A hundred times worse," said Tibo, "and much, much better."

Cesare said, "A good friend of mine once told me that there is not so much love in the world that we can afford to waste a drop of it, no matter where we find it. Your coffee's here."

Cesare took a cup from the waiter who now stood nervously at his shoulder and placed it carefully on the table in front of Tibo. "On the house," he said. "Enjoy." And he retreated to the coffee organ again.

When, a few moments later, Tibo finished his coffee and stepped out into Castle Street, Cesare did not acknowledge his going by so much as a nod. All that needed to be said had been said—there was no more to add.

Castle Street, The Golden Angel, White Bridge, City Square, none of it was usual or normal, everything had taken on a new colour for Tibo, as if he were seeing it for the first time, as if he were seeing it for the last time and then, when he arrived in his office, there was the letter, waiting on his desk. It was not signed but Tibo recognised the wide nib and the flamboyant hand. He had seen it only the day before on a piece of council stationery. It said, "Given all the hubbub of recent days, perhaps you should take a short holiday in Dash. Inform whomsoever must be informed. Leave all the arrangements to me. Until this evening."

Hubbub. A nice word. Tibo tried it out in his mouth a little, "Hubbub. Hubbub," and found that it tasted of huge carp sinking silently into dark green pools.

Tibo took another sheet of notepaper from Agathe's desk and wrote a letter to the Town Clerk. "Dear Gorvic, Not quite myself. I have decided on a few days in Dash for a change of air." He looked at it proudly. It was his first official lie.

Then, after he had answered some mail and written "The cheapest option is not always the best," across a query from the Parks Department, he found there was almost nothing left to do. So, after half an hour of wondering what it was that he had ever found to do, Tibo filled his pockets with ginger biscuits from the tin by the coffee machine and, munching them as he went, he walked home.

AGATHE WAS IN THE GARDEN. THE WIND had turned towards the south-west and the cold weather of the past week was gone. Dot lay washed in sunshine, enjoying a few last days of Indian summer before the Fire Brigade Band packed away its cymbals and its tubas, before the geese on the Ampersand sniffed the wind and turned their heads to the south and flew off, dragging winter behind them on their wings.

She had spent the morning lying in the cool, round shadow of a giant cotoneaster bush. The sunlight falling between the leaves left dark spotted shadows on her skin and she twitched away a tiny fly that landed on her ear. There was nothing to see. She liked that. She liked being low down and hidden, out of sight, safe. She liked not worrying about the washing, not fretting in case some kid in Canal Street kicked a dirty football against it. She didn't have to hide her purse any more. She didn't even have a purse, not even a pocket to keep one in—but she had enough to eat and she was loved and she wasn't afraid.

Lying in the shade, glorying in the heat and the blaze of green light that shone up from the lawn, Agathe thought, "This is nice." She stretched out and rolled on her back. The dry earth with its sprinkle of dead leaves left her clean and white. "This is nice," she thought. "I have Tibo to look after me and he lets me love him and he's not angry and I don't have to do anything. This is nice." She felt that she had awakened from a long dream where she had thought herself a woman, grown up, got a job, lived and loved and been happy and sad—sometimes very sad—and then, just when the dream had become too much to bear, she had come back to herself and real life as a dog. There was such a feeling of relief and contentment and she was amazed at herself and the life she had lived before. It was as if she had been brought up in some huge fairground hall of mirrors and only now, lying under a bush in the sunshine, could she see the world as it really was for the first time, without the bends and the wobbles.

Agathe rolled on to her tummy. She could feel warm blobs of sunlight on her skin where they fell through the tattered parasol of the bush. That fly settled on her ear again but this time she let it stay. There was the sound of a lawnmower slicing through the afternoon in the next garden but one. Slowly she went to sleep.

When Tibo got home to the old house at the end of the blue-tiled path, he walked through the kitchen calling her name, found the door to the garden open and sat on the grass watching her, enjoying her. He took another ginger biscuit from his pocket and broke it. The sudden crunch woke her.

"Want one?" he asked.

"I remember these," she said, as if ginger biscuits in the Town Hall belonged to a time years before and not the day before yesterday in Peter Stavo's lodge.

He offered her another. "Agathe, I'm going away soon."

"Yes, but I'll be going with you, won't I?"

"If you want to. Yes, I'd like that."

"That's all right, then."

"Yes, Agathe. I think that's all right." He held another ginger biscuit between his lips and she bit it away.

"Let's go in the house now, Agathe."

Tibo walked back to the kitchen door and, a little while later, she followed him in. They were still in the kitchen, Tibo sitting at the table, Agathe sitting under it when, towards ten that evening, the doorbell rang.

"Stay here," he said.

Tibo hurried to answer the door and he found Yemko, gasping

and almost unable to stand, demanding, "A chair, for God's sake, Krovic, a chair!" in insistent wheezes. "Your garden path is an interminable torment," he breathed.

Tibo ran back to the kitchen and returned with a straight-backed chair which creaked discreetly. Closing the front door, Good Mayor Krovic noticed the hearse-like bulk of Yemko's taxi, muttering on broken springs under a yellow street lamp, waiting, darkly.

He closed the door. "Can I offer you something?" he asked.

Yemko shook his head. He sat half-folded on the groaning kitchen chair, his hands dangling at his sides, his lawyer's briefcase at his feet until, in spite of Tibo's order, Agathe came out from the kitchen, came quietly down the hall and sniffed, gently, at Yemko's huge fingers and licked them.

He looked down at her and smiled. He said, "Once upon a time there was a dear lady to whom I pledged my friendship. Sadly, if she were here today and a fugitive from justice, I would have no alternative but to hand her over to the authorities but you," he said, stroking Agathe's head, "bring to mind her great loveliness and her many charms, although you are, quite obviously, only a dog."

Agathe said nothing to that but she held Yemko's gaze for some while until he said, "Dear God, Krovic, have you no softer chair than this and is there no brandy in the house of the Mayor of Dot?"

Tibo led the way to his sitting room where Yemko filled the couch, cradling an improbable glass of brandy. He seemed completely at home but, when Tibo went to draw the curtains and light the lamps, he hissed a warning. "Best not, old chap. Let's leave things as they are for now."

Yemko opened his briefcase and removed a blizzard of papers. "Am I right in thinking you are unknown in Virgule, Mayor Krovic?"

Tibo nodded. "I've never even been there," he said.

"All to the good." Yemko handed over the first of his documents. "This is a will dated six months ago and naming, as your sole beneficiary, one Gnady Vadim, commercial traveller of 173 Mazzini Street, Virgule. It nominates me as your executor and instructs me to sell this house and contents and to pass the proceeds and all pension entitlements to dear Gnady. It is properly witnessed and notarised and requires only your signature."

From his top pocket Yemko produced a fat black fountain pen and, with his left hand, flourished another sheaf of papers. "These documents identify you, indisputably as Gnady Vadim of 173 Mazzini Street, Virgule. This," Yemko waved a small book with a blue cover, "is his bank account and these," there was a faint, silverish jingle between his fingers, "are the keys to the flat at 173 Mazzini Street."

Good Mayor Krovic began to speak but Yemko silenced him with an eyebrow. "Do not interrupt," he said. "Tomorrow morning at seven, my taxi will arrive at your garden gate. The driver will get out. You and any companion of your choice will drive, with the blinds drawn, to catch the seven-thirty ferry sailing for Dash. On the ferry, you and any companion will remain, at all times, inside the taxi. You will speak to no one. Once at Dash, you will drive to this," he handed Tibo a brochure, "hotel, where a booking has been made in your name, inclusive of full garaging services for your vehicle. You will go to your room alone and any companion will remain in the taxi at all times. You will take dinner before taking charge of the very small, pitifully frail craft which has been provided for a relaxing night fishing trip—a trip which will end in tragedy and from which you and any companion will never return."

"Never return," said Tibo blankly.

"Never, because, if you use this," another small silver flourish produced a pocket compass, "if you use this and sail all night long then, with luck, you will find yourself in Virgule by morning. Sink the boat. Sink Tibo Krovic with it, walk ashore as Gnady Vadim, walk in your wet boots to Mazzini Street. Live there with the companion of your choice for a month or so—there's enough in the bankbook—and, very soon, you will come into your inheritance from poor cousin Tibo. Then you simply disappear."

After a long week of astonishments, Good Mayor Krovic found himself more astounded than ever. "Is any of this legal?" he said.

"Poor, poor Tibo Krovic. Poor Good Tibo Krovic still fretting over what's legal instead of what's right, still not sure if what's right is also what's good. Does it matter? Do you care? What difference does it make? Is it legal? No! But the question you should have asked is 'Will it stand up in court?' and I guarantee that it will. Now sign."

POOR TIBO LAY AWAKE ALL NIGHT, CHIDing himself for not getting plenty of sleep ahead of his long row to Virgule, fretting over his second official lie and listening to Agathe sleeping where she lay over his outstretched arm. She was a symphony of mutterings and twitches, strange little mewlings and lunges on the bed. "Chasing rabbits"—that's what they called it. He kissed her gently on top of the head and went back to listening to the dark.

At four o'clock, Tibo fell asleep. At five, his alarm clock went off and he awoke, more exhausted than ever. Agathe slept on.

Alone in the kitchen, Tibo made coffee and listened to the garden birdsong. He took his cup and wandered round the house, saying goodbye to things, his books, bits of furniture he had never cared for until now, ornaments, odd sentimental things that tied him to this house, to boyhood, to Dot. He was leaving and all of it must be left behind.

Tibo opened the door on his mother's old room, the cold bed, unslept in for years, the curtains that never closed, the picture of me with a beard like a hedge, everything calm and still and calm and damp and dusty. On the dressing table, there was a tiny photograph of his father—not the father he had known but a handsome, happy young man. With one finger, Tibo tipped it until it fell, face forward, on the rug. He pressed down on it with his heel until he heard the glass crack, then he went off to pack.

Tibo took only the sort of clothes that a man going for a relaxing weekend in Dash might be expected to take. He left his suits hanging in the wardrobe, his ties on their rack. There was no room in his duffel bag for the Mayor of Dot.

At six, Tibo made scrambled eggs on toast and shared them with Agathe, feeding her from his own plate. At six thirty, the dishes were piled on the kitchen drainer and Tibo was sitting on the couch, looking out the window. When it came into the street, the black taxi brought shadows with it. Tibo heard it stuttering down the hill all the way from the kiosk, the same insistent knocking that pursued him through nightmares, and then, with a final fart, it halted at the gate. The driver, a tall, lean man Tibo recognised from Yemko's bandstand picnic all those years before, got out and glared significantly towards the house. He took off his cab driver's cap with its numbered silver badge and, with a final nod at Tibo, he tossed it back through the open window and on to the driver's seat, hunched his shoulders and walked away.

"It's time," said Tibo. "Stay in the hall until I call you."

Tibo walked down the blue-tiled path carrying two thick blankets which he flung in the cab. He left the door standing open and went back to the house where Agathe was waiting in the hall. "The street's empty," he said. "Run."

Tibo picked up his duffel bag and her curtain bundle of clothes and watched as Agathe leapt into the taxi. She peered out at him, watching him from the blankets on the back seat as he locked up and carried the luggage down the path and then, disguised in the cabbie's hat, he drove off.

"Your bell is crying," she said.

"I know. I can hear it." He turned into Cervantes Street towards the docks and, a few minutes later, he was sitting on board the Dash ferry, nudging out past the lighthouse. Tibo gripped the steering wheel of the cab. He never moved from his seat. He kept the peak of his borrowed cap tugged down low. He kept his face fixed forward but his eyes were on the mirror and the image of Dot disappearing behind him. Smaller and smaller it grew, fainter and greyer and mistier, until it became the colour of the sea and vanished away into the waves and there was nothing left but the pale green dome of the cathedral and, finally, only me, glinting gold for a moment and disappearing like the crow's nest on a sinking trawler.

When the last of Dot had gone, Tibo looked straight ahead through the spray until Dash grew up out of the sea; first the thin grey plumes of its smokeries, then the unmistakable smell of fish carried on the wind, the chimneys poking up from the waves, the red roofs, the white houses and, soon, the quayside where the ferry docked.

Good Mayor Krovic took the hotel brochure which Yemko had given him and spread it open across the top of the steering wheel, fixed by his two thumbs. The directions he followed led him through the narrow streets of Dash town and out the other side to where the cobbles stuttered out in a narrow road of packed sand that wandered among hairy dunes to the far tip of the island. It was the last place in the world—a tiny inn at the end of a lost beach and, beyond it, the horizon and, beyond that, nothing but the sky.

Tibo drove the wallowing taxi into the courtyard where the double doors of the stables were open to receive him. He settled Agathe into her nest of blankets and kissed her again. "I'll be back in a few hours," he said. "Keep very still. Be quiet and try to sleep. The time will pass more quickly."

He made sure the blinds were firm on the windows and he had just finished closing the stable doors when a fat woman in black came bustling into the yard. "Are you Mr. Krovic?" she said. "We've been expecting you."

It was the first time in twenty-three years that anybody had called him plain "Mr." Krovic and it took the length of a smile before he said, "Yes, that's me," and walked into the inn.

THE QUEEN CATE WAS THE SORT OF PLACE where Tibo would have been happy to live all his days—dark and low-ceilinged, as tanned with smoke as any Dash kipper but sparkling from the sea-light that rushed in at the tiny windows with their panes of wrinkled green glass. It was haunted with wave-song, soothed by gulls and flavoured everywhere by the scent of Mrs. Leshmic's kitchen.

"You're in time for lunch, just about," she said and she put him at a table next to the fire where the coals dozed and muttered and where he ate hot meat pies and drank strong red beer and had good bread and cheese until he sighed happily and went to sleep.

But in the stables, in spite of what he had told her, Agathe did not sleep. She tried. She lay down on the broad back seat of the cab, her body folding awkwardly into the crater where Yemko had crushed the springs past their last squeak of resilience, but she did not sleep. After a while, with her nose down close to the upholstery, breathing in the smell of leather and bottoms and a galaxy of iced biscuit crumbs that had settled in the cracks between the cushions, Agathe sat up and squinted through the gap at the bottom of the blinds on her window. Her nose left a round mark. Her breath steamed the glass. Outside the car, the stable was dark and dusty. There was a broad, ragged streak of yellowish light coming under the ancient wooden doors but it was too tired and sickly to reach the corners of the room. She could see the worn brick floor, sunk in channels where cartwheels had rolled every day since horseshoes were invented, and a few strands of old straw that had blown in from somewhere and the usual rusty, greasy cans and tools that find their way into garages and that was about it. Nothing to look at. Tibo had been gone barely ten minutes and already she was bored. She bounced across the back seat and looked out the other window. There was nothing on that side but a wall with a bit of old sack hanging on it. Boring. Nothing to look at. Nothing to sniff. Nobody to play with. Boring.

"What's the bloedig point?" she asked. "What's the bloedig point of being a dog if it's no fun?"

She poked her nose through the little arch cut in the window dividing the driver from the passengers and searched for some hint of Tibo but there was none, just the old wool smell of the cabbie's hat and the tarry linger of his pipe. No Tibo. No love. Just a smell of "lonely."

Agathe fought the urge to howl, turned three times on her blankets and whirled them into a pile like the meringue nests Mrs. Oktar used to sell at her cake counter and, with a little whimper that sounded like "Tibo," she lay down with her chin on the leather cushions.

Hours passed. The line of sunshine under the stable door lengthened briefly then edged away into shadow again. Inside the taxi, it grew dark but was only when the first of the evening's customers came into the bar and the door banged in the wind and a tiny avalanche of sand spilled in from the beach and whispered on the stone floor that Tibo woke up.

Mrs. Leshmic was smiling at him from behind the bar. "Looks like you needed the rest," she said.

Tibo rubbed his eyes with the heels of his hands. "What time is it?"

"Just after six, my dear. Another beer? How about some rum? It's famous round these parts."

Tibo ordered a coffee, without the rum—"Maybe later"—and announced, "I should really go and unpack now." The regulars at the bar hunched a little closer to their drinks as he made for the door and Tibo imagined they spoke of him, "a stranger round these parts."

He found Agathe waiting for him eagerly in the darkened taxi and he gave her the biscuits he had saved from coffee. "Just a few hours more and we'll be on our way," he said. "It's a fine night for a sail and we'll be home by morning." He kissed her on the nose again, hoisted his bag on his shoulder and went back to the inn.

Tibo did not bother to unpack. He left his bag on his bed and spent the next hours by the window in the bar, watching the sea, watching the waves, watching distant sails. At eight, as clouds thickened around the edge of the world, he asked Mrs. Leshmic to pack some food for the night's fishing and went outside—"Just to take the air."

The courtyard was deserted but, in the taxi, Agathe was ill-tempered and almost frantic with boredom. "I have decided that being a dog is very much like being a little girl again—always waiting for the grown-ups, always having to do what you're told."

"But I thought that was what you wanted. I thought you wanted to follow me home so I could look after you."

"That's not what I meant at all," she said. "All day long, I've been stuck in here. How much longer?"

"Just one more hour," he promised. "Only a little while more." He took her bundle and hurried away from the inn, slipping through the empty dunes to the very end of the island and out of sight of the Queen Cate.

"I don't need those things any more," Agathe had protested.

"But we can't leave them for anybody to find. They must come with us."

Standing there, at the very edge of Dash, Agathe's bundle hidden in the bushes at his feet, Tibo looked back the way he had come. There was nothing to see and, in the darkness, not even the glow of Dot's street lamps would point the way back.

The time was drawing close. Tibo walked slowly to the inn and got dressed in double layers of clothing. "A fine night for fishing," he told Mrs. Leshmic. "Might I have those sandwiches now?"

She handed him a blue enamel tin—much like the one Agathe had bought for herself in Castle Street—and two bottles of beer.

"Just row off the headland, Mr. Krovic, that's my advice, just past the end of the island. That's where the boys find the fat ones. She's tied up at our little jetty. Will you need any help?"

Tibo refused modestly and said goodnight with a smile. There was a soft patter of fine sand against the door as he shut it and then he hurried back to the taxi and to Agathe.

"Time to run again, my darling," he said. "Straight for the dunes and I'll see you at the end of the island in a little while."

Tibo kissed her on the nose one last time and watched her race into cover and then, with two blankets round his neck, he climbed the steps down to the jetty alone.

It was hard work getting away from the little wooden pier. Tibo was no oarsman and he was dreading the thought of a whole night at sea. His nervousness showed. The boat tipped and wobbled as he settled himself on the centre line and he had trouble fixing the oars in their rowlocks. There were dark faces at the windows of the inn. Tibo tried not to look terrified and pulled away.

It took him about a dozen half-hearted strokes to get out of the inlet by the Queen Cate but, once he made it past the rocks, what wind there was blew towards the end of the island, Agathe and, eventually, to Virgule. When he reached the headland, Tibo began turning his boat towards the beach, whistling "The Boy I Love" as he paddled along lopsidedly until he heard Agathe's answering howls and saw her bounding along, pale in the dusk, amongst the beach grass.

Tibo rowed harder until the boat jarred against sand. He felt the crunch and grind of it running through the timbers and he leapt out on to the shore.

Agathe came splashing to meet him. "I'm here! I'm here!" she said, kicking up the spray as she ran.

"Yes, darling, I see you, I see you, clever girl. Now get in the boat. I have to find your clothes."

Tibo hunted about in the bushes for a time, beating his way up and down the beach and tearing his hands on brambles but without finding Agathe's bundle until, unbidden, she appeared at his side and pointed. "Honestly," she said, "it's right in front of you! Typical man."

They walked back to the boat together and Tibo wrapped her in blankets and fed her from Mrs. Leshmic's tin box while the stars came out.

"Do you know where we're going, Tibo?"

"More or less," he said.

"Can you find your way?"

"More or less."

"We haven't a chance, have we?"

"We never had a chance, Agathe, and this is the best chance we ever had."

"We'd better go, then."

Tibo gripped the rope at the boat's prow, turned her into the waves and pushed off the beach. Somehow, having Agathe to watch him was different from having the fishermen at the inn looking on. They made him nervous, she made him confident; they wanted him to fail, she wanted him to succeed. He put Yemko's pocket compass on the plank in front of him, looked up at the stars and pulled hard on the oars. There was nothing much to say. He looked at Agathe, she looked at him, the moon came up and shone on the water and Tibo rowed.

"The owl and the pussycat went to sea," said Tibo. He sang it all the way through to "They danced by the light of the moon" and Agathe loved him for it.

"But I am not a pussycat," she said.

"No, and I am not an owl."

"Oh, you are, Tibo! You are, you are!"

And that's how things were as they rowed away through the night.

Perhaps there should be more to tell about a night voyage in an open boat—particularly in a story which has gone on for pages about a concert in a bandstand and bothered to note how a simple postcard made its way from a pillar box on City Square, all the way to the Central Post Office and back again. Neither of these are events of great interest or adventure and, since anybody can see we must be getting near the end of this story, you might think that sailing to Virgule deserves a little more attention. You may be right. The truth is that the sea can be very boring. It tends towards flatness and there's a lot of repetition—one wave generally follows another and, when they do, they are much alike in size and shape and colour, especially at night, which this was.

Anyway, this story is much more about the telling than the things that happen in it so, can we just agree that things carried on much the same for the next few hours until a little after midnight, when Tibo had been rowing for fully three hours and he was beginning to feel really quite tired?

Tibo was not a rower, he was the Mayor of Dot. He had never pretended to be an athlete and he had no idea how far he was supposed to row, only that the lawyer Yemko Guillaume, who could barely walk the length of a garden path, said they would be there by morning. Tibo's arms ached and his hands were blistered. He found himself stopping more and more often "just to check the compass" and he began to wonder if Yemko had not simply sent them to their deaths. After all, if there was one Gnady Vadim ready to inherit his house, why should there not be another? He thought back to the scowling taxi driver—an ideal accomplice—and he kept rowing.

But, before he had time to stop and check the compass bearing again, Tibo felt that same crunch and grind of sand under the boat. And, because hope will always overcome plain common sense, he ignored it and rowed again. The boat stayed still. He rowed again and his oar juddered on harsh sand.

"Are we there?" Agathe asked although she knew the answer.

"I don't think so," he said, although he knew they were not.

There was nothing to see. Tibo stood up to get a better view and, just then, the moon came out from behind a cloud and showed him a huge, flat ellipse of water with angry waves biting away all round the edge of it.

"We've hit a sandbank," he said. "It doesn't matter. We'll just push ourselves off and find a way round."

But, when Tibo got out to push, their little boat tipped over to one side, nearly all the way into the water and, from right along at the other end of the sandbank, a wave came, getting bigger and more spiteful as it came, and it fell into the boat and lay there, a cold grey lump of water. Tibo fell over into the sea. The cold of it made him gasp. It flooded every fibre of his clothes. It weighed him down like chains flung around him and, by the time he got to his feet, wave after wave had hit the boat and swamped it. It made sickening little lurches and burrowed deeper into the sand with every one and Agathe sat on the thwart at the back wailing, "Tibo, Tibo."

"It's all right," he said. "Jump out. Come to me. It's only ankle deep."

The sound of his voice—even though he had to gasp for breath between every word—made her brave and she splashed through the waves and stood beside him.

"Don't. You. Worry. My. Darling," he said. "We can just roll the boat over a bit and get the water out."

But he couldn't, of course. Half full of sand and seawater, the little boat might as well have been made of lead. Tibo heaved and struggled but it wouldn't move. With the last of his strength, Tibo managed to climb over the side and back into the boat where he used his hands to shovel water back into the sea but the waves were coming faster and he couldn't keep up. Luckily, he was too wet and the night was too dark for the tears to show on his face and he was so wet and so tired that his breath came in sobs anyway. And then, when an especially big wave came shining and glistening out of the moonlight, glittering with all the flat dead malice of a shark's eye, the little boat swung to receive it, tipped, went under, came up and righted itself bravely but without its two oars.

Agathe stood on the sandbank, howling and defeated. Tibo crawled and swam and waded and wrestled out of the boat to sit, slumped in the water, beside her. He wound one end of the rope around her body and knotted his hand through it. "At least," he thought, "if they ever find our bodies, we will be together."

"We'll simply have to wait here until the tide goes out and try again," said Tibo.

But Agathe said, "It's up to my knees already. I think it's coming in."

"I'd hoped you wouldn't notice for a while," he said and he put an arm round her and said, "Agathe, I have nothing and nobody in the entire world. I have signed away all that I ever owned to a man I never heard of and, in a short time, when I am dead, there is not one single soul who will know it or care but there is nowhere else in the world that I would rather be than here with you, who knows how many sugars I take in my coffee. Now, let me hold you, because I am very frightened."

That was quite a pretty speech and Good Tibo Krovic should have felt entitled to hear something at least as nice in return—perhaps something about sticking by her and loving her, even when she had become a dog—but all that Agathe said was, "Look over there." And, when Tibo did not move, she said, "Look over there," again, until he did look. "I know where we are," said Agathe.

Coming through the water towards them, splashing knee-deep along the sandbank out of the darkness like a train over the winter steppe, there was a long line of figures and, first in the line, huge and solid like a tree walking, came a giant figure in a leopard-skin rug with an enormous handlebar moustache. Over his shoulder, he carried two oars.

He said not a word but, with gentle fingers, he uncoiled the rope from round Agathe's body and wound it round his own then, walking backwards towards the middle of the sandbank where the water was shallowest, he dragged the boat from the waves, heaving it up, bouncing it out of the water like a huge, defeated fish. But it was still far from afloat. The sea was lapping just inches from the gunwales and the boat was still full of water. The strongman set his jaw grimly, squatted with his back against the stern and began to lift. His feet shifted in the sand, his face contorted in an agony of effort but the boat began to tilt, it began to lift forward on its prow and the water poured away. The little boat rose clear of the sea and, with a gentle smile, the giant helped Tibo and Agathe back on board. Then, his huge hands on the stern, he pushed the boat off and sent it nodding away into the waves.

Tibo and Agathe hung over the side, looking back at the circus people standing in a row on the sandbank, waving. Already the water was up to their waists. The boat drifted on. The moon went behind a cloud. When it came out again, the circus people had gone and there was nothing to see but moonlight shining on a flat, smooth sea.

Tibo and Agathe were too tired to row, too cold and wet. They simply floated in the dark, looking towards the one bright star that still shone through the clouds.

Eventually, after a long time, Tibo said, "I have something very important to ask you, Agathe." When she said nothing, he took that as a signal to ask. He said, "My darling, did you know Hektor is dead?"

"Yes, Tibo, I think I did." After a moment, she said, "I don't think he was a very nice man."

Tibo said, "Does that mean that you think it was a mistake to become a dog?"

"I think becoming a dog was probably the wisest thing I could have done. On the other hand, I have decided to change back to being a woman as soon as possible—in fact, probably as soon as the sun comes up."

Tibo and Agathe were very far from Dot by then, too far even for me to see them, and nobody ever heard from them again. Nobody ever knew how their journey ended but every morning at 7:30, just before The Golden Angel opens its doors, I know that Mr. Cesare kneels quietly by my tomb where he says a prayer for the peace of the soul of his friend and never fails to leave a bag of mints.

And everybody knows that a portrait of Good Mayor Krovic, painted from his many likenesses in the archives of the *Dottian,* still hangs proudly in the Town Hall he served so well.

And the whole world knows that the celebrated twelve *Unfinished Nudes* of Hektor Stopak, stolen from his home, sold off hither and yon, passed from hand to hand, collected and reassembled at enormous cost into one perfect magnum opus, now hang together as a permanent exhibit in the Krovic Memorial Wing of Dot's Municipal Art Galleries.

Legend says there is a thirteenth Stopak but only the lawyer

Guillaume knows that it hangs in the sitting room of No. 43 Loyola Street, in a very private collection shared with no one and definitely not on show to the public, displayed on new wooden stretchers with its canvas expertly restored. And only the lawyer Guillaume knows that, on the shelves of the same room, there is one solitary book—a signed copy of *On Rice* by the celebrated author Gnady Vadim, who lives happily with his wife in a large white house on the coast of Dalmatia where they spend their days drinking wine and eating olives and speaking of Homer to their beautiful children.

About the Author

ANDREW NICOLL has spent his working life as a journalist. He has had short stories published in *New Writing Scotland* and other magazines. He lives in Scotland.

About the Author

ANDREW NICOLL has spent his working life as a journalist. He has had short stories published in *New Writing Scotland* and other magazines. He lives in Scotland.